**"It's possible we've had an intruder on board,"
Janeway said.**

"B'Elanna discovered that the artifact given to me by the Monorhans when we left their planet, the Key to Gremadia, is actually made up of living sporocystian remnants. They are currently resonating, similar to the way the Caretaker's remains did when we encountered Suspiria. We haven't ruled out the possibility that another Nacene might be nearby."

"That adds a decidedly unsavory piece to the puzzle," the Doctor observed.

"I agree. Keep me informed. I'll be on the bridge," the captain said, following him out of his office.

The Doctor halted in their approach to Naomi's biobed, where Phoebe stood over the girl. Turning to Janeway, he asked, "Captain, who is this woman?"

"Is that supposed to be a joke, Doctor? You know my sister," Janeway replied, gesturing toward Phoebe.

"Captain . . . I . . ." the Doctor stammered, and blinked out of existence.

STAR TREK VOYAGER®

STRING THEORY

BOOK 2

FUSION

HIRSTEN BEYER

Based upon STAR TREK®
created by Gene Roddenberry
and STAR TREK: VOYAGER
created by Rick Berman and Michael Piller and Jeri Taylor

POCKET BOOKS
New York London Toronto Sydney Gremadia

An *Original* Publication of POCKET BOOKS

POCKET BOOKS, a division of Simon & Schuster, Inc.
1230 Avenue of the Americas, New York, NY 10020

Copyright © 2005 by Paramount Pictures. All Rights Reserved.

STAR TREK is a Registered Trademark of
Paramount Pictures.

This book is published by Pocket Books, a division of Simon & Schuster, Inc., under exclusive license from Paramount Pictures.

ISBN-13: 978-1-4165-0955-4
ISBN-10:   1-4165-0955-0

First Pocket Books printing November 2005

10 9 8 7 6 5 4 3 2 1

POCKET and colophon are registered trademarks of Simon & Schuster, Inc.

Cover design by John Vairo, Jr.

Manufactured in the United States of America

For information regarding special discounts for bulk purchases, please contact Simon & Schuster Special Sales at 1-800-456-6798 or business@simonandschuster.com.

For David,
without whom I would not be possible

I celebrate myself, and sing myself,
And what I assume you shall assume,
For every atom belonging to me as good
belongs to you.

—WALT WHITMAN, "Song of Myself"

Prologue

She should have insisted that her personal cabin contain a window. It would have been simple enough to add to the design of the ship, and her children would have enthusiastically seized any opportunity to provide their *rih-hara-tan* with the most extravagant comfort, let alone a small portal to the stars.

Instead, her last living glimpse of the constellations of the Monorhan system, intricate designs she had been taught to name almost as soon as she could speak, was stolen as she had been all but carried by her *shi-harart*, Naviim, and three terrified *harans* through the dank, lifeless corridors of a forsaken alien space city into the docking bay where her ship was berthed. The sadness of this realization didn't hit with full force until she found herself locked securely in her cabin aboard the vessel she had christened *Betasis* twelve . . . *could it have been only twelve?* . . . short rotations ago, when this catastrophic journey had begun.

"Oweninum's Belt," she whispered to the darkness. On the homeworld, this cluster of seven stars had shown brightest in the final days of the harvest. Weeks later, the first crystals of *wantain* would blanket the fields in luminescent temporary death, until they were melted away by the timeless dance of Monorha's two suns, Protin and her partner, the Blue Eye, at the dawn of the planting season.

She activated her silent cabin's internal lights with a thought and turned her attention to the hand-painted star chart that covered the wall behind her personal command console. So well attuned was the *Betasis*'s organic circuitry to her mind and body that the dimness she now traversed as she crossed from the entrance alcove to the magnificent rendering of a thousand stars seemed to eerily echo her despair. Or perhaps her ship simply knew, as she did, that the task she was now determined to complete was best accomplished in the faintest hint of light.

"Is this, truly, the price of heresy?" she asked, gently caressing each of the seven stars of Oweninum's Belt that had been lovingly re-created by her *ati-harat*. It would be her final question of the Blessed All-Knowing Light, though she was uncertain if she still had the right to speak His name, let alone address Him in prayer.

The library of scrolls sat along the far wall, swathed in rich and ornately woven casings. Technically the property of the entire tribe, they were traditionally entrusted to the care of the *rih-hara-tan* for her private study. The original twenty-seven letters of Dagan that had been the hope of her people for countless generations, and the inspiration behind this final doomed voyage into the unknown, rested in a place of honor among them.

Steeling herself against the wave of nauseating rage that threatened to overwhelm her with thoughts of Dagan and his cursed visions, thoughts that would easily transform her into a frantic-braying *kuntafed* if given leash, she forced herself to draw a ragged complete breath and reached for the scroll of Jocephar. There she would find the invocation to meditation required to begin the ritual.

She was certain that what she was about to attempt hadn't been contemplated in Jocephar's time. But if anything of her or her people was to survive the next few hours, she had to try. She had miserably failed them once. She would not permit herself to do it again.

This ritual of transference was meant to be the final gift from one *rih-hara-tan* to the next. It gave the tribe a seamless continuity as the wisdom and experience, the very essence of its leader, were bestowed upon the next in the line of succession when it was clear that the *rih-hara-tan* was near death.

But her last potential successor, Lynarra, a mere child of eight cycles, was dead already; dead, along with ten thousand others, almost the entire population of Monorha's Fourteenth Tribe.

"And for what?" she asked herself.

For the ravings of madman was the only answer that came.

Even as this blasphemous thought knifed through the surface of her mind, she saw the face of Klyrrhea before her. Time had carved gentle lines around the deep green eyes of the *rih-hara-tan* who had preceded her. But those incandescent pools where she had often found understanding and comfort taunted her now, asking, "Where is your faith, child?"

But Klyrrhea had never been asked to witness the senseless death of her people in a matter of days. She hadn't been forced to watch the fear and anguish in the eyes of their loved ones, as the first of her brothers and sisters who had explored the city had succumbed to the slow, wrenching death that those *creatures* had inflicted upon them. She had not stood by, helpless as they fell, one after another, silently infected by the parasites. These instinct-driven, nonsentient life-forms should have died out centuries ago, when their makers or keepers had abandoned this place she had mistaken for the promised city of Gremadia.

But the parasites had been only the first assault her people had faced. As the nightmarish days had passed, another threat had made its presence known to her and the few who managed to avoid infection. They were invisible, but their presence was powerful and terrifying. Their chaotic thoughts and feelings, inarticulate and constant, reverberated within the part of her mind that had been reserved for the unique and sanctified connection between the *rih-hara-tan* and her tribe. Her people knew this connection intimately. They experienced it within the safety of their *hara*. What separated a *rih-hara-tan* from any other Monorhan was the ability to extend that connection to include the entirety of her people. This made her mind more vulnerable than her children to the frightful intense *need* of the invisible presence.

She had attempted once to open herself up to the presence, in hope that some form of communication might be possible. But that first attempt had been such a brutal and violent sullying of the most sacred spaces of her mind that she had abandoned all thought of the presence or its needs. That door within her mind was shut and sealed. But there was still the vulnerability of her body to the inevitable and inexorable approach of the parasites that remained.

My rih? Naviim's thoughts interrupted her own. . . . *danger* . . . She did not hear the rapid patter of his lower tongue muscle against his palate, but the vibration entered her mind at the exact same second as his greeting. *He is terrified,* she realized, almost tasting his fear.

I am here . . . her mind answered, as she did her best to distance herself from his terror, knowing as she did so that he did not deserve the brusqueness of her tone.

They have breached the inner hull at deck nine, section twenty-one, he began, the feelings interwoven among his words threatening to drown her in a surge of cascading waves of anger and fear.

"Enough," she barked aloud, silencing him. She knew his last memory of her, proximate mother of every member of the Fourteenth Tribe, would be of an impatient, brisk crone, but she didn't care. If she could trade her name and reputation, the way in which she would be remembered for all eternity, for even a fraction of the numbers of her children already dead, she would gladly have given her own life in peace.

There was no more time for pleasantries. No more time for pride. There was only this one desperate chance that she could transfer her consciousness into her ship's organic circuitry. The telepathic gifts of her tribe had been tested in the past, though she was certain a transfer had never been attempted, let alone completed between a living, breathing Monorhan and an organic construct like the *Betasis.* She knew it was risky. But she also knew it was possible. To succeed, she would first have to recall the wisdom of the ancient schools she had been raised in from infancy to completely separate her mind from her body. It required absolute peace and internal harmony. And it would be shattered completely if she had to hear one more time about what "they" were doing to her ship.

Secure the memory core and get to your preservation pod, she demanded of Naviim, careful to add as much . . . *peace* . . . *and . . . safety . . .* as she could to her thoughts. And then she was alone again, within her mind.

The *Betasis* had been Klyrrhea's dream, a dream she had nurtured to reality with the help of a brilliant scientist named Gora. So fervent was Klyrrhea's literal belief in the existence of Gremadia that she had marshaled the unimaginable resources of two generations of her tribe in the construction of a ship large enough to carry them from the surface of Monorha to the space between the stars where the All-Knowing Light was said to have constructed the promised city. There, His true followers would join Him to do final battle with the Others for the freedom of them all.

Or so they had believed.

The Fourteenth Tribe's adherence to this belief, first set down in the letters of Dagan, had sustained their faith for thousands of years, even as the other thirteen tribes of Monorha shunned them for this heresy. Over time, members of the Fourteenth Tribe had been restricted then forbidden by law to hold public office or participate in the intertribal council. Their lands had been "redistributed," or more accurately, stolen by the other tribes, and they had been banished to a nomadic existence, difficult at best to eke out from the least hospitable regions of their otherwise fertile planet.

But Klyrrhea's vision had been the dawn of a new era for her people. She had managed to convince them all that the Time of Knowing was upon them. Monorhans had finally gained the skill and technology needed to travel beyond the surface of their planet to the stars around them. Talk had begun within the council of colonizing new planets, though no suitable candidates had yet been discovered. When Klyrrhea had offered to end the tension and occasional violent disruption that her "heretical" kinsmen wove into the otherwise placid fabric of Monorhan culture, the council had agreed almost too eagerly to aid her in her quest to build a city-ship, capable of transporting the entire Fourteenth Tribe to the new home they believed the protector of them all had created for them.

Mainstream Monorhan culture had always looked

upon the writings of Dagan with thinly veiled contempt. The idea that the All-Knowing Light had fought and lost a battle with beings as powerful as He implied first that there could be other beings that were all-knowing, and this was simply unacceptable. But Dagan was a child of the Fourteenth Tribe, a seer gifted beyond any who had come before or since, so legend told. Unable to simply disregard his difficult teachings, his tribe had embraced him and his beliefs, and now, thousands of years later, had paid the price: total annihilation.

As she laid the scroll of Jocephar upon her workstation, weighing down the edges with ceremonial stones, dimly aware that she had subconsciously begun the long, low hum that initiated the transference ritual, Dagan's words sprang unbidden to her mind. She would have given anything to wipe them forever from her thoughts, but they rose stubbornly, just as she had recited them, hundreds of times in tribal assembly, piercing her heart with their sad beauty. Even as she wished that they had never been written, as they wound their way through her mind, she saw them for the first time in the light of these last days, and found in them an unexpected measure of comfort.

I, Dagan, Linuh-harat *of the Fourteenth Tribe of Monorha, record this true vision of* The First and Last Battle *to honor the* Rih-hara-tan *Montok.*

. . . The battle was lost, but not the war. The stench of death suffused the air, chilled by the absence of the suns, as the All-Knowing Light surveyed the fruits of His labors . . . the remains of His brothers and sisters scattered on the purple dunes of the Galhada Wastes. Darkness crept closer, threatening to overwhelm this cursed field that had never

known life, and He feared that this darkness would be the last.

And then He remembered.

Fear was for the lesser beings, whose regrets of the past and desires for the future blinded them to the reality that this moment contained more than the substance of then, now, and beyond. The battle had been lost tomorrow. The war would be won thousands of years ago. Time flowed and bent and danced and vibrated with infinite possibility that only the All-Knowing could truly appreciate.

He would begin again.

The Others might choose to subject themselves to tortured exile, but He would preside over the days to come in this new world and rip from the darkness shards of light to guide Him to victory for all His kind.

He gathered the bodies where they had fallen. Their flesh had already begun to nurture the field and He knew that in years to come new life would rise, even from this desolate present. He knew the Others would forbid it, but He cared not. Life was never meant to be contained. That was the simple truth that made time and its variations insignificant.

Then He turned His face to the heavens and, raising His right hand, He chose the space between the stars where He would make His final stand.

"I GO!" He cried in defiance. "And those who come after will know to follow. I will guide them through the darkness, when they have reached the Time of Knowing. Together, we will smash the gates that divide us from the Others and return to the infinite flow that will never again know the absence of light."

He blessed those who had fallen with these words: "All that are of us will once again taste life beyond time. Their sacrifice will transform this desolate place. I will make from

*their remains the Key to our victory. And when my follow-
ers reach the gates, knowing that to be bound to one existence is to be a slave, I shall show them their first glimpse of
freedom. This place I will prepare . . . I will call it . . .
Gremadia . . ."*

The rage was gone. Fearless acceptance had entered
her heart in its place and calmed her tormented mind.

The battle was lost . . . but not the war.

Although she could no longer light the way for her
own people, she could live on. The soulless parasites
could never reach her within the organic circuitry of the
Betasis. The ship would remain forever in one of the
dozens of docking bays of the alien city she had thought to
be Gremadia. And she would remain with it, a prisoner of
eternity.

One final thought consoled her. If there was an All-
Knowing Light, and if the life-forms that rose to consciousness on Monorha were truly His chosen followers,
then perhaps the members of the Fourteenth Tribe had already found the freedom they had been desperately seeking, not in life, but in death.

A motorized whine that signaled the failure of the *Betasis's* security grid alerted her to the fact that Naviim's defensive measures, however thorough, had been no match
for the parasites. Time was short.

The soft clanging of her door chime confirmed this
truth, though the largest part of her no longer cared. She
had begun the transference ritual the moment she opened
the scroll of Jocephar, an unnecessary aid to her meditation.

The gentle thrumming sensation that accompanied
complete alignment of her mind and body began to rise
from her toes, warming the bones of her legs, the lean

muscles of her thighs, and the hollow center of her birthing canal, which would never know the spark of a new life force growing within her. With the last conscious fragment of her mind she willed the door to open, granting Naviim access.

"My *rih*?" he asked reverently, well aware that access to her mind would be denied him in this sacred moment.

"Is the *Betasis*'s memory core secured?" some distant disembodied voice asked from a mouth that was somehow her own, and at the same time completely disconnected from her.

"It is," he answered, trying desperately to maintain the composure rigorously ingrained in a *shi-harat.*

"And are the three *harans* secured in their preservation pods?" came again from the voice not her own.

"They are, my *rih,*" he replied.

The *harans* might yet survive to return to Monorha. They probably wouldn't. The preservation pods were only equipped with rations capable of sustaining life for six rotations at the most, and it had taken twice that time to travel the distance from the homeworld. But even this no longer troubled her. The legacy of the Fourteenth Tribe as keepers of the flame of Dagan's truth would die here, or a few light-years away, but from its ashes a new purpose would rise. The hostile life-forms that had decimated her people would never again wreak pain and destruction upon sentient beings. If she could survive within the *Betasis,* she could warn away any future trespassers, Monorhan or otherwise, from this slow-spinning circle of death. And if the data-interface cables that tethered the *Betasis* to the station could be traversed by thoughts powerful enough, she would find a way to destroy the station from within.

Naviim stumbled, involuntarily grasping the entrance

alcove's railing with a free hand as the *Betasis* shook beneath him.

Structural integrity has been compromised, she thought painlessly.

As Naviim regained his balance, she saw the simple devotion of the man who had been her *shi-harat* her entire life, and wished she could reward him with something other than certain death.

"Go," she commanded.

Naviim bowed his head, but remained rooted to the floor.

He will not desert me, even now. Her final comfort would not be a view of the stars of her home, but instead, the sight of the love and loyalty of her most faithful servant.

Accepting this, she turned to the few remaining strands of thought that connected her mind to her body.

With her two powerful arms designed but rarely used for manual labor, she took hold of the command console before her and ripped it in one piece from its casing. Naviim averted his eyes, in deference to the sight of her two delicate interior arms as they emerged from the pouch sewn into the back of her ceremonial robe. Extending the long tapered fingers that were meant to embrace her mate, she thrust them into the sparking wires that still pulsed with life within the console.

"Be at peace, Naviim," she whispered. "The transference has begun."

These were the last words that Assylia, *rih-hara-tan* of the Fourteenth Tribe of Monorha, and commander of their finest achievement, the *Betasis,* ever spoke in the flesh.

Chapter 1

Tuvok was conscious of the song from the first fraction of a second that he began to emerge from his meditative state. He gradually roused himself through the stages of alertness; awareness of the weight of his limbs, his slow, rhythmic breathing, the hum of the shuttle's engines, the soft caress of the environmental controls setting the cabin temperature much warmer than most humans would be comfortable with. Finally, as he recalled where he was, and how he had come to be here, the intensity of the music threatened to plunge his Vulcan restraint into chaos.

With the precision only years of rigorous training in the Temple of Amonak had given him discipline to master, he forced the passion, the longing, and the unutterable pain into the recesses of his mind, and only when he was certain that he, and not the music, was in control did he open his eyes.

"Computer . . ."

The computer replied with a chirp, awaiting his command.

"What is our current heading?"

The cool voice devoid of all emotion answered as expected. *"Current heading remains unchanged: one six seven mark one four."*

"Estimate arrival at the singularity."

"One hour, twenty-seven minutes, eleven seconds."

Exactly as he had anticipated.

With great care, Tuvok rose from his knees next to the shuttle bunk, and sat on its edge. He shifted his focus inward, until he had counted exactly one hundred times the quarter of a second between each beat of his heart, and satisfied himself that no matter what, it would continue to beat at precisely the same rate, substantially slower than the normal Vulcan resting heart rate, until he allowed it to do otherwise.

He then turned his attention to the corner of his mind where he had placed the music. It had been a desperate struggle over the last nine hours to maintain his ability to perform even the most rudimentary exercises of piloting the shuttle, but finally he had forced the living presence that now shared his mind into a section of his consciousness that he could examine at will.

He was certain he was experiencing a telepathic communication, source unknown. He had considered the possibility that he might be suffering from an as of yet indefinable side effect of the strange properties of Monorhan space and subspace to which he and all of *Voyager*'s crew had recently been exposed. And after careful consideration, he had dismissed that theory.

The presence that called to him was alive. Its life, though painful and somehow disconnected . . . no . . . *stuck in between* . . . whatever that meant . . . was more than life, at least life as he had known it during his hundred-plus years of existence. And somehow, it knew him.

Tuvok.

Vulcan.

Head of security.
Husband.
Father.
Friend.
Traveler far from home.

It saw beneath the disciplined walls of self-control that fortified him against passions and emotional extremes that most humanoid species could only imagine, but all Vulcans knew intuitively as the enemy of stability, logic, and reason. It lived in these extremes and somehow managed to survive them without fear. It contained . . . no . . . experienced all that was possible, and merged that reality into harmony that his mind could almost, but not quite, hold. But it was somehow incomplete. The deepest notes, which pounded discordantly against the simplicity and beauty of the rest of the song, were sounds that spoke of yearning . . . need . . . desperate   painful   desire . . . for *home.*

But what would an entity of such vast and incomprehensible variety call home?

It was pointless, for now, to even attempt to imagine. It was enough for Tuvok that this presence had effortlessly compromised the deep and secure defenses of pure logic and reason that guided every moment of his life, and forced him to face the desires that he had never allowed himself to feel. They met upon this common ground. They both wanted . . . needed . . . desired *home.*

He was absolutely confident that when he found the source of the song, he would be able to somehow translate the nature of the communication and enter into dialogue with it.

That or it would drive him mad.

Either way, it was a journey best undertaken alone. Whether he succeeded or failed, he felt obligated to fully understand the nature of the presence and any threat it might pose to *Voyager*. Though to be absolutely accurate, part of him knew already that *Voyager* was not of intrinsic interest to it, because *Voyager* was an object with which it could not communicate. It needed someone to know . . . to help. It needed Tuvok.

The possibility that he would not survive this mission was very real. But, he reasoned, he had already been given up for dead on more than one occasion by his family, both genetic on Vulcan, and adopted in Starfleet. While he was certain they would mourn his loss, in time they would come to terms with their grief and integrate it into themselves in a way that brought meaning to both his life and theirs. That was the worst-case scenario. Much more likely, he would return from an unauthorized absence of a few days, give a full report of his findings to the captain, accept an official reprimand on his record, and return to his duties.

Had he been capable of feeling irony, he would have found it appropriate to describe the reality that the four years he had spent facing violent death at almost every turn while serving as Captain Kathryn Janeway's chief of security on *Voyager* had bought him, and all of the colleagues who had made that journey with him, a certain amount of latitude. It was not as if any deviation from standard protocol would be looked on lightly, but experience had shown that their odds of survival would have been seriously reduced were it not for the creative thinking and occasional renegade impulses that seemed required of most of the senior officers from time to time. Such ingenuity had saved their lives on more occasions than Tuvok cared to count, seventy-nine, all told.

Such simple evaluations of actions and consequences were one of the many tools, which had allowed his highest logical functions to assert themselves over the cacophony of sounds that threatened unrestrained abandon at every microsecond.

Point-two-five seconds. Beat. Point-two-five seconds. Beat.

Choosing an ancient visualization technique, a simple, non-automated door became the focus of his thoughts.

His hand was on the doorknob.

Point-two-five seconds. Beat.

Clockwise turn, seventeen degrees.

Point-two-five seconds. Beat.

Regulated intake of breath, diaphragm release, lungs filled to capacity.

Beat.

Biceps contract, pulling door forward five degrees.

Sound rushing like wind through his physical being, resonating not in his mind, but in his *katra*. Temptation, almost unbearable temptation to throw the door open and allow the symphony to swallow him whole. It would be so easy. Just like falling off a cliff.

Exhale.

Point-two-five seconds.

Beat.

His course heading had been accurate. He was almost there.

Kathryn Janeway strode purposefully into her ready room off the bridge of the *Starship Voyager* and found not one but two unanticipated visitors waiting within.

Her first officer, Commander Chakotay, sat comfortably on the long bench that lined the far wall beneath a large window, engrossed in a sheet of drawing paper. Next to him, occasionally indicating some point of interest on the drawing with the fingers of her right hand, stood Naomi Wildman, the half-human, half-Ktarian daughter of Ensign Samantha Wildman, and the first child ever born aboard *Voyager*. Though Naomi was little more than two years old, the combination of her human and Ktarian DNA resulted in a child who looked more like five or six and had already demonstrated the cognitive skills of a child nearly twice that age.

As Naomi struggled to answer a question posed to her by Chakotay, scrunching her forehead lined with small pointed horns running vertically from her hairline to the bridge of her nose, and absentmindedly pulling the end of her long strawberry blond braid to her mouth, Janeway noticed that in her left hand, Naomi held a large mug of a steaming beverage that looked, and dare she hope, smelled gloriously like coffee.

"I hope I'm not interrupting something important," Janeway offered casually.

She noted with an inward smile that as Chakotay rose automatically to his feet, handing the paper back to Naomi and greeting her with a warm "Not at all, Captain," Naomi's eyes grew involuntarily wide. The child stood at a miniature version of attention, managing to maintain both the drawing and the mug, though her hair remained fixed in her mouth as she waited, appropriately, for the captain to address her personally before she spoke.

"Good morning, Miss Wildman," Janeway began, not wishing to put Naomi through one more moment of discomfort.

"Captain," Naomi replied seriously, extending her left hand and offering the mug to Janeway as her braid mercifully dropped from her mouth and returned to its proper alignment running straight down her back.

"Thank you very much," Janeway smiled, as she took the mug, her senses calming instinctively as she took in the aroma of the steam rising from the dark liquid.

Definitely coffee.

"Neelix . . ." Naomi began, but then paused as if unsure as to whether or not she should continue.

"You have just made my morning, Miss Wildman," Janeway offered graciously, placing a gentle hand on the child's shoulder. "Please speak freely."

Naomi relaxed a little as she drew a deep breath and continued. "Neelix was helping me finish this star chart over breakfast when he saw that you had left your quarters and were going straight to the bridge . . ." She paused before adding, ". . . without stopping to eat."

Janeway threw a playful glance at Chakotay, who was obviously enjoying this exchange tremendously.

"Am I to understand that Neelix monitors my every move?" Janeway asked with mock seriousness.

Naomi appeared to realize her error immediately.

"No!" she blurted out before she noticed that the captain was still smiling. "It's just . . . he's programmed the computer to tell him when you get up in the morning . . . so that he can make sure your coffee is hot."

Janeway stood upright and took a sip, thankful that the morning's brew was replicated and not one of Neelix's usually interesting and completely undrinkable variations on the coffee theme.

"You may tell Mr. Neelix that I am very pleased with his work," Janeway said, as Naomi's smile grew bright enough to light the entire room. "And thank you for delivering this to me."

"Will there be anything else, ma'am?" Naomi asked, apparently oblivious of Janeway's unwritten rule that she be addressed as "ma'am" only in a crunch.

"May I see your drawing?" Janeway asked.

"Sure! I mean, yes, ma'am," Naomi answered, pleased. Examining the broad strokes of deep purple and blue that filled the page, Janeway was impressed to see that Naomi had actually created a very fair approximation of the stars of the Monorhan system.

"What do you think, Chakotay?" Janeway turned to the commander.

"I think Seven of Nine might want to add this to our astrometric database," Chakotay replied.

"High praise, indeed," Janeway acknowledged, "although, I wonder . . ." she mused, taking the drawing and placing it on the wall next to the door in a position where she could have an unobstructed view of it from her desk.

"What do you think?" she asked Naomi. "Would you mind very much if I were to hang this here, for the time being?"

The child's sweet, prideful smile was all the gratitude Janeway needed.

"I wouldn't mind at all, ma'am."

"Thank you for this lovely addition to my ready room, Naomi."

"You're welcome, Captain," Naomi grinned.

"You are dismissed, Miss Wildman."

With a curt nod, and a bounce in her step, Naomi took three long strides toward the exit before breaking into a full skip as the door opened to the corridor that would lead her back to Neelix and her day of study and play.

As Chakotay watched Naomi's braid dance in rhythm behind her, Janeway noted the deep lines of worry etched in his tattooed brow. He was still smiling faintly, but the smile no longer touched his eyes.

Nothing about humans irked Seven of Nine quite as intensely as their frequent inability to retain even the simplest series of instructions and perform them to her specifications without demanding infinitely more in the way of explanation and justification than she was ever of a mind to give. In a colleague who had earned her respect, B'Elanna Torres, for example, she had learned to restrain her irritation because she finally understood, largely owing to their recent away mission on Monorha, where they had been forced to function in a "mini-collective" state, that B'Elanna's questions were not meant to irritate, or to imply any ignorance on Seven's part, but instead were part of a process of intelligent debate that often resulted in a better solution than Seven might have arrived at on her own. Naturally, she was confident that she would have eventually seen the same issues B'Elanna would raise, but that was because B'Elanna had a natural gift for thinking ten or eleven steps ahead of any problem. This had earned her the right, in Seven's opinion, to interrupt her course of action, and consider at least a few other possibilities before fully committing herself.

The same could not be said for Ensign Brooks. He was one of a team of engineers who had been assigned to assist her in evaluating the viability of adding quantum slipstream technology to *Voyager*'s arsenal of not-quite-by-the-book modifications. Though to Seven's mind, there were infinitely more pressing matters before *Voyager*'s crew at the moment, Commander Chakotay had insisted that all senior staff were to provide him with regularly scheduled updates of all current projects now that things had returned to something vaguely resembling "normal." She had every intention of obeying Chakotay's request, despite the unpleasant fact that it would throw her into Brooks's path first thing after completing her regeneration cycle.

Brooks was obviously highly regarded by Commander Chakotay. Seven was certain, however, that should he ever be asked to engage in activities that went beyond the theoretical and more toward the practical applications, he would have made Harry Kim's frequent tendency to come within an inch of his life look like textbook procedure rather than innocent excess.

Ensign Brooks was speaking. Reluctantly she forced herself to focus on his question.

"But if the housing of the coil is reinforced with a static forcefield, won't that limit the distribution of the reaction and reduce capacity?" he asked.

Resisting the urge to extend her assimilation tubules and simply spoon-feed him the data he required, she began again, in the most patient voice she could muster.

"The forcefield is a necessary defensive measure. The limited vulnerability is weighted higher than the .0075 capacity reduction that you refer to, and would result in an insignificant reaction increase."

"In your opinion," he continued.

Seven paused.

"In the opinion of a collective of millions of beings who assimilated and then perfected quantum slipstream technology before finding transwarp travel more efficient." She made a mental note to review Starfleet Academy entrance requirements, and determine, if possible, who had felt it was prudent to make Ensign Brooks an engineer.

"Right. The Borg are obsessed with efficiency. But no matter how you look at it, the static field is not the most efficient option," Brooks observed.

"Ensign, if you were to engage the slipstream coil and begin flying at that speed, should the coil be transported from its station by a hostile party, it would result in the immediate disintegration of your vessel. Insignificantly decreased reaction potential is a small price to pay for the safety the static field provides. I can assure you that in the unlikely event you should ever fly that fast, finding a way to move at a higher velocity will not be a primary or even secondary concern."

"I was just saying . . ." he began, but her level gaze told him he might be taking his life in his hands if he chose to continue.

The next sound that Seven heard was the chirping of her combadge.

"Torres to Seven of Nine."

"Go ahead," she replied.

"Meet me in astrometrics."

"I'm on my way." She toyed with the idea of asking Brooks to realign the coil-locking dampers, but opted to complete the procedure herself when she returned. "Ensign Brooks, please review the coil distribution parameters using the following three antineutrino variances. I will expect your report when I return."

"Yes, ma'am," he stammered, obviously still unsure how one addressed a former Borg, now human, who had spent more time aboard a starship than he had, if you counted the various Borg cubes she had served on, but had never officially accepted a rank aboard *Voyager.*

Seven had almost reached the door when she remembered to turn and say, "Thank you, Ensign." It was an unnecessary nicety as far as she was concerned, but she had realized in the last eleven months how much more efficient working conditions could be when one observed these simple pleasantries.

"When was the last time you slept, Chakotay?" Janeway began, as soon as the door was closed.

"I could ask you the same question," he replied simply. Chakotay was not at all surprised to see that in the space of a breath, the jovial woman who had just lingered lovingly over a child's drawing was gone and in her place stood the most determined leader ever to ride point on a Federation vessel. Sometimes he thought they had survived this long in the Delta Quadrant only through the sheer force of her will. And now she had her game face on.

"You left the bridge less than two hours ago. It's not as if standing over the conn will get us to Tuvok any faster. As long as we're in Monorhan space . . ." he began.

"I know. Impulse engines only," she finished bitterly. "And he's got a good head start. At this rate he'll probably reach the singularity at least a few hours ahead of us."

"I am pleased to report that we're becoming much more proficient at navigating the unusual space and sub-space curvatures of the Monorhan system. It should cut some time off our pursuit course," Chakotay said.

"And we shouldn't have to worry about any more ships suddenly popping up right in front of us?" Janeway asked.

"Seven has assured me that we should not," he replied.

"Well, that's something," Janeway acknowledged. With a frustrated sigh, she settled into the chair behind her desk, placed Naomi's drawing on her credenza, and pulled the most recent operations reports up on her monitor.

"What could Tuvok possibly be thinking?" she asked rhetorically. "There are several crew members I could easily see charging off on some foolish errand if they felt there was no alternative course of action, even some of our bridge officers, come to think of it. But we're talking about Tuvok. He spent the better part of our early years together making sure I lived up to every comma, semicolon, and period, never mind letter of Starfleet regulations. Tuvok doesn't leave this ship without reporting to at least one of us where he's going and why."

"There was that incident with the Sikarians," Chakotay reminded her.

"I haven't forgotten," she replied, sadness and anger warring for dominance on her face. "But he wasn't the only one who tried to bend the Prime Directive that day. Hurt as I was by his choice, I understood why he did it."

"And you've been absolutely certain, since then, that he would never disappoint you like that again," he finished her thought.

Janeway nodded in silent assent.

"Then you might be a little relieved to hear that the Doctor has completed his report," Chakotay continued, placing a padd in front of the captain, before crossing to the replicator and ordering a cup of orange juice while he waited for her to read its contents. "That's why I stopped by this morning on my way to the bridge."

Janeway scanned the Doctor's findings related to Tuvok's stay in sickbay just prior to the time he left *Voyager* for reasons unknown. "A neurochemical imbalance in the mesiofrontal cortex?"

"That's the part of the Vulcan brain that regulates their ability to suppress their emotions."

Janeway cast a suspicious eye toward her first officer. "Studying up on Vulcan physiology in our copious spare time?"

Chakotay cleared his throat before offering, without a hint of defensiveness, "I know things."

"This made as much sense to you the first time you read it as it does to me, right?" she asked.

"Right. I asked the Doctor for some clarification."

"What's this about music?" she continued.

"When Tuvok went missing I accessed his personal logs for the past few days. Shortly after we destabilized the Blue Eye, Tuvok noted that he was hearing something he could only describe as music. The Doctor couldn't explain it, though its occurrence seemed to correspond to the decrease in neuropeptide production in the limbic system. He was particularly alarmed by this specific neurochemical imbalance because he's only seen it in Tuvok once before."

"When was that?" Janeway asked in a way that suggested she was not certain she really wanted to know the answer.

"A little over two years ago, when Tuvok initiated his series of mind-melds with Ensign Lon Suder."

"Well, terrific," Janeway said, tossing the padd to her desk and taking an extra-large sip of coffee before rising to her feet. "I mean aside from turning Tuvok into a homicidal maniac, that worked out okay, so I guess there's really nothing to worry about."

"The Doctor believes the 'music' Tuvok was referring to might have been some sort of telepathic communication."

"From whom?"

"He's not willing to speculate at this time."

"Anyone who could force Tuvok to ignore his duties to this ship, never mind altering his normal brain functions . . ." Janeway said before pausing long enough for Chakotay to see at least a dozen possible scenarios and their probable outcomes play out across her face. "If the circumstances were different, I'd just as soon give them a nice wide berth. In any event, I've seen enough of the peculiarities of Monorhan space and subspace to last me a good long while."

"I agree," replied Chakotay. "But since that's not really an option."

"Take the ship to yellow alert."

Chakotay assented with a slight nod, and started toward the door that accessed the bridge, pausing at the threshold to say, "Don't worry, Kathryn, we'll find him."

Janeway replied with a wan smile as he left her to her thoughts.

"Good morning, B'Elanna," Seven said as she walked briskly into astrometrics, almost faltering in her apparent attempt to establish a conversational tone.

B'Elanna forced herself not to smile too broadly as she felt . . . no, she corrected herself, *remembered* . . . what it was like to live within Seven's conflicted consciousness. Although the residual effects of their linked state had finally passed, the experience of sharing Seven's mind had given B'Elanna an entirely new perspective on her own internal struggles. "I thought I had a rough time of it, balancing my human and Klingon natures," she had recorded in her first personal log once the Doctor had separated them. But Seven's battle to refrain from constantly acting on her own, usually superior impulses, and instead interacting within the limitations of verbal communication among *Voyager*'s crew until a consensus had been reached, made her own occasional bouts of temper seem pale in comparison. *At least she's trying,* B'Elanna thought, surprised at the sensitivity and genuine warmth she now felt from time to time when she looked at Seven.

"Don't worry," she said aloud. "I'm not much of a morning person myself."

"You require my assistance?" Seven asked as she joined B'Elanna at the astrometric display control console and added softly, "Perhaps for the next four or five hours?"

This time B'Elanna didn't bother to repress her smile.

"You've been working with Ensign Brooks again this morning, haven't you?" she teased.

Seven's reply was uncharacteristic, due more to the heat than the speed with which it was delivered.

"I have, and if I am forced to return there in less time

than I have suggested it is my belief that at least one of us will end up reassigned or on temporary medical leave."

B'Elanna knew the feeling all too well. The only shocking thing was to see evidence of it or any other decidedly emotional response in the former Borg. Facing Seven with a hand on her hip, B'Elanna asked, with feigned seriousness, "Are you certain that all of the residual effects of our linked state have dissipated?"

"Why do you ask, Lieutenant?"

"Because I don't think physical violence was ever on your short list of interpersonal problem-solving alternatives before," B'Elanna said, turning back to her workstation.

Seven managed to resist the temptation to rise to B'Elanna's bait. "How may I assist you, Lieutenant?"

"By taking a look at this for me," B'Elanna replied, increasing the magnification of their most recent sensor sweep of the singularity and its surrounding environs. Fun as it was to tease Seven of Nine, there were definitely more pressing matters at hand.

"Does this remind you of anything?" B'Elanna asked, stepping aside and crossing her arms at her chest as Seven analyzed the sensor data and added the readings to her visual scan of the magnified sector.

Finally she confirmed B'Elanna's suspicions. "There is a construct of almost fifty billion cubic meters revolving around the quantum singularity."

"I can see that," B'Elanna responded tersely, "but that's not what I asked. Look at the power distribution signatures. What do they remind you of?"

Seven studied the readings in question again and to B'Elanna's annoyance almost immediately tapped her combadge.

"Seven of Nine to Captain Janeway."

"Go ahead, Seven."

"Please report to astrometrics immediately," Seven stated simply, in a tone that was more an order than a request before closing the comm channel.

B'Elanna shook her head and sighed deeply.

"What?" Seven asked in a manner that B'Elanna could have sworn dropped the temperature in the room by at least a few degrees.

"Nothing," B'Elanna replied, turning again to the analysis.

"I have offended you," Seven continued, obviously oblivious of B'Elanna's attempt to drop the subject.

"No, not me."

"Lieutenant Torres," Seven began in her most condescending voice.

"Look, Seven, she's the captain. She doesn't take orders, she gives them. Would it kill you to ask her to join us, rather than making it sound like you're the one who's really in charge around here?"

"I didn't mean to imply . . ."

"No, Seven . . . you never mean to imply anything. But you just . . . never mind. We're not having this argument again. You'll just stand there, a picture of frigid inflexibility, and I'll end up wanting to break your nose, and at the end of the day, we've really got much bigger problems than your unbearably inflated ego!" B'Elanna spat hotly, unsure if she was more annoyed with Seven, or herself for once again allowing Seven's implacable demeanor to destroy every good feeling she had ever had about the woman.

The Key to Gremadia, a gift that had been presented to Janeway by Kaytok, one of the scientists who had aided *Voyager* in their recent successful attempt to destroy the

Blue Eye and escape from a subspace fold, sat in front of its intricately carved case in the captain's cabin, precisely where she had left it less than twenty-four hours earlier. It shared a place of honor among some of the other personal souvenirs that Janeway had collected during *Voyager*'s long journey in the Delta Quadrant, among them a coin—actual currency used on Earth in the mid-twentieth century—given to her by Amelia Earhart before they had left her and the other 37's on the planet that had been settled by their descendants; a necklace that had belonged to the wife of an Alsaurian resistance fighter named Caylem, who had mistaken Janeway for his daughter in the last tortured days of his life; and a rock that had played an integral part in her journey on the Nechani homeworld to find the ancestral spirits in order to save Kes's life. Once she had completed the ritual, her Nechisti guide had suggested she keep the rock as a reminder that oftentimes our experiences are limited rather than enhanced by our expectations.

To the naked eye, the Key was roughly the same size as the Nechani rock, though it had formed or been carved into a perfect circle. Janeway fully intended at some point to analyze the extremely hard yet porous sphere for any scientific or archaeological data it might reveal. But since Tuvok's strange departure had forced them to leave Monorha abruptly, she had scarcely given the gift a thought. Nor had she noticed that almost as soon as she removed it from its ornately carved case and placed it on a small glass table beside her door, it had begun to vibrate almost imperceptibly.

By the time the first intruder had entered her cabin, emerging from the bulkhead in the form of dozens of plasmatic energy tentacles that oozed down the walls, seeking the strange vibrating sphere, the Key to Gremadia had begun to glow as if lit by an internal pinkish gray light. The second intruder barely arrived in time to activate an energy barrier around the Key, protecting it from the one who it knew instinctively had come to destroy the Key, and anyone who got in its way.

"Bigger problems than inching through a section of space that seems to defy every law of physics in search of our head of security, who has gone absent without leave?" Janeway asked, entering the astrometrics lab and the fray at the same time.

B'Elanna and Seven turned to face the captain simultaneously, and Janeway couldn't help but think that at this particular moment these two eminently capable women resembled nothing so much as errant children who had been caught with their hands in one of her mother's antique cookie jars.

B'Elanna looked to Seven, who nodded with only slightly condescending grace to indicate that she should begin their explanation to the captain.

"Well . . . ? " Janeway demanded.

"I've been scanning the singularity, Captain. So far the gravimetric interference has made it difficult to get any clear readings, but in the last hour or so, I've managed to clean up enough of the signal to see this."

Janeway spent a few moments studying the readings, but quickly turned her attention to the large display screen beyond the workstations that bordered the room. Walking calmly up to the staging area just in front of the display, she allowed her mind to integrate both the visual image and the numeric data scrolling beside the image at the same time.

Finally she spoke, almost reverently. "It's a space station, orbiting a black hole."

"Not just orbiting, Captain," Seven chimed in.

"No," Janeway continued, examining the readings more closely, "you're right. It's powered by the singularity. Amazing, isn't it?"

"Captain," B'Elanna said quietly, "it's a little soon to say definitively, but even from this distance, the power signatures appear to be similar to those we saw when we encountered the alien relay stations that had been coopted by the Hirogen."

Janeway turned abruptly. "Have we detected any Hirogen vessels?"

"No, Captain," she answered, "but with the interference, we might not detect them until we were right on top of them."

Janeway considered for a moment before resolving, "I'm confident that the *understanding* we reached with the Hirogen after our last encounter will hold for the time being. And even if they have somehow discovered this, I don't see how or why they would want to make use of it. The relay stations allowed them to stalk prey over much wider areas of space while maintaining communications. Unless this station is filled with beings the Hirogen would find challenging to hunt, I doubt we'll get any trouble from them," Janeway said as she turned back to the display. Finally she asked, "Can we date this technology?"

Seven quickly ran the data through a dozen different algorithms before replying, "The station is at least eighty thousand years old."

Janeway shook her head, awed. "So we have another mystery to add to those we've already encountered in the Monorhan system. It's possible that whatever ancient civilization managed to safely harness the energy of microscopic singularities and build the communications arrays we discovered several months ago didn't stop there."

"You're saying the next step was stabilizing a singularity large enough to power a space station?" B'Elanna asked, clearly ready to rethink her earlier supposition in light of this intriguing hypothesis.

"The relay stations were at least a hundred thousand years old. And the similarity in the power signatures is more than the complex mechanics of harnessing the energy of a singularity. I don't think it's a huge leap to suggest that both the arrays and this station were built by similar, if not, the same hands. The size of it, though," Janeway continued, her eyes glued to the viewscreen image, "It's so much larger than any space station the Federation would ever consider building. It's more like . . ."

"A city," Seven finished.

All three women stared silently at the image of the massive circular construct that orbited slowly around a singularity large enough, by all rights, to have sucked it into oblivion ages ago. Though none of them posed the question aloud, Janeway knew that both Seven and B'Elanna were as curious as she to know exactly what kind of stabilization field would be necessary to keep a piece of engineering that size intact around the densest and one of the most powerful gravitational forces known to the universe.

Finally Janeway broke the silence with a simple order. "I want continuous scans running on every sensor array we have until we reach this. Reroute internal sensors if you have to. We need to know everything we possibly can about it before we get there."

"I wonder if anybody's home, and how they'll feel about our stopping by?" B'Elanna mused aloud.

"We're about to find out," Janeway sighed, resigned. "Because Tuvok's headed right for it."

Chapter 2

Lieutenant Tom Paris, *Voyager*'s senior conn officer, had been ordered by Commander Chakotay to get some rest. He'd pulled more than his fair share of extra duty shifts since they had arrived in Monorhan space, and under normal circumstances would have been grateful for the brief respite. He knew that, even at impulse, *Voyager* would overtake Tuvok's shuttle in a few hours, and he would certainly be called to the bridge when their mission became, as his gut told him it would, more than a simple shuttle recovery. But right now only B'Elanna's firm warm presence nestled against him and her soft rhythmic snores could have guaranteed him a decent chance at sleep. Since B'Elanna was already on duty, he tossed and turned, grateful that at least her musky scent remained on the pillow beside him, arousing pleasant memories of the last night they had shared when she returned from Monorha and was given a clean bill of health by the Doctor. Finally he accepted that any pursuit of rest was probably a lost cause.

"That's it . . ." he resolved, allowing the mischievous demons that had ruled so much of his life to once again wrestle his better angels into submission, ". . . there will be plenty of time to sleep when I'm dead."

Rising from his bed, he considered dressing and heading down to the mess hall to see what frightening dish Neelix had managed to concoct from hydroponic vegetables and his favorite staple, leola roots. But his stomach rebelled at the thought. He had been saving replicator rations for days, planning to surprise B'Elanna the next chance he had with breakfast in bed: banana pancakes for two, a dish she had told him was one of her childhood favorites, but which she had been strangely reluctant to order for herself lately. Doing a little quick math in his head, he rationalized that if he was willing to forgo breakfast for himself for the next few days, he could still surprise B'Elanna and manage to indulge himself a little right now.

Standing over the replicator, he opted for one of his guiltiest pleasures, "Two slices of pepperoni pizza . . . cold." Moments later, seated comfortably in an armchair and savoring every single bite, he searched through his personal padds until he found the one that had most recently captured his imagination.

The padd in question contained everything in the ship's database concerning a series of stories created on Earth in the twentieth century. They were known as "serials," and were usually long and involved action-adventure pieces that chronicled in brief installments the exploits of larger-than-life heroes, their faithful sidekicks, and maniacal madmen bent on destroying the world. Each segment, or "chapter," invariably ended with the hero and his friends trapped in circumstances that could result only in certain death. But week after week, the heroes managed to survive, rescue the beautiful girl, and foil the evil villain.

Tom had spent most of what little free time he'd had of

late searching for the perfect serial to adapt into his next holodeck program. He had already received assurances from Harry that he would grudgingly participate, and if he could drag B'Elanna away from the Klingon martial-arts programs that she had recently begun to fill her free time with, he was certain his efforts would be rewarded with hours of fun for all three of them.

But which one, he wondered to himself, until his gaze fell upon one file on the list he hadn't had time to open yet. Smiling to himself, he read aloud, "Captain Proton, Space Man First Class, Protector of Earth, and Scourge of Intergalactic Evil."

His amusement turned to full-blown glee as he began the first installment of the series, *Captain Proton and Chaotica's Ray of Doom.* Captain Proton was, of course, the hero, his best friend a reporter called Buster Kincaid. But his joy was not complete until he had seen the description of Proton's secretary, the voluptuous Constance Goodheart, who often found herself embroiled in the direst of circumstances while wearing little more than a cocktail dress.

"It's perfect," he said, rising to change into his uniform. The moment he reached his combadge he activated it: "Paris to Kim."

He hardly noticed as he was dressing that he got no response.

The sensors aboard Tuvok's shuttle were nowhere near as sophisticated as those aboard *Voyager,* but all he needed was his bare eyes to know that the object he was approaching as quickly as full impulse would allow was both extraordinary and unique. The massive ring that spun slowly around the singularity he had used to set his course was so much larger than any space station ever constructed by the Federation. Even at this distance, the sensors were also reading densely woven layers of energy fields that, he could only assume, kept the station from being crushed by the gravity of the singularity. The computer could not make any substantive analysis of the molecular structure of the metals or alloys of which the station was composed. Life-form readings were unintelligible.

Nonetheless, Tuvok was absolutely certain that whomever or whatever he had been in contact with was aboard the station. When he allowed the music to break the surface of his conscious mind, he could hear a distinctive change in texture and complexity. It was as if a string quartet had suddenly been overrun by a full symphony orchestra. The delicate harmony lilting above the urgent bass, which continued to pound with the force of its constant voracious need, had become scattered, dissonant . . . as if the various musicians could no longer agree upon a piece to play and instead opted to throw out their sheet music altogether in favor of individual variations. For the first time since this journey had begun, Tuvok found himself wondering whether he might be facing one telepathic entity, or hundreds.

Forcing aside the intensity that commanded him to abandon all restraint, he slowed the shuttle's impulse engines to stationkeeping and began to calculate the safest approach to the station.

"Computer," he ordered, "begin transmitting friendship messages on all subspace bands."

The computer complied with a chirp as Tuvok turned his attention to the navigational controls and began to plot his course.

He was briefly startled—

beat, beat, beat

—when the computer announced, *"Incoming transmission, audio only."*

He took a moment to focus again on his breathing in order to slow his suddenly unruly heart rate, waiting until he was once again in absolute control of his faculties before he ordered, "Computer, play transmission."

A sharp burst of static echoed through the shuttle, though Tuvok noted with satisfaction that his heart rate remained steady as he lowered the volume a few decibels. Tuvok could faintly make out some semblance of a voice through the shrieking of electromagnetic interference, and he set about methodically weeding out the unnecessary signals that were garbling the message.

A few minutes later, he had three words, only one of which had any meaning to him. *"Assylia . . . Monorhan . . . Betasis."* As he put the message on continuous low playback, hoping that the computer might find another word or two, he considered the possibility that he was picking up the transmission from another vessel in the area. Although he was well outside the range that Monorhan ships were thought to have traveled, it was not inconceivable that one of their ill-fated transport vessels had wandered into the region and found itself trapped, or unable to return home. But after he compensated for the gravimetric interference of the singularity, a quick sensor sweep told him that his was the only ship in the immediate vicinity.

Returning his attention to the conn, he entered a new heading, one that would take the shuttle slowly toward the station on a line that followed the curve of the singularity's gravimetric displacement. He believed that this course would allow him to come close enough to the station to find a point of ingress while using the station's own magnetic stabilization field to keep him from falling into the event horizon of the singularity.

The shuttle began to buck and rattle as he neared the

station. Inertial dampers held him relatively steady, though the power drain required to maintain course was unacceptably high. As he methodically began powering down unnecessary systems to compensate, he saw that what had appeared from a distance to be one large ring was actually two rings that turned at the same rate in opposite directions, one on top of the other. An invisible magnetic field held the rings in their orbit, their motion obviously part of the stabilization design. Extending from the rings at regular intervals toward the singularity were dozens of long metal struts. Though he couldn't be certain, it seemed logical that these spokes of the wheels might channel the stabilization field to and from the rings, maintaining its motion and delicate balance.

Power reserves were holding steady, and his course seemed to be leading him toward a series of what could be docking bays, when the shuttle's alarm klaxon began to wail.

Despite his rigorous efforts, Tuvok had misjudged his course. Sensors indicated that he had stumbled upon the edge of the singularity's event horizon, but that seemed impossible. Every calculation dictated that the event horizon should exist within the magnetic fields that bordered the interior of the station's rings. Otherwise the rings should logically have been crushed by the gravity of the singularity. As he was still several hundred kilometers from the outer edge of the rings, he should have been at a safe distance. Nonetheless, the abrupt change in the gravitational pull on the shuttle told Tuvok in no uncertain terms that within moments, he would pass through the singularity's outermost fringe, exposing himself to the mercy of its inexorable pull.

His first instinct was to increase the shuttle's impulse engines to maximum and alter course in a straight line away from the station. It was a tug-of-war he was almost certain to lose, but the only logical option in the moment.

"Warning, shields at fifty percent," the computer called. A second later, *"Warning, shields at thirty percent."*

The engines protested loudly as every ounce of power at the shuttle's disposal was engaged in tearing it free of the singularity's intense pull.

Moments later, his shields were gone. Tuvok tried to route all remaining power to structural integrity, even as consoles began exploding all around him.

In the midst of the chaos, the barrier Tuvok had erected between his mind and the music shattered like glass. For the first time, the feelings were more overwhelming than the sounds. The aching need Tuvok had associated with a single powerful being came rushing forth in a wave of intensity that made him feel as if he had just entered into a mind-meld with a thousand people at the same time.

A few seconds more . . . and he would lose control of more than his shuttle.

The last thing Tuvok heard distinctly through the chaos of sound and light that now enveloped him was the final word of the transmission that the computer had managed to translate before it automatically rerouted all power to inertial dampers, structural integrity, and life-support.

"Gremadia."

"Computer," he choked.

There was no response. The main console erupted in a brilliant flash of light, and Tuvok released himself to the blackness and knew no more.

It wasn't that Harry hadn't heard Tom calling over the comm system. *Voyager*'s ops officer was a notoriously light sleeper who had endured no end of ribbing for his nightly use of an eye mask to ensure the darkest darkness possible when he slept. He had, in fact, started awake at the sound of his name. He just hadn't been particularly inclined to answer. He knew Tom. Whatever he wanted could certainly wait until they were on duty, and if it couldn't, surely the next voice he'd hear would be Chakotay's or the captain's.

"Paris to Kim."

Harry loved Tom like the older brother he'd never had, but sometimes the guy just couldn't take a hint.

Confirmation of that thought arrived a few seconds later when a loud pounding on his door began to reverberate through his cabin.

"Come on, Harry, I know you're in there!" Tom called.

Harry managed to muffle the curses that escaped his lips when his shin impacted something quite heavy, possibly a chair or table leg, en route to answer his door.

"Is the ship in danger?" Harry asked groggily when the doors slid open, a slight spark of indignation lighting in his stomach as Tom's eyes managed to silently mock the pajamas he was wearing, navy flannel plaid that had been a gift from his mother, and, of course, the eye mask hanging around his neck.

"Of course not," Tom answered cheerily. "Although we are at yellow alert, and that's never a great sign."

Harry perked up momentarily at this. "Have senior officers been ordered to the bridge?"

"No. Not yet. And unless I'm mistaken, we won't be for at least another three hours, or until our next duty shift begins, whichever comes first."

"Then, go away," Harry replied, turning back toward his room in an attempt to preempt any further discussion.

Tom managed to slide into the darkened room before

the doors slid shut behind him and immediately called, "Computer, increase illumination."

As the computer responded and the lights in the cabin rose to standard work settings, he continued, "You know it's not a good idea to walk around in the dark, Harry. You might break something."

Harry was already back in bed. And just in case Tom intended to be exceptionally obtuse, he had reset his eye mask and placed two pillows firmly over his head.

Perching himself on the edge of Harry's bed, Tom checked the computer's chronometer before saying, "Come on, Harry, you've been off duty for six hours already."

Through the muffling of the pillows Tom probably barely made out Harry's "And I have two more to go, so get out!"

But Tom was never this easily deterred.

"Harry, do you remember that time you were trapped in a parallel universe or alternate time line or, whatever, back on Earth and only an incredible act of self-sacrifice, that resulted in my death I might add, allowed you to return to your proper . . ."

"That wasn't even you!" Harry screamed into his pillows.

"Yes, but it was a version of me, and the way I see it, I pretty much saved your life, so . . ."

Unwilling to give in to the inevitable, but still determined to make his point, Harry sat up, scattering the pillows, and removed his mask.

"You know, I didn't even have to tell you that story. You would never have known . . ." he began.

"But isn't it great to think that that's the kind of friendship we have? I'll bet that in almost every conceivable time line out there, we've always got each other's backs," Tom continued.

Harry had successfully deluded himself for almost two minutes that he would be able to sneak in another hour of sleep, but the twinkle in Tom's eye made it perfectly clear that whatever scheme Paris had in mind, Harry was already an integral part of it.

"This is one of those 'resistance is futile' moments, isn't it?" Harry asked.

"I'm afraid it is," Tom replied.

"Where are we going?"

"To build a rocket ship and save the galaxy!"

Harry smiled in spite of himself.

"Could be fun."

The first intruder isolated the dissonant electromagnetic discharges it encountered on contact with the energy barrier that had been erected around the Key and dispersed them into harmless static. The atomic particles suspended in the atmosphere of the cabin snapped with a sudden charge before the static began to dissipate. Although this process was temporarily unbalancing and therefore . . . *painful* . . . the intruder did not concern itself with the unpleasantness of the experience. Instead, it threw the entirety of its being against the energy barrier and endured until it recognized the futility of this approach.

A part of it retained an ethereal imprint of sensations that the organic beings who inhabited this dimension referred to as "feelings." It had briefly inhabited this spacetime reality in an alternative form once before. It knew all too well that the longer it spent here, the more vulnerable it would become to mistaking those sensations for "feelings" of its own.

It identified the "feeling" washing over it at the moment as rage. Soon, the angry tumultuous energy spasms that resulted in these "feelings" would overwhelm it, and decrease its ability to counteract the forcefield.

As it re-formed itself into a sharp directed-energy beam that might puncture the barrier, the hostile and disturbing misplaced energy "feelings" were heightened dramatically when yet another series of vibrations were detected in the mix.

It could not remember why these vibrations were so unsettling. Countless moments had passed since it had last encountered them. Turning its attention to the source of the vibrations, it sensed that the one who had erected the forcefield was still present. It had taken a form that mimicked the other types of sentient life that had erupted in this dimension. *A lesser being.*

The form was a little less than two meters high. A soft, flowing, brightly patterned fabric composed of a combination of organic and synthetic polymers covered its four appendages, two that rooted it to the floor for balance and two that extended from its upper torso for the purpose of crudely manipulating solid matter. A round formation with several vulnerable openings sat atop the torso, and it was from one of these openings that the disturbing vibrations were emanating.

Finally, it found the distant memory it was seeking.
She is laughing at me.

"I know why you've come," the being that was so like itself and yet so different said. "You may as well go back, because you won't succeed."

Every moment brought fresh reorienting memories to the surface of its awareness. *Human. She has taken human form.* Though it could easily manipulate the matter of the fragile humanoid brain that regulated the functioning of its body's systems, it knew that such tactics would have no effect on the other, despite appearances.

"That's right," she said, answering its thoughts. "And I do not wish to hurt you either."

It gathered all of the distasteful "feelings" that had percolated inside it from the moment it had crossed into this reality, and directed them toward the other, engulfing her in the vise grip of its fluid tentacles as if it could force a more appropriate response from her.

She had been ready for just such an attack. She did not resist, conserving her energy and using it instead to send her own flow of powerful intentions into its consciousness. Where the two forces met, its rage and her acceptance, there was, for an instant, a delicate balance of energy.

Peace.

It knew this place too. But there could be no peace as long as she protected the object that was vibrating and glowing behind the energy field.

She was struggling to continue speaking. Bound by some of the laws of her form, she could not easily continue making the vibrations she was using to communicate as long as she was held in its powerful grasp.

It knew that if it persisted in this manner, she would defend herself. She was more than capable of repelling any "physical" attack presented.

"Release . . . me . . ." she was struggling to say.

Finally, a thin protective barrier closed over two of her facial openings, soft watery organs that some humanoids used to interpret visual stimuli. This action seemed to allow her to focus more sharply on her own intentions.

She did not speak again; nonetheless, it knew in a flash of insight that she wanted it to remember how to take human form, so that they could communicate more easily.

There was no time.

"There is always time," she struggled.

It slightly released the pressure of its tentacles, and allowed them to explore the humanoid form. Moments later, it had achieved a fair approximation of a human woman, a mirror image of the other that stood before her.

"Thank you," she said, as her respiration returned to normal.

"I do not want your gratitude," it replied, amazed at how quickly it was falling back into certain knowledge of every aspect of the form it now inhabited.

This was followed by an uncomfortable silence. Long ago, countless others had stood in precisely this place of opposition. It was pointless to begin the old arguments again, knowing all possible outcomes.

"You are an individual for the moment," she began. "Would you like a name?"

"I am not a lesser being," it replied scornfully. "I do not appreciate or require individuality. You forget us, and yourself."

The edges of her mouth curved slightly upward in the beginnings of more laughter. Laughter was a sign of amusement or pleasure. What positive feelings she could possibly be taking from this encounter were beyond it, but to argue over such a trifle seemed wasteful.

"I have learned more in my time here than I have forgotten," she countered, "and if you will not choose a name for yourself, I will choose one for you. I was always fond of Vivia. And you may call me Phoebe."

"This designation serves no purpose," Vivia snapped.

"I assure you, my designation is essential to my purpose, and to yours, unless this is a purely social visit," Phoebe replied placidly.

Vivia was momentarily disoriented by the reference.

Finally she realized that this "sarcasm" was a form of pointed laughter. As much as she longed for this temporary captivity to end, she understood that to show anger at Phoebe's game was to empower her further and to divert her attention from more significant issues at hand.

"Very well, Phoebe," Vivia began. "You have broken our agreement. We are aware of the breach and are working, even now, to repair it. Nor will this crude device you have fashioned aid you in your quest to return to the existence you forswore long ago. You will destroy it now, or you will allow us to do so."

Phoebe retorted sharply. "For a transdimensional sentience, you are surprisingly obtuse."

"You cannot insult me, Phoebe," Vivia replied. "I have no feelings to be hurt."

"I was not trying to hurt you. I was merely pointing out that you have come here with assumptions which are incorrect. But this has always been so, hasn't it?" Phoebe did not pause for Vivia's imminent contradiction. "We did not create the breach. Your precious artificial construct had obvious deficiencies. You were warned that this would be the case, but you chose to ignore those warnings. Life has emerged in this system. Life will not be contained, nor will it hesitate to defend and preserve itself. Those who created the rupture did so in an honest effort to sustain their existence and are unaware of the consequences of their actions."

Phoebe's words were disconcerting for two reasons. The first was that as long as they maintained their restrictive human forms, they were incapable of mingling their essences as was more appropriate to their natural state. In that state subterfuge was impossible. Vivia silently wondered if this was not the precise reason that Phoebe had insisted they communicate in this manner. More troubling was the possibility, however, that Phoebe was speaking the truth.

"If lesser beings are responsible, they must be eliminated. Their ignorance does not mitigate the threat they obviously pose," Vivia replied. "But no lesser being could have created the resonance focusing object you are attempting to protect. It is of us."

Phoebe bowed her head. "Of course it is. But it poses no threat to you."

"Then destroy it, and I will deal with the lesser beings."

"I cannot," Phoebe replied simply. "All things here are more complicated than you are accustomed to. No resolution can be achieved by force alone."

Vivia took a moment to consider her surroundings. The simplistic and fundamental atomic compounds that resulted in solid matter of varying hues, shapes, and densities were no match for her manipulative abilities.

"I could destroy this primitive vessel with a thought," she warned.

"As could I," Phoebe replied. "Since I have not, you should consider the possibility that I might have a good reason for not doing so."

"I do not care for your reasons."

"But you should!" Phoebe shouted. "They concern us all."

"You have only ever been concerned with yourself," Vivia argued. "Your presence here is evidence of that. Prove that you are also of us by assisting me."

"You would destroy what you do not understand," Phoebe reasoned. "I cannot allow that."

"You care for these lesser beings?" Vivia shot back. "You have been tainted by your exposure to them."

"I have been expanded by my dealings with these beings and others like them. I have gained knowledge and experience that is beyond you because you choose to be a slave. I will honor your choice, but you must also honor mine. And you must believe me when I tell you that destroying this vessel and the Key that I am protecting will only hasten that which you have spent your entire existence trying to prevent," Phoebe replied.

"That is not possible," Vivia said. "Why are you lying to me?"

"I'm not," Phoebe said carefully. "You are well aware that our interaction with all matter and energy in this dimension has consequences," she continued. "The Key is capable of focusing energy across the barrier that divides us, but the power to use it is now imprinted upon one of the beings who inhabits this ship. It was an unforeseen effect. I take no more pleasure in it than you do."

"Which one of these beings is it, and where are they now?" Vivia asked.

Vivia watched the wave of disconcertion rumble across Phoebe's face. Phoebe had obviously betrayed something she had not intended. Vivia realized in an instant that Phoebe was weaker than she appeared and this knowledge gave her . . . *pleasure*. Then she remembered how to laugh.

The Doctor was, once again, seriously considering taking a name. In four years of almost continual operation, he had toyed with and for a short time adopted more than one—Salk . . . Schweitzer . . . Shmullus . . . Mozart—but these were other men. Great men, to be sure. Their individual accomplishments had lent glory to their names in the eyes of their respective worlds, or those who loved them. But they just weren't . . . *him*. And so, they had been abandoned.

This was hardly the first time he had wrestled with the

Who Am I? question. Each time the subroutines that ordered his cognitive processes worked through the equations involved in answering such a question, the results
were either black and white or nonexistent. The "black
and white" option was, Emergency Medical Hologram
Mark One, AK1 Diagnostic and Surgical Subroutine
Omega 323, operating aboard the Federation Starship *Voyager.* The nonexistent option was a bit more disturbing,
if a hologram could even be "disturbed." He was programmed to display lifelike human emotions in conjunc-
tion with his practice of medicine. But neither he nor
anyone else could say definitively whether or not in dis-
playing those emotions he was actually *feeling* them.

The fact was, however, that what lay beyond the official
designation for his program, a definition of self he had long
ago determined was insufficient, was an emptiness that
sometimes created an unsettling processing loop. It left
him wondering whether or not, without such a definition,
he could even be said to actually exist. Often as not, the se-
lection of a name seemed the first and most important step
in filling that emptiness. But he didn't want somebody
else's name, however lauded. He wanted his own.

It had never really occurred to him that none of *Voyager*'s crew had ever faced his dilemma. Most humanoid
species did not allow their offspring to choose their own
names. Their names were given to them by those who
spawned them. Early on he had realized that as long as
Voyager was in the Delta Quadrant, he was going to have to
think of himself as more than a supplemental program,
but as the ship's chief medical officer. At Kes's urging, he
had asked the captain for a name. There were many subsequent days when he seriously wished that she had taken
him up on that request, rather than leaving him to make
the determination on his own.

Maybe Jim. It was short and simple, shouldn't be too hard for the crew to remember. But Jim was short for James, and there were few Starfleet officers as highly regarded as James Tiberius Kirk.

Adam? It had a nice ring to it. Long ago, certain sects of humans on Earth had believed that Adam was the first man created. As the first continuously functioning and self-aware EMH Mark One, he found a synchronicity in the choice that appealed to him.

But if he was going for simple, why not Matt, or David, or Paul? Having been made in the image of his human creator, Dr. Lewis Zimmerman, he hesitated to move too far beyond the realm of human names. Some of the Klingon and Romulan names contained in his databases also had a certain appeal, though they often sounded as if they were missing a few vowels when they rolled off his simulated tongue.

He had been processing the question for seventy-nine uninterrupted minutes when his aural subroutine alerted him to a faint high-pitched hum emanating from one of the storage cabinets in sickbay.

Crossing to the row of cabinets, he pinpointed the sound. It came from storage unit alpha one. The medium-sized drawer contained the first alien artifact he had ever catalogued and stored, the sporocystian remains of an entity known as the Caretaker.

Though most of the crew thought of the Caretaker as the less than caring alien being who had stranded them in the Delta Quadrant, this was not, strictly speaking, true. The Caretaker had used coherent tetryon technology to transport *Voyager* a distance of seventy thousand light-years from the Alpha Quadrant to the Delta Quadrant, but it was Captain Janeway who had made the decision that left them there. She had intentionally sacrificed *Voyager*'s way home to save the lives of an entire species. Knowing Janeway as well as he did now, the Doctor realized that faced with the alternatives, he could never have expected her to make another choice. The convenience of 146 Starfleet officers and Maquis crewmen did not tip the scales in their favor when weighed against tens of thousands of innocent Ocampa. Though the challenges posed in attempting to cross the seventy thousand light-years that separated them from their homes in the Alpha Quadrant had been arduous, it was to this exact set of circumstances that the Doctor owed what he considered "his life." He, for one, didn't blame the captain. Deep inside his matrix rested a simple subroutine he had labeled "gratitude," which he recalled whenever he considered *Voyager*'s unique circumstances and the opportunities those circumstances had given him.

Nonetheless, he was more than a little disturbed by the vibrating sound that was growing louder every second in storage cabinet alpha one. The last time the Caretaker's remains had done anything other than sit there like the inert, irregularly shaped formation of bioremnants that it was had been Stardate 49164.8. He recalled the day vividly.

Voyager had encountered the only other "Caretaker" they had known of, the original's mate, who called herself Suspiria. She was tending to her own flock of Ocampa, on an array several thousand light-years from that of the original Caretaker. When the ship had come within a certain proximity to her presence, the Caretaker's remains had begun to vibrate, much as they were doing now, and Lieutenant Torres had used readings of those vibrations to accurately pinpoint Suspiria's location.

If the benign and somewhat befuddled creature described in *Voyager*'s logs as the Caretaker was one extreme of his race's temperament, Suspiria was the other. Hostile

and deranged, she had almost succeeded in destroying the
ship in her rage to revenge herself on those she believed
had killed her mate. Although the captain had managed to
thwart Suspiria's murderous rampage, Janeway was never
certain whether or not she had convinced Suspiria that no
one aboard *Voyager* could be held accountable for the
Caretaker's death. He had died of whatever passed for natural causes among his people, the Nacene.

Suspiria had ultimately left the ship and returned to the
subspace layer she inhabited when she did not exist in normal space. When Kes had described the dark and bloody
range of emotions she had experienced when in brief
communication with Suspiria, the Doctor had silently
recorded his hope that *Voyager* never cross her path again.

So it was with no small amount of trepidation that the
Doctor slowly opened the cabinet labeled alpha one, and
removed the spherical transparent container that now
shook with the strange vibrations emanating from the
Caretaker's remains.

He was about to activate the shipwide Emergency
Medical Hologram override channel to alert the captain to
this frightening development when the irregularly shaped
rock began to glow with a faint pinkish light. In the space
of a few seconds, the light burned furiously bright. He
didn't even have a chance to set the container on his desk
and activate an emergency forcefield before the Caretaker's remains exploded violently, ripping through the
storage container and covering the Doctor's photonic
body with sporocystian dust.

It wasn't that Phoebe was unaware of the identity of the
Key's new owner. *Voyager*'s captain, Kathryn Janeway, had
been presented with the Key a little over a day earlier, and
with typical human arrogance and stupidity, the first thing

she had done was remove it from its ceremonial case and give it a cursory visual examination. One touch was all that was required for the Key to sense its new owner and imprint itself upon her.

The emotional spasms she was struggling to contain came from the certainty that Vivia had neither the patience nor the wisdom to do anything other than threaten the owner of the Key with oblivion should she refuse a request. But Phoebe had been watching this Captain Janeway and her crew since the transfer of the Key had taken place. She already knew everything that could be known about these humanoids and their *Voyager*, and she had no doubt that Janeway would willingly die before being coerced into anything.

"You must leave this to me," Phoebe replied, refusing to answer Vivia's question. "I will sever her connection to the Key, but it will take time. Only then will I be able to destroy it."

"And what of the rupture?" Vivia demanded.

"You have said you are already working to seal it. I trust you will succeed, and the peace and balance between us will be maintained."

"You have three days," Vivia replied as she began to release herself from the restrictive and distasteful human form. "If you fail, the Others will return with me, and we will deal with these beings as we see fit."

Phoebe knew this was possible. It was a huge risk, but one she could easily see Vivia and the Others accepting.

As she watched her mirror image dissipate in a mass of flowing, undulating plasmatic energy, she was abruptly thrown to the ground by the unexpected release of highly charged particles that were displaced by Vivia's transformation.

"Dammit," she hissed, picking herself up. *Voyager* possessed highly refined internal sensors. There was only so much she could hide from them. Vivia's unnecessary show of force had surely alerted *Voyager*'s crew to her presence by now.

Although Phoebe had already formed her plan and done much to put that plan into effect, there was still more to do, more than could be done in three short days.

But three days was all she had. Either the captain would do exactly as she said, or they would soon be on a collision course with the unimaginable.

War.

Phoebe took some small comfort in the knowledge that Vivia had, for the present, accepted her less than thorough accounting of the problems at hand. Phoebe did not like to lie. It was usually an unnecessary complication. But in this case, the whole truth had been a risk she was not willing to take.

Turning to examine one of the many crude matter-generation devices that were common on the ship, she paused for a moment over an image that rested on the captain's desk. It was a framed photograph of three women, one obviously older than the other two. All shared the same bright blue eyes and auburn hair. The face of the eldest was marked with slight furrows, particularly around the eyes and mouth, and her hair was streaked with gray, but the physical resemblance among the three was still striking.

"Gretchen," Phoebe said, tracing the older woman's face with a finger. "Mother of Kathryn, and Phoebe," she finished. As she replaced the photo and set to work on the captain's replicator, she decided that of the three, Phoebe Janeway definitely looked the happiest. Perhaps that was a good sign.

Chapter 3

Chakotay had been less than pleased when he called to Tom's quarters and found that he was not, as he had been ordered, getting some extra rest. Chakotay was decidedly uneasy about how the next several hours were going to develop, and he wanted his helmsman in top form. The captain's urgent call for him to gather the senior staff and meet in astrometrics had done nothing to allay his sense of foreboding, but he tried to put it aside as he entered the holographic research lab and found Tom and Ensign Kim conferring with Ensign Brooks. Chakotay suspected that Seven had been pulled from the quantum slipstream drive project earlier to consult with whatever had been found in astrometrics, so perhaps Tom's presence there wasn't evidence of willful disobedience, he reasoned. He was able to sustain that hopeful delusion until he stepped close enough to overhear the subject of their discussion without alerting any of the other three men to his presence.

"Tom thinks there should be multiple settings increasing in intensity, but I'm thinking . . . hey, this is a ray gun. It's only got one purpose—to blow up a planet. Do you see where I'm going with this?" Harry was saying.

"But more settings would allow for a broader range of uses," Brooks replied tentatively, then almost swallowed his tongue when he caught sight of Chakotay standing directly behind Tom and Harry.

"Really, Ensign Brooks?" Chakotay said tersely. "And which part of our quantum slipstream drive will the ray gun in question be attached to?"

Tom and Harry turned in unison to face their first officer. Harry immediately attempted to stammer out some excuse but Tom, as usual, was quicker on his feet.

"I'm sorry, Chakotay. Brooks here was doing a great job on the new drive. I asked him to set it aside for a minute to help us . . . I mean me . . ." he faltered.

"Imagine my surprise," Chakotay replied.

"And it isn't a real ray gun," Brooks added in an attempt to be helpful, "It's for Chaotica's mountain base."

"And Chaotica is . . . ? " Chakotay asked.

"A character in a holonovel," Brooks replied, chagrined.

"Right," Chakotay snapped, certain that all three were now sufficiently apprised of his displeasure. "As you were, Ensign. Lieutenant Paris, Ensign Kim, you're with me. We're needed in astrometrics."

Tom and Harry moved quickly to keep pace with Chakotay as he strode briskly out of the lab. A few steps from the door to astrometrics, Tom's stomach let out a growl of protest loud enough for all to hear. Without missing a step Chakotay inquired, "Are you feeling all right, Mr. Paris?"

"Absolutely, sir," Tom replied. "I was just making a mental note to rethink cold pepperoni pizza during yellow alerts."

"I've heard worse ideas," Chakotay said as the door to astrometrics slid open and he caught the first glimpse on the large viewscreen of the technological marvel *Voyager* was approaching.

B'Elanna, Seven, and the captain were conferring quietly over one of the display panels. Chakotay overheard B'Elanna saying, ". . . at full impulse we'll reach the array in approximately two hours, twenty-eight minutes," before the captain turned and acknowledged his presence with a nod.

"Well, Commander, Lieutenant, Ensign," she asked, gesturing to the main viewscreen, "what do you think?"

Chakotay didn't get a chance to formulate a response. Suddenly the image of the amazing construct circling the singularity was replaced by the Doctor's face looming large on the main display.

As the Doctor was authorized to override main channels only in the event of a serious emergency, Chakotay didn't expect that he was contacting them with pleasant news. But what really piqued his interest was the sight of the Doctor covered head to toe in a thick white powder.

"Sickbay to the captain," the Doctor said.

"Go ahead, Doctor," Janeway replied, as her eyes grew involuntarily large at the sight of him. Before he could continue, she asked, "Doctor, is there a problem with your holographic imagers?"

The Doctor replied with the world-weary tone that Chakotay had come to know and occasionally love. "No, Captain, but thank you for asking. I am, as you can see, covered in a foreign substance."

"How can we assist you, Doctor?" the captain asked impatiently.

"By sending someone, preferably Lieutenant Torres or Seven of Nine, to sickbay," he replied acerbically. "A few moments ago the remains of the entity known as the Caretaker began to vibrate. Within seconds they had exploded. I stand here, just as I am, so as not to disrupt any of the evidence that might lead to a better understanding of just what might have caused this unusual and, dare I suggest, unsettling event."

As soon as the words "Caretaker" and "exploded" had fallen from the Doctor's lips, Chakotay's mind began to automatically render and prioritize possible scenarios that could account for such a thing. As usual, the captain and B'Elanna were also immediately in the hunt. The moment their eyes locked they began to speak in the fragments and clipped sentences that Chakotay had grown accustomed to between these two women whose passion for science was surpassed only by the apparent effortlessness with which they dug their teeth into a complex problem.

"B'Elanna . . ." Janeway began.

"I'm checking the sensor logs now," B'Elanna said. After a brief pause, she went on, "The explosion was the result of an internal change in the resonance of the molecular structure of the Caretaker's remains. The last time we saw something similar to this, the vibrations were created when subspace dissonance waves impacted the molecular bonds, temporarily destabilizing them. We were able to calculate the intensity of the wave force to guide us to the Caretaker's mate. But even when Suspiria was on board *Voyager* the vibrations weren't sufficient to completely break down those bonds."

The captain studied the display of *Voyager*'s sensor grid as she added, "None of our sensors are detecting any subspace dissonance waves now."

"Could the gravimetric interference generated by the singularity be impacting subspace?" B'Elanna posited.

"It's possible, but you would think whoever designed the stabilization field around the array would have compensated for that," Janeway replied. "How else would they maintain structural integrity?"

"Maybe they did," B'Elanna continued, "but only in a highly localized area. The stabilization field surrounding the construct must be strong enough to dampen the intensity of the force generated by the singularity, but only in its immediate vicinity."

"So at this distance, both space and subspace might be affected, but our sensors wouldn't be able to distinguish between the effects on each of them," the captain finished.

There was a brief pause as Chakotay worked diligently to wrap his brain around the nuances of the discussion. As usual, however, Seven was way ahead of him and did not hesitate to join the conversation.

"What you are suggesting could also account for the irregular collapse of the white dwarf," she said.

Janeway immediately picked up the thread.

"She's right. Since we didn't consider any excess gravitational flux in our calculations, we weren't prepared to see the formation of the microsingularity. The white dwarf acted as a natural barrier between our sensors and this array."

"It would also explain why the microsingularity is growing at an unexpected rate," Seven added.

"What?" B'Elanna and Janeway snapped in unison.

"The microsingularity has grown to approximately one hundred times its original size in the last twelve hours," Seven replied serenely.

Chakotay studied the readouts that Seven had pulled up on her display screen. "It should have taken at least two hundred years for it to reach its current size, and it is continuing to expand at an accelerated rate," he said tensely. "Captain . . ."

"I know," Janeway said wearily. "For the time being,

Monorha is safe, but if it continues to expand at the rate we're seeing that will change in a matter of months."

"Oh, Captain . . ." the Doctor interjected.

"I'm on my way, Doctor," B'Elanna said, receiving a slight nod of approval from the captain. "I want to analyze the debris and confirm our hypothesis."

"Captain . . ." Chakotay began.

But before he could continue, the ship buckled beneath their feet. Everyone quickly placed a secure hand on whatever was closest and firmly attached to the deck to avoid landing on the floor.

Naomi sat up straight in her chair as Neelix placed the grilled cheese sandwich garnished with two slices of pickled leola root in front of her.

"And what would you like to drink, my dear?" Neelix asked warmly.

"May I please have a cup of coffee?" she asked.

The faint brown spots that covered her Talaxian godfather's head and neck darkened a little as he replied, "Not under any circumstances, young lady. You're much too young to drink coffee."

"But Neelix," she whined, "the captain drinks coffee all day long."

"And when you're the captain, you can have anything you like. But as long as you're a little girl and I'm in charge of the mess hall, your choices are water, juice, or milk."

Naomi wrinkled her nose in faint disgust as she decided that this was probably not a battle she was going to win.

"Milk, please," she said.

Neelix returned moments later with a tall glass of cold milk, and seated himself across from her. She took a dutiful sip before digging into her sandwich with real gusto.

Her mother loved grilled cheese sandwiches. There were other human foods that Naomi had no stomach for, strawberries, broccoli, and scrambled eggs among them. The Doctor had told her that it was probably the Ktarian half of her that didn't like these foods—the half of her she had inherited from the father she had never known.

She wanted to be just like her beautiful, kind mother. So she had forced herself to try and eat everything her mother ate, even when she ended up in sickbay for two whole hours once when she couldn't stop throwing up after inhaling a dessert called "strawberry shortcake." She had been thrilled to discover that melted cheese on toasted, buttered bread was something she and her mother could enjoy together. Even though her mother wouldn't be able to join her and Neelix for lunch today, she had intentionally requested grilled cheese. She would save half to share with her mother when her duty shift was done.

But there was a problem.

Half the sandwich was already gone and Naomi was still hungry. As she considered the half she had mentally reserved for her mother, a third option sprang to mind.

"Neelix?" Naomi asked.

"Yes, my dear?" he replied.

"Do you think you could make me another half a sandwich?"

He smiled. "Of course," he answered, rising to go to the kitchen. "I'll wrap it up for you. Your mom will be pretty hungry when she gets off duty. It will make a perfect snack."

Naomi grinned broadly as she took a huge bite of the rest of her lunch. It was nice having a godfather who could read her mind.

She was glad she had picked up her sandwich when she

did. Moments later, her seat shook violently beneath her, spilling the still mostly full glass of milk all over her plate.

Once the disturbance had passed, Janeway quickly tapped her combadge.

"Janeway to the bridge. What was that?" she snapped.

"We don't know, Captain," Rollins replied. *"We're reading some kind of electromagnetic discharge."*

"Is it coming from the singularity?" was Janeway's next question.

"Negative, Captain. It originated within the ship. It might have been an overload in the power relays. Give me one moment."

Janeway could feel her anxiety rising to a fever pitch.

"Lieutenant Rollins?" she finally asked, unable to contain herself any longer.

"Captain, the discharge originated in your cabin."

Janeway started immediately for the door as she called out, "Send a security team to meet me at my cabin. I'm on my way there now."

"Understood," Rollins replied.

"Commander," she said as Chakotay moved to join her, "I need all available personnel monitoring the array and the microsingularity."

"I'll see to it," he replied.

Less than two minutes later, Janeway turned the corner to find three security officers standing outside her cabin, both their phasers and their tricorders at the ready.

"Report," she ordered when she reached them.

All three of them seemed puzzled by the readings they were getting. Ensign Maplethorpe was the first to offer, "There's a life-form in there, Captain. For a minute, it looked like more than one, but our tricorders don't seem to be calibrated properly. I've never seen interference like this."

Janeway grabbed her phaser as she called to the computer, "Computer, can you identify the life-form in my cabin?"

She was momentarily stunned at the computer's reply. *"Phoebe Janeway."*

With her free hand Janeway entered the code to unlock her cabin door. When the door slid open, Ensign Maplethorpe and the others fell into formation behind her as she entered.

Phoebe sat cross-legged on the floor in front of Janeway's replicator. The front panel had been removed and placed beside her. She was pulling a damaged piece of conduit from an exposed, sparking wire.

Janeway shook her head in disbelief.

"Phoebe," she asked. "What are you doing here?"

Tuvok stood bathed in a bright white light. The source of the light was directly over his head at a distance of several meters, if the diameter of the circle on the floor around his feet could be used as any indication. Beyond the circle was an inky darkness. But it was not empty.

They're waiting for me to begin.

He didn't know how he knew this. But he was absolutely certain that a few arms-lengths beyond the circle of light, hundred . . . maybe thousands . . . were waiting in rapt attention for his next move.

And then it hit him.

He could no longer hear the music.

It should have been a relief. But somehow the strange symphony that had first called to him hours ago had carved out a space of its own within his mind. Its absence left him feeling more than empty. He was suddenly incomplete.

His continuing sense of the presence was a small comfort. He consoled himself with the thought that perhaps this was the next logical step in establishing communication with those that had called him here.

"I have come," he said quietly. "What do you want with me?"

Each moment of silence that followed added exponentially to the agony of his exquisite loneliness. He wanted to step beyond the circle of light, but somehow he knew that he would not reach them physically. A deep chasm separated him from those he had come to find.

He closed his eyes and attempted to reach out to them with his mind.

Nothingness enveloped him.

The next thing that rose to his consciousness was the 289th verse of *Falor's Journey*. Tuvok had sung the epic poem to his children when they were young. He wasn't certain if this fragment of his past seemed suddenly important because of its haunting melody, or because of this verse's subject.

> *Falor entered the temple of Kir*
> *Certain that at last his journey*
> *Had brought him to this place of peace*
> *So that his burdens and sorrows*
> *Could be lifted from his weary mind*
> *But all that greeted his newfound hope*
> *Was silence, only silence.*

Tuvok began to sing. The words pulled from his distant past were difficult to find at first. He let the melody lead him forward, until the story of Falor's encounter with the monks of Kir and the lesson Falor had learned from their silence poured forth as easily as it had when he had sat beside his eldest son's bed, and used the tale to lull the infant Sek to sleep.

A faint hum of recognition seemed to thrill his audience. He wanted to stop singing, so that he could focus more clearly on their response. But he was afraid to break the subtle connection he was beginning to forge.

He continued, noting with relief that as he did so, the circle of light grew brighter, its range wider, giving powerful support to his rich baritone voice. A little more, he believed, and the light would extend to a range that would illuminate those he was trying desperately to reach.

His right eye began to burn. There had been an uncomfortable stinging sensation present there since the moment he had awakened within the circle, but it was becoming more difficult to ignore. Determined to continue, he wiped his eye, attempting to remove any foreign substance that would account for his discomfort. When he touched his eye, he realized that it was caked almost completely shut by some hardened substance. A warm liquid oozed from the area above his eye, pouring into the small opening that remained, causing the unpleasant burn. He pulled his hand away to examine his fingers and discovered that they were covered with blood . . . green blood . . . his blood. He gently allowed his fingers to explore his forehead above his eye, and his alarm was intensified when he discovered a large gaping gash that was the source of the blood pooling into his eye. He was instantly alerted to a dull throbbing that intensified as he focused on it, making it impossible for him to continue singing.

Suddenly, the pain was everywhere.

His right arm was on fire. Tuvok had suffered his fair share of plasma and radiation burns in the years he had served in Starfleet. He estimated that the burn on his right arm was probably third-degree, while the one that covered much of his chest was second-degree. Mentally cataloguing the rest of his body, he realized that he couldn't feel his left leg. His first thought was nerve damage. A sharp blow to his cervical spine could account for the lack of sensation, but as he turned to focus his one good eye on his left leg, he realized that he simply could not see it.

What he could see was that the circle of light, which had begun its tentative expansion, had snapped back to the small spot surrounding his feet.

And then, the light was extinguished.

Tuvok lay on the floor of his shuttle. It was cold in the cabin. It was logical to assume that his body had not been the only thing ripped apart in the explosion, which was the last thing he could remember. But he could breathe. Whatever the damage to the shuttle, wherever he was, he was grateful that he had not yet been exposed to the vacuum of space.

He gingerly raised his left arm and again began to explore his face. Wherever he had just been—in a dream, or in an alternate reality created by the presence that had drawn him here—he had not imagined the severity of his injuries.

He tried to sit up. The shock of sensitivity in the exposed nerve endings of his abdomen that had been flayed by the plasma explosion beneath the main console of the shuttle almost caused him to lose consciousness again.

Taking as deep a breath as the pain would allow, he attempted to slowly turn his head slightly down and toward the left. He could move his neck. That was a good thing. Perhaps the lack of feeling in his lower left extremity was not the result of cervical damage after all.

Though the shuttle's standard and emergency lighting systems were obviously damaged beyond repair, there was a faint bluish glow present in the cabin. Allowing his eye a moment to adjust to what little light there was, he peered into the dimness around him, hoping to assess the injury to his leg. He was not startled, more disappointed when he made out his left leg bent at an impossible angle at the knee, jutting up toward his thigh. Obviously it was broken, almost in half.

He tried to calculate the odds that from his present position he would be able to pull himself through the cabin and find the emergency medical kit that came standard with every Starfleet shuttle. They were dismally low. But even this was not enough to completely shatter his resolve.

He had managed to grab hold of a random piece of solid metal within range of his left hand and force the resulting wave of nausea to a section of his mind that could ignore it before he realized that the physical injuries he had just sustained were not the only part of the vision he had just experienced that was real.

The music that had become as much a part of his mind and body as the air he breathed and the blood that flowed in his veins had left him. The presence that had become his constant companion was gone. He tried to focus on it, willing it to appear again in his mind. But the torrent of pain overwhelmed every other aspect of his consciousness, leaving no room for such exertions.

For the first time in his entire life, Tuvok felt the loneliness that his Vulcan discipline had never before allowed him to experience. He didn't know why he could no longer sense or hear the presence. Perhaps the injuries to his body actually paled in comparison to the physical injuries of his brain. It was likely that the music was still present. He had felt a tentative connection forming only moments ago. But if the centers of his brain that linked him to the alien presence had been damaged, that would more than account for his inability to hear them now.

All he knew for sure was that he might still be able to survive his physical pain. He retained enough of himself to force his mind beyond it. But he could not survive the loneliness. He could not imagine how anyone suffering a similar sense of loss could ever survive it.

Tuvok's hand released the metal support he had grasped, and he felt the wind knocked from his lungs as his upper body slapped back to the floor. Alone in the cold blue darkness, he began to weep.

As he tidied up Naomi's spilled milk, Neelix affectionately considered his beautiful and good-natured charge. He couldn't believe how quickly she was growing up. It seemed like only yesterday she had been cradled in his arms, a wriggling cooing slice of pure joy. Most of the time, he counted Naomi as one of the greatest blessings he had ever received. But as part of his brain fretted over the disruption that had overturned her milk, he felt a pit of concern tighten in his stomach again.

Much as he loved Naomi, and much as he could no longer imagine his life without her, he had to acknowledge that no starship, even one as marvelous as *Voyager,* was any place for a child.

Before Naomi was born, he'd never understood the affection others had for children. He had long ago resigned himself to a solitary existence, which had changed only when he met Kes. He had even summoned the courage to agree to have a child with Kes when the *elogium* had come upon her prematurely. But he hadn't been able to hide from Kes or himself the niggling doubts that shrouded that difficult decision. To this day he believed that they had both been relieved when the *elogium* had passed, and the Doctor had assured them that she would probably be able to conceive in a few years, as was normal for an Ocampa.

But Kes was gone. The life that he had imagined for both of them was a distant memory. Naomi hadn't replaced Kes in his heart. That would have been impossible. But the love he had found in nurturing *Voyager*'s only child had been a soothing balm in the dark days after Kes had departed.

He watched her eat, satisfied that she was obtaining as least most of the nutrients her growing body needed from her lunch, and thumbed through the drawings she had worked on throughout the morning.

The one she had obviously spent the most time on was a copy of the starfield she had given to Captain Janeway that morning. He had barely been able to contain the deep pride that welled in his heart when Naomi had recounted in every detail her meeting with the captain and her request to hang Naomi's drawing in her ready room. But Naomi had intended that drawing for her mother. She had been momentarily alarmed when she realized that by giving it to the captain, she would be denying this special gift for Ensign Wildman, and Neelix had tactfully resolved her dilemma by suggesting that she had plenty of time to make her mother another one before her duty shift ended late that afternoon.

Neelix had an eye for detail. It had been developed in his years as a "junk" trader, one of many occupations he had attempted before his fortuitous encounter with *Voyager.* One man's junk was another man's treasure, if you knew what to look for. As he cast his eye over Naomi's new drawing, he puzzled over a large empty black area near the center. He couldn't say for sure, but he believed that this was different from the first drawing he had so carefully helped her begin the night before and finish up that morning. Of course it was possible that Naomi had simply chosen to draw the stars of the Monorhan system from another vantage point, but the rest of the drawing was so close to the original that he doubted this was the case. And despite Naomi's age, she had already shown herself to be an intensely detail-oriented child. He didn't believe she had made a mistake. But he also had a hard time believing that a star that had been so prominent only a few hours earlier was simply no longer present.

He turned to look out one of the mess hall's large windows, carefully studying the area of space Naomi had duplicated. Comparing her drawing with the stars, he realized that she had, once again, drawn the view from the window quite precisely. There was, in fact, a large area, devoid of stars, right where her drawing indicated.

And then it hit him.

The small void in question was either the exact area or very near the spot where, only a few days ago, the Blue Eye, one of Monorha's two suns, had been. He had read the reports without dwelling on the details that recounted the work *Voyager*'s engineers had proposed to collapse the star to slow the outpouring of radiation that was poisoning Monorha. Since their emergence from the subspace field where they had been trapped for several harrowing hours, he had spent more than a fair amount of time gazing out upon the area, both because he'd had a nice view of it from the mess hall, and also because it had inspired such a sense of awe and wonder to consider the miracles his crew was capable of achieving.

Maybe he was imagining things. But part of him felt certain that apart from the Blue Eye, which he knew was gone, there should have been another star there.

Shaking off the tiny voice in his head insisting that this

was not a good thing, he made a mental note to mention the matter to the captain or Commander Chakotay the next chance he had. Surely they would know what was to be done about it.

As Janeway gazed curiously at her sister, Phoebe rose from her position on the floor, straightening the folds of her floral tunic so that it fell gracefully from the sash that gathered it around her waist.

"Since when do you need a security detachment to accompany you to your quarters?" she asked sarcastically.

"Since when do you enter my quarters without asking permission?" Janeway snapped back. "This isn't our house back in Indiana. But I guess some things never change."

Phoebe cast a disparaging glance at Ensign Maplethorpe and the other officers who still had their phasers aimed in her general direction. Janeway noted this, and calmly nodded, indicating that the others could go, before she holstered her own phaser and assumed the position Phoebe guessed was the one she usually found herself in when confronting her sister about anything: hands on her hips, jaw set, and eyes staring determinedly into those that could have been a mirror image of her own.

As the security officers retreated, Phoebe decided it would be best not to antagonize Janeway too much at this point. She had armed herself with every memory stored in Janeway's conscious and unconscious mind about her sister, but she lacked the data that could be gained only by actual experience or interaction with the captain. She opted to tread carefully for the moment.

"I thought you always said I made the best coffee of anyone in the family," she said simply.

Janeway shook her head in disbelief.

"You do," Janeway acknowledged. "But you don't

know the difference between a power conduit and an iso-linear chip. Did you honestly think you could come up with a better cup of coffee by trying to rebuild the replica-tor?"

"I thought it might be worth a try," Phoebe offered.

In fact, she had been searching for a plausible cause for the electromagnetic discharge that she knew would even-tually attract someone's attention. Mucking around in a primitive system that she supposedly had very little knowledge of had been the best she could come up with on a moment's notice.

"I don't have time for this, Phoebe. Go back to your quarters and stay there."

"But Kath," Phoebe pleaded, hoping to unearth some of the sisterly affection she knew was present in Janeway's heart.

"No, 'but's," Janeway commanded. "The ship is at yel-low alert right now. It isn't safe for you to be roaming around. You'll just cause more trouble."

In some ways, this was going well. For the time being, Janeway obviously accepted the fabricated memories that Phoebe had implanted in her mind and the minds of the crew so that they would accept her presence on board the ship. The alterations she had made to their computer were also functioning perfectly. It took a great deal of energy to maintain this illusion, but Phoebe knew she didn't have to do it for long.

She had chosen to assume a form that Janeway would find comforting and familiar. Having never had a "sister," she had not anticipated that the depth of affection she knew that Janeway and the real Phoebe shared would be mitigated by so many other powerful conflicting emotions. Seeing Kathryn through Phoebe's eyes, she realized that despite the similarity in their outward appearances, their respective temperaments were markedly different.

Searching through the catalogue of memories she had lifted from Janeway's mind, she found a tactic that might be more suited to her immediate needs.

"Why don't you let me help you?" Phoebe asked.

Janeway looked puzzled.

"Help me?" she said slowly, overenunciating each vowel and consonant sound. Crossing her arms defiantly she asked, "How do you propose to do that?"

"I don't know. Tell me what's going on and maybe I could . . ."

"Paint me a picture?" Janeway chided.

Phoebe allowed her face to fall, and smiled inwardly as she heard Janeway silently curse herself. It was a definite advantage that even while wearing a human form, she possessed the ability to understand all that Janeway said, whether aloud or in the privacy of her mind.

I'm snapping at everyone this morning, Janeway was thinking. *Patience has never been one of my many virtues, but there's no reason to take my frustrations out on the artist of the family.*

Phoebe mused at how different two women who shared so much genetic history could be. Although Phoebe was a few years younger then Kathryn, the older they got the less noticeable this fact was. She knew from Janeway's memories that others had often remarked at the striking similarities in their features: the deep blue eyes that turned a stormy gray when they were angry, the high forehead crowned by fine flowing auburn hair. But Phoebe had their mother's full lips, and like Gretchen Janeway, smiled often. The two most significant women in Kathryn's life shared the innate ability to find the humor in most of life's challenges, whereas Kathryn, like her father, spent less time laughing about life than she did trying to conquer it.

"I'm sorry, Phoebe," she sighed. "Tuvok left the ship several hours ago and he's headed for some kind of alien space station that orbits and is powered by a singularity."

"Tuvok? Your tactical officer? The Vulcan?"

"You're asking like you've never met the man," Janeway said.

"Of course," Phoebe covered quickly. "I don't mean *which* Tuvok. I mean, I can't believe he would do something like that."

"Neither can I," Janeway replied.

"You're worried about him, aren't you?"

"Of course I am."

"I'm sorry, Kath."

Phoebe opened her arms and saw Janeway's eyes glistening with tears as she fell into the comfort of her sister's embrace.

Much better, Phoebe thought.

Time to change the subject.

"You know I was talking to Master da Vinci, and he suggested I might go back to realism for a while," Phoebe offered quietly.

"You couldn't ask for a better mentor, Phoebe, even if he is a hologram," Janeway said genuinely, disentangling herself from Phoebe's arms while continuing to clasp her hands warmly.

"It was very thoughtful of you to create him for me," Phoebe added.

I didn't, Phoebe heard Kathryn think.

Phoebe paused. Janeway should be accepting everything she suggested without resistance. But to her relief, the captain didn't dwell on it. Instead, she mentally chalked it up to the length of time since her last cup of coffee. She couldn't imagine where this abrupt and ungenerous thought had come from and was only too relieved she hadn't said it aloud.

"I actually came by looking for some inspiration," Phoebe continued. Crossing to the small glass table where the Key rested, she paused over it.

"What's this?" she asked as innocently as she could.

"That was a gift from the Monorhans. They called it the Key to . . ." Janeway's brow furrowed as she tried to remember. ". . . something or other."

"It doesn't look like a key."

"I know," Janeway smiled, crossing to Phoebe. "I don't think they meant it literally. I assumed it was symbolic . . . like the key to a city being given to a visiting dignitary."

"Can I have it?" Phoebe asked.

Janeway was obviously taken aback. The real Phoebe wasn't one to think before she spoke, but even so, this might have seemed unusually blunt.

"No," Janeway replied, with a half-smile. "Phoebe, it's a sphere. If da Vinci wants you to explore realism, I think he'd be a little disappointed with such a simple subject. Don't you want something a little more challenging?"

"I suppose," Phoebe shrugged. "I didn't think it was that important to you. I mean, you can't even remember what it's called."

Janeway considered the Key. "It's not the object, Phoebe," she said gently. "It's what it represents—the gratitude of an entire planet."

"I understand, Kath," Phoebe replied.

"But if you seriously want to use it . . . if it inspires you . . . go ahead. Take it to Master da Vinci and see what he says."

Phoebe considered for a moment. Borrowing the Key would not suit her purposes.

"I'll think about it," she finally answered. "Can we have dinner tonight?"

Janeway gave her sister's hand a warm squeeze. "I certainly hope so . . . but I wouldn't count on it."

The Key was barely an arm's length away from Phoebe, but it might as well have been buried beneath a frozen ocean on the other side of the galaxy. It was still vibrating, but at a rate so slow that the human eye would not normally detect it.

Once Janeway had left, she placed her hands around the sphere, absorbing some of the energy it was displacing. The effort cost her more than she had anticipated. Casting herself beyond the limited subatomic particles that were organized to form the substance of the ship and its crew, she searched for the source of the disruption the Key was responding to.

It didn't take her long to discover the abominations. Trapped between this dimension and the existence Phoebe had forsworn long ago, they waited patiently for someone or something to guide them home. Somehow Tuvok had also been alerted to their presence. He could not have grasped the faintest fragment of their truth, but nonetheless she sensed the rapidly unraveling tether that bound his mind to theirs.

Their existence changed everything. She set out immediately for the array that she and so many others had devoted much of their existence to building and was determined to spend the remainder protecting.

For the moment, Janeway and the Key would have to wait.

Chapter 4

Seven of Nine rarely found anything shocking. Every significant fact of time, space, and quantum reality that could be calculated was contained within her mind. As a Borg, she had been privy to the experience of billions of others, and added their knowledge to her own. Though she was now severed from the hive mind, she had retained every facet of their collective knowledge, culled from the millions of sentients who had been assimilated into the Borg collective.

But there was no other word to adequately contain the disbelief with which she viewed the latest sensor logs *Voyager* had compiled as it neared the array. Although she no longer sympathized with the Borg imperative that perfection was attainable through assimilating unwilling individual life-forms, she took a moment to consider the fact that had the Borg ever encountered the array she was studying, and been able to successfully assimilate it, they not only might have achieved perfection, but would certainly have become a force against which no civilization in the galaxy including the Federation could have stood for long.

Scrolling through the data summarized on the padd

she had brought with her to the captain's ready room, she was almost at a loss to determine where exactly to begin her report.

"Seven?" the captain asked, her tone clearly communicating the concern awakened by the hesitant confusion plain on Seven's face.

"I was able to compensate for the gravimetric interference that was blinding our sensors to the array's interior," Seven began, "and have compiled a complete schematic."

"Go on," Janeway encouraged.

"It is difficult to know where to begin. The array is unlike anything I have ever seen," Seven continued. "To be more precise, it is unlike anything I would ever have believed possible."

Janeway rose from the seat behind her desk and gently took the padd from Seven's hand, perching herself on the desk's edge as she began to examine its contents.

"This has to be a mistake," Janeway said slowly.

"I assure you, there are no errors," Seven replied.

"You expect me to believe that this array is capable of manufacturing and storing every single element in the known universe . . . even a few we've never seen . . . and refining them into pure energy sources?" Janeway asked.

"Belief is irrelevant," Seven said simply. "One of the two rings that comprise the array is dedicated completely to the accumulation, storage, and processing of atomic particles ranging from the simplest to the most complex. There are hundreds of power transfer conduits which branch out from the central refinery so that energy can be distributed throughout the array's various systems. In addition, there are forty-seven docking bays equipped with storage tanks and fueling systems which would appear to be compatible with all known starship propulsion engines and power grids."

"This doesn't make any sense," Janeway said, shaking her head.

"The singularity that the array orbits, like many singularities of its size, would theoretically contain all of the elements we are reading in some form. Though I cannot speculate as to how they are able to gather, stabilize, and process those elements . . ."

"That's not what I mean," Janeway cut her off. "Consider the point of view, or the goals and aims of a species of sentient beings who would construct such a thing. Set aside the 'How did they do this?' question for the moment. Typically, once a civilization becomes capable of interstellar travel, they utilize the elements that are accessible when they develop their propulsion and power systems. In the case of Starfleet, for example, our matter-antimatter reactors require dilithium to harness their energy, which is relatively common within the Federation. Our scientists are constantly seeking new and more efficient energy systems, and as breakthroughs are made, Starfleet vessels are upgraded to incorporate new developments and the others are discarded. What we are seeing here suggests that the array's builders anticipated the fact that multiple vessels using hundreds of different propulsion and power systems would, at some point, need to use the array for fueling."

"Perhaps many different species participated in the construction of the array," Seven offered.

"Perhaps," Janeway mused, "but that doesn't change the fact that while this is a marvelous and brilliant system, it is also incredibly impractical."

Seven could not argue the point, nor did she wish to. The energy systems she had discovered were only one of the many marvels the sensors told her were present aboard the array.

"At this time we do not possess enough data to form any complete hypothesis as to the motivations of the array's designers," Seven said. "However, I believe there is evidence to support the position that the array was intended to be used by multiple species."

"What makes you say that?" Janeway asked.

"The second ring that comprises the array contains life-support systems for every species contained in the Federation database, as well as every race the Borg ever encountered."

Janeway tried and failed miserably to hide the level of shock generated within her by Seven's characteristically stark and simple description of a technological miracle as Seven continued her report.

"In addition, the array's computer core contains trillions of gigaquads of data stored in densely compacted information retrieval buffers. I calculated the system requirements for a core that could contain data including planetary composition, interstellar phenomena, complete astrometric mapping, and life-form analysis for our galaxy alone. This system exceeds those requirements by a factor of ten."

"Where to begin, indeed," Janeway said, as if finally understanding Seven's initial inability to begin her report. "You said there are life-support systems present," she continued. "Does that include human life?"

"There are many areas within the array that currently contain an oxygen/nitrogen atmosphere which would allow us to explore without environmental suits," Seven replied. "In addition, there is evidence that the environmental systems aboard the array are adaptive."

"Adaptive?" Janeway asked.

"There are sensor grids in the airlocks which connect the docking bays to the rest of the array that are set to detect the precise life-support requirements of any individual who comes on board and adjust the internal atmosphere accordingly."

"How thoughtful," Janeway quipped, before asking the obvious question. "What about life signs?"

Seven's brow furrowed. "It is difficult to say."

"Why?"

"*Voyager*'s sensors are calibrated to detect consistent life signs. Even when those signs are faint, they are detectable as long as they remain constant for one second or more. Within the array, there are indications of life, but they fluctuate too rapidly for definitive analysis."

"You mean in less than a second, a life-form may be alive, and then dead?" Janeway asked.

"A more accurate explanation, based on the readings I have collected, would be that in less than a second the potential life-forms I am reading exist, and then cease to exist."

"It might be a sensor glitch," Janeway suggested.

"It might. The sensors have been operating at maximum since we encountered the array and our systems could be overloading, though every diagnostic I have run suggests otherwise."

"So it's possible the array is devoid of life, at least humanoid life . . ." Janeway began.

"Or it is possible that there are thousands of different life-forms currently occupying the array," Seven finished.

"What about Tuvok?" Janeway asked.

"We have pinpointed Lieutenant Tuvok's shuttle and life signs within one of the docking bays. His life signs are growing weaker."

"Dammit!" Janeway vented.

"We will be within transporter range within the next fifty minutes," Seven said, softening the blow as best she could. "Even if the lieutenant has sustained serious injuries, we should be able to transport him to sickbay in time for the Doctor to . . ." She hesitated to finish the statement with the words "revive him."

Janeway nodded, eliminating the need for her to find a more comforting phrase.

"There is one more thing, Captain," Seven said.

"What's that?"

"One of the other docking bays is currently occupied."

"Can you identify the vessel?"

"It is Monorhan . . . but . . ."

"Go on," Janeway said.

"Its technology does not conform to the specifications of the Monorhan vessels we have already encountered in several significant respects. There are organic components to the design which are unusual, and their propulsion system is somewhat primitive by current standards."

"An early transport vessel perhaps?" Janeway suggested.

"One of the Monorhans I worked with while Lieutenant Torres and I were on the surface told me of a group of Monorhans who left the planet almost fifty years ago. They were members of the planet's Fourteenth Tribe. They were seeking something known as Gremadia, a city built by their god."

"The Key to Gremadia!" Janeway said, apropos of nothing that Seven could see.

As the ocular implant that almost surrounded Seven's left eye rose quizzically Janeway explained, "Phoebe was asking me about the Key a little while ago and I couldn't remember what it was called."

"What is your sister's interest in the Key?" Seven asked.

"She's bored and looking for a new subject to paint, or sculpt."

"The Key is a perfect sphere," Seven said as if no further information were required.

For Janeway, none was.

"I suggested she find something more challenging," she replied, before returning to the more interesting and intriguing topic of the array. Finally she said, "If the Monorhans were looking for a city built by a god, based on these readings anyway, it looks like they might have found it."

Seven's face fell skeptically. Surely the captain did not seriously believe that the array was constructed by an alien deity.

"If this tribe was searching for Gremadia, why didn't they take the Key with them when they left?"

"I believe there was a dispute among members of the *hara* who had the Key. Not all of the members of the Fourteenth Tribe left the planet. Nor do I believe that the Key was required to gain access to Gremadia. Its significance was primarily as an artifact which imparted visions of the true nature of their gods to the ancient Monorhans."

"Torres to Captain Janeway," B'Elanna called over the comm.

Janeway sighed heavily before tapping her combadge to reply, "Go ahead, B'Elanna."

"Are you available to come to engineering, Captain?" B'Elanna asked. *"We found something you need to see."*

"I'll be right there," Janeway said, closing the connection and returning the padd to Seven. "For the moment the religious beliefs of the Monorhans will have to be set aside. I want you to show this to Commander Chakotay. I want teams organized before we reach the array to board it and gather as much data as we can."

Seven nodded in acknowledgment.

"And Seven," she continued. "As long as we're stopping

at the biggest fueling station in the quadrant, we should determine whether or not we can use this technology to replenish our own systems."

"Agreed," Seven replied.

Only after Janeway had left, en route to engineering, did Seven realize that the captain did not require her *agreement*. As B'Elanna would no doubt have pointed out to her, a simple "Yes, Captain" would have sufficed.

Tuvok was floating.

He moved through the air, held aloft by invisible hands. The pain was still present, but somehow, his mind was no longer engaged in the struggle to overcome it. He hadn't accepted it. He hadn't been able to lock it securely behind a door in his mind where it could be ignored. Logic dictated that the severity of his injuries should have rendered him unconscious long before now.

But he was awake; at least, he felt awake. He could feel his left leg dangling useless, though the hands were careful to hold it in place and prevent it from impacting anything that might cause it further damage as he was carried along. The sensation of movement in the absence of a fixed perspective caused his gorge to rise, so from time to time, he opened his left eye. Bright white light assaulted him the first time he made the attempt but after that he did catch periodic glimpses of a regular pattern of archways. He believed he was moving farther into the structure, but had no sense of direction to indicate where he was in reference to where his shuttle had entered the station. His mouth was filled with a pungent metallic-flavored liquid, which he associated with the taste of his own blood. A dull clanking sound met his ear at fairly regular intervals, possibly the result of a misalignment of some mechanism within the structure.

With so many of his sensory organs responding to stimuli that related specifically to what he knew of his present circumstances, he had to conclude that he was conscious. This made the fact that he could not see anything of the hands that carried him, or their owners, faintly disturbing. From what he could see, they didn't even cast a shadow on the walls as they moved silently through the structure.

Finally, their journey came to an end. Tuvok felt a solid, slightly cushioned surface meet with his back. Slowly, he felt the ambient temperature begin to rise. This small comfort added immeasurably to a sense of peace within him. Unless the owners of the invisible hands possessed advanced medical technology, it was unlikely that they would be able to repair the damage to his body. But their efforts to make the last moments of his life as pleasant as possible seemed generous and well intentioned.

This belief in their benevolent nature was confirmed when a few moments later a light blanket was thrown over him, adding to his warmth.

He had not forgotten about the music. And the silence in his mind was as deafening as it had been the first moment he had become aware of its absence. But there was something else. It could not be compared in intensity to the haunting sounds that he had first called "the music," but nonetheless he felt certain that someone or something was moving through his mind. The connection was not at all akin to a mind-meld. Nor was it a telepathic attack. Rather, it seemed that some external force was gently searching his mind for the clusters of cells which, when activated, produced powerful feelings of well-being. There was no sound associated with their ministrations, but from time to time, a word or short phrase would wash over him.

Be at peace.

He could not be certain if he was meant to construe the intentions of those who were tending to him in these words, or if they were a product of their work within his damaged mind and body. Ultimately he did not care. They seemed to be doing all they could for him, and for this, at least, he was grateful.

Too much damage.

Growing weaker.

A gentle hum washed over him. He had never been so near dying that he could say for certain, but this seemed to be the beginning of the release he believed could only end in death. There was no fear. He was no longer troubled by the loneliness. What he was experiencing was both gentle and somehow appropriate.

He did not believe he would be capable of speaking, or producing any sound that his caregivers would understand. But he did not wish to die without trying.

Parting his dry and cracked lips, he willed enough air to flow from his lungs over his vocal chords to say all that he could.

"Thank . . . you."

He surrendered himself to the inevitable long before the next wave of knowledge burst through the failing pathways of his mind.

Danger.

The captain entered engineering to find B'Elanna hovering around the diagnostic station where the Key to Gremadia had been encased in a level-ten forcefield.

Janeway was more than a little dismayed.

"This thing has been sitting in my cabin for almost two days. Why is it behind a forcefield in engineering?" she demanded.

"It's resonating on a subspace frequency that is barely detectable," B'Elanna replied evenly. "Our internal sensors didn't even pick up on it until I calibrated them to a precise resonance frequency."

Janeway shuddered slightly as the significance of the frequency rose vividly to her mind.

"Would that be the same frequency that disrupted the Caretaker's remains?" she asked.

"Yes, Captain. I completed a thorough investigation of sickbay with the Doctor's assistance. When I analyzed the debris from the explosion I discovered that even though the particles had been disrupted, the molecular bonds of the powder that remained were still highly resonant. I tested the resonance frequencies of all gravimetric distortion waves present within the system, those emanating from the singularity around the array, and those generated from the microsingularity closer to Monorha. None of them are distorting subspace in the way we anticipated. Of course, there are dozens of anomalous factors which utterly defy analysis, but until I began to search for the precise frequency still emanating from the remains, I couldn't find anything to account for their sudden disruption."

"And now . . . ? "

"There is a small subspace dissonance field emanating from this sphere. I recalibrated the sensors and was able to see that for approximately fifteen seconds in the last three hours that field expanded to include the entire area of your cabin. That time period corresponds exactly to the moment when the Caretaker's remains disintegrated."

"What caused the field's expansion?"

B'Elanna slammed her palm down on the diagnostic table and replied wrathfully, "I don't know! The two events are linked. They have to be. But I'm missing something." B'Elanna massaged her forehead ridges with the palm of her hand as if willing the answer to form itself in her mind. After a moment she said, "There was an electromagnetic discharge in your cabin a few minutes later . . ."

"That was Phoebe doing some work on my replicator," Janeway informed her.

"So the sensor logs showed me. But it doesn't make any sense. We're closer to the array now than we were then, so it doesn't seem likely that our proximity caused the sudden expansion. Phoebe was in your cabin the entire time, and she didn't report anything unusual. But this . . . *thing,*" she spat venomously, "sent out a dissonance field more powerful than any I've ever seen given its size and composition, and I can't tell you how or why."

"All right," Janeway replied calmly, "let's look at what we do know. I assume you've analyzed its structure. What is it made of? Is it organic to Monorha?"

"It isn't Monorhan," B'Elanna replied. "Its molecular structure doesn't correspond with any known elements in the planet's composition, or any other elements we've detected in the system."

"Is it sporocystian?" Janeway asked.

"There are similarities in the molecular structure of the Caretaker's remains and the Key, but the Key is significantly more dense."

"Computer," Janeway called, turning to the diagnostic control panel, "display analysis of the Caretaker's remains from stardate 48398."

When it came up on the screen before them, she saw that B'Elanna was correct. There were properties that suggested a sporocystian origin, but there were also significant variances that defied definitive comparison.

"Wait a minute . . ." B'Elanna said, tapping the diagnostic panel. The display of the Caretaker's remains was reorganized as B'Elanna instructed the computer to extrapolate the molecular structure of more than one sporocystian life-form integrated into a solid form similar to the Key.

Janeway watched, fascinated as the molecular composition of a single sporocystian remnant reacted in the hypothetical presence of another. But even after the process had been duplicated over fifty times, the simulated results bore only a cursory resemblance to the Key.

As the simulation continued, B'Elanna crossed her arms over her chest and said, "Maybe I'm just ignoring the obvious because I don't like to even consider the possibility."

"What do you mean?" Janeway asked.

"Maybe we encountered another Nacene," B'Elanna suggested. "We know their presence disrupts subspace. The Key might just be reacting to the dissonance field a Nacene would have created, but its density prevented its destruction."

"Unlike the Caretaker's remains," Janeway finished.

"And the fact that it's still vibrating might mean that a Nacene is still nearby."

Janeway didn't like that possibility. But it was hard to dismiss.

"I assume you're aware of the Key's cultural significance to the Monorhans?" Janeway asked.

"Of course," B'Elanna replied. "Everything Seven of Nine learned while we were linked on the planet is also . . . part of me now," B'Elanna added. "In some ways it was one of the few high points of the 'collective experience' for me."

"Why is that?" the captain asked sincerely.

"Because the more I knew, the less we had to discuss," B'Elanna replied tersely.

Janeway smiled faintly and continued, "So how does an object that at least shares some similarities with Nacene bioremnants end up thousands of light-years from the only other areas of the quadrant where we've seen Nacene activity?"

"And how does it get folded into the culture of the Monorhans?" B'Elanna added. "The Key has been on the planet since before their recorded history. It was discovered by a farmer who touched it and became some kind of prophet."

"Well I touched it too," Janeway said simply, "and if anything, I know less about the future now than before."

"Of course, you're not telepathic," B'Elanna said. "All of the Monorhans share low-level psionic capabilities, but among the Fourteenth Tribe, those abilities were uniquely strong." She shook her head as she continued ruefully, "It's a shame that tribe never returned from their search. I imagine they reached the edge of the system and disintegrated like the first transport we encountered."

"They didn't," Janeway corrected her. "We've already found their ship. It's docked on the array."

Torres stared at her. "Captain, I'd like to get a look at that ship."

"So would I," Janeway replied. "Meet with Seven as soon as you can. Retrieving Tuvok is our first priority, but I have a feeling we're going to spend at least a few days on board the array. The sensor data we've collected so far is overwhelming."

B'Elanna nodded.

Before she could enquire further as to the nature of the sensor's findings the computer chirped, indicating that the simulation it had been running was complete. As both women turned instinctively to check the results, however unpromising they would surely be, they shared a moment of breathless awe when they saw that the computer had been able to create an exact duplicate of the Key by following B'Elanna's hypothetical parameters. What was amazing and disturbing was the estimation of the number of sporocystian life-forms that would have to be integrated in order to produce the Key.

"That's not good," Janeway commented.

"No, it isn't," B'Elanna agreed. "If this is right, the Key is comprised entirely of sporocystian remains . . . almost a hundred thousand of them."

The thought was intriguing. Everyone who had actually met the Caretaker had grown used to thinking of him as a highly unique life-form. True, they had also met his mate, but the idea that at some point in time there had been enough Nacene within the galaxy to result in the formation of the Key with no other record or evidence of their activities seemed incomprehensible.

"No wonder it wasn't destroyed," B'Elanna said. "I can't even imagine how many Nacene it would take to disrupt subspace enough to completely destabilize this."

Janeway was absorbed in an analysis of the subatomic alterations of the fusion process that were required to stabilize the bond between the remains. It suggested something even more disturbing.

"This occurred naturally," she finally said.

"Captain?" B'Elanna asked, studying the same analysis.

"No external force short of dozens of suns going supernova at the same time could have forced the kind of fusion we're seeing here."

"You're saying that tens of thousands of Nacene somehow fused together of their own accord as they were dying?" B'Elanna asked.

"Possibly," Janeway said. "Or maybe . . ." she said, choosing her words extremely carefully.

"What?"

"Maybe the reason they are still resonating is because they aren't dead."

This was a fringe hypothesis, even for B'Elanna.

"We know the Caretaker died. That's why he brought us here, along with Kahless only knows how many others. That's why Suspiria tried to kill us. His remains were only resonant in the presence of another Nacene, but their molecular structure was constant."

"But if thousands of Nacene were also near death, this might be the only form they could survive in," Janeway posited.

B'Elanna seemed anxious to disprove this possibility. She instructed the computer to scan the Key for anything remotely resembling life, saying, "This is the one scan I didn't bother to initiate from the beginning because it simply hadn't occurred to me to do so. The first time the Caretaker's remains started to vibrate we mistook that for life signs too. I didn't want to make the same mistake twice. At any rate, I still think it's much more likely we simply encountered another Nacene."

"Phoebe was in my cabin the entire time," Janeway argued. "She's not the most observant person I've ever met, but I don't think she would have missed an intruder boarding the ship right in front of her."

"She's pretty focused when she's working," B'Elanna teased. "She kept me waiting outside holodeck three for over an hour last week while she was working on something in your da Vinci program. She swore she didn't hear me, but . . ."

"Point taken," Janeway smiled. "I suppose we could

just ask her. Captain Janeway to Phoebe," she called, tapping her combadge.

There was no response.

"Computer, locate Phoebe Janeway."

The computer's reply was inconceivable.

"Phoebe Janeway is not on board Voyager."

There wasn't time to address this impossibility, as, a moment later, the diagnostic display confirmed Janeway's hypothesis.

The Key was alive.

Phoebe hid herself between the second and third electrons orbiting the phosphate atom contained within a molecule of ioxicyllic phosphatase in a remote deck plate within the array. Though the abominations could theoretically find her here, she did not believe they would do so. They were still such simple creatures. For all the potential that lay within their grasp, they had been unprepared to receive the spores and consequently behaved like the infants of primitive races. They had barely scratched the surface of their new existence and remained bound to perverse and irrelevant notions. Their call to Tuvok had been idiotic. He was incapable of grasping the nature of their existence and therefore incapable of rendering aid. Their desire to return *home,* as they put it, indicated that much of their humanoid existence and values were still thoroughly enmeshed with their evolved essence.

All of this might have been forgivable. There was a time when it might also have been interesting to witness their first halting steps into a larger existence. But in their rashness, they had taken something that did not belong to them, and by doing so, had damned countless others to a half-life within a space-time reality that was not theirs.

Had she been capable of weeping in her disembodied state, she would have cried fierce hot tears. The work, the planning, the purposefulness with which the array had been constructed and the spores had been created were now for naught. *How could this have happened?* She tortured herself with guilt. The last time she had returned to the array for rejuvenation had been so recently. True, it had been almost six hundred years, but that was the blink of a god's eye.

She allowed the rage at this senseless waste to move through her. If she was going to salvage anything from this desperate turn of events, she would have to think beyond her anger. She had learned long ago that however unpleasant an emotional state was, it could be released only if it was first accepted and experienced. Denial, though often easier, was ultimately counterproductive.

They were arguing with one another. Tuvok's fragile brain would never have been able to translate their communication. He would have sensed the constant pounding need that was the sum total of their collective desire for release. But his mind would have interpreted their discussion in the same way that he had first understood their call. It happened in the space of a human breath. His mind would have perceived the sound, but no mind, bound by matter, would have been capable of deconstructing the sound in a way that would have communicated its truth beyond a vague sensation of gratitude, doubt, and fear of the unknown.

But to Phoebe, their words were perfectly clear.

His people are coming for him.

They will be too late.

Not with our aid.

What can we do?

Show them the way.
They are not our kind.
Neither was he.
He was part of them.
Not as we are part of one another.
He came for us.
He is dying.
Perhaps not.
We cannot protect him.
We shouldn't try. Let the unknowing one come.
Will he become our kind?
It is his only hope.

Phoebe was intrigued. *It is his only hope.* At first, she could not imagine what they might be referring to. What hope was there for Tuvok? His body was injured, quite possibly beyond his own people's abilities to repair it. With each fraction of a second that passed, his tenuous connection to the abominations grew thinner as his mind began to shut down, a few neural pathways at a time.

What did they know that she didn't?

Opening herself beyond the scope of their conversation, she searched for their hope, and was instantly flooded with relief when she found it.

She sensed its frenzied approach . . . and knew peace. She watched in delight as the one . . . *the unknowing one,* they called it . . . found Tuvok, grasped him roughly around his torso, and bending its face to his, implanted the spore that it carried within it into Tuvok's mouth.

The convulsions that marked the first stage of transference of a spore into a humanoid body began instantly. Tuvok writhed in apparent agony, as his muscles contracted, seeking to dispel the foreign body from his esophagus.

Phoebe shared their overwhelming joy when, a few moments later, Tuvok ceased to struggle . . . and opened his eyes.

Burning with the hope that this unforeseen possibility presented, Phoebe returned, undetected, to *Voyager*. She found a quiet corner of the deserted mess hall and immediately began reorganizing her thoughts.

The spores were gone. They had been awakened from their dormant state by the Monorhans who had stumbled upon the array they called Gremadia. But the new lifeform generated in the process of the transformation was capable of creating the spores anew. The abominations would bow to her will, and the will of those for whom the spores had been intended. Even if they did not, there was at least one . . . the unknowing one . . . who would suit Phoebe's purposes perfectly. Now all that remained was to keep Janeway ignorant of the Key's true purpose until she was able to contact the full number of her companions and bring them to the array.

She had stood alone in her dark corner of the mess hall for several minutes, pondering the view of the array that loomed large through the windows, when her tranquil reflection was shattered by a piercing screech.

Turning to the door, she saw a small humanoid standing in the entrance. *A child.* She was female, a hybrid of some kind, and her tiny fists were balled at her sides as she continued to scream.

Obviously the girl was terrified, but this shouldn't be the case. Phoebe had resumed her human form the moment she returned to the ship. Every member of the crew should be seeing her exactly as Janeway did. They should accept her presence as normal. The memories of "Phoebe" and her interaction with the crew that had been implanted were not threatening in the least. In fact, she had made herself truly liked by the crew, to limit any conflicting interaction.

But the girl was still screaming.

Something was obviously wrong.

She didn't take the time to consider all of her options. She knew the alarm that the girl was sounding would not go unnoticed for long. With a thought, she entered the girl's mind, searching for a way to calm her. The moment she had done so, she realized her error.

This one is different.

Her next action was uncharacteristically rash, though she decided later that it had been her only choice at the moment, and probably a result of her inability to reason without emotion while she assumed a human form.

Crushing the neurological pathways that supplied the impulses that directed oxygen to the girl's brain, she silently hoped that there were no others like her aboard the ship. Though Phoebe saw no intrinsic value in the lives of Kathryn's crew, the only hesitation she felt as she took the girl's life sprung from the certainty that Kathryn did.

She couldn't afford to kill them all.

Yet.

Chapter 5

Neelix was multitasking. He had spent the last few minutes gathering gear for his impending away mission. En route to the mess hall to lock down the supplies he had already prepped for lunch and dinner, he walked with his nose buried in a padd, reviewing the section of the array he and Crewman Dalby would be analyzing within the hour.

He liked Dalby. The somewhat distant Maquis who'd had such a difficult adjustment to life aboard *Voyager* was gone. In his place was a capable and disciplined officer in the making. That had earned him Neelix's respect. More important, Neelix trusted Dalby for one simple reason. Dalby was unflinching in his honest estimation of Neelix's food. Although taste was ultimately less significant than nutritional value, Neelix strove daily to serve the crew the most delicious and satisfying food available. Tom Paris's colorful jests aside, most of the Starfleet personnel accepted their meals stoically, as if eating, no matter how unpleasant, was a duty. He knew they were appreciative of his efforts. But also knew that without honest evaluations of his work, there was little he could do to improve their culinary experience and with it their morale. On more than one occasion, Dalby had quietly pulled him aside to offer suggestions ranging from "a little more spice" to "never again, please."

Yes, Neelix liked Dalby.

At the same time, he was also considering the arrangement of supplies stored in cargo bay three. Most of the expansive space had been reserved for some of the crew's personal possessions and nonperishable food. The majority of those contents could be divided between bays one and two, leaving bay three as a potential space for raw matter storage they were sure to find aboard the array.

Come to think of it, there were a number of emergency ration packs in bay three which should probably be brought to the mess hall right now. He was running a little low, and with much of the crew assigned to the upcoming away mission, it was probably a good idea to have plenty on hand. If he diverted his steps to the nearest turbolift, it would take only a few moments . . .

"Aaaahhhhhhh!"

The shrill, piercing scream that echoed through the hall was temporarily disorienting. It sounded like it was coming from the turbolift, behind him. The second scream caused the blood to drain instantaneously from his extremities, but it also made it easier for him to determine where it was coming from.

Naomi!

Neelix ran for his life. He found strength and speed he hadn't known since he was a young boy, chasing his sister, Alixia, through the forest that ran behind their home.

His worst fears were confirmed when he turned the final corner that led to the mess hall entrance and saw Naomi crumpled on the floor.

Before he had even reached her, he tapped his combadge.

"Neelix to sickbay. Medical emergency."

Naomi was curled on her right side. She didn't appear to be breathing and her face and hands had a faint purplish blue tinge. As Neelix gently touched her left hand, and felt, as he had expected to, its horrifying chill, he called out again over the comm.

"This is Neelix. Something has happened to Naomi. Request emergency site-to-site transport. Get us to sickbay . . . NOW!"

Seconds later, Neelix and Naomi materialized in sickbay. The Doctor immediately lifted the child from the floor and placed her on a biobed.

Neelix was at the Doctor's side instantly. He was shaking with fear, but the Doctor moved quickly and efficiently around him to render the necessary aid. He didn't take time to calm the terrified Talaxian, or to force him out of the way.

"She isn't breathing. Her airway is probably obstructed," the Doctor diagnosed immediately. "Naomi is an otherwise healthy child. Since she was found near the mess hall, the most likely scenario is that she ate something and began to choke."

But as he passed his medical tricorder over her upper torso and neck, Neelix noted the flat series of beeps emanating from the device, which indicated a negative result.

His alarm was heightened when the Doctor tossed the tricorder aside, a decidedly disgruntled scowl on his face, raised the biobed's medical arch over Naomi's upper body, and initiated an immediate infusion of oxygen into her system.

"What . . . what . . . what's wrong with her?" Neelix stammered.

"As I said before," the Doctor replied evenly, "she isn't breathing."

"Why not?"

The Doctor turned his attention to the scans of the child's central nervous system as he said, "I don't know."

"Is something wrong with her lungs?" Neelix asked, "Because she can have my lung if she needs it."

"No, she can't, Mr. Neelix. You only have one lung left and that is a transplanted Ocampan lung. Her body would reject such a transplant, even if my ethical subroutines did not preclude the possibility of taking your life to save hers."

"But the Vidiians did it!" Neelix shouted.

"Do you see any Vidiians in sickbay at the moment?" the Doctor asked sarcastically. "Though I am well versed in the procedure you are describing, I do not possess the resources they had at their disposal to perform the transplant."

"But . . . there has to be something . . ." Neelix offered, at a loss. The prospect of his own death was not nearly as terrifying as the idea of standing by, helpless, watching Naomi die.

"If there is, I will find it, Mr. Neelix."

"Can I help?"

"Yes," the Doctor said calmly. "You can move out of my way."

Neelix quickly repositioned himself on the other side of the biobed, noting with faint relief that Naomi's small face was returning to a more normal color thanks to the oxygen infusion she was receiving.

"Aha!" the Doctor said as the final results of the neural scan appeared on the monitor before him. Without another word he moved quickly to a storage cabinet and removed a small neural stimulator.

"It's a good thing I equipped sickbay with emergency medical equipment specific to the needs of a human and

Ktarian child shortly after Naomi was born," he said as he returned to the child's side.

He then placed the neural stimulator on the left side of Naomi's forehead and began carefully resetting the small components that controlled the stimulator's programming.

"What are you doing to her?" Neelix asked quietly.

"I am repairing the damage to her brain."

"Her brain?" Neelix asked, as if this was the last thing he had expected to hear.

"Yes, Mr. Neelix. Naomi has suffered a series of collapses in her neural pathways. I am attempting to stimulate new pathways that will restore the normal functioning of her respiratory system."

"But why?"

"Because it is the only way to save her life."

"Of course," Neelix said, "but what could have caused such a thing?"

"At the moment, I have no idea," the Doctor replied, "although as soon as Naomi's condition is stabilized, I do not intend to deactivate myself until I find out."

"Is there anything I can do?" Neelix asked.

"Yes," the Doctor answered. "Please contact Naomi's mother."

Neelix nodded and made his way on shaking legs toward the door. News such as this had to be delivered in person.

Chakotay was faced with a complicated task. According to the schematics provided by Seven of Nine, the array they were approaching contained hundreds of kilometers of corridors and other spaces to be searched on foot. Had all of *Voyager*'s roughly 150 crewmen been at his disposal, a thorough search of the array would take weeks. Given the fact that at least one-third of those crew members would be required to maintain *Voyager*'s systems, rotating duty shifts with the other two-thirds to allow minimal time for them to eat and sleep, apart from the senior officers that left less than forty people at his disposal at any given time to form his search teams. This meant that they might easily spend at least three months aboard the array and still not see everything there was to see.

He was every bit as intrigued by the possibilities of the array as the captain and Seven of Nine were. The power reserves alone were worth a thorough examination. At no time since *Voyager* had left the Alpha Quadrant had all of their reserve systems been completely replenished. A few months of less restrictive replicator rationing would go a long way toward boosting crew morale. He even let himself hope that some of the technology they were sure to find could be adapted to *Voyager*'s. Obviously they would not have access to the primary source of power, the elements found in the singularity at the center of the array. But most of those elements had existed in normal space before they had been sucked in by the immense gravity of the black hole. The array's most valuable asset would be the converters used to transform simple elements into complex fuel sources. With that at their disposal, *Voyager*'s return to the Alpha Quadrant might still take decades, but they would be comfortable decades.

The difficulty in assigning and scheduling the away teams lay not in prioritizing their goals. First they would find Tuvok, and then they would begin a thorough exploration of the array's power systems.

The problem would be Kathryn.

They had been faced in the past with opportunities to settle on hospitable and welcoming Class-M planets. Invariably the consensus was that returning home outweighed the comfort and ease of the life they could easily have built for themselves anywhere in the Delta Quadrant. Time and again the crew had pushed themselves to the brink of oblivion rather than avert their gaze from the shining beacon of the Alpha Quadrant.

But the array offered them something that no Class-M planet ever had. The possibilities for advancing their scientific knowledge well beyond current Federation standards might just be the siren call that Janeway would find most difficult to resist. Colonizing a safe planet in an uninhabited region would have been challenging, but at the end of the day would also have been settling for less than they were capable of as individuals and a Starfleet crew. But the challenges and promise of the array were more difficult to weigh on an objective scale. Chakotay intuitively sensed that until Kathryn had pried every last secret from the array's grasp, she would find it a moral imperative to continue their research. And he firmly believed such a task would take decades.

He saw the good in both sides. He was, for the most part, content with the life he had found on *Voyager.* Spending the rest of his life working by Kathryn's side, whether traveling through space or plumbing a mystery as vast as the array, was all he really wanted anymore. But the same could not be said for the rest of the crew. Many of them had left family and friends behind. Though they would certainly be intrigued by the mysteries of the array, their enthusiasm was sure to wane as the weeks wore on.

Rumbling beneath the surface of these contemplations was another disturbing thought. Though they had located Tuvok's life signs, the readings clearly showed that he was seriously injured. He was not altogether certain that boarding the array would be a simple matter. Though the bulk of the shuttle Tuvok had taken was now on board the array, fragments of debris had been detected within a hundred kilometers of it, and Chakotay wondered what price Tuvok had paid to gain entrance. Further, there was the reality that Tuvok had not been drawn here of his own free will. Chakotay agreed with Kathryn that the Doctor's findings, coupled with Tuvok's uncharacteristic behavior, pointed to an external force exerting itself on Tuvok's better judgment. If that force and the mysterious hands that had built the array were one and the same, there was no way to know whether or not it would look favorably on their arrival. If Tuvok had been "invited" and barely survived, he shuddered to think how such a force might react to unwelcome trespassers.

For the moment, these musing had to be set aside. Once he had entered his initial search-team assignments into the interface console that was embedded in the arm of his chair on the bridge, he turned to Ensign Kim at ops. Kim and Paris had reported directly to the bridge from their truncated briefing in astrometrics and had quietly and efficiently begun to plot the safest course for entering the array. Seven assisted them from the bridge's tactical station.

"Ensign Kim," Chakotay asked, "do we have a heading yet?"

"I suggest we alter course to two five seven mark four, Commander," Harry replied.

"Is that were the shuttle's impulse trail leads?"

"It is. It appears Tuvok followed the trajectory of the graviton flow to maximize his distance from the theoretical event horizon," Harry replied.

"Theoretical event horizon?" Chakotay asked.

Seven interjected before Harry could continue, "Because the array is drawing power from the singularity, it is difficult to precisely calculate the absolute edge of the singularity. Based on the singularity's size, it should extend far beyond the space occupied by the structure."

"But if that were the case, the structure would be crushed in the gravity well," Chakotay finished for her.

"Precisely," Seven affirmed. "Therefore we must assume that the actual event horizon begins somewhere near the inner side of the rings. As our sensors cannot pinpoint that exact location, our calculations must include the 'theoretical' variable which we refer to as the theoretical event horizon."

"We've picked up signs of debris," Chakotay said, "which suggests that Tuvok's shuttle took a beating along that course. Are we making the same mistake he did?"

"Our shields and the size of our ship will make it much easier for us to compensate for the gravitational density than Tuvok's shuttle," Harry advised. "It might be a rough ride, but we should be fine."

Chakotay stared for a moment into the tumultuous swirling mass of matter and energy that was the singularity. Somehow, "should be fine" wasn't as comforting as he would have liked when he considered the sheer and overwhelming force they were approaching.

Harry adjusted the display on the main viewscreen so that a small section of the upper ring was visible in greater detail. "These are the docking bays, Commander."

"Will our present course take us into one of those bays?" Chakotay asked.

"Yes, sir," Harry answered.

"Are we within transporter range yet?" Chakotay asked hopefully.

"Yes, sir," Harry replied, "but . . ."

"I would not advise using the transporters, Commander," Seven interrupted him evenly.

"Why not?"

"At this distance, the gravimetric interference could easily destabilize the annular confinement beams. We could compensate by moving into position closer to the structure, but at that distance it would no longer be advisable to drop our shields."

Chakotay was accustomed to making quick decisions. His consideration of the available options was brief. "Mr. Paris, adjust course to two five seven mark four, and take us in."

Paris's hands flew gracefully over his controls as he made the course adjustment. "Course laid in," he said.

"Nice and easy, Mr. Paris," Chakotay added.

Paris nodded in acknowledgment, falling into seamless, almost symbiotic harmony with the helm. Chakotay was comforted in the knowledge that their odds of safely reaching their destination were increased exponentially with Paris at the helm. Chakotay had piloted his fair share of vessels. Technique could be mastered. Skills could be practiced. But the delicate touch, the subtle, sometimes prescient adjustments that could mean the difference between successfully navigating such a precarious patch of space and oblivion, were beyond the ken of any manual or simulation. The minuscule movements Paris made as *Voyager* approached the structure came from a subconscious place inside him, a place where he and his ship became one. Chakotay knew that the helm of a ship was the one place where Tom Paris knew certainty. And no pilot had ever known a ship as well as Tom knew *Voyager*.

"Commander," Harry called from ops, "incoming transmission, audio only."

"Incoming from where?" Chakotay asked.

"It's coming from the array."

"I guess somebody's home after all. Let's hear it, Mr. Kim," Chakotay ordered.

Harry muted the initial burst of static that spiked his readings into the red and compensated for all interference until his display showed the clean, narrow band of a clear comm signal.

" . . . *Assylia,* rih-hara-tan . . . *Monorhan* . . . Betasis."

"Is that all of it?" Chakotay demanded.

"The signal has degraded, Commander. I'll see if I can reconstruct any more of it," Harry replied.

In the tense seconds that followed, Chakotay noted with approval that though Seven seemed inclined to assist Ensign Kim, she remained rooted to her station, allowing him to complete the task rather than doing a quicker and more efficient job of it herself. Chakotay couldn't help but marvel at the vast positive changes he had observed in the newest addition to their crew over the past eleven months. In the early days, Seven wouldn't have thought twice about bucking Kim out of the way and finishing the job herself.

"There isn't much more, Commander," Harry finally sighed, resigned. "The signal has been transmitting continuously for fifty years, and its proximity to the singularity . . ."

"Just give me what you have, Ensign," Chakotay interrupted.

"I am Assylia, rih-hara-tan *of the . . . Monorhan . . . vessel . . .* Betasis *. . . array . . . in search of Gremadia . . . turn back."*

Chakotay leaned back in his chair, gently massaging his tattooed brow. The fragmentary transmission could easily be read in two ways: either as a routine message to other Monorhan vessels who might pass this way or as a warning.

Chakotay knew that a Monorhan vessel had been located aboard the array. The age of the transmission tracked with what little he knew of Monorhan history and the mission of their Fourteenth Tribe. But without more information, it was difficult to say with any degree of certainty how to best construe the garbled transmission. The words lost between "Gremadia" and "turn back" were all important. He said a silent prayer that the rest of the message was a benign recounting of their course and journey, despite the lingering foreboding that it probably wasn't.

"Chakotay to Captain Janeway," he called over the comm system.

"Go ahead, Commander." Her voice resonated through the bridge.

"We've laid in our course for our approach to the array, and we've discovered a transmission, possibly from the Monorhan ship," he informed her.

"I'll be right there," she replied briskly, ending the communication.

As Janeway closed the comm channel she cursed silently at the war raging within her between family and duty. She was needed on the bridge, but Phoebe was missing. For the moment, her sister took priority. She was momentarily shocked at the computer's announcement indicating that Phoebe was not on board, but she refused to allow herself the luxury of panic. She couldn't count the number of times in the past four years she had imagined returning to Earth, only to have her most joyful reunion, the one she anticipated with her mother, tainted by the news that while *Voyager* had been lost, she had failed to protect the life of her sister.

Wait a minute.

Her sister was supposed to be on Earth.

No, Phoebe had been on Earth, but at the last moment asked to join Janeway on what was supposed to be a brief rescue mission in the Badlands. She had been commissioned to do a painting of the unusual and beautiful plasma eruptions in the Badlands and had begged her sister to give her the opportunity to see them firsthand.

Setting the disquieting thoughts aside for the moment, she was about to dispatch a security team on a deck-by-deck search for Phoebe when her mingled fear and anger were dissipated by the relief of seeing Phoebe walking calmly toward her.

"Where have you been?" Janeway demanded savagely.

"What do you mean?" Phoebe replied, obviously slightly annoyed by Janeway's tone.

"I asked the ship's computer to locate you a few moments ago and you weren't on board."

"Yes I was."

"Phoebe . . ." Janeway began fiercely.

"Where would I go, Kath? I've been in my quarters since the last time I saw you. The computer made a mistake."

Janeway considered this. Her sister was aggravating, self-centered, and occasionally irresponsible, but she wasn't a liar. On the other hand, the ship's computer was incapable of lying.

It doesn't matter.

The thought, like the vibrant memory of Phoebe's face the day she pleaded with her sister to take her on *Voyager*'s maiden trek, didn't feel organic. Of course it mattered.

As she wrestled with herself, wondering at her reticence to call Phoebe to task for her improbable explanation, she saw that Phoebe's gaze was fixed on the Key.

"Kath, what have you done to the Key?" Phoebe demanded.

"That isn't your concern," Janeway snapped. A slight wave of nausea rose abruptly from her stomach. Grasping the edge of the diagnostic display table, she willed the nausea to pass, along with the dizzying sensation that now accompanied it.

Yes it is.

She heard the words clearly in her mind, but could not imagine where they were coming from. The next wave of nausea that assaulted her almost brought her to her knees.

"I'm sorry, Phoebe," Janeway murmured softly.

"It's all right," Phoebe soothed. "Tell me what you have done to the Key."

"Nothing, for the moment. We're keeping it behind a forcefield to contain the subspace dissonance waves emanating from it. It appears to be alive."

Janeway was suddenly conscious of a firm hand grasping her arm. It was B'Elanna.

"Captain, are you all right?"

Get rid of her.

Janeway didn't know how she knew, but nonetheless she was certain that as long as she obeyed that strange voice, the crippling sensations coursing through her would cease.

"I'm fine, Lieutenant," she said. "Continue your work."

B'Elanna uttered a faint, "Aye, Captain," and moved away, leaving Janeway and Phoebe somewhat alone.

"If the Key poses a danger, give it to me, and I'll remove it from the ship," Phoebe offered.

"I can't do that," Janeway replied, still hazy, "and neither can you. I need to know . . ."

"What?" Phoebe asked.

"When you were in my cabin earlier . . . did you see anything unusual?"

"Of course not," Phoebe lied.

"Phoebe, this is important . . ." Janeway persisted.

No . . . the voice insisted . . . *it isn't.*

It was obvious that Kathryn was strong. Her resistance, even now, was impressive. But that resistance was inflicting subtle and potentially serious damage to the tissue of her brain. Phoebe knew that she could force the captain's mind to accept her words. But the more she shrouded the captain's actual thoughts and inserted those required to meet her ends, the greater the risk she ran of damaging Janeway beyond repair. Though saving Janeway's life was not of any ultimate importance, she had to keep the captain alive and functioning for the time being.

For the moment, however, the priority was to divert Kathryn's attention from the Key. They had detected the disruption. This was frustrating, but not completely unexpected. It was unacceptable, however, that they had also learned that the Key was, as they crudely understood it, "alive."

In the interest of getting Janeway as far from the Key as possible, Phoebe suggested, "Kathryn, you don't look well. Perhaps you should see your doctor."

"There isn't time . . ." Janeway said with forced deliberateness. "Have to get to the bridge."

"Kathryn," Phoebe said softly, "you are under a tremendous amount of pressure. You haven't had a good meal or a good night's sleep in days. Let me take you to the Doctor, on your way to the bridge. It won't take any time at all."

Of course the moment they arrived in sickbay Phoebe fully intended to incapacitate the captain in such a way that she would remain confined in the ship's medical bay for at least the next forty-eight hours. That should be just enough time.

"Will you come with me?" Phoebe asked, demanding internally that Kathryn comply.

"Of course," the captain nodded.

As Phoebe helped Janeway to sickbay, a firm arm circling her waist, she gently began to remove some of the manipulative threads she had been using to exert her will over the captain.

She was at first shocked, then enraged when they arrived and found Naomi Wildman sleeping quietly on a biobed, her mother and Neelix standing tensely on either side of her, each holding one of her hands and taking turns patting her head lovingly.

She seethed within as all thoughts of further incapacitating the captain fled from her consciousness.

This was impossible. The hybrid girl had obviously survived. Though Phoebe's powers were vast, there were only so many battles she could fight at once. Releasing Janeway's mind completely, she moved closer to Naomi. Though the child posed no immediate danger while she was unconscious, Phoebe would have to find an appropriate time to finish what she had started. For the moment, however, she would have to bide her precious time.

Once Janeway's mind was again her own, the captain stood for a startled moment wondering how she had ended up in sickbay. It was as if a thick mist had lifted before her eyes, and to her vast relief, her stomach too seemed much calmer. She wanted very much to know what had just happened and how she had gotten here, but at the first sight of Naomi's frail figure resting on the biobed before her, all concerns for her own well-being evaporated. She approached Naomi and asked of no one in particular, "What happened?"

Ensign Samantha Wildman's face turned to hers, her milky skin awash with bright red blotches, her eyes rimmed with tears. "We don't know."

"Where's the Doctor?"

Neelix gestured with a nod to indicate that the Doctor was in his office. As Janeway turned toward the partition that divided sickbay from his workspace, she saw through the window the Doctor bent over his workstation studying a display.

She barely heard Phoebe's faint murmurs of concern directed toward Neelix and Samantha as she turned briskly and went to confront the EMH, who did her the courtesy of rising when she entered his office.

"What happened, Doctor?" Janeway asked with palpable concern.

"I believe Naomi was attacked," the Doctor replied.

Though Janeway's brow shot up in disbelief, he continued, "Someone, or something, intentionally disrupted the neural pathways in her brain that coordinate her respiratory system. In the hands of a lesser hologram, she would certainly have died."

The captain reached for the Doctor's desk, perching on its edge. Raising a hand to her head, she gently massaged her temples to relieve the dull throbbing that usually indicated the onset of a major tension headache.

"Are you certain she didn't fall, or hit her head on something?" Janeway asked, adding, "She's a very active little girl."

"Her skull was not fractured. There was no edema or localized damage to a distinct area of her brain, as would be typical in a traumatic percussive head injury. There are no pathogens present in her system. There are no genetic causes, nor are there any known disease processes that could produce the effects I've seen. Specific neural pathways were targeted and disrupted. It's as if something reached into her mind and forced her to stop breathing."

"Could this have anything to do with whatever drove Tuvok to leave the ship?" Janeway wondered aloud.

"There are certainly telepaths who would be capable of damaging the minds of others. But Tuvok's brain wasn't injured, despite the neurochemical imbalances. I won't be able to make a more definitive analysis until I am able to examine him again."

"I understand, Doctor," the captain replied. "Is Naomi going to be all right?"

"After a few days of bed rest, she should be fine. I'll keep her here under observation for the next few hours at least."

The captain nodded, thoughtful. "It's possible we've had an intruder on board," she said. "B'Elanna discovered that the artifact given to me by the Monorhans when we left their planet, the Key to Gremadia, is actually made up of living sporocystian remnants. They are currently resonating, similar to the way the Caretaker's remains did when we encountered Suspiria. We haven't ruled out the possibility that another Nacene might be nearby."

"That adds a decidedly unsavory piece to the puzzle," the Doctor observed.

"Exactly. You should replicate supplies of the toxin we developed to counter a Nacene attack and keep some on hand, just in case."

"I agree," he said, moving toward the door.

"Keep me informed. I'll be on the bridge," she said, following him out of his office.

The Doctor halted in their approach to Naomi's biobed. Turning to Janeway, he asked, "Captain, who is this woman?"

"Is that supposed to be a joke, Doctor? You knew my sister," Janeway replied, gesturing toward Phoebe.

"Captain ... I ..." the Doctor stammered, and blinked out of existence.

Phoebe heard the soft footfalls of Janeway's approach, but did not face her directly until she and the photonic being were almost standing beside her. She had spent the last several moments studying the atomic structure of the hybrid girl, all the while whispering soft comforting words and thoughts to the two humanoids who obviously felt the greatest attachment to her. She had discovered the difference that made the girl immune to the memories she had implanted in the minds of the rest of *Voyager*'s crew and to her alarm found herself powerless to correct the slight phase variation in the girl's molecular structure. She was considering more invasive options when she heard the Doctor's unnerving question directed toward Kathryn.

Alerted immediately to the possibility that there might be more like the hybrid girl, it took her less than a second to completely analyze the atomic structure of the being known as "the Doctor" and conclude that here, too, was an unforeseen threat.

In the analysis of *Voyager*'s systems and crew that preceded her choice to assume the role of "Phoebe" she had, of course, discovered the holographic generators. They were regulated discreetly from the primary ship's systems and computer memory, and since she had no intention of interacting with any recreational holograms during what she hoped would be her brief stay aboard the vessel—she found particularly distasteful the loud and garish simulation of some kind of outdoor, tropical club—she had elected not to adjust those systems to accept her presence. It would have been simple enough, now, to add to the

Doctor's program a subroutine similar to one that she had already inserted in the main computer to acknowledge her existence and fabricated history. But a closer look at this "Doctor" told her that in this case, nothing simple was going to be effective.

Though he was composed of photonic particles, generated by the primitive holographic imagers, there was also something more to him, something almost ineffable. It was small, just burgeoning into existence, but it was unmistakably there. Phoebe had never encountered such a thing, even in the most complex artificially created lifeforms, and she realized in an instant that she could not manipulate this "Doctor" as easily as she manipulated the minds of the rest of the crew.

Searching the holographic database for an alternative, she quickly stumbled upon a few other versions of the Doctor's program. Most of them had been created fairly recently, automatic backup systems, she speculated. There was only one that might suit her purposes. So it was with a thought that, as the Doctor and Janeway approached the biobed where Naomi lay, Phoebe chose the path of least resistance and simply overloaded sickbay's holomatrix long enough to destabilize the Doctor's program and activate an earlier version of the Emergency Medical Hologram, the only one she could find that was not yet tainted by the intrusive ineffable quality.

As the Doctor dissolved out of existence, and was replaced by this earlier version, Phoebe added several comforting thoughts to the minds of those present so as not to alarm them in any way. She was relieved when no one reacted to the momentary destabilization of the Doctor.

"Please state the nature of the medical emergency," the Doctor intoned when he rematerialized.

She was further relieved when as the Doctor reappeared only Neelix was troubled by the fact that the Doctor rarely, if ever, used this particular greeting anymore. Forcing that thought out of the Talaxian's mind, she had all but begun congratulating herself on her work when she was thrown to the floor as the ship turned abruptly at a sharp angle and sickbay was plunged into darkness.

Chapter 6

Janeway made her way to the bridge with difficulty. The red alert ordered the moment the gravimetric interference generated by the singularity began to buffet *Voyager* about like a sailboat caught in a typhoon left the corridors bathed in a deep crimson glow.

When she finally arrived at deck one and immediately called "Report!" she noted with small satisfaction that at least the ship's fire-suppression systems were operating at peak efficiency. With a firm hand placed first on the rail that separated tactical and ops from the step that led down to her chair, she gingerly took her seat amid the waning vapors of smoke most likely triggered by the explosion of the tactical panel to her right, which now gurgled and sputtered . . . a tangled mass of plasma relays and conduit.

"Shields are holding, Captain," Chakotay said tensely. "Inertial dampers are at maximum. It's going to be a little rough until we reach the docking bay."

Turning her attention to the main viewscreen, she could see their destination. One-third of the array's upper ring now occupied the full screen, and several active force-fields along the exterior gleamed like tiny blue beacons. Anxious as she was to enter the array and explore the promise of its unique technology, she silently wondered whether or not this was the most appropriate course of action. At the end of every day, *Voyager*'s safety had to come first.

Turning to Chakotay who sat at her left hand, she saw the firm set of his jaw and knew he shared her concerns.

"Commander," she asked, "is it possible to retrieve Tuvok without boarding the array?"

"Seven of Nine assures me it is not," he replied evenly. "But don't worry. Harry thinks we should be fine."

Janeway caught the faint flicker of a smile. She trusted Chakotay as she had never trusted another first officer, and she had served with her fair share of fine and eminently capable ones. She did not doubt for a moment that in her absence, he had evaluated every possible course of action at their disposal. If he had chosen this path for them, odds were it was the safest and quickest way to accomplish their goal.

"That's good enough for me," she replied with a wry smile as the ship continued to rock and buck.

Scanning her readouts of the array, she asked, "No shields . . . no weapons?"

"Apparently not," Chakotay replied. "There are a number of unusual alloys present in the hull and interior of the array. It's possible that they provide sufficient defense against conventional weapon attack."

"But anyone who wished to destroy the array wouldn't have to target the construct itself. A properly targeted photon torpedo would destabilize the singularity and their structural containment systems," Janeway theorized. "You would think at the least they would have created a countermeasure for that."

"Self preservation, perhaps," Chakotay suggested.

"What do you mean?"

"If you were willing to destroy the array by targeting the singularity, you would also have to be willing to die in the attempt," he said.

"No you wouldn't," she argued. "You'd just launch the torpedo and go to warp . . . oh," she said, as the simple brilliance dawned. "You can't go to warp within the system."

They both paused as Janeway added new information to the fragmented picture she had created in her head of the alien or aliens capable of creating the array and, for all she knew, the entire Monorhan system.

"That's one anomaly of the system we've yet to explain," Chakotay said finally. "If we're right . . . if the entire system was created by some alien design, and if part of the purpose was to protect the array . . ."

Janeway picked up the thread. "The evolution of life on Monorha was unexpected. Since it shouldn't have happened, we've been operating on the premise that it was a flaw in the design. But if the designers knew that life would evolve . . . if, in fact, they intended it . . . then the placement of the white dwarf which kept the Monorhans from detecting the array might only have been the first level of defense. Making warp travel within the system impossible could be the second."

"We picked up a transmission from the array sent by the *rih-hara-tan* of a Monorhan tribe. Her name was Assylia," Chakotay informed her.

"Do we know anything else about her?" Janeway asked.

"No."

"But the ship carrying the Fourteenth Tribe only left Monorha fifty years ago, right?"

"Yes, and the message has been transmitting for almost that long."

"So it's possible they're still there," Janeway hoped. Whatever else they were about to find on the array, Janeway's limited experience of the Monorhans told her that they could be rational, when they wanted to be. At this point, they could use all the allies they could get.

Finally she asked, "What was the message?"

"It's hard to say definitively, but the suggestion is that they believed the array to be Gremadia," he continued.

"Their mythological holy land," Janeway added pensively.

"The rest of the message was a little disturbing," Chakotay finally said.

"Go on."

"The last words were 'turn back.' "

Janeway watched as the view of the array's docking bays engulfed the entire viewscreen. Within moments, they would be on board.

"It's a little late for that now, don't you think?" she offered.

"I do," he agreed.

"B'Elanna found the cause for the explosion in sickbay. The Key to Gremadia, the gift Kaytok gave me before we left, is made up of sporocystian remnants," Janeway told him. "It's literally the remnants of thousands of Nacene, and we have reason to believe they may still be alive."

Chakotay shook his head. "We don't know much about the Nacene. We do know that their technology was far beyond ours. And both the Caretaker and Suspiria built arrays from which they carried out their experiments."

"But those arrays were nothing like this. The only thing we've found in the Delta Quadrant that even resembles this technology were the communications arrays that the Hirogen were using powered by microsingularities."

"The Caretaker called Suspiria his mate," Chakotay said, "but neither of them ever said they were the only Nacene to enter our galaxy. They were explorers. Maybe they weren't alone."

"That's what I'm afraid of," Janeway said finally.

"May I make a suggestion, Captain?" Chakotay asked.

Janeway replied with a sharp nod.

"I know this technology is fascinating. We could spend weeks studying it and barely scratch the surface. But given the fact that Assylia's message could be construed as a warning, that it's possible that the Nacene have had either a hand or an interest in creating this system and the array, I think it would be wise to simply find Tuvok and get out of here as soon as possible."

Janeway considered this carefully. The array was alluring. But she shared Chakotay's concerns. Finally she said, "Once we're on board we'll transport Tuvok directly to sickbay, and we'll send an away team to the Monorhan ship. Otherwise, we'll hold off on any purely exploratory missions for the time being."

Chakotay relaxed a little. "Yes, Captain," he said, and set about sending revised orders out to the teams he had already assembled.

The ship suddenly rocked forty-five degrees on its axis, throwing Janeway from her seat. Through the explosion of several plasma relays, she saw Lieutenant Paris clawing his way from the floor back to the conn. The bridge was bathed only in the red-black darkness of the emergency lighting system.

Pulling herself up on her hands and knees, Janeway shouted, "Report!"

Ensign Kim's was the first voice she heard through the confusion of alarms.

"We've encountered the singularity's event horizon, Captain," he shouted.

She felt the firm grasp of Chakotay's hand on her arm, helping her to her feet. In the space of a few seconds, Paris had regained his seat at the conn and the bridge had been returned to an angle that made standing, or at the very least staying in your seat, possible.

Tossing a glance toward the main viewscreen, she saw that her relatively placid view of the array's docking bays had been replaced by the swirling vortex of the singularity.

"We're still outside the array. How is this possible?" Janeway demanded.

Harry's hands were flying over the controls.

"I don't know Captain. According to our calculations, the existence of the horizon at any point outside the area of the array's rings was theoretically possible, but highly unlikely."

Voyager rocked again, but Janeway noted with some satisfaction that most of the bridge crew was prepared to hang on this time.

"Mr. Paris, adjust our heading to take us away from the array and go to full impulse."

"Yes, ma'am," Tom managed through clenched teeth as he willed the ship to hold together long enough for him to lay in the new course.

Harry's voice was strained, but controlled as he informed the bridge, "Shields at sixty percent."

"Mr. Paris?" Janeway asked.

"Going to full impulse . . . now."

The ship shuddered violently beneath them.

"Shields at forty percent."

"The new course is laid in, Captain, but our impulse engines can't pull us free of the gravity well."

Janeway cursed silently as *Voyager* slipped inexorably toward the center of the singularity.

"B'Elanna," Janeway shouted over the comm, "reroute all available power systems to the impulse drive."

"It's already done, Captain! Impulse engines are running at forty percent over maximum capacity now!" B'Elanna screamed over the chaos.

Janeway was running out of options.

The loneliness was gone. The pain was gone. Tuvok stood on the ridge of a vast, barren plain. Below him, hundreds of thousands of beings were dancing. They moved in couples, and small groups. They came together, and flew apart, as if compelled by the rhythm and harmony that sounded all around him.

The sadness of the spectacle he was witnessing was as overwhelming as it was inexplicable. The chaos of their movement shuddered through him, as the song began to lose its coherence. He could make out the shapes of those who had fallen. The others danced on, oblivious of the carnage.

Finally the truth hit him. This was not a dance. This was a battle. There were no directed-energy weapons. The forms he had earlier thought to be people did not actually possess arms or legs for punching or kicking. Nonetheless, the violent frenetic masses swarming the plain were obviously capable of inflicting mortal wounds upon one another. Their rage and hatred of one another was palpable.

"This was the beginning of the end," a soft voice whispered beside him.

Turning, he saw a Monorhan male standing beside him on the ridge. Although he had never met him, Tuvok knew him in an instant. His name was Naviim.

"Are you the one who brought me here?" he asked.

Naviim's dark gray eyes clouded over momentarily.

"In a way. You heard our call . . . sensed the urgency . . . but you would not have been capable of helping us."

For the first time since the music had taken hold of his mind in sickbay, Tuvok found it relatively easy to focus. It seemed that his mind was, once again, his own.

"The music . . . is that the call you refer to?"

Naviim's long jaw dropped slightly as the edges of his mouth crept upward and his ears flattened against his skull. Tuvok recognized the Monorhan smile.

"What you experienced as music contained much of our truth. Your mind interpreted the call in a way that brought order to the dissonance. There are mathematical properties to music that underpin some of our truth. You are fortunate that your exposure to complicated musical patterns gave you this context. Our telepathic gifts were different. When we came and the first of us were exposed to the gift, our sense of the emergence came not in sound, but overwhelming feelings of fear and danger."

"Where am I?"

"Your body is on Gremadia. But you are no longer merely the sum total of your biological processes and simple matter. Your body is no longer relevant. What you are becoming . . . is all."

"I do not understand," Tuvok replied simply.

"Nor will you, for a time. But surely you sense that you are no longer what you once were?" Naviim asked.

Tuvok took a deep breath, bathing in the cool clear peace that the ability to separate thought from emotion gave him. Searching deeper, he was suddenly aware of the truth of Naviim's words. He was no longer lonely . . . because although the music was gone, he was not alone. Blossoming within him was something new. He did not fear it, though its alien presence was faintly disconcerting. Instead, he considered it dispassionately, not as something that should not be there. But as a thing that in some impossible way . . . by taking the place of the music . . . completed him.

"You are Monorhan," Tuvok observed. "Are you also on Gremadia?"

"I was, and am, though not as you see me now. I was the last taken. As such, it falls to me to welcome you to your new life. You see me now in the only form that your limited mind can still accept. It will not always be so."

Tuvok was intensely curious. Yet somehow he grasped intuitively that the answers he would have of Naviim were already within him . . . that in time . . . he would know all. For the moment, he was content to allow the mystery to unfold.

"What is this place?" he finally asked.

"You are experiencing a memory of us. I have not visited this place in a very long time," Naviim replied.

A split second later Tuvok felt a white-hot searing pain slice into his head.

Do not resist.

He heard the words clearly, though the largest portion of his mind denied their truth. That which caused pain must be resisted. Logic dictated that if there was something he could do to prevent this, he should. The instruction of the voice flew in the face of that logic. And yet, somehow, that voice was also his. It was part of him. And part of something infinitely larger than him.

With no ready alternative, he chose to heed what he hoped was the voice of some sort of higher reasoning. He accepted the pain, and in that same moment, its power vanished.

"I am sorry," Naviim said as the pain subsided. "The

transition before you will be difficult at times. As you see, acceptance is the easiest course. We would not have you suffer unnecessarily."

"What have you done to me?" Tuvok demanded.

"We have done nothing. Though we are all capable of sharing the gift with you, we would never force it upon you without your consent, as it was forced upon us. But there is one among us who does not share our ability to make such distinctions. We allowed it to pass the gift along, as the only means to guarantee the continuation of your existence. We were grateful that you came. It would have been wrong for such a noble impulse to end in oblivion."

"Will you stay with me?" Tuvok asked.

"You will pass into darkness soon," Naviim replied. "As your body dies it will be difficult for us to continue this communication. But do not be afraid. We will not leave you, and when you awaken to your new existence, I and the others will be here to greet you. We await that moment with joy."

With those words, Naviim vanished.

Tuvok turned again to the plain below. The battle was over. Vague, shapeless masses were strewn about the field. Many appeared to be in the final throes of death. The light around him began to fall. The field was bathed in deep purple gauze. In the distance, Tuvok saw a figure, rising from among the dead. A fierce wail, equal parts agony and defiance, rocked the earth beneath Tuvok's feet. The sound was everywhere, within and around him, searing heat that threatened to pull him apart.

Phoebe left sickbay as quickly and unobtrusively as she could, leaving the Talaxian and the hybrid girl's mother sitting their uneasy vigil. As she made her way back to engineering, she realized that she had fallen into an old habit, underestimating humanoids. Having spent so much time among the life-forms of this dimension, she had grown used to thinking of them as *lesser beings*.

It hadn't started out that way. When she had made a choice to turn her back on the Others, she had done it with a firm sense of the possibilities that this dimension would hold. For thousands of years she had marveled at the complexity of life, and its seemingly limitless potential. But their tendency toward sameness, the mistakes she had seen countless different races make time and again, as if they had no interest or intention of learning from the wisdom of others, or even their own histories, had gradually soured her on the experience.

She had yet to encounter a humanoid species that even approached the limits of their own abilities. They evolved at a torturously slow rate, and were hindered, of course, by their mortality. Though it was true that Phoebe and her kind were "mortal" in a sense, their life span could be extended almost to infinity if the proper measures were taken.

She had made the same early mistakes as many of those who had once shared her passion for exploration. She had intervened in the normal development of countless life-forms, helping them enhance their natural abilities, artificially extending their life spans, restructuring their environments to make them more hospitable to their evolution.

But time and again, she had been disappointed.

Perhaps the Others had been right about that much. The consequences of interference could be harsh, but to simply witness senseless death and wasted potential seemed equally inappropriate. Why exist, if one's existence did not make a difference?

But she was still a long way from accepting the choice of the Others. Every moment still held the possibility that another solution to their mutual problem might exist. She had no intention of giving up, but she had long ago concluded that no humanoid life-forms would play any role in the ultimate solution. If her current circumstance was any indication, quite the opposite might be true. These humanoids in particular, could be the undoing of them all.

Captain Janeway unknowingly held the literal and metaphorical key to the most devastating possibility Phoebe had ever faced. The worst part was there was almost no way that Phoebe could even begin to make her understand what was at stake. Humans like Janeway didn't even have words to describe the reality that hung in the balance. Though they were more evolved than many, they were millions of years from even a rudimentary understanding of the true nature of the space-time construct that they inhabited.

The only possibility for communicating the truth to Janeway lay in a course of action Phoebe instinctively found unacceptable. But if worse came to worst, she wouldn't have a choice. She hadn't passed along knowledge of the sort required to such a lesser being in a very long time. But she couldn't predict what Janeway would make of the array, or the spores that had been placed there when it was created and ultimately taken by those that became the abominations. She assumed Janeway would perceive the abominations as a threat. Anything a humanoid could not understand was often classed as hostile. She would have preferred to keep Janeway and her ship far from the array until the last possible moment, but only a massive show of force would stop the captain at this point. She could contain the rest of the crew. She would kill them if necessary to protect the precious cargo contained within the abominations. Their value was incalculable. But she knew that Janeway would never agree to help her if she was responsible for the wholesale slaughter of the humanoids who were under the captain's protection.

More troubling were her own mistakes. She had been away from the array for too long. Though it was not her primary responsibility, she and many others had made periodic visits to ensure the safety of the spores and to shed the inevitably wearying fabric of the one or many lifeforms they mimicked while exploring this realm. Some had chosen to enter stasis rather than continue this cycle, content to leave the difficult work of solving the problem to those with more energy and enthusiasm for it. In the process they had added whatever new data they had collected to the array's systems, evidence in the case they would ultimately make to the Others of the value of their choice.

When she had first encountered *Voyager*, her course of action had seemed obvious. The lesser beings were no match for her abilities. She would deceive them as long as necessary to protect the Key and its owner. Though she could not have anticipated the anomaly presented in the hybrid girl, she should have been more thorough in her analysis of the holographic doctor. He could have been her undoing. It was a careless mistake and she was unaccustomed to making such mistakes. Her solution would probably wreak havoc on all she had planned.

Perhaps when *Voyager* reached the array there would be time for her to renew herself. There were dozens of suites designed for this purpose, and she took a moment to anticipate the welcome release and reinvigoration that would accompany the reorganization of the subatomic fabric of her existence.

First, however, she must protect the Key. Janeway had

already learned too much. The "sporocystian" label she had placed on it was predictably simplistic, and altogether too close to the truth. Phoebe knew full well that once the Key was in closer proximity to the abominations, the subspace dissonance field emanating from it would increase exponentially. Janeway would most certainly misunderstand this, and might go so far as to destroy it.

When she entered engineering she noted with relief that all the crewmen present were busy tending to their respective duties. Their heightened state of alarm and alert, given the strain on the ship resulting from its proximity to the singularity, made her all but invisible. Nonetheless, she encouraged them with a thought to pay no attention to her as she moved toward the Key still sitting tranquilly behind its forcefield.

Even in her true form she would not be able to deconstruct the Key in order to remove it. Its very nature made that impossible. Had this not been the case she would simply have enveloped it and taken it back to an uninhabited area of Monorha, similar to the field where it had rested undisturbed for so long. For now, she could only use the primitive technology at *Voyager*'s disposal. Standing before the diagnostic station, she pulled up the ship's transporter controls and searched for an appropriate hiding place. It did not take her long to find the only location within the ship where the Key would go unnoticed for a time. *Voyager*'s warp core had been deactivated for several days, since they entered the Monorhan system. But the residual antimatter swirling within it would shield the Key temporarily from their sensors. As long as the warp drive was not active, it would pose no danger to the Key. Phoebe could think of no reason why the warp engines would be brought online in their present circumstances, and breathed a sigh of relief when a few moments later the Key dematerialized behind the forcefield and the transporter log, deleted as soon as it appeared, indicated that it now rested at the base of the warp core.

Her relief was short-lived. Within seconds of the transport, the ship careened at an impossible angle as klaxons began to wail.

Static burst across the main viewscreen, briefly distorting the image of the spinning vortex that threatened to crush *Voyager* and her crew.

Through the open channel between the bridge and engineering Janeway was conscious of a fierce debate raging as B'Elanna and her staff proposed and discarded one potential possibility after another. She heard Seven's normally calm voice raised almost to the point of shrillness as she joined their efforts.

Strangely, the bulk of her mind, however, was calm. This was the difference between a Starfleet captain and the rest of the crew, no matter how experienced. In such a moment, as the rush of adrenaline caused most people's bodies to kick into a hypersensitive yet often unproductive state, a good captain could find a safe harbor in the eye of the storm, where the idea that meant the difference between life and death was invariably to be found. Dipping into the well of experience, Janeway searched for the idea. A moment later, she had it.

"B'Elanna," she shouted over the din as the rest of the bridge grew silent, "bring the warp core online."

"But, Captain . . ." B'Elanna began.

"Just do it," Janeway cut her off. "I'll explain later."

Janeway knew full well she might never get the chance to explain. But she also knew she was right. She had just spent an uncomfortable several hours trapped in a subspace fold of the Monorhan system. Several of the properties of that layer were similar to those contained within the singularity. Although it was impossible to create a stable warp field within the layer, it was possible to create an unstable one. The difficulty lay in determining their exit vector. They had considered but ultimately rejected this course of action a few days earlier, unwilling to run the risk of exiting the subspace layer at an indeterminate point. The singularity was probably the only other area of Monorhan space where a similar field could be created. She was counting on it.

As she waited for confirmation of the successful execution of her orders, she took a moment to hope that Tuvok would forgive her choice, assuming he was still alive. If what she was about to attempt worked, the odds were dismally low that they would be able to attempt another rescue mission. She knew that he would have been incapable of feeling pain or regret at her choice. She wished she could be sure that he knew the lengths she had taken to rescue him. Although it wouldn't have comforted him, she knew he would have seen her gesture, however futile, as an appropriate testament to the level of respect and love they shared in their many years of friendship.

Assuming they survived, she would have time later to regret her choice and to transform the guilt and torment into something that at least vaguely resembled acceptance. Like so many others, it would be her lonely burden to bear.

"Captain," B'Elanna's voice interrupted her thoughts, "I can't activate the warp engine. I'm locked out of the control system."

"What?" Janeway demanded, attempting to rise from her seat.

But she didn't get an answer to her implied question. A moment later the ship was struck hard by an unknown force, and instantly the viewscreen was bathed in a deep green glow. Simultaneously, the tumultuous jarring ride they had endured since crossing the event horizon ended, and with the help of the inertial dampers, the ship resumed a calm, smooth course.

"Mr. Kim, what happened?" Janeway asked, certain that he was already searching for the answer she was seeking.

"We're caught in a tractor net, Captain. It's coming from the array. We're being pulled into one of the docking bays."

Relief battled with concern as she considered this development. On the one hand, it was an entirely unexpected reprieve. For all she knew, it might be the only way to safely enter the array. On the other hand, she instinctively hated turning over control of her vessel to unseen hands.

"Harry, can you show me where we're headed?"

Instantly the view of a docking bay came up on the screen. Janeway noted with some alarm that the entrance glistened with a faint blue forcefield, but she could only assume that if the tractor beam had been automatically activated, the station's controls would also drop the force field as they approached. A moment later, her suspicion was confirmed, as the field blinked out of existence.

An eerie calm settled over the bridge. The alarms had been silenced, the smoke had cleared. All they could do now was wait.

Chapter 7

The bridge was silent. Janeway watched with an unmistakable sense of foreboding as *Voyager* cleared the entrance to the docking bay, and came to rest within its cavernous depths. She was so accustomed to facing the unknown with stoic faith in her crew's ability to overcome any challenge presented that she didn't even flinch at the heavy metallic clanging of alien docking clamps securing *Voyager* to the docking bay. She did, however, involuntarily release a faint sigh of relief as the bright green web that had drawn them here finally flickered out of existence, leaving the main viewscreen lit by only the faint bluish glow of the bay.

She was the first to speak.

"Status, Mr. Kim?"

"The docking clamps are secure and the forcefield has been restored. Damage reports are coming in now. Impulse engines and shield generators are offline."

"Chakotay?"

"A few minor injuries, none life-threatening."

"Ensign Kim, do we have a lock on Tuvok's life signs?"

"Yes, Captain."

"Janeway to Tuvok, do you read?"

She held her breath, awaiting Tuvok's reply.

None came.

"*Voyager* to Lieutenant Tuvok . . . if you are receiving this transmission, I order you to respond," Janeway said more forcefully.

Again, no reply.

"Janeway to transporter room one," Janeway called over the comm.

"*Transporter room one reporting.*"

"Lock on to Lieutenant Tuvok and transport him directly to sickbay."

There was a brief moment of silence as she waited for confirmation of the successful transport.

"*Transporter room one to Captain Janeway.*"

"Go ahead."

"*Transport failed. We can't establish a lock.*"

Janeway rose from her seat.

"What's wrong?"

Throughout this exchange, Seven of Nine had been busy at tactical. "I believe I may have an answer, Captain," she said in her maddeningly calm voice.

Janeway closed the distance between herself and Seven in a few quick steps and examined the readings.

Seven began to speak as Janeway reached her. "There is a mineral compound of unknown origin contained within the metal that comprises over ninety percent of the station. It acts as a natural barrier to our transporters. It seems designed to repel any directed energy beams, including those used for the transfer of matter."

Fascinating as all of this was, Janeway refused to be sidetracked for long.

"Would pattern enhancers help?" she asked.

"It is impossible to tell," Seven replied.

"We'll take them anyway, just in case," Chakotay said.

"Commander," Janeway ordered, "assemble your rescue team. I'm sorry we couldn't make it easier for you, but at least we know where Tuvok is."

Chakotay had already risen to his feet, presumably expecting this command as soon as Seven made her report about the transporters.

"We'll be back as soon as we can," Chakotay nodded assuredly. "Mr. Kim, Mr. Paris, you're with me."

As the doors to the turbolift slid shut behind them, the bridge was suddenly bathed in a bright white glow.

Seven was the first to diagnose the situation. "Captain, we are being scanned."

"By what?" Janeway demanded, shielding her eyes from the blinding light.

"A coherent tetryon beam," she replied, oblivious of the instinctive alarm this raised in Janeway, and most likely in every member of the crew who had been aboard *Voyager* the day they were pulled into the Delta Quadrant.

A few seconds later, the beam was extinguished.

"Let's hope whoever activated that scan liked what they saw," Janeway observed.

"I believe it is an automated system, Captain," Seven informed her as she switched the image on the main viewscreen to a multipicture view of several areas of the docking bay.

The bay was lined with dozens of power nodes. Long black cables were wound neatly at the base of each node. As Janeway looked on in awe several of the cables that had been wound innocuously on the walls appeared to unwrap themselves and seek out external ports along *Voyager*'s hull. Their movement was slow but precise. The eerie dance reminded Janeway of the hypnotic movement of a cobra, charmed from a wicker basket by an Indian shaman. She had never seen the spectacle in person, but

Chakotay had shown her a holovid of such a scene, research he had collected after a particularly disturbing vision quest. The only thing missing in the moment was the gentle whistle of the lute that the snake charmer had used to coax and then regulate the motion of the deadly cobra.

With a series of barely audible clicks and hisses, the cables attached themselves to ports along *Voyager*'s hull.

Janeway called to engineering. "B'Elanna," she asked, "are you detecting the activity along our hull?"

"*Yes, Captain*" she replied. "*Most of them are power-transfer cables. However, there is also one dataport being compromised. I believe the array's computer system is attempting to interface and synchronize with ours. Should we attempt to disengage them?*"

Janeway was torn. Everything she already knew about the array suggested that this could be an opportunity they might never have again. It had been years since all of their reserve systems had been stocked at maximum levels. But a nagging voice of doubt in the back of her mind persistently reminded her that nothing, even in a society that had eliminated currency, came without a price. She would have preferred to initiate and oversee any power transfers from the array. It appeared, however, that she wouldn't have that chance.

"Monitor the levels closely, Lieutenant. At the first sign of an overload, disengage them by force if necessary."

"*Understood, Captain,*" B'Elanna replied as Janeway moved toward ops and pulled up the same readings that B'Elanna would be seeing in engineering. Within moments the interface procedure completed its operation, and the green bars on the display that indicated *Voyager*'s reserve supplies began to climb.

As Seven peered over her shoulder Janeway said softly, "It's amazing, isn't it? While humans were still wearing animal skins and living in caves, an alien race designed a system that could anticipate the needs of every spacefaring vessel."

Seven nodded silently.

Once the power transfer was complete, all of the cables with the exception of the data-transfer cable disengaged themselves automatically. Janeway pulled up several different external views of the docking bay, and her breath caught in her throat at the sight of the power cables neatly wrapping themselves up along the walls.

"B'Elanna," Janeway called, "the power transfer is complete. Why is our dataport still connected to the array?"

"The port is still active in order to allow us to send commands to the array's systems." She paused before adding, *"Since I'm assuming we'll want to leave the array at some point, I don't think we should disengage it. I'm seeing limited command controls, including those that control the docking clamps and forcefield active in this bay."*

"Understood," Janeway replied. "Leave it active for now."

She turned her attention to the sensor displays. "Seven, life-form readings are still unclear. Take B'Elanna and go as quickly as you can to the Monorhan ship. If you encounter any of them, contact me immediately."

"You do not trust me in a first-contact situation?" Seven asked innocently.

"It's not that, Seven," Janeway chided. "It's a matter of protocol."

Though obviously dissatisfied with Janeway's curt response, Seven nodded dutifully and directed her steps toward the turbolift. Once Janeway had given B'Elanna her orders and set about overseeing repairs in her absence, she silently wondered whether or not it was a good idea to send B'Elanna and Seven into a potentially hostile situation again, so soon after their misadventures on Monorha. Brilliant as they both were, they usually mixed as well as matter and antimatter. In controlled amounts, they generated significant power, but it was a delicate balance. Not for the first time, she wondered how they had survived as a mini-collective.

Once she had assured herself that repairs were progressing at an appropriate pace, Janeway retreated to the solitude of her ready room. Replicating a cup of coffee, she took a moment to pause over the drawing that Naomi had left her. She made a mental note to check in with sickbay as soon as possible, then turned her attention to the schematics of the array's power systems.

Prickling at the back of her mind was the coherent tetryon scan that had preceded the energy transfer. The Caretaker had used coherent tetryon technology to pull *Voyager* across seventy thousand light-years in the wink of an eye. The Key was generating a subspace dissonance field, possibly in response to the presence of another Nacene. All of the evidence at hand certainly pointed to the possibility that the Monorhans, like the Ocampa, might have been unwitting victims of Nacene manipulation. But any substantive understanding of the Nacene's intent in designing the system and the miraculous array eluded her.

Her musings were interrupted by a call over the comm system from Neelix.

"What is it Neelix?" she asked.

"I'm sorry to disturb you, Captain, but I believe there's a problem with the Doctor."

Chakotay, Tom, and Harry stood tensely as the ramp lowered from *Voyager*'s lower hull. They walked quickly

down, once it had settled firmly on the floor of the docking bay. Chakotay and Tom were armed with compression
rifles. They walked on either side of Harry, who carried
his phaser in one hand and his tricorder in the other.
Harry couldn't help but feel an unreasonable sense of vulnerability. If his brief history aboard *Voyager* was any guide,
he was certainly the crewman most likely to suffer a
painful and violent death at the hands of an unknown hostile alien. But he had to acknowledge that this arrangement was the most practical. Chakotay and Tom were
better shots than he was, and he would more efficiently
gather as much sensor data as he could along the way. As
tense as the knot in Harry's stomach was when they
stepped onto the solid plating of the docking bay's deck,
he was also certain that they were going to need as much
information as possible at their disposal to safely leave the
monstrous structure. Falling into step beside Tom and
Chakotay, both dimly illuminated by the reassuring glow
of the bay's forcefield separating the atmosphere within
from open space, he struggled to put his fears and doubts
aside. Maybe this time it would be different.

"Welcome to Black Hole City," Tom said quietly, as
they started toward a ladder which climbed toward a cat-
walk into the darkness above them. The only doorway
leading to the interior of the station was a few meters beyond the top of that ladder.

"Very funny," Harry replied, to Tom's feeble attempt to
lighten his mood.

At several points along the walls of the bay, black power
cables were wound and stored in their places. As their eyes
adjusted to the dim blue lighting, *Voyager,* suspended by
four large docking clamps, cast large looming shadows all
around them. The bay seemed to pulse with energy. It
could have been tension, the seriousness of their mission

combined with the strangeness of their surroundings. Though Harry didn't voice his thoughts, he was struck by the almost palpable currents running through the air, as their boots whispered softly across the floor.

Data was streaming into Harry's tricorder faster than his processor could organize it.

"Commander," Harry murmured, overwhelmed.

"Yes, Ensign?"

"I've pinpointed the location of the tractor net system. There are generators present every hundred meters or so along the outside of the array, but they are routed to a central processor located in what looks like an engineering center."

"That's fascinating, Harry," Tom jibed, "but what about the life-form readings?"

"I've still got a lock on Tuvok. He's stationary, approximately twenty-five hundred meters from our present location."

"So he might be injured," Chakotay offered.

"And there's another problem," Harry added.

"Of course there is," Tom said with obvious dismay.

"What is it Harry?" Chakotay asked.

"Tuvok isn't in this section of the array. His life-form readings are coming from the other ring."

"So how do we get there?" Tom asked.

"I don't know," Harry answered. "There are no direct access points anywhere on this level. The rings move independently of one another. There's no physical connection between the two as far as I can tell."

"But we know that ring is filled with living quarters, don't we?" Chakotay asked.

"Among other things, yes," Harry replied.

"So if these are the only docking bays, there has to be a way," Chakotay said firmly. "Tuvok's shuttle, or what's left of it, is currently housed in this ring. He must have found a way onto the other ring. I suggest we make our way to the engineering center. If they have transport technology it might be there, or at the very least, point us in the right direction."

"The engineering hub is located approximately twelve hundred meters from our present location," Harry said.

"Then we'd better move fast," Chakotay replied.

As Tom slung his rifle over his shoulder and began to quickly ascend the ladder, which was easily a hundred meters high, Harry thought he caught a flicker of movement in the shadows to his left. Dropping his tricorder to the ground, he instantly fell into a crouch and aimed his phaser into the darkness.

Chakotay followed suit, but after a breathless second it seemed they were both jumping at shadows.

"What is it, Ensign?" Chakotay asked.

"I thought I saw something, Commander," Harry replied, still crouched.

Bending gingerly to retrieve Harry's tricorder, Chakotay leveled it toward the darkness. The readings showed a data-transmission junction with a large cable attached to its base.

"It's a dataport. I'm not picking up any life signs, Harry," Chakotay said gently.

Swallowing hard, Harry rose and confirmed the readings. As he holstered his phaser and tricorder to begin his own climb, Chakotay clapped him on the shoulder saying, "But you can't be too careful."

"Are you guys coming?" Tom panted from above.

"Right behind you," Harry called, hoping the exertion of the ascent would dissipate some of the adrenaline pounding through his system and willing himself to get a grip. He relaxed a little more when he saw Chakotay standing with his back to the ladder and his rifle leveled, covering him and Tom as they climbed.

Several minutes later, all three had gained the top. As they directed their steps toward the heavy door that stood between them and the rest of the station, they took a moment to catch their breath over the spectacular and unusual view of their ship afforded them from this vantage point. Even without her exterior running lights aglow, the fluid grace of their starship buoyed Harry's spirits.

Before leaving the ship, they had been apprised of the miraculous energy infusion *Voyager* had received in the time it took them to collect the gear they required for their rescue mission. By the time the entered the docking bay, the power-transfer cables had coiled themselves neatly back into place. Harry didn't know whether he was more disconcerted or relieved when the airlock door opened automatically as the away team came within a meter of it.

B'Elanna and Seven made good time, reaching the Monorhan vessel housed two bays over in a little less than thirty minutes. They, too, carried pattern enhancers, in the event that this would make the return trip on foot unnecessary. The docking bay where the vessel, easily twice the size of a *Galaxy*-class Federation ship, rested was similar to the one where *Voyager* was berthed, but it appeared that it had been the scene of a brutal conflict. Sections of hull plating, striated by weapons fire, were visibly scorched and charred. Power conduits and plasma relays no longer belched smoke or residue, though telltale trails of grit and exposed circuitry tangled with huge chunks of fuselage made traversing the distance from the docking-bay door to the ship something like walking through a densely overgrown mechanical forest.

The Monorhan ship had been a lean and graceful piece

of engineering in her day. Composed of synthetic polymers and familiar Monorhan alloys, two fin-shaped ex-
tensions fused seamlessly on either side of the cylindrical
mass that made up the central body of the ship and housed
its propulsion system. It appeared to have been built with
as much a sense of beauty as utility. B'Elanna wasn't aware
of any ocean-dwelling creatures native to Monorha, but in
looking at it, she could not stop mentally imagining a huge
stingray that had been taught to fly. Sensor networks that
would be heavily shielded on a Starfleet ship ran along
every surface of the ship like pores. There were no sharp
edges, no obvious doors or windows. In short, apart from
the technological components that her tricorder and common sense told her were present, it looked like a beautiful,
almost fragile living thing.

"So how do we get in?" B'Elanna asked. Extending her
hand toward the hull, she took a chance and tapped lightly,
as if knocking on a door.

"I do not believe anyone will answer," Seven observed.

"You're telling me it wasn't worth a try?" B'Elanna
asked pointedly.

"There are no life-form readings aboard this vessel. Although our sensors cannot penetrate most of the array, I
can verify that there are no other living beings within this
docking bay," Seven advised her.

"There were supposedly thousands of people aboard
this ship when it left Monorha. Fifty years later, there's
nobody home. That's disturbing, don't you think?"
B'Elanna asked.

"Any sense of foreboding at these circumstances is irrelevant. Although I agree, it is curious."

B'Elanna nodded and began circling the aft of the vessel. Seven was the first to find an entry point. The ship
rested on four landing struts, and beneath the central

mass, which rose only a few meters from the floor, a spherical pod hung precariously.

"This appears to be an emergency evacuation device," Seven noted as she scanned the small vessel. "Its separation from the ship was not completed."

Running her hands along the smooth cool surface of the pod, B'Elanna found a small inset latch. She tugged it gently, and a faint whoosh of dank air was released as a door, barely large enough to crawl through, opened in response. At the same time, a similar door within the body of the main ship also opened.

"Found an airlock. Give me a boost," B'Elanna requested, catching either side of the exposed frame of the door in her hands and relying on Seven for the extra momentum she needed to pull herself through it. Once inside, she returned the favor, securing her legs on one side of the door frame and leaning both of her arms out to Seven.

The corridor they found themselves in was shrouded in darkness, though the end of the hallway was faintly lit by a slowly pulsing yellow light.

"Curious," said Seven as they picked their way cautiously toward the light, "there are no obvious command consoles present in this area. There is a dense network of fibers beneath the hull plating, indicating the presence of partially organic relays, but there does not appear to be any obvious way to access them."

"The members of the Fourteenth Tribe were telepaths," B'Elanna said. "Their abilities were far beyond those of most Monorhans. Maybe their systems only respond to mental commands."

"Or vocal ones," Seven added.

B'Elanna shrugged, "Also worth a try." As they turned

the corner into a much wider corridor, and several open doorways came into view, she called, "Computer?"

There was no response, though to B'Elanna's eye, the pulsing of the only ambient light seemed to quicken for a moment, as if a heart, suddenly startled, began to beat faster.

The first doorway they came to led to some sort of passenger cabin. There were eight bunks built into the walls, surrounding a small common area strewn with a few low cushions they both recognized as Monorhan chairs.

"This level is filled with similar cabins," Seven announced, studying her tricorder. "There are two hubs that appear to be processing centers eight decks above us."

"I don't see any Jefferies tubes," B'Elanna noted.

"I do not believe they utilized them," Seven replied, pointing to the far end of the corridor where a circular staircase wound its way up.

They climbed the stairs in darkness, B'Elanna taking the lead. The stairs were not wide enough for two to walk abreast. When they reached the top, they found themselves in a large circular room. Four archways loomed before them, but it was easy enough to see that the second archway to their left led to some sort of command center. It was illuminated at standard working light settings, though the light still pulsed ever so faintly.

One large chair dominated the room. Many-hued lights blinked and flashed at several low display stations around the room, though it was clear that whoever might once have been responsible for monitoring those stations had done it from the Monorhan equivalent of a standing position. The absence of any other stools or chairs made it clear that only the captain of this vessel was ever seated while on duty.

B'Elanna bent to study the displays, gently tapping the consoles in hopes of eliciting some sort of response. A few frustrated minutes later she said, "The main computer core is locked down. I can't access any primary or secondary systems."

"Continue working," Seven suggested. "There is another staircase in that corner. I will search the area."

B'Elanna nodded, too engrossed in her task to worry much about what Seven might encounter there.

Leaving B'Elanna to her work, Seven cautiously followed the winding staircase down into dimness. The first sight her wrist beacon exposed were the fragmented skeletal remains of a Monorhan male lying prostrate over the entrance to another large room at the end of the corridor. Seven started toward him automatically, pausing only when her light caught the walls. Unlike the other corridors she had passed, the entire hallway was covered with an intricate design formed from small pieces of colored glass. She was able to make out small figures within the designs, also Monorhan. Playing her light slowly over the intricate piece of art, she discovered several scenes from what she could only assume were Monorhan history, or legend. Most striking was a vast field beneath a purple sky, covered with thousands of dead. On a rise above the field, a figure wearing robes of light was pointing to the heavens above.

She took a few moments to scan the images into her tricorder, then continued toward the doorway. Stepping gingerly around the bones, she entered the room. An entire wall was devoted to shelves that housed dozens of scrolls rolled into ornately woven cases. She pulled one from the first shelf on the right and gently opened it. The parchment was brittle in her hand, and broke in two places. Nonetheless, she could clearly make out Monorhan script on the parchments.

Something sparked in the darkness behind her. Turning, she saw a low desk, where a display station, similar to those in the command center, must have been housed. The display had been torn from its housing, and fragments of the panel were strewn about the desk and on the floor nearby. The entire level was shrouded in darkness, but the circuitry of the display still pulsed with power. Extending from deep with the guts of the display, delicate skeletal fingers protruded upward. Seven stepped slowly toward the desk, scanning the area with her light. Though the arms of the hands that were embedded in the display had broken off at the first joint, the rest of the body to which they had once been attached was crumpled on the floor behind the desk, still swathed in a finely embroidered robe.

As Seven bent low to get a closer look at the body, the lights of the cabin pulsed into a bright harsh glow.

B'Elanna studied the alien control panel. She had been attempting to enter simple commands, using her tricorder to decrypt what she could of the strange system. Frustrated, she set it aside and tried to think like a Monorhan. Playing her fingers intuitively across the panel, she entered a series of strokes that would have made sense to her, had she designed the system.

Suddenly, a square section of what had been a solid wall opposite the command chair began to glow. It was immediately obvious that this was some sort of viewscreen. A bright flash of static illuminated the room and the face of a Monorhan female appeared before them.

"*I am Assylia,*" she began. But as she continued to speak, the message blinked in and out, garbling the rest of her words beyond understanding.

"This is the source of the transmission we picked up before we boarded the array," B'Elanna said to herself, studying the controls. Following her instincts, she began to work to clear up the distorted image.

It took only a few more tries for B'Elanna to restore the transmission. She set it to replay, then stood back, wiping from her fingers the dust that she had collected while working the controls that had obviously been untouched for some time.

Her momentary satisfaction turned quickly to alarm as Assylia spoke.

"*I am Assylia, rih-hara-tan of the fourteenth Monorhan tribe and commander of this vessel, the Betasis. There is a hostile, parasitic life-form present on this array. It took the lives of almost ten thousand of us in a matter of days. We came in search of Gremadia. We found nothing but death. If you attempt to board the array, you will meet our fate. I beg of you, turn back. Do not make the same mistake that I did.*"

After a brief moment of silence the message began again.

"*I am Assylia . . .*"

"Seven?" B'Elanna shouted into the darkness, slapping the panel to abruptly end the transmission.

When she received no reply, she followed the path Seven had taken down the winding stairs.

She found Seven pulling dozens of scrolls from a musty shelf in a brightly lit cabin at the end of the corridor.

"These scrolls contain data of historic and religious significance to the Fourteenth Tribe. Several of them mention the Key. We should take them back to *Voyager,*" Seven said as B'Elanna entered.

"We have to get out of here," B'Elanna said.

"Were you able to retrieve any data from the computers?" Seven asked.

"We don't have time. It will take hours to crack their security codes and I'm not staying here that long. The message . . . the transmission we received . . . it was a warning from the captain of this vessel. The reason we aren't picking up any Monorhan life signs is because they all died within days of boarding the array."

Seven's eyes widened.

"It is our duty to collect as much information as we can while we are here. We may not have another opportunity to examine the files contained in their computer system," Seven said.

"I agree, but if we don't live long enough to make it back to *Voyager*, what's the point?" B'Elanna replied, agitated.

Turning back to the fragmented display console, Seven paused. Then, resolved, she stepped back toward the desk and closed her right fist, extending her assimilation tubules into the exposed circuitry.

"Seven, what are you . . ." B'Elanna began, pausing when a spasm of shock momentarily convulsed through Seven's body.

Undeterred, Seven maintained the connection. Low, guttural sounds, formed in the back of her throat, began to pour from her mouth like a dull growl as her eyes rolled into the back of her head.

"Seven!" B'Elanna demanded, stepping closer, but too disconcerted to touch her. "Seven, can you hear me?"

The growls became more like hisses, as Seven struggled to form words.

Silently cursing Seven's rash actions, B'Elanna steeled herself and firmly grasped Seven's right arm with both hands, determined to sever whatever link she had just made by force.

A voice, Seven's, but lacking her irritating inflection and infinitely more menacing, escaped Seven's lips.

"Get . . . off . . . my . . . ship," it said.

B'Elanna had no idea who or what Seven was communicating with but she already knew she didn't like him, her, or it one bit. For a few seconds, Seven's face was again her own.

"Not until we retrieve the data we require," Seven said forcefully.

The next words that came from Seven's lips only served to strengthen B'Elanna's initial dislike of the entity.

"Then . . . you . . . will . . . die."

The first long corridor that Chakotay, Tom, and Harry entered after clearing the docking bay's airlock was as dull and utilitarian as any Tom had ever seen. Though reasonably well lit, it appeared that no creativity of design or decoration had been considered in its construction. He could hear a rhythmic clank echoing within the walls every few meters, but Harry's tricorder offered no indication as to the mechanism that might be the source of the noise.

A few hundred meters later, he no longer noticed it. They were approaching a fork in the path ahead. One well-illuminated corridor led to the engineering center. The other was shrouded in darkness, but Harry paused as they approached, scanning the area.

"Commander," he said softly, "I'm detecting minute traces of tetryon radiation emanating from this corridor, maybe a hundred meters down."

"Suggesting what?" Chakotay asked.

"This might be our transport," Harry replied. "There

are dozens of junction points where the configuration of the relays is similar to the coherent tetryon transporter used by the Caretaker. We don't have much data on that system, but the similarities are striking."

"Let's check it out," Chakotay decided, leading the way into the darkness. Harry stepped aside for Tom to follow as he recalibrated his tricorder, looking up when Tom did not immediately fall in line.

"What is it?" Harry asked.

"I don't know," Tom answered. "We have a perfectly well-lit corridor here to our right that we know leads to the engineering center. And on our left, we have the dark spooky hallway. You want to check it out? You first, my friend."

Harry shook his head and followed Chakotay, Tom trailing behind.

They soon came to a large control panel embedded into one of the walls. Stretching beyond it on either side were dozens of alcoves. As he waited for Harry to analyze the panel, Tom thought of Tuvok. He knew that every moment they spent trying to reach him might be a moment that Tuvok couldn't spare. He had been alone and injured for several hours. Tom and Tuvok weren't exactly friends. It was hard to crack that stoic Vulcan veneer, though Tom was more sensitive than some to Tuvok's well-shrouded depths. He could have hated him, however, and still not wished him a lonely death. Tuvok had worked tirelessly for four years to keep *Voyager* and her crew safe. He deserved better than this.

Suddenly more anxious than he had been at any time thus far to find Tuvok and return him to the ship, Tom stepped quietly past Chakotay and Harry, who were murmuring to one another over Harry's tricorder readings. As he passed the plane where the first two alcoves on either side of the wall sat opposite one another he was suddenly engulfed in a bright white light.

He barely heard Chakotay call out his name in alarm. "Tom!"

The flash of light took both Chakotay and Harry by surprise. Harry had all but determined that this was some sort of transporter, but the control system was too complicated for him to make immediate sense of. Harry could sense Tom's frustration. From the corner of his eye he saw Tom move past him into the darkness.

A split second and a flash of light later, Tom was gone.

Chapter 8

Janeway approached sickbay to find Neelix standing outside, nervously shifting his weight from one foot to the other. The moment he caught sight of her, he rushed toward her as quickly as his short legs would carry him.

"Captain," he stammered, "I swear to you, I didn't do this."

"I believe you, Mr. Neelix," Janeway replied as calmly as she could under the circumstances. "What didn't you do?"

"I didn't break the Doctor."

Janeway almost smiled. The reality was that there was precious little Neelix, or most anyone else on board, could do to "break" the EMH. They had expended considerable resources over the years supplementing and securing his program. The few instances when his survival had been at risk had forced them to consider the possibility of completing their journey without a dedicated physician, and that had been simply unacceptable. Between the backup modules they had created and the Doctor's personal holoemitter, he was more stable at present than he had ever been.

"Neelix," she sighed, "if you could just tell me what happened."

"After your sister left, the Doctor was deactivated. I couldn't understand why he would have done that, so I re-activated him and he had no idea who I was, who Samantha was, or who Naomi was. He operated on her brain less than four hours ago," Neelix said, his voice rising in pitch and force, "and he didn't remember treating her!"

Janeway's brow furrowed. *This is a problem.*

"And that's not the worst part," Neelix continued.

"It isn't?" Janeway frowned.

"No! Once he had examined Naomi and pronounced her well on her way to recovering, he asked me to deacti-vate him!"

The Doctor had been in control of his activation sub-routines since the early days of *Voyager*'s journey. If he was truly unaware of his program's parameters, Janeway was forced to conclude that he might be facing another cascade failure.

"Where is he now?" Janeway asked.

Neelix paused, at a loss. "I didn't want to deactivate him, but he insisted. He's . . . wherever he goes when . . ."

Janeway raised a hand to halt him as she fortified her-self with a deep breath and entered sickbay, Neelix right on her heels. Naomi still rested peacefully on her biobed; her mother had fallen into a light slumber, her head rest-ing on crossed arms at the foot of Naomi's bed.

"Computer," Janeway called, "activate Emergency Medical Hologram."

Her initial fear that once he had been deactivated he might not be immediately recoverable was allayed when the Doctor materialized before her. But her other con-cerns were heightened when his first words were "Please state the nature of the medical emergency."

Although his standardized programming included this automated activation greeting, he had long ago dispensed with it, unless he was in a particularly peevish state.

"Doctor," Janeway began, "what is the last thing you remember before you were deactivated?"

The Doctor inclined his head to one side in a gesture Janeway had come to recognize as his body language for *You can't possibly have summoned me here to answer such an idiotic question?*, but answered, "I checked the vitals of the half-human, half-Ktarian female in that biobed and asked this rather garishly attired gentleman to deactivate me."

"Doctor," Janeway continued, "do you know who I am?"

He paused briefly and said, "Based on the insignia on your collar I assume you are the captain of this vessel."

"But you don't remember ever meeting me?" she persisted.

"No," he said perfunctorily.

"What about my sister, Phoebe Janeway?"

"Phoebe Janeway is your sister?" he asked. "I shall add that to my records, though she should also inform your chief medical officer."

Janeway was flabbergasted. "Doctor, you are our chief medical officer," she said.

"That's impossible," the Doctor replied. "My program is not designed to . . ."

"Yes, I'm well aware of that, but in the past four years, you and your program have adapted to *Voyager*'s unique circumstances," Janeway said.

"What circumstances are those?"

Throughout this exchange Janeway had grown more concerned with every response the Doctor gave. Although she had faith in the Emergency Medical Hologram, she knew full well that much of the Doctor's expertise had been gained in the trenches of their voyage. A brand-new hologram would have neither the wisdom nor the ability to treat the crew, Naomi in particular, without the benefit of those experiences. Not to mention the fact that this brief exchange was a visceral reminder of just how far the Doctor had come in four years. Painful memories of the Doctor's acerbic and somewhat hostile early bedside manner came flooding back to Janeway. They left a taste in her mouth like burnt coffee.

"Captain . . . if I may?" Neelix interjected.

"Yes, Neelix?"

Neelix addressed himself to the Doctor. "May I ask, sir, on what stardate were you first activated?"

The Doctor replied without missing a beat. "Stardate 52004.2."

Janeway and Neelix exchange knowing glances. The correct answer to that question was stardate 48315.6, almost four years earlier.

"Now, if you wouldn't mind," the Doctor continued, "what unusual circumstances . . ."

"Computer, deactivate EMH," Janeway ordered.

Without another word, Janeway went to sickbay's control console and pulled up the Doctor's file. A cursory examination told her that the program currently running was, in fact, the least sophisticated of the backup modules that had been created in the past year. The Doctor standing before them wasn't lying, and he wasn't damaged. But he was also not *their* Doctor.

Next, she set about locating and recovering the real Doctor's program. At first frustrating blush, it appeared to have been deleted from the database. But a closer analysis revealed that the situation, while dire, was not as bad as all that. The Doctor's program had been fragmented. It was no longer intact in a workable form, but had been broken into several large—and in some cases corrupted—data blocks. Though the captain could have reversed this process with several days' work, she knew that B'Elanna or Seven would likely have the real Doctor up and running in a matter of hours. She opted to leave the problem to their more capable hands as she turned to the next major question.

How had this happened?

"Mr. Neelix," Janeway asked, "when was the first moment you noticed anything different about the Doctor?"

Neelix turned the question over in his mind a few times, determined to give as accurate an answer as he could.

"Let's see . . . after Naomi's surgery he spent a long time in his office. Samantha had just arrived and we were discussing the Doctor's prognosis. She was crying . . . of course . . . I asked if she needed anything and offered to run down to the mess hall . . ."

"Mr. Neelix," Janeway said with a bit more urgency.

"Oh . . . right . . . sorry. I did check with the Doctor a few times. He was examining the scans he'd just taken of Naomi's brain and muttering about . . . well, something about another fine mess you've . . . but I'm sure he wasn't talking about you. At any rate, then you stopped by with Phoebe. She's such a kind person. But then I guess you know that since she's your sister. Truly, though . . . she was so concerned about Naomi, and so comforting to Samantha . . ."

"So up until that point, you are certain the Doctor's program was intact?" Janeway asked, attempting to move the natural-born storyteller along.

"Well, you spoke to him next, didn't you?" Neelix asked. "Did you notice anything funny about him?"

Janeway shook her head, no. The Doctor she had spoken to just before *Voyager* had boarded the array was definitely *their* Doctor.

"So, I guess . . . after you left . . . he spoke briefly with Phoebe," Neelix suggested hesitantly.

Janeway checked the ship's chronometer and logs. It coincided almost precisely with Neelix's estimation. In fact, the Doctor's program had been altered and the backup module activated just a few seconds *before* Janeway had left sickbay.

Given the fact that only Neelix, Ensign Wildman, and herself were present and conscious at that time, and that none of them would have had a motive or vested interest in damaging the one person on board who could save Naomi's life, the only other likely suspect was Phoebe. But Phoebe didn't know the first thing about holographic programming. Something like this was far beyond her rudimentary skills. She recalled the first time she had introduced Phoebe to Master da Vinci, one of Janeway's favorite simulations. Phoebe had been amazed and impressed with the depth and reality Janeway had achieved and had immediately set about studying with the Renaissance master.

No she hadn't.

There it was again. That strange voice of doubt that had been pestering Janeway almost every time she talked with or thought about her sister.

"Captain," a soft voice interrupted her thoughts.

Across the room, Naomi had regained consciousness.

Both Janeway and Neelix walked quickly to her side as her mother stirred awake and smiled with relief.

"How are you feeling, Naomi?" the captain asked gently.

"I have to speak to you . . . alone," Naomi said.

Janeway cast a questioning glance toward the others,

then nodded as they all moved away from the biobed. This seemed to cost Samantha dearly, but Neelix quickly put a protective arm around her shoulders, whispering silent assurances.

Janeway bent closer to Naomi to limit the exertions the child would have to make in continuing their conversation.

"What is it?" she asked.

Naomi's eyes were alert. She did not seem in any way deranged or incapacitated by her ordeal or the medications the Doctor had given her to relieve any residual pain. Nonetheless, Janeway found it difficult to accept the child's next words.

"Captain," Naomi whispered solemnly, "there was a monster in the mess hall."

Harry and Chakotay paused for a confused second after Tom disappeared before their very eyes.

"Where did he go?" Chakotay was the first to give voice to thought.

Harry turned first to his tricorder.

"I've got him, Commander," he said with definite relief. "He's in the other ring. And he's within a few meters of Tuvok's signal."

"The system is obviously automated," Chakotay theorized. "It's probably set to transport directly to a similar area in the other ring. Tuvok must have made it this far. He might have transferred to the other ring accidentally."

"Or, he might have been trying to reach one of the medical bays situated there," Harry added.

"I'll go next," Chakotay offered. "Confirm my transport, and then follow me," he ordered, stepping toward the first pair of alcoves.

"Yes, sir," Harry replied.

As Chakotay vanished in a second flash of light, Harry gave his tricorder a cursory glance to confirm that the commander's life signs were still present, and with a deep breath and a silent hope that they would not be too late to save Tuvok, stepped into the path of the alien transporter.

A second later, Harry found himself in the middle of one of the most horrifying scenes he had ever witnessed.

The room was easily a hundred meters wide and at least half again that high. It was lit by a faint blue glow and filled, floor to ceiling, with the skeletons of countless dead Monorhans. Unseeing eyes peered at him from every corner. Many had been piled facedown, and from some of their backs the strange secondary arms indicative of female Monorhans hung lifeless, like broken insect wings.

Months earlier, *Voyager* had been boarded and briefly occupied by a pack of Hirogen hunters. They had used the ship's holotechnology to create brutal scenarios used to stalk the crew over and over again for pure pleasure. Time and again Harry's friends and comrades had been placed in these grisly fabricated realities, hunted to near death, revived by the Doctor, and hunted again. Though Harry had been kept outside the simulations in order to constantly maintain and upgrade the system *very much against his will,* he had seen most of the holographic environments and the programmed scenarios. In one of the more disturbing simulations, captured prey were hung in cold rooms on large hooks used in Earth's distant past for meat storage, until almost all of the blood had been drained from their bodies. *Slaughterhouses,* he remembered. Apart from the absence of the hooks, this room had the same feel. What was most overpowering was the sense of waste.

Harry had broken out into a cold sweat at first sight of the room. As his central nervous system debated the options of either collapse, or hyperventilation to counter the shock that was engulfing him, Harry was slapped back to the present by Tom's urgent call.

"Harry!"

Tom was kneeling over a body that Harry did not immediately identify as Tuvok. The face and uniform were caked green with blood.

"Get over here and give me a hand," Tom demanded.

Harry willed his legs to step through the throng of bodies. A med kit lay open beside Tom, who was busy taking readings from a medical tricorder.

"He's alive . . . but just barely. His left leg is shattered and he's suffered second- and third-degree burns over a third of his body, but he's breathing," he reported.

"His eyes are open," Harry observed. "Is he conscious?"

"No," Tom answered. "His pupils are fixed, but not dilated. We have to get him out of here. Where are the pattern enhancers?"

Harry knelt and opened his rucksack. With shaking hands he began to assemble the three pattern enhancers they had carried with them, in hopes that they would boost the transporter's signal through the otherwise impenetrable alloy.

Tom tapped his combadge. "Paris to *Voyager.*"

"This is Rollins. Go ahead, Lieutenant."

Tom smiled, relieved. "We've found Tuvok. We're almost ready for transport. Stand by."

Harry completed the perimeter and joined Tom beside Tuvok. He was about to signal for transport when the same troubling thought dawned on him and Tom at the same time.

"Where's Chakotay?" they asked each other.

"He came through before me," Harry began.

"You transported here just a few meters away from me. Almost the same spot where I materialized," Tom said.

"So where did Chakotay end up?" Harry asked, pulling out the tricorder he had just stowed. After a few seconds, he had it. "He's here. He also transported to this ring."

"Where?"

"He's almost five thousand meters from our present position."

Tom grabbed the tricorder and slung his rifle over his shoulder. "You go with Tuvok. I'll find Chakotay."

Harry didn't like the idea, but there was only one alternative and Tom didn't look like he was in a mood to discuss it.

"Paris to *Voyager* . . . transport Ensign Kim and Lieutenant Tuvok directly to sickbay."

For a few interminable seconds it looked as if the pattern enhancers would not be sufficient to cut through the array's natural barrier. Finally, Harry felt the vague tingling sensation that often accompanied the onset of transport. The last sight he saw was Tom collecting his gear before the makeshift morgue vanished.

Chakotay materialized in a darkened corridor. For a moment he worried that the transport had not been successful. Through the dimness ahead, he could make out the junction of the corridor connecting to a well-lit adjacent hall. Reaching automatically for his tricorder, he remembered that Ensign Kim had been carrying all of their equipment aside from Tom's med kit. He had designated himself as the team's defender without seriously considering the possibility that they would be separated.

He walked double-quick toward the light, his senses heightened by the very real vulnerability he now felt.

When he reached the branches of the hall, a quick glance told him that at the very least, he was now in a different part of the array. He hoped that he was also on the second ring, but his first priority had to be locating the others. Taking careful mental notes of his location, he started down the hall toward the right. He debated the wisdom of calling out for Tom or Harry. If they were close, they might hear him. But then, so would anything else that might be here, and he wasn't keen to give his position away to any potentially hostile aliens. The inconclusive life-form readings they had taken both before and after boarding the array led him to believe that it was certainly possible they were not the only living things here. He could hope, but not state absolutely, that whomever or whatever he might encounter would be friendly.

His years in the Maquis resistance had heightened the survival skills ingrained in him by his father and the elders of his tribe. It was almost an afterthought when he remembered to reach for his combadge.

"Chakotay to Ensign Kim," he said softly.

There was no answer.

"Chakotay to Lieutenant Paris," he tried.

Again, no answer.

As he started down the hall he realized immediately that it bore little resemblance to the corridors he had traversed when they entered the array. Far from utilitarian, the doors spaced along the hall were awash in vibrant flowing colors. Vivid oranges and purples in swirling designs gave a sense of motion in their stillness. Farther down a similar pattern in varying hues of green and yellow wound itself into infinity.

It occurred to him that, however unlikely, it was possible that Tom, Harry, or Tuvok might be behind one of these doors. He didn't relish the thought of searching each of these rooms, but soon resigned himself to the inevitable.

He began with the purple and orange door. There was no obvious lock or entrance pad, so he raised his hand and placed his palm in the center of the swirling design. The design on the door began to move. Stepping back, he watched, transfixed as the colors dissolved into blackness.

Suddenly, through the door frame he saw a vast, still desert. It looked like many holographic simulations he had seen. It was obvious from the size of the room and its proximity to the next door that the pale white sands could not stretch as far as they appeared to. It was also obvious that none of his crewmen were within.

Resisting the urge to explore the strange environment, he moved to the green door. Again, placing his palm in its center, he waited for the pattern to dissolve and reveal what lay beyond.

This time, a milky violet liquid rose from floor to ceiling. It was faintly disorienting to see the gentle undulating motion held in place rather than flowing out through the open door, but he had certainly seen stranger things.

He continued on, searching one alien landscape after another. He didn't pause again until he opened a door that revealed a lush green tropical jungle. His steps were halted by the vividness of the picture before him. Rich spices invited him to explore the fragrant depths, and in the distance he was certain he could hear the faint gurgling of a small stream dancing through rocks. But somehow, the perspective of the view was wrong. Unlike the other vistas he had observed, this one had the uncanny appearance of a painting. Stepping back, he focused on several different points but was unable to shake the illusion that he was somehow seeing a two-dimensional representation of three-dimensional objects.

He told himself he must press on, but something about the room kept him rooted to the ground. Raising his right hand, he reached out carefully and allowed his hand to pass the plane that separated the hallway where he stood from the jungle.

The searing pain that assaulted his senses was dizzying. He heard and felt the bones of his hand crunch and crack as his hand was forced into the two-dimensional reality of the scene. For a moment he saw his flattened hand, and part of his mind marveled at the fact that he was somehow existing in two dimensions and three at the same time. But that moment was brief. With all his might he pulled his hand back from the door frame. He could have sworn that the whoosh and pop that accompanied the freedom of his hand was an illusion, but the pain was all too real. As he extracted his hand, wincing at the sight of his flattened palm and fingers, the fire of the initial injury became a dull aching throb. Once it was restored to the normal space outside the door, however, his hand returned to its familiar, three-dimensional shape, though it continued to ache incessantly.

There was only one door left along this hall. At first he thought it had no design, but upon closer examination he saw that the same swirls and whirls covered the door in very faint hues of black.

Raising his left hand this time, Chakotay opened the door and instinctively drew away. He stood at the brink of nothingness. The blackness before him had no depth or texture. It was simply absence.

As he stepped away, his combadge chirped to life. It was one of the most beautiful sounds he had ever heard.

"Paris to Chakotay, do you read me?"

"I'm here, Paris," Chakotay said.

"I'm a little less than two thousand meters from your position, Commander."

"You have the tricorder?" Chakotay asked.

"Yes, sir. We found Tuvok. He and Harry have transported back to the ship. I have the pattern enhancers with me. Can you meet me halfway?"

"Just tell me where to go, Lieutenant. There's no way for me to get a sense of direction."

"You're at a dead end, Commander," Tom said.

"You're telling me," Chakotay replied under his breath.

"Head back down the corridor. Three hundred meters or so down you will see a three-way intersection. Turn to your left. And leave your comm channel open."

"Understood," Chakotay replied, and began walking as quickly as he could away from the black room. "I tried to reach you earlier, Tom, but I couldn't get a signal."

There was no response.

"Tom? Tom?"

Chakotay quickened his pace and continued to call for Paris. Once he had cleared the corridor of swirling doors he found the first intersection and turned toward the left, just as Tom had instructed. He was rewarded a few moments later by a burst of static over his combadge.

"Chakotay?" Tom was calling.

"I can hear you. There's some kind of interference. It keeps cutting our signal," Chakotay replied. "I've found the first intersection and taken the left turn."

"I can see your signal, Commander," Tom replied. *"And I think I've found a shortcut. There's a door at the end of your corridor. It leads to a large room, probably a cargo hold of some kind. Go straight through, and I'll meet you on the other side. I have a little farther to go than you, so wait for me."*

"Understood, Tom. I can see the doorway now."

Unlike the other doors Chakotay had encountered, this one had an elaborate locking mechanism embedded in the wall to the right of the door. Chakotay tried a few random variations of picking the lock before he stepped back, resigned, and leveled his compression rifle at the door. It disintegrated in a wave of fire and sparks and Chakotay stepped gingerly over the bottom lip of the frame, entered the inky blackness of the room, and activated his wrist light.

Playing the light along the right side of the room, he immediately saw a long, low bank of consoles. They were dead. No faint hum or dim light betrayed an operational status. There was a clear path before him and as he began to jog forward, he focused the light to his left and almost tripped over his own feet.

He was staring at a Hirogen hunter. It took him a second to realize that, though the hunter glared back at him with dark penetrating eyes, he was standing behind a transparent barrier. Moving closer, Chakotay confirmed that the Hirogen was in some kind of stasis chamber. To the hunter's right was another alien that Chakotay did not recognize, also in stasis. This creature was bipedal, but with two long necks that extended from its torso, one slightly taller than the other. Its skin was a dull shade of copper. Perched atop one neck was a bulging head covered with small spikes. The other was topped with a larger head consisting of small circular indentations layered with fine cilia.

Chakotay retraced his steps but slowed his progress through the room. The stasis chambers, each containing a distinct alien species, ran the length of the room and at least twelve high. Chakotay was uneasily certain that there were probably more rows, but their placement exceeded the power of his wrist beacon. Continuing on, he recognized a Borg drone, a Talaxian female, an Illiderian, a Sikarian, a member of Species 8472, and a male Ocampa among countless others. It seemed that every alien race *Voyager* had encountered on their journey thus far through the Delta Quadrant, and many more that they had not, was represented in this strange and somewhat gruesome collection.

After walking for over five minutes in this way, he stubbed the toe of his boot against a panel that was embedded in the floor. Stepping back to examine it, he found himself on the border of a circular construct that was at least twenty meters in diameter and raised a little less than one meter off the floor.

Casting his beacon into the circle he saw suspended by invisible means a massive brownish sphere. It had been ripped open in several places, and from the direction of the tears that edged the gaping wounds it appeared that the rips had been directed from inside the sphere outward.

The sphere was made up of a fine, thin substance, almost like paper, though he suspected that it was sturdier than it looked. As he cautiously made his way around the sphere, he found himself imagining the possible composition of whatever it was that had emerged from it. Each vision was more chilling than the next, and once he had passed it, he broke into a run, refusing to pause until he reached the far side of the massive chamber.

He blew his way out of the room the same way he had entered and paused to catch his breath.

"Chakotay to Paris," he panted.

"I'm right here, Commander," Tom shouted, turning the corner at the far end of the hallway where Chakotay rested. For his part, Chakotay had never been so glad to see Tom Paris in his entire life.

~

Janeway stood beside Naomi, trying to absorb her words.

A monster in the mess hall?

Bending close to the child, she said softly and reassuringly, "You're safe now. You don't have to worry."

"I know," Naomi said, "but you have to believe me."

Janeway paused. "Can you tell me what it looked like?" she finally asked.

An involuntary shudder coursed through Naomi as she closed her eyes and attempted the most accurate description she could muster.

"It was like water when it moves. It had arms, like an octopus. It was all arms. And it was clear. I mean, I could see it, but I could also see through it."

Janeway's head pounded. She had seen something similar, only once before.

"Thank you for reporting this to me, Naomi," Janeway said seriously. "Now I want you to try and get some rest."

"Yes, ma'am," Naomi nodded dutifully.

Gesturing for Neelix and Ensign Wildman to resume their posts at Naomi's bedside, Janeway entered the relative solitude of the Doctor's office and turned his computer interface panel toward her. Her heart was in her throat as she pulled up the sensor logs from the mess hall at the time of the attack on Naomi. She was neither surprised nor relieved when the log showed that the only crewman present in the mess hall at that time was Phoebe Janeway.

Though everything Janeway believed to be true strained against it, she was forced to accept the possibility that her sister might not be what she appeared. There was only one way to be sure.

"Computer, activate the EMH," she called.

"Please state the nature . . ." the Doctor began. Upon seeing her, however, he said, "Oh, it's you again."

"Yes," Janeway retorted with as much patience as she could muster.

"I realize that I am only a program designed to serve your needs, but don't you think it's a little rude to deactivate someone midsentence?"

"I apologize," Janeway managed through gritted teeth.

The Doctor paused, a faint flicker of alarm crossing his face. Though he hadn't known the captain long, he seemed to sense that he would be taking his subroutines in his hands if he chose to antagonize her further.

"Well . . . thank you," he said as genially as possible. "Do you require my assistance?"

"I do. I want you to run a full neurological scan."

"Of whom?" he asked, reaching toward a standard medical tricorder situated on a shelf behind his desk.

"Me," she replied evenly.

"You appear to be in good health," the Doctor said as he began the scan. "Are there any troubling symptoms you would like to share with me?"

"I believe that my memory may have been tampered with," she replied.

"Very well," he said. "I assume there are records of previous engrammatic scans in your medical file."

He set the tricorder down and moved to his diagnostic panel to pull up images of the scan he had just completed and the last similar scan on record.

Janeway peered at the results over his shoulder. Though she was not as well versed as the Doctor in engrammatic analysis, it was obvious that there were significant discrepancies between the two scans.

"It appears your concerns are well grounded, Captain," the Doctor said. "There are significant portions of your memory centers that have been displaced."

"What does that mean?" Janeway asked.

"It means that your true memories, whatever they may be, are buried beneath a layer of artificially implanted memories. The good news is that if we can safely purge the implanted memories, you should recover your true memories almost instantly. If, for example . . ."

"Thank you, Doctor," Janeway cut him off. "I want you to perform the same procedure on Mr. Neelix, Ensign Wildman, and Naomi."

A few tense minutes later, the scans were complete and the results were telling.

"Mr. Neelix and Ensign Wildman have also had their memories tampered with; however, the young girl is unaffected," the Doctor announced.

"Can you hypothesize as to why?" Janeway asked.

"Without more data as to the source of the altered engrams, it would be difficult," the Doctor said simply. "There are many differences between your species which could account for . . . What is this?" the Doctor interrupted himself.

"What?"

"There is a subtle phase variation in the molecular structure of Naomi Wildman which she does not share with you, her mother, or Mr. Neelix. Can you account for this?"

A theory was formulating in Janeway's mind and the Doctor's discovery crystallized it. "Almost two years ago, the day Naomi was born, in fact, our ship encountered a subspace scission and every particle of matter on board was duplicated, including the crew. The Naomi who was born on this ship did not survive, but the duplicate child did, and before the other ship was destroyed, she was brought on board."

The Doctor was nonplussed. "May I inquire again as to the nature of *Voyager*'s mission?" he asked. "You have no chief medical officer, you harbor duplicate crewmen and non-Starfleet personnel . . ."

"As I said, Doctor, our circumstances are unique. We were pulled into the Delta Quadrant against our will almost four years ago. We lost a number of our senior officers and in the course of our journey . . ."

"The Delta Quadrant!" the Doctor shouted.

"We are doing everything we can to return home as soon as possible!" Janeway snapped.

"And yet you had time to stop and investigate a subspace . . . what did you call it . . . *scission*?"

"We didn't so much stop as run right into . . ." the captain tried to interject as the Doctor continued.

"Where are we now? Are we traveling at maximum warp on the shortest conceivable course back to the Alpha Quadrant?"

Janeway was about to end the discussion by once again deactivating the EMH when B'Elanna and Ensign Maplethorpe entered sickbay, carrying a faint Seven of Nine between them.

"Who is this woman?" the Doctor asked, as Seven was placed on the nearest biobed. "Is she another duplicate . . . or another alien we've picked up along the way?" After initiating a cursory scan he turned exasperated on the captain to say, "Are you aware that this woman has Borg implants?"

Curiosity furrowed the space beneath B'Elanna's cranial ridges and the bridge of her nose, but she had no time to ask any of her obvious questions before Janeway said, "Report."

"We found the *Betasis,* the Monorhan ship," she said, "and Seven made contact with someone, or something inside of it."

"Who was it?"

"I don't know and I'm not sure I want to," she replied.

"Did you discover anything about the Key?" Janeway asked.

"We're still analyzing what we found. But we also discovered the rest of the transmission." B'Elanna swallowed hard before she continued. "The Monorhans who came here fifty years ago were wiped out by some kind of parasite. Ten thousand died in a matter of days."

Janeway inhaled sharply.

"Captain," B'Elanna urged. "We have to get off this array."

"I agree," Janeway nodded. "But we're not leaving without Tuvok and the away team."

"They're not back yet?"

"No. And for the moment, I can't spare you on analysis of the information you just gathered. We have another problem."

B'Elanna turned to the Doctor, who had begun treating Seven while muttering several uncharacteristic epithets.

"What's wrong with the Doctor?"

"That's not our Doctor. His program was intentionally sabotaged. I need you to get him back as soon as possible. That," said Janeway, indicating the EMH who was treating Seven, "is one of the backup modules we created."

B'Elanna nodded, crossing to the EMH diagnostic control panel. As she began to pull up the necessary files, she asked, "Captain . . . was there a reason you removed the Key from its containment field?"

Janeway shook her head.

"I didn't."

"Then you should add another problem to our list," B'Elanna said. "The Key is missing."

As Janeway struggled to maintain a sense of calm and

dignified command in what was quickly disintegrating into total chaos, Rollins called out over the comm.

"Sickbay, this is the bridge. Prepare to receive emergency transport from the array. Two officers incoming."

Everyone automatically moved to the edges of the room to clear as much space in the open center as the high-pitched wail of the transporter alerted Janeway to the imminent return of her away team. A split second later, Tuvok and Harry appeared before her, and Neelix immediately helped Ensign Kim heft Tuvok onto another available bed.

"Doctor," she called, "is Seven of Nine stable?"

"For the moment," he replied. "Several of her implants were overloaded with a series . . . ."

"Explain later," Janeway barked. "You have a medical emergency here!"

As the Doctor turned his exasperated attention toward his latest patient—saying just loud enough for Janeway to hear, "What kind of ship is this woman running?"—the captain caught her first glimpse of Tuvok and realized that their rescue had come not a moment too soon. She barely contained a gasp at the sight of Tuvok's blood-crusted face and mangled body.

Intense hope mingled with fear as she watched the Doctor raise the biobed's arch over Tuvok's body and begin his scans. It was frustrating but true that there was far less she could do for him than the Doctor at this moment. Realigning her priorities, she turned to Ensign Kim.

"Where are the others?" she asked.

"We were separated. Tom went after Chakotay. Given his position, it could take as much as an hour for them to return, even with the pattern enhancers."

"Dammit," Janeway spat.

"I'm sorry, Captain," Harry began.

"Don't apologize, Ensign," Janeway said, more sharply than she had intended. "I need to know something else."

"Yes, Captain?"

"Mr. Kim, do I have a sister?"

This was obviously the last question Harry was expecting at such a moment, and it showed on his face.

"Yes, Captain, I believe you do."

But Janeway's next question was even stranger.

"And have you ever met her?"

"No, Captain," he replied. "Isn't she on Earth?"

Janeway cast a quick glance around sickbay. The Doctor was tending to Tuvok; Seven was already sitting up and looked better than she had when she entered. B'Elanna was working over the diagnostic panel that regulated the EMH, all observed by Neelix and Ensign Wildman, who were occupied trying to shield Naomi from the worst of the unsettling set of circumstances.

"Mr. Neelix," Janeway ordered, "I think we should move Naomi back to her quarters at once. I want a security team posted at her door, and you and Ensign Wildman should stay with her at all times. Above all, you are not to allow my sister to come anywhere near her."

"But, Captain," Neelix began.

"That's an order, Neelix."

Neelix nodded. "Consider it done."

Crossing to Seven, she asked, "Are you able to return to duty?"

Seven hopped off of the biobed. She was pale and slightly shaken, but said, "I am."

"Get down to engineering. I need you to find the Key."

"Yes, Captain, but . . ."

"Yes, Seven?"

"I believe we are in serious danger. We must evacuate the array as soon as possible."

Janeway nodded. "B'Elanna already gave me the broad strokes. One crisis at a time."

"Understood, Captain."

Seven obviously had a great deal of information to impart and Janeway hated to delay her report. But there was simply no time at the moment.

Crossing to the Doctor's office, Janeway spent a few moments at his control panel, opened one of the storage cabinets, and removed two vials of a dark gaseous substance.

On her way out the door she turned to Harry saying, "Ensign, you're with me."

Harry fell into step beside her as they strode quickly out of sickbay.

"May I ask where we're headed, Captain?"

"I think its time you met my sister" was her cryptic reply.

Chapter 9

Chakotay's relief upon finding Tom was mitigated only by the disconcerting discoveries he had made while they were separated. Tom immediately examined Chakotay's hand and injected Chakotay with a hypospray from his med kit, which dulled the residual pain.

"How did you get here so fast?" Chakotay asked once the kit was stowed and Tom began to lead him back down the corridor that wound away from the room of specimens and the strange sphere.

"I think I've discovered something about the array's transporters," Tom said, obviously pleased with himself.

Taking another quick turn, Chakotay saw that they were headed for a row of alcoves, similar to those they had first encountered.

"What's that?" he asked warily.

"What were you thinking when you first stepped into the transport beam?" Tom asked.

"I don't know," Chakotay replied. "I guess I wasn't thinking about anything in particular. I was worried about you. But I was also wondering what the purpose of this place was."

"And you ended up where?" Tom continued.

"I came out near a corridor with dozens of doors which lead to artificial environments . . . most of them unlike anything I've seen before."

"When I first entered the transport, I was thinking about Tuvok . . . and how much I wanted to find him. I can't say for sure, but my guess is that when Harry entered, he was thinking the same thing, find Tuvok or find me."

"What's your theory, Lieutenant?" Chakotay asked.

"On my way to you, I found another transport station, and I took a chance. I was thinking about finding you, and when I entered, I came out only a dozen meters from your location."

Chakotay paused to consider this. "You're telling me you honestly believe that these systems determine our destination based on what we're thinking?"

"I do," Tom replied, grinning. "Want to prove me wrong?"

"Did you bring the pattern enhancers with you?" Chakotay asked.

"I did, but I'm telling you, Commander, I know this is how it works."

"Even if you're right, that might only apply to areas within the array," Chakotay suggested.

"*Voyager* is on board the array," Tom said. "I wouldn't try this otherwise. But if I'm right, we might be able to make use of it, or adapt our systems in a similar way."

Chakotay considered Tom with a level gaze.

"Make use of it how exactly?" he asked.

Tom sighed. "We already know that coherent tetryon technology is capable of transporting huge objects great distances . . . far beyond the range of our transporters, or any other technology we've found, including the space-folding fields the Sikarians could generate."

"You think we could adapt this technology to ours in order to get home?" Chakotay asked.

"I think we should find out. I'm willing to chance it. Keep the pattern enhancers with you," Tom said, laying his rucksack on the ground beside the alcove controls. "Use them to return to the ship if I don't make it."

"Then how will you get back?"

"At the very least, I know how to get from one ring to the other. If I have to walk a little farther to get back to the ship, that's my own fault."

Chakotay was reluctant. True, what Tom was proposing could mean the difference in the next several years of *Voyager*'s entire crew. But the potential benefits did not outweigh the risks.

"I don't think so, Tom. We'll transport back to *Voyager* using our technology, and if we have a chance, we'll return later to test your theory."

Tom was obviously disappointed, but unwilling to push the matter further.

"Yes, sir," he said as he began to unpack the enhancers.

"I'm not saying it's not an interesting idea, Tom," Chakotay said, trying to soften the blow.

"I understand," Tom replied.

Chakotay picked up the tricorder while Tom worked scanning the area for any new or interesting readings. The data they had already collected would keep them busy for days, but that didn't mean he should waste the opportunity to collect more as long as they were there. A sudden change in the life-form display caught his attention as it spiked and then stabilized.

Tom had paused in his assembly of the second enhancer. He sat frozen, like a spooked animal, as the color drained from his typically ruddy face.

"Tom?" Chakotay asked, turning to follow the direction of his terrified gaze.

Floating down the corridor toward them was a nightmarish translucent creature. The structure of the face was vaguely familiar. Two pain-filled eyes set above an extended jaw which opened to reveal rows of long pointed teeth. The grisly visage sat atop three circular sections of torso that tapered to a point at the bottom. There were no arms or legs. The creature glided on several pairs of tattered wings, which gave no grace to its movement. As it approached, long pincerlike appendages emerged from behind its belly, reaching toward Tom and Chakotay. A bloodcurdling screech flew forth from its mouth, and years of first-contact scenarios with strange alien races always given the benefit of the doubt were tossed aside as Tom rose from a crouch and reached for Chakotay's compression rifle.

Tom thumbed the setting to maximum and fired.

The creature was momentarily engulfed in the phaser blast, but kept coming. If anything, it seemed to Chakotay that the energy discharge might have made it angrier.

There wasn't time for anything else. Tom grabbed Chakotay and, pulling him toward the nearest pair of alcoves, screamed, "Think about *Voyager*!"

Closing his eyes and concentrating as hard as the panic inside him would allow, Chakotay entered the transport and willed himself to return to their ship.

The last thing he heard was the creature's infuriated shriek accompanying the bright flash of light signaling their transport.

Though Harry was easily several centimeters taller than the captain, he had to move quickly to keep pace with her as she made her way from sickbay to the nearest weapons locker located outside cargo bay one. He knew her well enough by now to know that she was furious, and he was grateful that her wrath was not, for the moment, directed toward him. In fact, he hoped fervently that he would never be on the receiving end of such intense displeasure from his captain.

He hesitated to intrude upon her thoughts, but memories of the Monorhan dead were still fresh in his mind. He addressed her as tactfully as he could.

"Captain, there's something you should know."

Janeway's pace did not waver, but she replied, "Go ahead, Ensign."

"When we found Tuvok he was in a storage room of some kind. The room was filled with thousands of bodies."

"Monorhans?" Janeway asked.

Harry swallowed and nodded.

"B'Elanna recovered the rest of the transmission we intercepted. The Monorhans who boarded the array were wiped out by an alien parasite."

Janeway paused long enough to throw open the weapons locker and began searching its inventory of modifiable compression rifles.

"Were your life-form readings while you were aboard the array any more definitive than those we already have?" she asked, reaching for two of the rifles she was seeking. In a matter of moments she equipped them with the vials she had removed from sickbay. Each small vial of concentrated toxin attached to the firing chamber, and Harry could only assume they were designed to incapacitate a specific enemy.

As Janeway passed one of the rifles to Harry and slung her own over her shoulder Harry replied, "No, ma'am. We did, however, find evidence of more coherent tetryon technology. It appears to play a significant role in their transport system."

Janeway nodded, as if this only further strengthened her resolve and certainty about the course of action she was pursuing.

Once they had secured the locker, Janeway used the nearest computer interface to request the current location of Phoebe Janeway. Harry was shocked to see her name appear on the computer's crew manifest.

The computer indicated that Phoebe was in "her quarters," deck eleven, section C-7.

"Captain, those quarters should be vacant," Harry informed her as she closed the interface and headed toward the nearest turbolift.

"I'm not surprised," she replied. "I no longer believe that the woman I have supposedly been interacting with for the past several years is my sister."

"Years?" Harry asked.

"The Doctor found evidence that my memory has been altered. If I'm right, so have the rest of the crew's, as well as the ship's computer. So far, the only person on board who can see Phoebe in her true form is Naomi Wildman. She was attacked several hours ago and up until now, I had no idea why."

"But why don't I have any memory of her?" Harry asked.

"What is the one thing you and Naomi Wildman have in common, Ensign?"

It had been a long time since Harry had thought of this ship as anything other than *his* ship. It had been disorienting for the first few days after the encounter with the subspace scission, and difficult to shake the thought that somehow he didn't quite belong here. But time had passed, and the disquieting sense of unbelonging had faded. Nonetheless, he realized immediately what the captain was referring to, and chided himself for not seeing it for himself.

"Oh," he said.

"I don't know why the subtle shift in your molecular phase variance made you immune to Phoebe's tampering, but obviously it did. I'll be relying on your eyes, Ensign. When we find her, I need you to tell me what you see."

Harry nodded, said, "Yes, ma'am," then asked, "Have you been able to determine how long she's been with us?"

"No. As far as I remember, she's been on board from the day I recruited Tom on Earth. I remember vividly her request to join us on our journey to the Badlands. She had been commissioned to do a painting and wanted to see the plasma fields firsthand. I'm realizing only now how absurd it would be for me to have granted any civilian such a request. I remember dinners, games on the holodeck, I even remember saving her life when . . ."

A mixture of sadness and anger surged within her and Janeway did not immediately continue. Finally she said, "What I don't understand is how she could have been so thorough. I don't see how anyone or anything could possibly re-create another human being, someone I know so very well, using only my memories of them."

"If she can implant memories in the minds of a hundred and fifty people at the same time, that doesn't sound like a huge leap," Harry suggested. "My question is, why? Who is she really, and what does she want?"

"I believe she may be Nacene," Janeway said.

Harry glanced at his phaser rifle. Suddenly he remembered the neural toxin Tuvok had developed a few years earlier when *Voyager* had encountered the Caretaker's mate.

They turned the corridor that led to "Phoebe" 's quarters and approached without another word. When they reached the door, Janeway took a deep breath and overrode the lock.

The door slid open.

Phoebe had been considering her options. She was tired of the charade. More important, she could not envision any circumstances wherein Janeway could be innocently induced to do her bidding. Phoebe needed help. But she had come to that conclusion much too late. Janeway's resistance to the implanted memories had been remarkable. Phoebe had sensed the splintering of the barrier she had erected in Janeway's mind and finally accepted that there was only one clear path before them both.

When the door opened, Phoebe was seated with her feet curled under her on a low bench running under the room's only window. Only the faint blue glow emanating from the docking bay outside illuminated her features.

In a low voice she said, "Kathryn, I've been waiting for you."

Harry heard the words, but did not see a human woman saying them. Instead he saw a mass of undulating translucent tentacles rising from the floor of the cabin and extending outward and upward for several meters. They writhed and danced in the eerie blue light, and for a split second he hesitated to fire into the terrifying spectacle.

"Harry?" the captain said softly.

"That's not your sister," he replied simply.

As Phoebe moved toward them, calling Kathryn's name, Janeway and Harry leveled their modified rifles and opened fire.

~

B'Elanna felt certain that this day was never going to end. It had started well enough. Though their entry into the array had damaged several crucial systems, she checked regularly with her engineering staff and was satisfied with their work. The energy reserve transfer they had received had buoyed her spirits as well. The sight of those green bars at maximum was one she had never dared allow herself to hope to see as long as *Voyager* remained in the Delta Quadrant. So much of her time in the past four years had been devoted to squeezing every last ounce of energy from their systems, finding creative ways to bypass Starfleet regulations, and just making the best of what they had. A complete restock felt like an embarrassment of riches.

Of course, since returning from the *Betasis* she'd had less time than she would have liked to let her mind roam freely through the myriad problems that had just been solved for her, and the new possibilities that were now spread before her. She had never been a patient person, but even she had to acknowledge that at the moment her efforts were best directed at more important and less pleasurable tasks.

"Excuse me, Lieutenant," the Doctor asked in a patronizing tone she had thought forever banished to the realm of bad memories.

"Yes," she replied, without bothering to hide her annoyance.

Just a few more subroutines to locate and integrate . . .

"Are you one of *Voyager*'s senior officers?" he asked.

"I am."

"Then would you mind using your security authorization codes to erect a level-ten containment field around this biobed?" he asked.

This caught her attention.

"Your program should allow you to do that," she replied.

"In a perfect world, I suppose it would, but as I am only a supplement to your medical staff and your chief medical officer in name only for the moment . . ."

B'Elanna quickly pulled up a diagnostic display of the backup module that was running and realized that because this particular backup predated the Doctor's initial activation, the upgrades that allowed for such decisions were absent. She dutifully added the appropriate subroutine and said, "Try it now."

"Computer, erect a level-ten forcefield around biobed one," he said, and the field automatically flashed into existence.

"Thank you, Lieutenant," the Doctor said, passing through the field and returning to Tuvok's side.

As she was about to reintegrate the remaining subroutines that should restore the *real* Doctor, B'Elanna realized that there were few conceivable reasons why the EMH would require such a containment field. Given what she had learned on the *Betasis,* she asked, "Doctor, why is the containment field necessary?"

"Because this man has ingested an alien parasite," he replied as if he were commenting on nothing more serious than the weather.

An icy chill shot down B'Elanna's spine.

"Can . . . can you remove it?" she stammered.

"Oh, I don't think so," he replied.

B'Elanna had often wondered whether or not her mercurial temperament was a Klingon or human trait. Both species, she knew, could flame with rage in an instant, though Klingon anger was typically more aggressive, an act-first, think-later kind of anger. Her human father and cousins tended to simmer quietly, though repressed anger could often be more damaging than that which was immediately expressed. In any case, the Doctor's attitude was definitely bringing out the Klingon in her.

"What do you mean you *'don't think so,'* " she bellowed. "You are talking about someone who is vital to this crew . . . someone who we care about."

"Then it is unfortunate I was not programmed to care in the same way that you do," the Doctor replied. "I have done what I can to repair the injuries he sustained before he was infected. I am actually of the opinion that were it not for the parasite, Lieutenant Tuvok would probably had died several hours ago."

"What!?!" B'Elanna demanded.

"I believe the parasite which entered the lieutenant's body is actually the first stage in the development of a new life-form. The organism which is now merging with his central nervous system was able to sustain critical neural pathways which, given his injuries and blood loss, were in the process of shutting down. Although I was able to stabilize those systems which were damaged, it is almost impossible and certainly unadvisable to separate the lieutenant's neurological tissue from that of the organism, which is also utilizing it to grow. Even if there were a way to remove the parasite from his body now, he would most likely awake from the procedure in a persistent vegetative state. As I have never seen an organism like this one, nor is there any record of one in our medical database, I am hesitant to speculate as to the kind of creature that will emerge from Lieutenant Tuvok's body once the gestation of the first-stage life-form is complete, nor can I estimate how long the generative process will take. Given all this, I believe the containment field offers the greatest protection for the rest of the crew."

B'Elanna's head was spinning. Tuvok had been infected by a parasite. The parasite was feeding off of his body and slowly killing him in the process. The part she was having a hard time with was the *kind of creature that would emerge from Tuvok's body when the gestation was complete.*

She needed more information. "Doctor, I thought most parasites lived within a host, feeding off of them perhaps, even to the point of death, but I've never heard of a parasite that ended up using a host to create an entirely new life-form."

"Then it was, perhaps, an excellent choice for you to become an engineer, rather than a physician," he replied without a trace of sarcasm. "The fact is that from what I can tell, the parasite is merging with Lieutenant Tuvok in a way that suggests at least some part of him will survive along with the new organism. His body will die, that much is clear, but the level of neurological tissue and biochemical signal transfer leads me to believe that rather than his body simply being used and then discarded, in some way Tuvok will be an integral part of the new organism."

B'Elanna didn't care. As far as she was concerned, saving *part* of Tuvok was not an acceptable compromise.

"Listen to me," she said, glaring at him through the containment field so intensely that the Doctor took an involuntary step back as she began. "You will do everything in your power to remove this thing from his body, no matter what the cost. That's an order."

"*Can* you give me orders?" the Doctor asked, his eyes seemed to focus on the provisional rank bars Janeway had assigned to the ex-Maquis crew members. "I am not certain that technically speaking you outrank me."

B'Elanna returned to the EMH programming panel. She was still several minutes away from completely restoring the Doctor who would not hesitate to act on her wishes or in Tuvok's best interest, but time seemed like the one thing she was running uncomfortably short of. Instead, she altered one of the backup Doctor's subroutines and said, "I said find a way to remove it . . . that's an order."

"Yes, Lieutenant." The Doctor nodded and immersed himself in the readouts of Tuvok's vital signs.

With a small sigh of victory B'Elanna refocused her thoughts and returned to her work, her fingers flying across the panel.

Phoebe's body was engulfed in the orange fire of Janeway's and Harry's rifles; but she did not dissolve on contact as pretty much any other solid matter would have.

Instead, Janeway saw her sister fall to the ground and begin to transform into the massive amorphous shape that she could only assume Harry had seen all along. She forced herself to ignore the abrupt spark of pain firing in her brain as Phoebe's hold upon her mind was completely shattered.

"Computer," she called, "erect a level-ten containment field around the nonhuman life-form in this room."

The computer complied, and with a chirp and buzz, Phoebe was surrounded by the strongest energy barrier at Janeway's disposal.

For a few seconds, it looked as if the situation was controlled, but just as Janeway was stepping haltingly toward the containment field, torrents of angry red energy shot through the field, disintegrating it. As Janeway watched in horror, the amorphous blob once again resumed its more organized flowing form and three tentacles shot toward Ensign Kim, enveloping him in a stranglehold.

Janeway raised her rifle to fire again, but stopped as Phoebe's voice, her sister's voice, echoed through the cabin.

"Put down your weapon," Phoebe demanded.

Harry had ceased to struggle.

"Release him!" Janeway cried.

"I have no wish to harm you or those you care for," Phoebe said, "but I will if I have to."

Janeway considered her words and, cursing herself for not including a full security detachment on this escapade, tossed her rifle across the room.

"Now let him go!"

Phoebe complied. Harry slumped lifelessly to the floor as the flowing energy withdrew from him, and Janeway rushed to his side.

She was able to confirm that he was still breathing and was about to call for an emergency medical transport when she looked up to see her sister, once again, standing before her.

"He will survive," she said simply.

"Who the hell are you?" Janeway said, rising to face the creature who had stolen her sister's form.

"Your query is imprecise. I promise, I will answer your questions as best I can, but your limited understanding will make clarity difficult," Phoebe replied.

"Are you Nacene?" Janeway asked.

Phoebe smiled as if she were humoring an impertinent child.

"I am of the Nacene," she replied, "but Nacene is what you have called us, not what we are."

"Then what are you?"

"There is no word in your language to contain us."

Janeway was growing more frustrated by the moment.

"Are you of the same species as the entity we encountered called the Caretaker, or his mate, Suspiria?" she asked.

"As you understand them, yes," Phoebe replied. "But you do not yet begin to understand us."

"Then enlighten me," Janeway said petulantly.

"Is that truly your wish?" Phoebe asked.

Janeway paused. Something in Phoebe's tone told her that this was a loaded question.

"Tell me first, why are you here?"

"I was called here by the object you refer to as the Key to Gremadia."

Janeway's brow furrowed as she realized that almost every time she had spoken to Phoebe in the past few days, the subject of the Key had been raised.

"What is the Key?" Janeway asked.

"Again, there are no words," Phoebe replied.

"Well, *find* some!" Janeway shouted.

"The knowledge you require cannot be transmitted through any means of communication at your disposal. If I were to enter your mind and attempt to transfer that knowledge to you, your fragile brain would be destroyed in the process. You must choose, Kathryn," she said. "Agree to use the Key exactly as I instruct you despite your ignorance of its nature and purpose, and I will not harm you or your ship. Surely by now you realize that if I wanted you dead, you would be."

Janeway considered this. It was obvious that Phoebe wielded power that was beyond that of the Caretaker and Suspiria. Her gut told her that Phoebe was more than capable of following through on her threat. But she instinctively rebelled at the thought of being used to an unknown purpose by such an entity.

"What will happen if I refuse?" she asked. "If you have the ability to destroy us, surely you can take the Key from us by force."

Phoebe's smile faded and Janeway knew instantaneously that though Phoebe was strong, this was, at least, one possible vulnerability.

"I could take it," she replied harshly. "But without your . . . there is no word . . . I will be unable to use it."

"And that would cause you pain?" Janeway pushed.

"Unless you agree, we, like you, will be always far from home."

Janeway wanted to believe her. It would be so easy simply to do as Phoebe asked and put an end to at least this much of the danger *Voyager* was facing.

But she couldn't.

"I'm sorry," she said, "I cannot agree to this unless you can tell me why you need the Key and what will happen if I do as you have asked."

"I cannot tell you," Phoebe replied. "I can only show you."

"Fine," Janeway said, wondering how much of this was a matter of semantics. "Show me."

Phoebe took the captain's hand, and a moment later Janeway found herself standing before a door she had never seen. It was completely black, though faint swirls of varying hues were subtly visible on its surface.

"Where are we?" Janeway demanded, turning to see several other similar doors decorated with more vivid splashes of color.

Phoebe raised her hand and placed it on the center of the door. Janeway sensed movement in the pattern, and then the door was gone and she was staring into emptiness.

"We are at the beginning," Phoebe replied. "Do you still wish to be shown?"

Janeway stared into her sister's eyes. Phoebe, the real Phoebe, had never led her astray. They'd had their fair share of disagreements over the years, but the foundation of their relationship had been love and trust. Somehow Janeway suspected that the creature who was leading her into darkness would not have chosen this particular form if the bond shared between Janeway and her sister had not been significant and powerful.

"To travel with me, you must take my hand," Phoebe said. "If we become separated in the process, call my name and I will find you."

Janeway nodded.

Phoebe gently grasped Janeway's hand again, and led Kathryn into absolute nothingness.

Tom and Chakotay materialized on *Voyager*'s bridge, almost colliding with Lieutenant Rollins, who had been left in command since they had boarded the array. The forward momentum generated when they threw themselves into the array's transporter was not dispersed by the transport process and they found themselves falling to the deck the moment they arrived.

As Tom helped Chakotay to his feet, Chakotay stammered, "What the hell was that thing?"

"I think I could live the rest of my life in peace even if we never find out," Tom replied, then turned to Rollins and asked, "Did Harry and Tuvok make it back to the ship?"

"Yes, sir," he replied. "And B'Elanna and Seven have also reported in."

"Rollins, where is the captain?" Chakotay asked.

"I think she's in sickbay," he replied.

"Chakotay to Janeway," he called, making his way toward the turbolift.

When there was no immediate response he asked the computer to locate her and was temporarily stunned at the computer's response.

"Captain Janeway is not on board."

"Where did she go?" Chakotay demanded. "Is she on the array?" he barked in the general direction of the ops station, where Crewman Dalby was working a shift.

"Scanning, sir," Dalby replied.

But if the computer's reply to his first question had been shocking, Dalby's answer to the second a few interminable moments later was like a sharp blow to the gut.

"Captain Janeway is not on the array."

Chakotay struggled to rein in the panic that was quickly rising within him. This was impossible. She had to be one place or the other.

"Computer, what was Captain Janeway's last known location aboard *Voyager*?"

"Deck eleven, section C-7."

"Have a security team meet us there," Chakotay barked to Rollins as he entered the turbolift, Tom at his heels.

When they arrived at the door to what had been Phoebe's cabin, Chakotay dispatched Paris to get the unconscious Ensign Kim to sickbay and ordered a deck-by-deck search of the ship for the captain and her sister. All security personnel were placed on alert.

Part of Chakotay knew that he had to get *Voyager* off of the array as soon as possible, and now he could. But there was absolutely no way he would do so until Kathryn had been found.

~

When B'Elanna decided that she was finally at a point where she could begin recompiling the Doctor, she initiated the process, stood back, and held her breath. She wasn't sure how much longer she could endure the presence of his less-evolved replacement.

At that moment, the door to sickbay slid open and Tom entered, gently guiding a disoriented Ensign Kim to a biobed.

B'Elanna caught Tom's eye and he gave her a familiar half-smile and a wink. Crossing to them, B'Elanna helped him assist Harry, and in the process Tom reached for her hand and gave it a firm squeeze. She should have been comforted and reassured. She wasn't.

She loved Tom. In the past such a simple and familiar gesture would have buoyed her spirits immeasurably. But this wasn't the first time in recent memory that she had been strangely unable to lose herself in the comfort of his love for her. There was something dividing them. She couldn't put her finger on it, but she was acutely aware that whatever was creating that distance was her doing, not his.

Releasing his hand, she asked, "What happened?"

Harry answered her question with one of his own.

"Where is the captain?"

"We don't know," Tom replied.

B'Elanna turned on him more fiercely than she intended.

"What do you mean you don't know?"

"She's been missing from the ship for almost ten minutes."

"That's not possible. Why would she board the array after I told her about the parasites?"

"What parasites?" Tom asked with alarm.

"It was her sister," Harry interrupted as Tom dutifully

ran a medical tricorder over him, verifying that he had suffered no permanent damage when he was rendered unconscious.

B'Elanna was puzzled. "What does Phoebe have to do with this?"

"It's not Phoebe. Phoebe's an alien, probably a Nacene," Harry replied. "Phoebe Janeway has never been on *Voyager.*"

"But . . . I remember . . ." B'Elanna started to say.

"Your memories were altered. Everyone's were. The captain figured it out."

"What parasites?" Tom asked again.

Before B'Elanna could answer, Chakotay called over the comm, *"All senior officers report to the conference room immediately."*

Tom turned to Harry.

"Are you up to it?"

"Absolutely," Harry replied, trying to jump down from the bed and almost stumbling into Tom's arms.

"Harry, maybe you should stay," B'Elanna suggested.

"Not a chance," he replied.

At that moment a chirp from the computer alerted B'Elanna to the fact that her recompilation process was complete.

"Tell Chakotay I'll be right there," she said as Harry and Tom headed for the door. She took a moment to recheck the diagnostic display and turned to the Doctor.

"Computer, deactivate EMH."

The backup Doctor turned on her, alarmed, and vanished. Taking a deep breath, she brought the remaining restored subroutines online, then called, "Computer, activate restored EMH."

The Doctor shimmered into existence beside her and said, "Please state . . . wait a minute." Turning to

B'Elanna, he demanded, "What happened? There was a woman here. The captain called her Phoebe. She said it was her sister but . . ."

B'Elanna raised a hand to silence him. "We know. It's a long story."

"Give me the short version," he said sardonically.

B'Elanna turned him toward Tuvok.

"We've had an intruder aboard, possibly another Nacene, who altered the crew's memories and pretended to be the captain's sister. As you can see, we've recovered Tuvok, but apparently he's been infected by an alien parasite. An earlier version of you who has been running for the past few hours doesn't believe he can be saved. We're still aboard the array and there is reason to believe that more parasites may be out there. Oh, and the captain is missing."

The Doctor raised a cynical eyebrow and retorted without missing a beat, "So in other words, it's a pretty light day aboard the starship *Voyager.*"

B'Elanna couldn't help herself. Smiling broadly she planted a kiss on the Doctor's cheek and said, "It's good to have you back. I really missed you."

Only once Lieutenant Torres had left did the Doctor add quietly to himself, "Someday someone really ought to write all of this down for posterity."

He turned to Tuvok and thoroughly examined the notes already logged by his temporary replacement, then did his own analysis of the scans of Tuvok's body. It didn't take him long to see that the backup EMH had probably been right. It would take a miracle to save Tuvok now, and advanced as he was, there was no subroutine in his program that allowed for the existence of miracles.

Chapter 10

There were grim faces all around as the senior officers, minus their captain and Tuvok, assumed their places around the oval table that took up most of the space in the conference room. Chakotay arrived last and, taking the seat at the table's head, began by informing them that a thorough search for the captain was still under way. Harry brought the room up to speed about Phoebe, and all were alternately shocked and disturbed to be told that memories of experiences with the captain's sister spanning four years were nothing more than fabricated reality. Strangely, the more they talked about it, the dimmer those memories seemed to grow for Chakotay, as if the alien influence that created them was slowly but steadily dissipating.

B'Elanna gave a brief synopsis of the backup EMH's evaluation of Tuvok and expressed cautious optimism that since the real Doctor had been restored, Tuvok's prognosis must be better. Chakotay briefly described the strange rooms he had discovered aboard the array, but before he or Tom had a chance to mention the hostile creature that had attacked them, Lieutenant Rollins entered and advised

Chakotay that the search for the captain had been completed without yielding any new information as to the captain's current whereabouts. Chakotay dismissed him with a nod and briefed the others as stoically as possible.

"The computer's logs show that approximately thirty seven minutes ago the captain left the ship. At the same time, the logs show a massive subspace dissonance field at her last known location, and that the entity we have known as Phoebe also disappeared," he said. "Although the life-form readings aboard the array are still inconclusive, we do know that *Voyager*'s sensors were able to detect Tuvok's life signs, as well as both away teams we sent into the array. So if the captain were there, we would know it."

"Are you saying the captain simply vanished into thin air?" Tom asked.

"We suspect that Phoebe was actually a Nacene. We know very little about them or their technology, but based on what we do know, I don't believe it's outside the realm of possibility to suggest that Phoebe could have taken the captain just about anywhere.

"So we are faced with a choice: Either we leave the array and hope that Phoebe returns the captain to us once we're gone, or we stay here and do what we can to find them," he finished.

"Surely we have to stay," Neelix said with obvious anxiety. "We can't just leave the captain behind."

"If there were no other dangers present I wouldn't hesitate to agree," Chakotay said, "But there are."

"What dangers?" Neelix asked.

"When Tom and I were aboard the array, we were attacked by an alien creature. Our phaser rifle had no effect on it."

"What was it?" Neelix was the first to ask.

"I don't know. We've analyzed the readings from Tom's tricorder and they suggest that there are multiphasic properties to it."

"Commander," Seven interrupted, "if it was a multiphasic organism, our sensors can be modified to track it. All of the potential life-form readings we have picked up from the array are difficult to analyze because they fluctuate so rapidly. If there are others like the creature you saw, and they are also multiphasic in nature, that would account for our inability to confirm their existence up to this point."

"She's right," B'Elanna added. "Maybe our sensors haven't actually been malfunctioning in respect to these life-forms. Even the slightest phase variance as they move in and out of our precise phase modulation makes it look like they exist and then cease to exist from one fraction of a second to the next."

"If we can track them, can we also count them?" Chakotay asked. "I'd like to know how many we're up against."

Seven rose, moved to the room's computer interface, adjusted the sensors to account for the multiphasic properties of the organisms, and said, "There are nine thousand, nine hundred and ninety-six creatures that share this signature aboard the array."

Chakotay and Tom exchanged a worried glance.

"Great," Tom said. "So, basically we're talking about an army of them."

"An army against which we're currently defenseless," Harry added.

"Not entirely," B'Elanna said. "We've restored the shield generators to full power and as long as the shields are up, we should be safe aboard *Voyager*."

"So you believe we can remain here indefinitely?" Chakotay asked.

"In theory," B'Elanna replied. "We might also be able to find some kind of a defense, in the event they find a way through our shields."

"Let's assume they will. Developing a defense needs to be our first priority right now," Chakotay said. "Setting that aside for the moment, let's also assume that whoever or whatever Phoebe actually is, her intentions are hostile. What was she doing here? And why go to such lengths to insinuate herself among us? What did she want that she couldn't have simply taken by force?"

"The Key to Gremadia," Seven said, as if everyone should already know that. When the others faced her with a mixture of irritation and disbelief plain on their faces, she elaborated. "The captain asked me to locate the Key, which was, at that time, missing. I discovered that shortly before we boarded the array, the Key was transported into our warp core. The transporter logs were deleted in a manner similar to the log alterations that Ensign Kim has described. Therefore I suspect that Phoebe was responsible for the transport."

"Why would she have done that?" Chakotay asked.

"As we have not engaged the warp engines in several days, it was a perfect hiding place. The residual antimatter in the core provided a natural shield for the dissonance waves that emanate from the Key, which have increased significantly since we boarded the array. It appears that her primary interest is not in us, but in the Key itself, and in making sure that we are unable to discover its purpose."

"So what does an ancient religious artifact have to do with us, apart from the fact that it was given to us as a gift?" was Chakotay's next question.

"We found a large collection of historical records aboard the *Betasis*. From that data it is possible to extrapolate at least a partial hypothesis," Seven continued. "The first and only Monorhan to ever touch the Key was the *haran* who discovered it, Dagan. It imparted visions to him of Monorha's ancient past, which he integrated into their existing religious mythology. Dagan died shortly after he touched the Key, and for reasons I can only speculate about, the Key became a sacred and terrifying object of reverence. It was encased in a box, the same box in which it was presented to the captain."

"Do you have a theory as to why the Monorhans were so frightened of it?" Chakotay asked.

"Much of the Key's history between Dagan's death and its retrieval by Kaytok's family is lost to us. However, I believe it is significant that according to the calculations we did when we first encountered the Monorhan system and the Blue Eye in particular, the gravitational shift which ultimately resulted in the destabilization of the star began at exactly the same time as Dagan's death."

"Did the Monorhans make a connection between the activity of the Blue Eye and Dagan's death?" Harry interjected.

"No, Ensign," Seven replied. "They were much more perturbed by the various ecological disasters that accompanied the death of Dagan. But given their limited understanding of interstellar phenomena at that stage in their development, it is unlikely that they would have. Perhaps more instructive is that fact that the name 'Blue Eye' was only given to the star after it began its unnatural collapse and came into common usage within a hundred years of Dagan's death."

"But do we know anything about the Key's purpose?" Chakotay asked, nudging Seven back to the point.

"In one of Dagan's letters he asserts that the Key is the final and crucial piece of a larger mechanism, one which he was unable to describe clearly given his limited understanding of complex technology. But he does say that the mechanism is located within the promised city and that the city will circle the ultimate darkness, which does suggest, at least metaphorically, the array. More important, he says that only the Key's owner will be able to put the Key in its proper place in the 'Time of Knowing' and open the conduit of light."

"That's fascinating, Seven," Tom interjected, "but what does it all mean?"

"According to Ensign Kim, Phoebe most likely arrived shortly after the captain was given the Key. It is logical to assume that since the captain is the first person in thousands of years to actually touch the object, that she is also its owner. If Phoebe were able to use the Key, she would have taken it from us long before now. But if the captain is the only person who can use it, Phoebe needs her. This might also explain why 'Phoebe' chose to assume the form of someone who is close to the captain . . . someone she would trust instinctively."

"Did the captain also see visions after she touched it?" Chakotay asked.

"No, Commander," Seven replied. "The Key had no obvious effect on her. But the Monorhans of the Fourteenth Tribe were highly telepathic. It appears that their vessel is equipped with an organic neural network which most likely responds to telepathic commands."

"So you have to be a telepath to see the visions?" Tom asked.

"Or hear them . . ." Chakotay suggested.

There was a pause as every face in the room turned to him curiously.

"The Doctor believed that Tuvok might have left the ship in response to a telepathic message only he could hear," Chakotay explained. "His proximity to the Key might have been the cause."

"But why would it have drawn him to the array? The Key has been aboard *Voyager* since we left Monorha," Tom said.

B'Elanna rose and joined Seven at the computer interface, calling up Seven's analysis of the data recovered from the *Betasis*. When she had found what she appeared to be looking for, she said, "I don't think the Key brought Tuvok here."

"Why not?" Chakotay asked.

"I think the Monorhans did."

"Explain," Seven demanded.

"Right now we're reading nine thousand, nine hundred and ninety-six multiphasic life-forms aboard the array. That is almost the exact number of Monorhans who came to the array aboard the *Betasis* fifty years ago. The backup Doctor believed that Tuvok is actually gestating a new life-form. If the Monorhans were attacked by the same thing Tuvok was, then perhaps these life-forms we are seeing were created when the parasites merged with the Monorhans."

"But the Monorhans are dead," Harry said. "We found Tuvok in a room that was filled with their bodies."

"And have you asked yourself how he got there?" B'Elanna asked. "Given the severity of his injuries, there is no way he could have left his wrecked shuttle on his own."

"You think the Monorhans somehow brought Tuvok . . ." Tom began.

" . . . to a place where he could also be infected and transformed, just like they were," B'Elanna finished. "The Doctor said that some part of Tuvok would be incorporated into the new life-form. If the same thing were true of the Monorhans, then perhaps they retain their telepathic abilities and used them to contact Tuvok."

"So what did they want with him?" Tom asked no one in particular.

It was a good question and one that no one seemed prepared to speculate on at the moment.

"There is one flaw with your premise, Lieutenant," Seven said finally.

"What's that?" B'Elanna retorted.

"I do not believe that all of the Monorhans were transformed as you suggested."

"What are you basing that on?" Chakotay asked.

"When we were aboard the *Betasis,* I attempted to interface with their computer core using my assimilation tubules. When I interfaced with the neural network of the ship, I discovered a presence there . . . a consciousness."

"How is that possible?" Harry asked.

"I hesitate to speculate as to how," Seven replied. "Nonetheless, it did communicate with me."

"Don't you mean *through* you?" B'Elanna demanded, obviously still irritated at Seven's rash actions when they had boarded the Monorhan vessel.

"That might be a more accurate description," Seven acknowledged. "The presence demanded that we leave the ship and threatened us with imminent death if we did not comply. Among the records we discovered were descriptions of Monorhan rituals that included the transfer of consciousness between certain members of the tribe. I believe that one of the Monorhans attempted such a transfer between themselves and the organic components of the *Betasis.* If they succeeded, then they are still alive in a manner of speaking, within the ship, and would therefore not have been infected by the parasites as the others were."

The others pondered this possibility silently for a few moments before Neelix asked the obvious.

"Well, if one of them is still alive, maybe we should try and talk to them again. They'll know more than we do about these creatures."

"I do not believe they will comply," Seven replied.

"Neither do I," B'Elanna agreed.

"What if we could offer them something they need?" Harry suggested.

"What's that?" Chakotay asked.

"A body," Harry replied.

The only thing Janeway could feel as she entered the blackness was Phoebe's firm, icy hand holding hers as if their lives depended upon remaining in physical contact. For a few disorienting seconds it seemed that the darkness around her was as impenetrable as it was eternal. She heard Phoebe calling to her, her voice echoing around her as if it were coming from everywhere at once, and not from the firm solid presence that walked beside her.

"The Beginning . . ." Phoebe called, over and over.

Suddenly Janeway found herself standing on the transporter pad of *Voyager*'s main transporter room. Admiral Patterson strode toward her, extending a warm hand as he said, "Welcome aboard, Captain."

Janeway had automatically reached out to accept his hand when he froze where he stood and Phoebe appeared beside him.

"What is this moment, Kathryn?" she asked.

Janeway didn't have to think to answer. It was one of her fondest and least complicated memories.

"This was my first day aboard *Voyager*," she replied.

"Not the day," Phoebe said patiently, "the *moment*."

Janeway considered briefly. "This moment . . . when I first appeared on the transport pad . . . was the beginning of my life aboard *Voyager.*"

"Fine," Phoebe replied. "It is a beginning. But not *the* beginning. Try again," she said.

"The beginning . . ." Janeway said softly.

The image of the transporter room grew dim and fractured. Colors and sounds whirled into blackness as Janeway closed her eyes and forced herself to focus on the word "beginning."

When she opened them, she found a familiar pair of blue-gray eyes staring lovingly into hers. Her arms and legs were bound closely around her, but the warmth and comfort she felt in this position overwhelmed any sense of danger at her sudden immobility. She couldn't speak, but as she looked beyond the beautiful eyes, she caught flashes of light and sound that some dim part of her associated with her first sight. Suddenly she knew that this moment was also a memory. This was her first moment of consciousness after birth. She quelled the instinct that came from she knew not where, to begin screaming and crying. Part of her sensed the emptiness in her belly and knew she needed nourishment. But the part of her mind that was still the fully grown Janeway could also experience the memory with some detachment. She acknowledged this moment as the beginning of her life.

Phoebe's face loomed large above hers, blocking out any view she had of her mother's eyes.

"Yes, Kathryn, this too was a beginning. Do you understand the difficulty . . . the imprecision of your most basic tool for communication . . . your language? This is the beginning of your life . . . your existence. But imprinted upon the strands of amino acids which form your DNA are memories which predate your life. You and every other living thing hold the memories of the beginning of all existence within you. Try again," she commanded.

Reluctant as Janeway was to abandon the warmth and comfort of her mother's arms, she obeyed and cast her mind into darkness, searching for a memory she had never known was part of her.

She found herself suspended in blackness, staring toward a tiny speck of light.

"Better," Phoebe said.

Turning toward the sound, Janeway could barely make out the vague outline of her sister floating in the darkness beside her.

"Where are we?" Janeway asked.

"Closer to the truth," Phoebe replied enigmatically.

"That's comforting," Janeway replied, hoping that saying the statement would make it real.

"I know this is difficult, Kathryn," Phoebe said. "The answers you are seeking are buried far beyond the parts of your mind and body where you normally seek them. Unfortunately I can only show you those things for which you have some sort of context, even if it is theoretical. Once we have established the limits of your knowledge, we will attempt to push past them. But I will only be able to present that knowledge to you in images that you can relate to experientially."

"All right," Janeway said, turning her attention again to the tiny speck of light that seemed to beckon in the distance. "So far I understand that we are looking for a beginning."

"That is correct," Phoebe said.

"And that the word 'beginning' is imprecise because from my particular point of view there have been several events which were, in fact, some kind of beginning."

"Also correct," Phoebe replied, then asked, "What is this beginning?"

Janeway studied the speck of light. She was already growing weary of the exercise. She remembered vividly her days in early school, and then Starfleet Academy. She had always possessed a visceral thirst for knowledge. It drove and defined much of her existence. But the moment just before a concept or new piece of information had been integrated into her larger understanding of the subject at hand, that casting about in the unknown searching for the thing which would anchor her in her search had always been painful. She realized in this moment how much of her drive and discipline as a student had been calculated avoidance of this exact feeling. She needed to know the answer, the correct answer to the question. Only that could stave off the inevitable physical discomfort of ignorance.

In a flash, these thoughts brought her to the appropriate memory. She had been seated in Professor Philemon's theoretical quantum mechanics course in her first year at Starfleet Academy. Philemon had been presenting a lecture on the origins of the universe, accompanied by a holographic projection of the moment still referred to in some circles as the "Big Bang."

The moment she realized where she was, the fleck of light began to dance before her. A split second later it burst forth in a cascade of light that enveloped the room.

Turning to Phoebe, she said, "This is the beginning of the universe."

"As you understand it," Phoebe replied.

"Are you telling me that this theoretical model of the formation of the universe is wrong?" Janeway asked. "That the basic principles of space and time which have allowed humanity and countless other species to venture out into the universe and safely explore space are . . . what?" she demanded.

"Incomplete," Phoebe replied.

Janeway planted her hands on her hips and asked, "In what way?"

"Look closer," Phoebe demanded.

Resigning herself to the attempt, Janeway considered the fragments of fiery light flowing out from the original speck that she had always imagined as the beginning of the universe. Suddenly, the shrapnel that had exploded forth reversed itself and rushed back into its formation as the tiny speck of matter that somehow contained in its densest form all matter that had eventually become the universe.

In her mind, Janeway saw herself examining the speck. As she did so, she found herself standing right in front of the speck. Reaching out, she grasped it in her hand and began to turn it one way and another, hoping to see some hint of what Phoebe was suggesting. Janeway visualized all 246 of the elements known to Federation scientists and imagined that they were contained within the palm of her hand. She saw their atomic structure. She had committed them to memory years ago and knew them the way a child of seven knew their multiplication tables.

"Closer," Phoebe demanded, and somehow Janeway knew that in this place even her thoughts were not her own.

She forced herself to see the atoms of the elements contained in the palm of her hand, the protons and electrons circling the nuclei of the atoms. Tiny circles zoomed in their stable orbits in a timeless dance that came as close to perfection as Janeway could possibly imagine. But her mind rebelled at the thought of anything beyond this. Certainly there were smaller, subatomic particles, and even as she thought this, she saw them weaving among the identifiable pieces of the atoms before her.

"Closer," Phoebe said again, and Janeway had to force herself not to send the atoms spinning in a fiery ball of anger toward her.

With a deep breath, she tried again, allowing the atoms to disintegrate until all she was holding was a ball of darkness. After a moment she said, "There's nothing here."

But just as the words escaped her lips a tiny wisp of light burst from her hand and began to dance all around her. She looked again at her palm and dozens of similar threads exploded forth, coiling and unraveling to join the first in its chaotic movement.

"What is this?" Janeway asked.

Phoebe smiled.

"The beginning," she replied.

Tuvok knelt before the fire. The subject of his meditation was the Vulcan principle of the *Kol-ut-shan*. Roughly translated, it meant infinite diversity in infinite combinations.

As the flames jutted and peaked, he considered first their motion, and then the chemical reactions that permitted this motion. He then considered the life of the fire. He contemplated its existence in its potential forms; the wood that fueled it and the oxygen that sustained it.

He resisted the urge to reach his hand into the fire. He recognized the childish and illogical nature of the thought, but some part of him honestly believed that he could touch it without coming to harm. He heard the rustle of the robes of the Vulcan master who watched patiently behind him.

Tuvok knew this place. He was a young man in the

Temple of Amonak. His father had brought him to the temple weeks earlier when he had confessed in a moment of weakness his desire to abandon logic and reason in favor of an emotional attachment to a young woman that all but consumed him.

The master was displeased. He knew Tuvok's thoughts, sensed their disorganized and fragmented nature, and strained with the force of his own discipline to impose structure and rigidity upon his young charge's mind. Tuvok felt the intense pressure weighing down upon him and took a deep breath, determined to begin again.

Infinite diversity . . .

The flames rose higher, their tempestuous motion a matter of calculable chemical conflagrations.

. . . in infinite combinations.

The pile of tinder beneath the fire was composed of shards of wood taken from dozens of different trees native to Vulcan. He separated each piece of wood in his mind, saw their source in a natural state, and examined the faint differences in the way they burned.

To understand the fire was to know the fire was to control the fire. His thoughts were like the pieces of wood that burned. They too could be separated, examined, and placed in a logical order. Logic and order were the gateway to the mastery of his passions, and to peace. Only in peace could he truly understand the *Kol-ut-shan*.

Two black eyes stared at him across the fire. They were his eyes, but jostling their placid depths was an enticing mischief that Tuvok did not recognize in himself. Tuvok saw his young and troubling face gazing intently at him. His mirror image seemed unconcerned with the master's reproachful rustling. The image raised his hand and placed it in the fire.

To his amazement Tuvok saw that the hand, his hand,

became part of the fire without being burned by it. Intrigued, Tuvok raised his own hand, and reached for the hand of the mirror. He could feel the immediate increase in temperature as his fingers grazed the flame's edge. Logic dictated that to touch the fire was to be consumed. But the promise of the eyes said that there was something beyond logic, something that he had yearned for but never touched. Here was a place where his emotions could live alongside his reason . . . *in peace.*

He wanted the fire. He knew the truth of its promise. He had sought it in quiet contemplation for more than a hundred years of life. And he had never before been so close to it.

Trusting an instinct that was so new as to be indefinable and yet so certain as to be irresistible, Tuvok reached his hand into the darting flames and grasped the hand that waited for him there.

Kol-ut-shan, he said . . . and almost knew.

The connection was severed in a moment of slicing agony. The fire and the eyes vanished into the oblivion where Tuvok now flailed like a drowning man caught in a tempest. The darkness choked him, assaulting his senses from all sides even as he struggled to return to the warmth and truth of the fire.

Tuvok opened his eyes. The light was blinding, suffocating. Blinking rapidly, he tried to force his senses to adjust. He thought of Naviim and his promise that the transition he was undergoing would be difficult. He longed for the passage, resigning himself to endure whatever was required in the meantime.

The face of the Doctor moved into his field of vision. He was speaking. His lips were moving, but for a few seconds it was impossible for him to process the Doctor's words.

". . . feeling better?" he heard.

"Where . . ." Tuvok croaked through a parched throat.

"You are perfectly safe, Lieutenant," the Doctor replied. "You are in sickbay, and I believe I have found a way to reverse the process that was initiated by the parasitic life-form that has invaded your body."

Tuvok did not know where he found the strength to move, but as if his existence depended upon it, he focused every ounce of will on a single object and grasped the Doctor by the throat.

"You . . . will . . . not . . . continue," Tuvok demanded, adding the force of his hand to his words as the Doctor's eyes widened.

Suddenly the Doctor was gone. Tuvok twisted and turned, instinctively searching for the enemy. Seconds later something cold was placed on his neck, followed by the whisper of a hypospray.

The will to fight seeped slowly from his body, replaced by a numb heaviness. He groaned under the effort of keeping his eyelids open as the Doctor said soothingly, "Please don't be alarmed, Tuvok. I assure you, you're going to be all right."

"No," Tuvok muttered.

"Tuvok, if I don't proceed, you will die," the Doctor continued.

With the last remnant of strength and will at his disposal, Tuvok forced his eyes to open and focus on the Doctor, who was once again standing above him.

"It is my wish to die," he said, and before the Doctor could respond he said, "Computer, deactivate Emergency Medical Hologram, security override authorization Tuvok, pi, six, one, gamma."

He remained conscious long enough to see the

Doctor's shocked face dematerialize. A few moments later, he found himself once again seated before the fire.

All eyes around the table turned to Harry.

"A body?" Chakotay was the first to ask.

"Yes, Commander," Harry replied evenly. "The consciousness Seven is describing could theoretically be contained within a holomatrix," he said. "When we found the Vidiian doctor, Danara Pel, the Doctor was able to transfer her synaptic patterns into sickbay's holobuffers and then create a stable holomatrix which he used to interact with her."

"But she was unconscious when the Doctor did that," B'Elanna said. "She didn't have a choice. We're talking about someone, or something, that only wants to be rid of us. How are you going to force the synaptic patterns into our holobuffers?"

"By making its current environment inhospitable," Seven said.

"What?" B'Elanna asked in obvious disbelief.

"Most life-forms share a survival instinct. If the consciousness embedded in the organic circuitry of the *Betasis* were no longer able to live within that ship's neural network, it would be forced to seek an alternative. If we provide it with a suitable escape path, it would be forced to either take it or die."

"Like trapping an animal," Chakotay said. "But what would we use as bait? I mean to say, how would we make sure that the consciousness will choose the path we will lay out for it?"

"*Voyager*'s systems have a bioneural component. Our gel packs function in a manner which is similar to the neural network of the *Betasis*."

"But the gel-pack system is completely separate from the hologrid," Harry reasoned.

"I am not suggesting that we offer *Voyager*'s bioneural circuitry as the bait," Seven continued. "But we have sufficient spare gel packs to create a smaller neural network that could be linked to the hologrid for the purposes of attracting the consciousness. Once the consciousness is completely contained there, we simply transfer it to a stable holomatrix."

B'Elanna was quick to voice her next objection.

"How do you propose we destroy the neural network that the consciousness is currently embedded in?" she asked. "Do you want to blow up the *Betasis*?"

"No, Lieutenant," Seven replied. "If I were to infect the neural network with a sufficient supply of nanoprobes . . ." she began.

"You want to assimilate it?" B'Elanna shouted.

"B'Elanna," Chakotay barked in frustration. He could see the wisdom in what Seven was proposing, though he had to admit there was a time when he would have responded as sharply as B'Elanna had to any suggestion of using the Borg's invasive and destructive means of "reproduction" as a means to an end.

Seven cast an icy and disparaging glance at B'Elanna. "The nanoprobes could be coded to destabilize the neural network without affecting any of the ship's other systems. They would not be capable of assimilating the vessel, any more than the nanoprobes that were transferred into your body to save your life on Monorha were capable of turning you into a Borg," she retorted sharply.

B'Elanna paused, then said softly, "I'm sorry, Seven. That wasn't fair of me."

"Your apology is acceptable," Seven replied.

"You mean accepted?" B'Elanna half-teased.

Seven responded with a slight smile, further dissipating the tension between them.

Chakotay gave those present a moment to raise any further objections before he offered his conclusions.

"Very well," he said. "Seven, begin replicating the nanoprobes. Harry, get down to the holographic research lab and construct a stable holomatrix that will support the transfer. Use the holomatrix designed for Danara Pel as a template, but adjust the physical parameters to those of a Monorhan. B'Elanna, you'll work with me on our defensive capabilities. We still need an alternative in the event the life-forms aboard the array get curious about *Voyager*."

"Commander," Tom interrupted.

"Yes, Lieutenant?"

"With your permission, I'd like to conduct a more thorough analysis of the tetryon transport technology we discovered aboard the array."

Chakotay instinctively balked at the idea, but gave Tom a chance to make his case.

"To what end?" he asked.

"If we can't defend ourselves against those creatures, we'll need a way to get off this array in a hurry. Boarding the array was a disaster that I'm not anxious to see repeated. We barely escaped the singularity's gravity well. If the tractor net that brought us in hadn't activated, we wouldn't even be having this conversation right now, and at this point we don't know if that system was automated or controlled by something or someone else. We have to know that we can leave the array at a moment's notice, and I believe the tetryon technology can be adapted to do just that," Tom said.

"Fine," Chakotay replied, "although I'd also like as thorough an analysis of the tractor net system as we can get without going back aboard the array."

Tom nodded and smiled, "Aye, sir."

Chakotay turned last to Neelix.

"Neelix, I want you to study the historical information collected from the *Betasis.*"

"What am I looking for, Commander?" Neelix asked.

"The visions that reference the Key might contain information about the Nacene. You know more about the interaction between the Caretaker and the Ocampa than any of us. I want to know if there are any similarities between the Monorhans and the god or gods of their mythology and the Ocampa and the Caretaker. If Phoebe is Nacene, Dagan's visions might give us a clue as to where she and the captain have gone."

"I'll do my best, Commander," Neelix replied.

Chakotay took a moment to meet the eyes of each of his officers. Assuming the mantle of command was not difficult for him, but he'd have given anything for Kathryn's firm reassuring presence beside him as they faced these challenges. He knew the others shared his unspoken wish.

"I don't have to remind any of you what's at stake here," he said solemnly. "Let's get to work."

Chapter 11

B'Elanna was stumped. She knew that a few hours of sleep would revive her more effectively than the *rakta-jino* that was cooling at her workstation, but for the moment, the liquid stimulant would have to do.

She had spent more than an hour analyzing every piece of data they had been able to gather about the multiphasic life-forms and kept running up against the same solid problematic wall. The creatures were not stable. That is . . . they did not exist in any phase variation long enough for any weapon at *Voyager*'s disposal to have any effect upon them at all. She had reconfigured several phaser rifles to fire at randomized phase variances but the only way the weapons would be effective is if the phase variance of the rifle and the creature were exactly the same. She had added a phase calibrator to the rifles, but in every simulation she ran, the sensor could not detect the variance, lock on target, and fire before the phase variance of the creature shifted. She also had to face the unpleasant reality that like the Borg, the creatures might be able to adapt to randomized fire, making the highly advanced weapon she was developing practically useless.

Ensign Glenn, one of Tuvok's tactical munitions experts, had just started her duty shift, and B'Elanna silently hoped that a pair of fresh eyes might see what she was obviously missing.

A pop and sizzle from the rifle Glenn was configuring stirred B'Elanna from her thoughts.

"Careful," she chided.

"The sensor relay overloaded," Glenn replied. "I'll replicate another. Don't worry," she added as she crossed to the replicator. "I lost a few fingers at Menassa VI trying to deactivate a micro-mine. My biosynthetic digits are less sensitive. I didn't even feel it."

B'Elanna nodded as she absentmindedly pushed a few unruly strands of hair back into place.

A sonic shower and a few hours of sleep.

Instead, she reached for her *raktajino* and, grasping the cup, was rewarded with a quick burn on the first finger to touch it. She had ordered the beverage extra-hot and within a few minutes the mug had absorbed so much of the heat as to be temporarily untouchable. As she automatically thrust her index finger into her mouth to sooth the mild wound, she cast a glance at Glenn and reminded herself that any feeling in her fingers, no matter how unpleasant, was better than the alternative that Glenn had to live with. Only once in her life had she come close to losing normal sensations in her extremities: when she and the rest of *Voyager*'s crew had been subjected to a series of barbaric scientific experiments by a group of aliens who had turned the crew into unwilling lab rats. Their first round of experiments on B'Elanna had caused the alveoli in her lungs to stop processing oxygen. In successive genetic alterations B'Elanna's left arm, hand, and leg had been paralyzed. They hadn't been able to engage the aliens until they had discovered their hiding place.

Wait a minute.

B'Elanna removed her hand from her mouth and stared at it for so long that Glenn was moved to ask, "Lieutenant, are you all right?"

"I'm an idiot," B'Elanna replied.

"I beg your pardon?" Glenn asked, then added politely, "In my experience, Lieutenant, nothing could be further from the truth."

But B'Elanna was in no mood to hear or accept a compliment. "We don't need to calibrate our weapons to find the phase variance of the creatures," B'Elanna said. "We have to force them into phase with us."

Glenn's gaze dropped down as she considered B'Elanna's proposition.

"I don't . . ." Glenn began.

"The Srivani were able to conduct their experiments on us by hiding in a slightly variant phase," B'Elanna said. "All we needed was a precisely modulated hand phaser to bring them into phase with us."

Glenn quickly cleared a path as B'Elanna, consumed by her revelation, darted to the deflector dish controls and began a series of calculations as she continued.

"The same principle might apply here if we can flood the array with enough ionized particles."

As Glenn smiled with respect at the chief engineer, Chakotay entered engineering carrying several small vials and said, "We've got some good news, B'Elanna. We've found a way to intensify the toxin we developed to disable Suspiria, and hopefully now Phoebe. Tell me you've made some progress."

B'Elanna faced Chakotay her eyes ablaze.

"We have."

Seven of Nine entered sickbay in hope that the Doctor would be able to assist her in modifying the nanoprobes she had replicated in her cargo bay. It was delicate work, and his were the only hands other than hers that she trusted with it.

She was surprised to see that the room's lights had been dimmed well below standard work settings and that the Doctor was nowhere in sight.

"Doctor," she called, pausing to note that Tuvok lay unattended on his biobed behind an active forcefield.

When the Doctor did not appear immediately she asked the computer to activate the EMH. She was disconcerted when the computer replied, *"The Emergency Medical Holographic Program is unavailable."*

"Clarify," Seven demanded.

"That program is restricted. Security authorization is required for reactivation."

"Who restricted the program?" Seven asked.

"Lieutenant Tuvok," the computer replied.

Seven made short work of breaking Tuvok's security encryption and reactivating the Doctor. Nonetheless, a tight fist of worry formed in her stomach when she realized in the process that Tuvok had been unattended for almost an hour.

"Computer, belay that order!" the Doctor shouted as he rematerialized.

Seven inclined her head as she replied, "It might comfort you to know that the computer would not have accepted your request, had you found the presence of mind to utter it before your patient locked your program out."

"The computer should have accepted it," the Doctor replied with concern. "As chief medical officer I outrank all members of this crew in matters relating to their physical well-being."

"A distinction I have rectified so that Tuvok will no

longer be able to disable your program," Seven said simply. "The chief of security's override capability has been taken offline for the time being, though I am certain that it was only put in place for your own protection."

"Protection from what?" the Doctor asked annoyed.

"A hostile intruder who might wish to tamper with your program," Seven suggested.

"Well . . . thank you," the Doctor said, then turned to examine the progress of the parasite, adding, "Although I realize it is impossible to be prepared for every eventuality, I would hope that when the hostile intruder and the chief of security are temporarily one and the same, someone would take the time to inform me that he can override my autonomous subroutines."

"I am certain the captain would have addressed the issue, Doctor, had she not been abducted shortly after Tuvok was brought back on board," Seven replied.

"I'd like to think you're right," the Doctor said caustically, failing to convince either himself or Seven that this was true. "Despite the progress we've made over the years," he added bitterly, "I'm still usually the last to be considered, consulted, or informed until whatever crisis the crew was facing had gotten seriously out of hand."

Seven found that she could not honestly contradict him and decided that for the moment the Doctor's energies were best spent addressing Tuvok's condition, but as she started to return to the cargo bay and complete her work on the nanoprobes on her own, Chakotay called over the comm system, *"Attention all personnel, we are instigating a low-level ion sweep of* Voyager *and the array. It is possible this action will antagonize the creatures we have detected aboard the array. Red alert."*

As the computer responded, sickbay was bathed in a flashing red glow. Seven's implants tingled as a barely detectable hum cut the air indicating the presence of charged particles.

A few seconds later, the ion sweep was complete and Seven was halted at the door to sickbay by the sound of dismay in the Doctor's voice.

"Oh, my," he said.

Turning, Seven immediately saw the object of his alarm. Tuvok's torso, neck, and head were engulfed in a mass of flowing translucent tentacles that pulsed with volatile energy at several points where the tentacles penetrated his skin.

"Is that the parasite?" Seven asked.

"It is. Apparently it shares the multiphasic properties of the creatures aboard the array."

Seven shuddered involuntarily. She knew all too well what it was to have her body's systems invaded by a hostile entity. The Borg had perfected the technique. Though she was about to perform a similar procedure by infecting the *Betasis* with modified Borg nanoprobes, and was certain that the means did justify the ends in this particular case, she couldn't help but feel a pang of regret for the neural network that would be compromised and overrun, just as Tuvok's body had been violated by this parasite. For a moment, B'Elanna's initial revulsion at Seven's suggestion seemed not only comprehensible, but also appropriate.

Nonetheless, Seven completed the modifications within the next half-hour and forced the regret from her mind as she returned to the *Betasis* to all but assimilate its neural network.

Blessed be the All-Knowing Light. Through Him we are bound to what is and the beyond. Time cannot contain Him, but in its fullness will restore the harmony which was broken. Created in His divine image, we toil as one to

*expand our knowledge. We suffer as He suffered, oppressed
by those who fear His truth. We will not raise our hands in
violence against those who are blind. Our war is not with
them, but within ourselves. The path to peace is lit by the
fires of creation. We must strive daily to keep those fires
alive so that when He returns He will find us ready to
stand beside Him in Gremadia. Only there will we taste
life beyond time. To walk in His presence is to know eternity.*

Neelix read these words aloud, pondering their deeper
meaning. The Monorhan belief system contained within
the poetic images of Dagan was beautiful, to be sure—
more lovely than most, he had to allow. In his travels he
had encountered many such mythologies. Most races in
his experience grappled with a definition of self, and as
many as not found it comforting to ascribe their existence
to the efforts of some separate but benign entity. Neelix
had no personal context for such a belief, as Talaxians had
always framed their morals and values around personal responsibility and close family ties.

It had been many months since Neelix had faced his
darkest personal crisis of faith. A protomatter explosion
had actually killed him, and only through the intervention of Borg technology had his life been restored. He
had been raised on stories of the Great Forest and had believed fervently up until that day that when he died he
would begin his afterlife at the base of the Great Tree, welcomed into eternity by those members of his family who
had died before him. He had been revived with no such
memory and for a time had struggled with the possibility
that there was no afterlife. Although this belief had never
defined his life, he found it almost impossible to continue
living with the knowledge that at the end of one's life there

was nothing at all. In time he had come to see that whatever might or might not exist after one died, there was such goodness in life to cherish that to end one's life prematurely would simply be a waste.

Difficult as it was to relate to on a personal level, however, Neelix tried to put himself in the shoes of the Monorhans, particularly those of the Fourteenth Tribe, whose apparent suffering in Dagan's time would be given meaning at some distant future date when they would participate in a great battle fighting on the side of their god.

What struck Neelix most was that, if he was reading Dagan correctly, the Monorhans actually believed that they could interact with their supreme being while they were still alive. Turning his thoughts to the Ocampa, he considered their relationship to the Caretaker, comparing and contrasting it with that of the Monorhans and their All-Knowing Light.

"... *the harmony which was broken,*" he said to himself, and images of Ocampa before the disaster that had forced them into the underground caverns sustained by the Caretaker flooded his memory. His first stolen moments with Kes had taken place the night he entered Jabin's camp, as he had so many times before, and was introduced to the Kazon's new *servant*. As Kes tended the fire, well out of earshot of her sleeping captors, she had spoken in a rich whisper of the Caretaker and her people's love for him. Though Neelix had always given the Caretaker's array a wide berth, he had known that a powerful and technically advanced alien or aliens had inhabited it. To hear this beautiful woman-child speak of his benevolence and special relationship with her people almost made him long to share the confidence and faith such a relationship nurtured.

But even Kes had been wise or at least rebellious enough to see that the Caretaker need not be a divine being to enter into that relationship. What she had been less willing to accept at first, though had eventually made her own peace with, was that the entity she had been raised to believe acted only in the best interests of her people did so out of a tremendous sense of guilt. The Caretaker had been somehow responsible for the disaster that left the planet bereft of nucleogenic particles and unable to sustain life.

. . . the harmony which was broken.

That was it. The Caretaker had forever destroyed the natural balance and harmony of Ocampa. Perhaps the All-Knowing Light had been responsible for a similar disaster on or around Monorha. The battle that was to come was meant to restore that harmony. Monorhan space was an anomaly, much like Ocampa after the Caretaker's intervention. Perhaps the All-Knowing Light would return only when he had found a way to repair the anomaly that he had in part created.

But Dagan's visions were also filled with images of the "Others." These beings seemed to be every bit as powerful as the All-Knowing Light, and for reasons that eluded Neelix, they seemed to stand against the All-Knowing Light in his desire to restore the harmony that had been broken.

Neelix's musings were interrupted by a call from Samantha Wildman. Naomi was restless and asking for a story. A few moments later he found himself perched at her bedside, softly relating the story that always calmed her the most, that of the Great Forest.

Even if it was a lie, as big a lie as the All-Knowing Light and the Others, it was a lie that was at least filled with hope. The more Neelix turned the writings of Dagan over in his mind the less he found anything remotely comforting. Life itself was a battle, even if one did not involve oneself in the quarrels of beings who could destroy an entire planet or system. But the fate of the Monorhans seemed as intimately entwined with the fate of their All-Knowing Light as the Caretaker and the Ocampa. Dagan had obviously believed that his people were headed toward a cataclysm worthy of a Talaxian epic song.

As Naomi fell into a restless slumber, Neelix reached beyond his doubts and silently asked the spirits of his mother, his father, and his beloved sister, Alixia, to watch over his goddaughter in the days to come. If they were truly as dark as Dagan had foretold, and if *Voyager* was now to play a part in those days, they would need all the help they could get. To know eternity might be a good thing, but for his sake, and the sake of the angelic little girl who now possessed the largest part of his heart, he hoped they would not have to face it for many, many years.

For the exhausted Talaxian, bathing in the warmth of Naomi's soft, rhythmic breath, only this moment mattered.

Eternity could wait.

Kathryn stood on the porch of her mother's house. A replica of an ancient architectural form called "craftsman," the home was extravagantly large by the utilitarian standards of the Federation. But her mother had taken such pride in her meticulous maintenance of the house, and filled it with so many loving reminders of the people who inhabited it, that few who ever entered were cognizant of its size. What was overwhelming was the coziness of each room, the subtle patterns in the wallpaper bringing out the framed images of seascapes and snowcapped mountains that were her mother's favorites. Most of the furnishings were also antiques. There was no sofa as comfortable in the quadrant as the one in her family living room, which

Kathryn had fallen asleep on countless times as a young girl and teenager, usually with a book or padd lying across her chest.

But among the home's most welcoming touches were the aromas that always lured one from the entry hall straight through the dining room to the large kitchen. It was filled with the best the past and present had to offer in terms of appliances.

As Kathryn threw open the front door, she hoped that the first smell that would meet her nose would be Gretchen Janeway's famous caramel brownies. If the fates were really smiling on her, Phoebe would also be visiting, and waiting with a pot of coffee made from freshly ground beans.

The first thing she noticed, however, once she had closed the door behind her, was the absence of all sound.

"Mother?" she called curiously.

Only the stark incongruous silence answered her.

Stepping past the foyer into the living room, she saw that her mother, wherever she was, must have been doing her spring cleaning. Long-forgotten drawings, toys, and padds from Kathryn's childhood were strewn about amid half-packed boxes and plastic storage bins.

As she moved toward a box that was overflowing with soft plush animals, her face broke into a wide grin of reminiscence. She pulled from the pile a small green and purple mouse she had once named Sneakers. A favorite toy, it had been a gift from her father when she was four . . . perhaps five years old. For many months, Sneakers had accompanied her everywhere, perching at her small desk while she played basic math games on her padd, sitting on her shoulder while she read her first stories, and nestled into the crook of her arm when she curled into a ball of sleep at night.

The flood of pleasant memories was overwhelming. Turning toward the bay windows that lined the back of the room, she called again, "Mother, where are you?"

But again, there was no answer.

Instead, the panes of the window began to shimmer. Indiana summers could be ruthlessly hot, and on many occasions, seated beneath one of the shade trees in the backyard, Kathryn had watched fascinated as the heat rising from the earth became visible in flowing waves.

But the windows weren't the only things shimmering with heat. Turning to the closed doors that separated the living room from her father's study, she saw a small figure emerge from the doors before her. Though at first glance it seemed that this delicate being had walked through the doors from the study, Kathryn was certain that somehow it had once been part of the door. How it had freed itself, she could not imagine.

Kathryn's first assumption was that this was a little girl. The figure had long, flowing locks of silver and blue hair, flecked with tiny sparks that reflected light in all directions. But there was a decidedly masculine character to the child's face, and its soft gray smock betrayed nothing of its gender.

The child said nothing, only gazed contentedly at her with its solemn little eyes.

"Who are you?" Kathryn asked with friendly curiosity.

The child opened her mouth to speak, but the sounds that flew forth were an incoherent babble that Kathryn could make no sense of.

Undeterred, she tried another question.

"What are you doing here?"

Kathryn didn't know whether or not she was more surprised by the fact that when the child spoke again she could understand the words perfectly, or by the words themselves.

"I am holding up the doors."

Kathryn started to smile.

"Why would you do that?"

"What else is there for me to do?" the child replied.

Kathryn looked around the room, considering the multitude of childhood riches that sat before her.

"We have lots of toys. Would you like something to play with?" she asked.

The child looked about, and said, "I should really stay here and hold up the doors."

"Don't you ever play?" Kathryn persisted. "Here," she continued, holding Sneakers out to within the child's reach, "this mouse is one of my favorites. His name is Sneakers . . . why don't you play with him?"

The child cocked her head, considering the stuffed mouse. There was no innocent mischief in her eyes, only a cold calculating consideration that was too adult to belong on the small face.

"Go ahead," Kathryn urged gently. "We can play together if you like."

The child reached for the toy, and in a flash it was pulled from Kathryn's hand on an invisible thread and landed firmly in the child's arms. She petted it lovingly for a moment as Kathryn smiled. Then her head cocked to the side again in that strange quizzical fashion, and suddenly Sneakers was alive. Held in the child's firm grasp, a purple and green mouse nestled and burrowed, his whiskered nose sniffing the air greedily.

The child mimicked him, and to Kathryn's surprise she saw tiny whiskers sprouting from the child's cheeks at the base of its nose. The plain gray smock was streaked with wide swaths of purple and green, bleeding into existence as if they were sucked from Sneakers's flesh.

Then the child began to laugh.

If Kathryn had ever found laughter comforting or pleasant, those memories were blotted out as the eerie, shrieking laughter of the child echoed through the house.

Kathryn took an involuntary step back, suddenly feeling the urgent necessity of putting as much distance as possible between herself and the strange laughing creature. Her foot met something solid behind her. Turning, she saw another child reaching out to her.

This one was definitely more feminine than the first. Long jet black hair was coiled atop her head in dozens of looping curls, and her face was painted with bright streaks of silver and gold.

The girl reached past Kathryn and grabbed several wooden blocks painted with the letters of the alphabet and single-digit numbers. As Kathryn watched in alarm, the symbols on the blocks unhinged themselves at the girl's touch and rose in the air above her head, flying about the room. For a moment, Kathryn saw complicated equations forming and re-forming, but within seconds she could make no sense of the strange girl's game.

The mouse-child was still laughing, scurrying about the room on all fours, chasing Sneakers around, and in the process knocking over anything and everything in her path.

Instantly, there were children everywhere. Some emerged from thin air, others climbed out of the cushions of the sofa or the folds of the drapes her mother had made, others pulled themselves from the half-empty boxes and bins.

Each child had its own color and look. And each was as different as the elements. Some, like the first child, took on vague characteristics of the items they touched. Others blended and melted into one another as they found an object of mutual interest and struggled with one another to gain full ownership of it.

Within moments, Kathryn was standing in the midst of one of her worst nightmares. Many years ago, her sister had taken a position at a children's summer camp, and on a short break from the Academy, Kathryn had visited her sister there and watched with a firm sense of her own deficiencies as Phoebe had gamboled and tumbled with her young charges in an open field on a hot summer afternoon. She had understood instinctively that while children could be adorable and magical in their way, she was not constituted for their care. Phoebe had taken such delight in their games, while Kathryn's gut had cried out to impose some sort of order and discipline on their unstructured play.

What had been her mother's beautiful and cozy living room was now a full-fledged disaster site. The strange children were everywhere. Kathryn could not have cut a path through them even if she had wanted to. Finally, in a moment of desperate frustration, she cried out at the top of her lungs.

"STOP!"

For a moment there was silence as hundreds of curious eyes turned on her, waiting for her next command.

"You can't play like this in here," she said, tenuously grasping for a shred of control.

"Why not?" the silver-haired mouse-child asked.

"Because you are ruining everything," Kathryn replied automatically. She had no idea where her mother was, but when she returned and found her living room, Kathryn was going to have a lot of explaining to do.

"Where else should we play?" another asked.

"This is our home," a third chimed in.

"We like your toys," another called.

Janeway raised her hands to silence them. "Then take the toys and go outside."

"Where?" the mouse-child asked.

Turning to the windows Kathryn saw that what had been a tranquil afternoon beyond them was now a vast starless night.

Part of her felt a twinge of regret at sending the children out into the night, but the larger part knew instinctively that if she didn't act fast, the house would be torn from its foundation and pulled apart by their wild, unruly play.

"Outside," Kathryn said again, pointing at the front door behind her, adding, "NOW!" in a voice that left no room for argument.

The heads turned toward the door, and in a flood the children were taking their toys and rushing through the door. What had been a standard-sized door frame was ripped from its casing as they poured through.

Kathryn had expected that once they were gone, she would find herself again in the silence of her mother's living room. But as the last child rushed out into the warm Indiana night, she saw a soft light resting on the porch. The light bounced and vibrated, pausing at what had been the doorway, and after a moment rose from the porch and flew into the house. It came toward Kathryn, who instinctively raised her hands to shield her eyes from its unearthly brightness, circled her a few times, then darted past her, crashing into lamps, skewing pictures from the wall, and finally bursting through one of the bay windows and disappearing into the darkness.

Turning back to what had been the front door, Janeway saw dozens of similar lights floating toward her. Though she couldn't put her finger on exactly why, their approach filled her with an overwhelming sense of dread. Somehow she knew how wrong this was, yet the glowing balls kept coming.

Suddenly, Phoebe stood beside her. In a rush of memory, Kathryn realized that this could not be her mother's home. She was trapped in the Delta Quadrant, and this being who looked like her sister was, at best, a tour guide from hell.

"What is this?" Kathryn demanded, still shaking from her encounter with the children.

"This was our home," Phoebe replied sadly.

"No, Phoebe . . . or whoever you are . . . this was my home."

"As I told you before, Kathryn, I can only show you our truth within a context you will understand."

"Who were those . . . children?" Kathryn asked, wondering at her reluctance to call them the monsters she truly believed them to be.

"They are the beginning," Phoebe replied, "the first and most basic particles. Some of your scientists have another word for them."

"What word is that?" Janeway asked, searching within herself for a semblance of the answer.

"The strings," Phoebe said.

Janeway paused.

The strings?

"Are you referring to string theory?" she asked.

"You begin to understand some of your limitations," Phoebe congratulated her. "What you still call a theory is practical truth for us."

Janeway's mind reeled. She had, of course, studied string theory, along with fifty other equally plausible treatises on the nature of the universe. Though never proven, there were a number of serious and respected scientists who were pursuing it as the definitive answer to the question that had, thus far, eluded the best minds of the Federation: What is the exact structure, design, and function of the fabric of space and time?

Apparently the Nacene were no longer wrestling with this question.

"So you have proven that the strings are real?" Janeway asked. "You can actually perceive them?"

"Proof . . . belief . . . they are irrelevant. We know them, Kathryn," Phoebe replied. "And as with all things we know, we wanted them to be of us. Unfortunately, we made the same mistake you just did."

"What mistake was that?" Kathryn asked, truly curious.

"We engaged them, and tried to control them."

In a flash, Janeway had at least a part of the picture clear in her mind.

"You did what?" she asked incredulous.

"Can you blame us?" Phoebe said disdainfully. "You did the same thing. You understand where the impulse came from. It lives in you as well."

Kathryn took a moment to consider this. She vividly remembered her childhood, the early years spent exploring the mysteries of words and numbers, slowly learning to control and manipulate them. She remembered the thrill of each new piece of knowledge that came within her grasp, how she had longed for it, and her voracious hunger for more . . . always more.

If this was the truth Phoebe was trying to impart to her, it was certainly one to which she could relate.

"What happened to the strings?" she finally asked.

"They did what they are meant to do," Phoebe replied. "And then they did all manner of things that we never expected. They led us from our home, and in doing so, unbalanced everything."

Janeway looked about the disaster area that had once been her mother's living room. She recognized this place as the only true home she had ever known, and felt a surge of pain and anger at its senseless wreckage.

"The flashes of light . . . the things that were beneath the elements and atoms I saw before . . . those are the strings?" Janeway asked.

Phoebe nodded.

"Were they part of our universe before you let them loose?"

"They are that which binds all of the universe together. They sustain all that is, when they are functioning properly."

"And now they are completely out of control?" Janeway asked.

"No," Phoebe said. "Controlling them is not the problem for us that it is for you."

"Then what is the problem?"

"The imbalance," Phoebe replied.

"I don't understand."

"Of course you don't," Phoebe said sadly. "But you will."

Though Janeway knew she must continue in her "education," she felt a tingling of doubt and fear as Phoebe took her hand and led her through the splintered front door frame into the darkness.

Harry and B'Elanna stood before the interface console in the holographic research lab and examined their handiwork. Once the ion sweep had been successfully completed, several security personnel had been ordered to monitor every move the multiphasic creatures made, and for the time being, it seemed they were content to leave *Voyager* alone. With little else to do to shore up the ship's defenses, B'Elanna had joined Harry as he put the final touches on the holomatrix he had been assigned to develop.

They had successfully created a hologram of a Monorhan male *haran* of average size and weight, dressed in a light tunic and pants that were appropriate to Monorha fifty years ago. The holobuffer reserved for personal data and activity subroutines was large enough to contain as much information as a Monorhan brain could hold but for the time being was empty.

The basic image had been taken from *Voyager*'s transporter logs, but they had both gone to great lengths to adjust the physical parameters so that their creation was not an exact duplicate of any of the Monorhans who had briefly boarded the ship. Though the distinctions in eye color, size, and shape, mingled with the length of elongated jaw and neck, were in some senses "typical" Monorhan features, their intention had been to create a physical frame for the consciousness that would be as neutral as possible. The only gender-specific characteristic was the absence of the interior arms that were present only in female Monorhans.

A small frame holding five of *Voyager*'s spare gel packs linked through bioneural interfaces had been completed.

Both the "bait" and the "trap" were set.

"I think we're ready," Harry observed.

"Ready as we'll ever be," B'Elanna added, tapping her combadge.

"B'Elanna to Seven of Nine."

Seven stood on what she had termed the "bridge" of the *Betasis*. It was the large room she and B'Elanna had discov-

ered earlier that seemed, in structure and design, central to
the ship's functioning. The viewscreen where B'Elanna
had first seen Assylia's disturbing transmission was still
active, but the image of the Monorhan commander was
frozen. Seven had considered deactivating it, but preferred to disturb as little as possible, given what she was
about to attempt.

The assimilation tubules located in the implant integrated into her left hand had been stocked with the modified nanoprobes, and she awaited B'Elanna's notification
that the holographic matrix was ready for transmission. In
the meantime she had relocated the pattern enhancers she
and B'Elanna had used to evacuate the ship on their first
away mission from the chamber below to the bridge. It
had been agreed that the moment the nanoprobes had
been dispersed into the neural network of the *Betasis,*
Seven would use the pattern enhancers to return to the
relative safety of *Voyager.*

Once she received B'Elanna's call, Seven wasted no
time. Positioning her left hand above the ship's main computer interface, she extended her assimilation tubules and
easily compromised the synthetic alloys of the surface of
the interface. Once she had breached the casing, she
searched gingerly for the appropriate links to the neural
network. Steeling herself to withstand the flood of anger
she had experienced in her first connection with the ship,
she connected herself to the neural network and released
the nanoprobes.

For a moment, nothing happened. Seven could not
sense the presence she had felt before, nor could she determine whether or not the nanoprobes were having any
effect.

Only when the soft pulsing lights throughout the ship
began to quicken, then race, did Seven sense the approach

of the entity. She immediately withdrew the tubules and stepped back, just as the console exploded. Retreating to the perimeter of the pattern enhancers she had set up near the only chair on the bridge, she watched as every power console in the room erupted in a fiery sparks.

A moment later, she materialized in *Voyager*'s transporter bay and hurried to join Harry and B'Elanna in the lab.

It took almost two minutes for Harry to detect the imminent approach of the consciousness. In order to transfer the synaptic patterns from the *Betasis* to the smaller neural network they had rigged, they had decided to utilize the data-transfer cable that still tethered *Voyager* to the array via the dataport located in the docking bay after discovering that the *Betasis* was linked to a similar port in its wrecked bay. The connection to the *Betasis* was barely functional, degraded by time and several fused circuits, but Seven had been able to confirm that it would suit their purposes. There would be a brief lag while the patterns were forced to move through the array's systems, but given that they could survive for any length of time only within a bioneural construct, Harry had anticipated that the transfer would still be fairly quick.

His hard work was initially rewarded when the miniature gel-pack network was flooded with luminescent particles. It seemed to take only a few seconds for the consciousness to accept the fact that there was not sufficient space within the gel packs for it to sustain itself, and then the mute Monorhan hologram standing before them showed its first signs of "life" by blinking its long-lashed eyelids.

Harry turned to B'Elanna and caught her premature smile of satisfaction. But the moment of success was cut short as the hologram raised its hands and looked at them closely, as if it were seeing them for the first time.

"It's all right," Harry said gently, approaching the hologram cautiously.

The hiss of the doors alerted him to the fact that Seven had joined them, but Harry stayed focused on the hologram, fully aware of how disorienting this process must be for the consciousness they had just trapped.

He vaguely heard Seven ask disdainfully "What have you done?" before the hologram looked on him with dark despair and began to wail and groan, the clicking of its secondary tongue thrashing against its lower palate indicating what Harry believed was imminent danger or distress.

As the hologram fell to its knees it began to tear at the skin of its face with the dulled claws that jutted from its fingers. Dark blue blood poured from the rents in its face as its pitiful cry echoed throughout the room.

"Computer, deactivate holomatrix," Seven ordered through the confusion.

As Harry turned on her, B'Elanna said sharply, "You can't do that!"

But Seven was working furiously, reconfiguring the physical parameters of the holomatrix. "There is no alternative," Seven chided her, undeterred.

"The synaptic patterns are destabilizing," B'Elanna warned as the gel-pack network began to glow. "The patterns are attempting to return along the same path, but the temporary neural network can't sustain them."

As if to prove her point, one of the gel packs burst, spewing its contents onto the workstation. The others were expanding quickly and within moments would also be ruined.

"Computer," Seven called, "activate holographic file Kim Monorhan interface beta."

Another Monorhan shimmered into view. It bore a vague resemblance to the neutral Monorhan Harry and B'Elanna had created. Harry didn't immediately register the significance of the alterations Seven had made, but he could see that B'Elanna recognized the new template immediately.

"That's Assylia," B'Elanna said softly.

"Who's Assylia?" Harry asked, but there was no time for B'Elanna or Seven to respond. A second gel pack exploded, and for a moment it seemed that the consciousness would rather face extinction than another experience in the holobuffer. Harry reasoned in a flash that either way their options were rapidly disintegrating and shut down the miniature neural network.

The revised hologram came again to life. But this time it was as if it sensed the change in its physical form and found it more curious than frightening.

Hoping that Seven's assumption had been right, Harry added a full-length mirror to the room and placed it before the Monorhan.

The hologram was again examining its arms and hands, running its eyes down the length of its body with wonder. When the mirror appeared, its elongated jaw dropped open and its eyes grew large. Only when it had extracted and extended its secondary arms and swallowed with visible relief did Harry start breathing again.

Finally, hiding its secondary arms within a pouch in the back of its cloak, it turned to Harry, Seven, and B'Elanna and said, "How is this possible?"

Harry smiled slightly, still disconcerted by their first failed attempt to integrate the consciousness with a holomatrix, and said, "We possess technology that allowed us to re-create your body using something we call a holomatrix."

"Who are you?" the hologram demanded haughtily.

"My name is Harry Kim, and this is the starship *Voyager.*"

She cast a questioning glance at Seven and B'Elanna and said, "I am Assylia, *rih-hara-tan* of the Fourteenth Tribe of Monorha and commander of the *Betasis.* I would speak to you in private, Commander Harry Kim."

B'Elanna couldn't help but snicker softly before tapping her combadge and saying, "Torres to Chakotay."

Assylia jumped slightly as Chakotay's disembodied voice echoed over the comm.

"Chakotay here."

"Report to the holographic lab immediately. There's someone here who wishes to speak with you."

"I'm on my way. Chakotay out," he replied.

Turning to Assylia, B'Elanna said, "Our commander will be here in a moment. I'm Lieutenant Torres, and this is Seven of Nine."

Assylia looked more closely at Seven and said, "I know you."

Raising herself to her full height, Seven replied, "We have interfaced once before."

"You invaded my ship," Assylia said, her serpentine neck extending upward until her eyes were level with Seven's.

"We were looking for information," B'Elanna interjected quickly. "We need your help."

"How many of your people have died, Lieutenant Torres?" Assylia asked.

"None . . . yet," B'Elanna replied.

"They will," Assylia said sadly. "It is only a matter of time."

Chapter 12

Tom's first step in analyzing the array's tetryon transport system was to confirm that his initial hypothesis—that what one thought before transport was relevant—was accurate. He was able to confirm it in a way that satisfied him, but had your typical Starfleet scientist been shown his methods or results Tom was certain he would have been laughed out of his uniform.

Once the creatures had been made visible he took the unauthorized but, in his opinion, absolutely necessary step of returning to the array to test the system in its own "home." Given the size of the station he was able to use the schematics to pinpoint locations which he was certain were devoid of life-forms and move freely between dozens of transport sites and *Voyager.* Up to that point, his premise held. As long as he focused intently upon his destination just prior to stepping into the line of alcoves, he ended up at the precise coordinates he imagined.

Step two had been to remove a pair of the mechanisms in its entirety from the array in order to attempt to integrate it into *Voyager*'s systems. As a team of engineers set to work rebuilding the pair of alcoves in the main shuttlebay,

Tom analyzed the scans of the transports to determine as best he could why the mechanism worked. It would have been enough for him to know that it did, but he was going to need more than theory to sell the first officer on the plan he was about to propose. He was going to need irrefutable proof that the device could be used safely.

Poring over the sensor data from the transports, he began to form a rough theoretical premise which was so simple, yet so beyond anything he had ever imagined possible, that he almost scrapped it entirely and gave up. He silently wished that B'Elanna could spare a few moments to help him with his analysis, but at the same time was certain that based on what he had, she would dismiss the project out of hand as altogether too dangerous to pursue.

Ensign Brooks approached and informed him that the system integration had been complete. One of the two necessary transporter alcoves had been embedded within a wall of the shuttlebay. The other alcove was placed five meters opposite it but connected to its mate by a series of fine, fragile cables. Tom had decided that for his next series of tests, he would re-create as best he could the operating parameters of the alcoves as they were set up on the array. Putting enough distance between the pair to accommodate a shuttle was a hurdle he would deal with later.

Tom was now free to test the transporter again, but there was one insurmountable problem. He didn't need to transport himself or any other individual within either the ship or the array. He needed to use the mechanism to transport objects, a probe and in the very near future a shuttle, using the tetryon technology, and no inanimate object could "think." Even he was unwilling to risk just strapping himself in and mentally focusing on his destination as the beam intersected the shuttle. As best he could tell, he would successfully be transported to whatever co-ordinates in space he chose, but if he arrived without his shuttle . . .

Tom was daring, not suicidal.

The first several probe tests were disastrous. He programmed a series of coordinates into the probe's navigational array that should have transported it to a stable position several hundred kilometers beyond the array, and each time the probe remained stationary within the transport mechanism. It went absolutely nowhere. The same held true for any inorganic substance he placed within the transporter's beam.

He had all but given up when Harry entered, flushed with excitement, to tell him they had successfully made contact with the Monorhan presence they had detected aboard the *Betasis*. Though Tom was obviously pleased for Harry—any success at this point brought all of them one step closer to getting off the array—he couldn't hide from Harry his frustration with his own project.

"So . . ." Harry began, after Tom had halfheartedly congratulated him on his work, "how's it coming down here?"

Tom shrugged, dejected. "Don't ask," he replied.

Harry looked about the shuttlebay and soon saw the fully functional tetryon transport station that had been set up. "Tom, this is amazing," he said, crossing to examine its operational parameters, adding, "I didn't think you'd be able to get this far."

"I did," Tom replied. "But thanks anyway for your vote of confidence."

"So what's the problem?" Harry asked.

"You want them in alphabetical order, or order of importance?" Tom answered.

Harry returned to Tom's side and placed a conciliatory hand on his best friend's shoulder.

"Look," he said, "I don't know about you, but I haven't had anything but a couple of stale nutrient bars in the last twenty-four hours. Why don't we head up to the mess hall, grab a quick bite, and see if we can put our heads together on this?"

Tom accepted the offer with a nod. He wasn't giving up, but he doubted that once Harry had seen his results, the by-the-book ensign wouldn't waste any time in telling him to scrap it.

They entered the mess hall engaged in a mild disagreement they had every time they ate together and either one or both of them had replicator rations to spare. On days like this, more than anything, Tom would have preferred to replicate a meal. Though he appreciated Neelix's efforts in the mess hall, there were times he simply couldn't face the Talaxian's cooking, and this was one of them. Harry still felt, even after almost four years in the Delta Quadrant, that as senior officers they were required to constantly set a good example for the rest of the crew, and that included eating, heartily and without complaint, anything Neelix chose to put in front of them.

Tom saw a good omen in the fact that once they arrived, they found several of their fellow crewmen eating replicated dinners. Given the enormous power transfer they had received the day before and the fact that Neelix was otherwise occupied, Chakotay had left a standing order that until further notice, the kitchen was to be closed and the replicators made available to all personnel, regardless of the number of replicator rations they had at their disposal.

As Harry, carrying a tray of grilled salmon over a bed of

sliced leola-root slaw, joined Tom and his double serving of macaroni and cheese, Tom stopped in midbite to ask, "Harry, what are you thinking? *Leola slaw?!?*"

"I like it," Harry replied defensively. "Now shut up and tell me what the problem is."

Tom continued shoveling food into his mouth. He hadn't realized until he started eating just how famished he was, and macaroni and cheese was the ultimate in comfort food.

"The problem is I understand the mechanics of how the tetryon transporter works, but what I can't figure out is why."

Harry thumbed through a padd filled with the preliminary test results. He paused, a forkful of salmon halfway to his mouth, when he reached the equations the computer had generated to show in mathematical terms exactly how the transporter worked.

"What's this 't' variable?" Harry asked.

"Thought," Tom replied simply.

"That's impossible."

"No it's not."

"Yes, it is."

"You have the results right in front of you, Harry!" Tom snapped, rising to replicate some fresh melon to follow his dinner.

Harry read and reread the equations before him. By the time Tom had returned to his seat, Harry had pushed the food in front of him away and begun to modify Tom's equations into something resembling reality as he knew it.

Finally he muttered, "Dazhat's Theorem."

"I beg your pardon," Tom replied.

"Dazhat was a Cardassian defector," Harry explained. "He gave a lecture at the Academy just before I graduated."

"How many people were in the audience?" Tom joked.

"Not many," Harry conceded. "He had spent most of his life studying the Breen."

"From a safe distance I hope," Tom interjected.

"The Breen use organic ships, and are capable of achieving warplike fields without antimatter. He was relegated to a minor role in the Cardassian scientific community because all they were interested in were the weapons that were attached to the ships, but Dazhat believed that the ultimate strength and greatest vulnerability of the Breen might lie in their reliance on the organic component of their ships' navigation and propulsion systems."

"And this has exactly what to do with . . ." Tom began to ask.

"Dazhat detected traces of tetryon particles in the wake of Breen ships going into their version of warp. The Federation has never delved too deeply into the use of tetryon particles because they are so unstable. Dazhat believed that the instability was a result of the interaction between space and time in the presence of tetryons. It wasn't that the tetryons were unstable, it was that they made space-time unstable."

For the first time since Harry had mentioned the name Dazhat, Tom was intrigued.

"In concentrated quantities, tetryons actually created curves in space-time reality. The Breen ships weren't actually moving through space, or subspace as we do. Their propulsion system actually bent space. No one has ever been able to prove this, but his analysis showed that it was theoretically possible."

"You think these transporters are bending space?" Tom asked.

"I do. And I know why your inorganic experiments aren't working."

Now it was Tom's turn to push his plate of food away.

"Monorhan space can't be bent to accommodate the tetryon field. We can't even create a stable warp field in this system. The array seems to be immune to the system's anomalies, and as long as *Voyager* is aboard the array, the space inside our ship is too. But no matter how many times you try, you aren't going to be able to use the array's alcoves to transport anything from this ship into Monorhan space."

"But beyond Monorhan space . . ." Tom began.

"Exactly," Harry finished his thought.

"But how do we teach a probe to think?" Tom went on. "Even if we can transport something outside the system and track it on our sensors, we still aren't past the '*t*' factor."

"Yes, we are," Harry said rising. "Come on. I'll show you."

Harry and Tom returned to the shuttlebay. Less than twenty minutes later, with a little help from B'Elanna, they had completed their first successful probe transport.

Assylia's first request after her introduction to Chakotay was that they speak privately. After instructing Seven to create a holographic seating area filled with the low cushions the Monorhans preferred, Chakotay dismissed the other officers and joined the *rih-hara-tan* in what was for him an extremely uncomfortable half-squatting position on the pillows. Chakotay was relieved to see that she seemed content and surprisingly at ease as she began to pepper him with questions. Although he did not immediately warm to her, her carriage and demeanor demanded that he respect her right off the bat.

"How did this vessel discover the space city?" was her first question.

"One of our crewmen left the ship while we were in

orbit around Monorha. He did not explain his actions and we were forced to follow him. His trail ended here," he answered honestly.

"Are all of your crewmen so undisciplined?" she asked, adding a faint click of her tongue which Chakotay interpreted as disdain.

"They are not," he replied quickly. "His actions were out of character and cause for great concern. We believed then, as now, that he might have received a telepathic communication from someone or something aboard the array."

Assylia sighed deeply. Chakotay sensed regret.

"*They* called to him," she said with emphasis. "*They* have led you all to your death."

"*They* being the parasites that attacked your people?" Chakotay asked.

"No. *They* are not the parasites. I know of whom you are speaking. *They* may be the parasites' keepers . . . I do not know. In the years that have passed since my people were annihilated I have sensed their presence. I have lived in constant awareness of them. Their pain is all-consuming. Their desires are insatiable. Like the parasites, they are of this place, but they are not the primary danger you are facing, nor is your crewman the first *they* have called to. He is merely the first that answered, and I assure you, you will die regretting his choice."

"For the moment we appear to be safe," Chakotay said simply. "Our sensors have detected thousands of creatures which we assume are the parasites you spoke of. We chose to try and free your consciousness from your ship in hopes that you might be able to tell us something more about them, as well as anything you might know about an object called the Key to Gremadia."

Assylia's eyes widened as a series of sharp clicks echoed

through the room. "You have discovered the Key?" she asked with awe.

"It was given to us by your people," he replied.

"That is impossible!" she stormed, rising from her seat and beginning to pace. "The Key was lost generations ago. And no Monorhan would have given you something which is so precious to us."

With as much humility as possible, Chakotay explained their first encounter with the Monorhans and the lengths to which he and the crew had gone to save the planet from imminent destruction. His story ended with the presentation of the Key to Captain Janeway.

"They were fools," Assylia stated flatly, once his story was done. "The Key has meaning only for my people, and those we left behind had no right . . ."

"Kaytok seemed sincere," Chakotay interjected. "He believed he had seen a real vision of his grandfather, Gora."

"Gora died, just like all the others," Assylia said menacingly. "And the Key was not Kaytok's to give."

Chakotay silently wondered whether or not Assylia's cooperation might hinge on the return of the Key to its rightful owners, but hesitated to offer it, even as a conciliatory gesture, until the potential Nacene connection could be verified. As far as their enemies went, Chakotay still believed that the Nacene posed a greater threat than Assylia for the time being.

"What is the Key's significance?" he asked.

"That depends entirely upon who you ask," she replied.

"At the moment, I'm asking you," Chakotay said diplomatically.

"The Key was a gift from the Blessed All-Knowing Light to His true followers. The *haran* who discovered it was given wisdom beyond that of any Monorhan who had come before or since. Dagan was a prophet who told us the truth about our God."

"What truth was that?"

"That the Blessed All-Knowing Light was not alone. That He did not create Monorha and fill it with life so that we could simply honor and revere His name. The All-Knowing Light created Monorha so that those who rose to life on its surface could join Him in His battle with those who oppose life and help Him overcome them."

"As I understand your history, that was a difficult concept for most of your people to accept," Chakotay offered.

"It was. The members of my tribe were ridiculed and then punished for holding to that belief. But the All-Knowing Light foresaw our struggle. He created a place for us between the stars where His true followers would find Him."

"Gremadia?" Chakotay asked.

Assylia nodded.

"And do you believe you found that place?"

"Of course not," she hissed. "In the dark days that followed our discovery of this station I came to believe that perhaps the others were right and that Dagan was, at best, insane."

"What is the purpose of the Key to Gremadia, and why did you leave it behind when you left the planet?" Chakotay asked.

"Dagan wrote of a conduit of light which the Key would unlock. This would mark the beginning of the final battle between the Blessed All-Knowing Light and the Others. Although we based our faith on Dagan's visions, we were never naive enough to take every word he said in a literal sense. The Key was lost to my people hundreds of years ago. We assume that the light he spoke of was the light of truth. The Key had unlocked the true vision of our people and our destiny which should have been Gremadia. But we have failed our God. We did not find Gremadia."

"Are you certain?" Chakotay asked gently.

"You know what became of my people," Assylia said with barely concealed contempt. "If this place were the promised city, our All-Knowing Light would never have allowed any harm to come to us while we were here."

Chakotay hesitated to reply. He had his own theories about Assylia's All-Knowing Light and how the array might fit into their mythology, but he hesitated to provoke her further.

"I'm sorry for your suffering," he said simply. "It is the most difficult thing imaginable to lose lives that have been entrusted to your care."

"If that is true, why did you not heed my warning?"

"Our captain has disappeared. We believe she has been taken by a life-form which has a specific interest in this array and the Key. Unless we can determine what that interest is, we may never find her."

"It is only a matter of time until the parasites find and attack you. Your captain would, no doubt, gladly sacrifice her own life for the safety of her people."

"You are right," Chakotay nodded. "But we will not abandon her without the certainty that she is beyond our help."

"If she boarded the array, the parasites have undoubtedly found her already," Assylia said. "For all you know this creature that took your captain might control the parasites. It might be in league with the presence that called your crewman here."

"Several of our officers have boarded the array over the last two days. Only one, the first to arrive, has been infected by a parasite," he replied. "I have seen one of the parasites myself. I do not doubt their hostility. But our officer who was attacked had psionic abilities, similar to those of your people. I believe this may have some significance. Otherwise it is inconceivable to me that all of the parasites we have detected have not already attacked this ship."

Assylia considered his words. After a moment, she said, "What did the creature you saw look like?"

Chakotay struggled to find words Assylia could relate to. *Hideous butterfly* came to mind, but he didn't know what the universal translator would make of that.

"The creature floated on several pairs of ragged wings. When it began to attack, a small set of pincers emerged from behind it. I hardly saw its face. I believe it was humanoid, but devoid of any compassion or beauty," he finally finished.

"That was not a parasite," Assylia replied flatly.

"Then what was it?" Chakotay asked.

"I do not know," she replied honestly.

"What do the parasites look like?" Chakotay asked.

A series of clicks and pops accompanied Assylia's next words. "They were small, wormlike . . . does that . . . ? "

"Go on," he urged.

"We found them in a large spherical sack, suspended within a biological preserve."

Chakotay shivered as he remembered the huge room he had discovered and the torn sphere still suspended within it.

"Did you disturb the sack in any way?" he asked.

"Of course not," she replied. "I was not present when the sack was discovered, but I was told that the moment the first *hara* approached, the sack began to glow and pulsate. The parasites emerged and flew toward my people. They were ingested before anyone knew what had happened. The first died within moments."

Finally Assylia faced Chakotay squarely and said, "This discussion is irrelevant. I understand your choice to capture me in this body, but I have no intention of remaining here. You must return me to my ship so that any others who approach may be prevented from arriving, and you must take your ship and leave this place at once. If you release me from this form we may be able to help each other."

"How?" Chakotay asked.

"In all the years I have been trapped here, I have only desired one thing . . . to destroy the array. You could help me do that," she said venomously.

A new thought struck Chakotay as she said this.

"When we attempted to board the array, we were almost pulled into the gravity well of the singularity. At the last moment, a tractor net pulled us safely into the array. Did you . . . ?"

Assylia's jaw retracted in a slight grin. "I have lived for fifty years within the organic components of my ship. In that time I have learned to exert my will on the controls of this station through the data-interface cable that connects my ship to the station. I sensed your approach and disabled the station's guidance system. *They* reactivated it at the last second and brought you aboard. I bear you no ill will, Chakotay. I would only have spared you the fate I suffered. At least your death would have been quick and painless."

Chakotay's jaw tensed as he became fully aware of the lengths Assylia would go to achieve her warped ends. He pitied her. No one could have endured what she had without suffering from serious mental instability. By giving her this new "life" he suddenly wondered whether or not he had placed *Voyager* in even greater danger than they were already facing.

"Computer," he called, before she could say another word, "freeze program."

Assylia stood before him, suspended in time.

"Computer, is there sufficient memory within the holobuffers to sustain every aspect of this hologram if the program is ended?"

"Affirmative."

Chakotay paused then said, "Computer, end program."

The Doctor examined his readings for the third time and concluded that if his plan was to have any chance of succeeding, he would have to act without further delay. The parasite had already compromised over sixty percent of Tuvok's central nervous system. The new life-form that was being created as a result of this merging now completely enveloped Tuvok's head, neck, and torso, and was growing larger with each hour that passed. Once the creature had been forced into a stable and visible phase, its progress had slowed a bit. The Doctor realized that the multiphasic nature of the organism was intrinsic to its development, though he was unsure exactly why. For the present, it was enough that the ion sweep initiated by B'Elanna had bought him more time to save Tuvok's life.

The separation protocol he had devised was as risky as any he had ever conceived. Under any other circumstance, he would have rejected it out of hand. But the bottom line was there were no other alternatives. Tuvok had not regained consciousness since his last attempt to lock out the Doctor's program, and it was doubtful that unless the transformation could be halted he would never awaken again. The levels of neural stimulation in his brain were beyond any he would have thought a humanoid could survive. The chemicals that regulated normal brain functions were being created and dispensed into his system at unimaginable rates, and surprisingly, if the most recent brain scans were any indication, at least part of Tuvok was thriving. The centers of the brain that controlled complex calculations and creative thought were functioning well beyond any quantifiable capacity. This alone might account for Tuvok's initial resistance to the Doctor's efforts. But the Doctor could clearly see that Tuvok was reaching a point where these functions would have to be taken over by the new life-form in order to be sustained. At that point, Tuvok's death would be inevitable.

Seven of Nine entered briskly and said, "You requested my presence?"

The Doctor verified that the neuropeptide infusion he had begun to replicate was almost complete before he replied, "Yes, Seven. Thank you. I will require competent support in order to initiate the separation protocol which I have devised, and you are the only member of this crew with sufficient dexterity to assist me."

Seven smiled faintly at the compliment. "Explain the procedure, and I will comply," she replied, joining him at the display station so that she could examine the readings as he spoke.

"The creature that initially infected Tuvok remains intact, and requires healthy neural tissue in order to sustain its transformation. I believe the only way to drive the creature from Tuvok's body is to make what little tissue had not yet been compromised less 'appetizing' to it."

Seven immediately understood the potential risks in what the Doctor was proposing.

"How do you intend to keep Lieutenant Tuvok stable

while you are effectively poisoning the rest of his neural tissue?"

"The creature seems to have adapted itself to a specific chemical balance within Tuvok's neural tissue. As it encroaches upon each new area, there is a significant decrease in neuropeptide levels. I believe that these neuropeptides might be harmful to it in large quantities, however, as they are appropriate to Tuvok's normal brain functioning, the tissue we are targeting should not be adversely affected in the long term. I am simply trying to distract the creature long enough to prevent it from attacking us as we slowly poison it."

"How do you intend to do that?" Seven asked.

"At the same time I am regulating Tuvok's neuropeptide levels, you will be introducing minute doses of the neural toxin we developed to counter the creatures we discovered aboard the array. I will need you to monitor those levels. If we move too quickly, the creature will undoubtedly try and defend itself. By attacking it slowly on two fronts it is my hope that we will render it unable to effectively counter either course."

"I understand. Are you ready to begin?" Seven asked.

The Doctor rechecked the simulations of the procedure one last time and nodded.

Moving to the biobed where Tuvok and the creature now rested, he raised the arch and studied the areas of unaffected neural tissue indicated on its display. He noted with an approving glance that Seven had already armed herself with a hypospray of the toxin to be injected into the creature and taken the position opposite him.

Their eyes met one last time and then, in concentrated silence, they began to work.

Initially, the procedure followed the exact course predicted by the simulations generated by the computer. Just

as the Doctor had anticipated, the parasite avoided all neural tissue where the Doctor had increased the neuropeptide levels. Its rate of expansion slowed by twenty . . .
fifty . . . and then almost eighty percent.

The toxin Seven was injecting directly into the creature seemed to have little effect. As the Doctor watched
the organism's cells absorb and integrate the poison she
was introducing into its system, it occurred to him that in
such small doses this particular formulation was unlikely
to seriously damage the creature.

Once the creature's expansion had been reduced to almost nothing, Seven slowly began to elevate her injection
levels. For a moment, the Doctor was intensely pleased to
see that the parasite did not seem to perceive the tissue he
had treated as a viable source of continued growth. Only
when Seven reached forty-five percent of maximum did
the procedure come to an abrupt halt.

A whip-thin appendage burst from its place just below
Tuvok's shoulder and sent Seven reeling. The Doctor
barely escaped the same fate, automatically reverting to a
permeable form before the tentacle aimed at him sliced
through the air.

As Seven recovered her balance and approached the
biobed more cautiously, the Doctor watched with per-
plexed alarm as the creature's growth rate began to expand
more rapidly than it had at any point thus far.

Several decks away, in engineering, Ensign Vorik, the only
other Vulcan member of *Voyager*'s crew, was busy calculating the actual event horizon of the singularity based upon
the course the ship had taken in boarding the array when a
searing pain arced from the top of his head down through
his chest. He immediately dropped the padd he had been
using and fell to his knees, then to his side, cradling his

head in both hands as Ensign Peterson called for an emergency medical transport.

Kathryn had always despised the rigid and uncomfortable testing facilities where Academy cadets reported quarterly for technical examinations. This was due in equal parts to the design and purpose of the rooms where the examinations were given. The inevitable anxiety that knotted within her each time she crossed the threshold to that room all but consumed her, no matter how well prepared she was for her tests.

Long benches with low desktops circled two-thirds of the room, arena-style. The distance between the cadet's seat and individual workspace was calculated to the specifications of each cadet's weight and body structure to provide maximum ergonomic support during the long and rigorous exams. Nonetheless, as the exams stretched into the sixth and, in some cases, seventh hour, Kathryn, like most of her fellow students, found herself hunched over, head resting on the desktop as she struggled to pry something resembling a coherent response from her lethargic and uncooperative brain.

Resigning herself to the task before her, Kathryn sat at attention and waited for the proctor to distribute the examination padds. An irritating creaking noise was coming from behind the podium where the proctor usually stood to announce the test section, and the room was filled to capacity with eager faces, but as Kathryn searched in vain for the source of the creaking, she realized that she did not recognize anyone else in the room. She toyed briefly with the possibility that she was in the wrong room. Perhaps she had found her way into a first- or second-year examination.

At that moment she realized that she had no business

being here. She had graduated from the Academy years ago.

Creak . . . creak . . .

That sound again. There was a slow, soothing rhythm to it, which did little to mitigate its grating tone.

Creak . . . creak . . . creak . . .

Kathryn rose from her station and craned her neck to look past the rather tall humanoid seated in front of her, but was unable to see beyond the podium to the source of the sound. She searched in vain for the small comm button embedded in each station to alert the proctor to the fact that a student had completed a section or required assistance. Frustrated, she was about to simply make her way down to the exit aisle when a padd and small holographic image of a Class-M planet appeared before her. Similar items materialized at each station, and rather than disrupt the others, she chose to resume her seat.

Though she was certain that she wasn't supposed to be taking this test, her curiosity got the better of her and she picked up the padd and began to read over its contents.

The series of equations that streamed across the padd were relatively simple. These were calculations that provided for the planet's density, gravity, and composition. With a sigh she decided that this had to be a first-year exam. But as she continued to read she saw that each successive equation was more complex than the last. The equations suggested that the planet was infinitely more than any single planet could possibly be. In its present form it existed, theoretically at least, in not three but seven different dimensions.

Eight.

No . . . nine . . .

Creak . . . creak . . .

Scrolling to the bottom of the padd, she struggled to

wrap her mind around the nature of the question being posed in the exam. As she didn't recognize the construction of most of the algorithms before her, this was an almost impossible task.

A subtle radiance caught her attention. Turning to her right, she saw that the cadet seated next to her had placed his hands around the holographic planet before him. Glancing at his padd, she watched the equations shift automatically as the planet grew brighter and brighter. Moments later she had to avert her eyes as the planet became a glowing ball of fire.

The cadet removed his hands and returned his attention to his padd, shaking his head. The moment his hands were gone, the planet returned to its natural—or, in this case, decidedly unnatural—form.

Creak . . . creak . . .

Turning from the cadet on her right, Kathryn studied the planets that were being manipulated by the rest of the cadets taking the test. Some of them glowed as the one on her right had done. Others were covered with sheets of ice. Some were several times smaller or larger than they should have been, and a few had left their static position on their respective workstations and were zinging around the room, crashing into one another and exploding in bursts, dissolving into liquefied masses, or being duplicated by factors of ten or more.

This was ridiculous. Apart from the fact that there was no obvious point to this exam that she could see, it didn't appear that any of the others were having better luck than she was.

Kathryn moved as gingerly as she could behind the seats of the others and made her way to the center aisle. From this vantage point she could see a wooden chair behind the podium. The chair had gently curved slats at its base which allowed the person seated to rock gently back and forth. Here at least was the source of the annoying creaking sound. But she could not see who was seated in the chair.

Striding briskly down the steps that separated her from the podium, she saw hands, hundreds of hands at the ends of hundreds of arms all attached to the same torso, moving almost quicker than her eye could perceive. Their motion was hurried without being frantic. As the hands moved, huge folds of fabric unfurled at the base of the chair.

Kathryn moved slowly around the edges of the fabric, which lapped toward her like waves carried in by a surging tide. She had to see the face of the one who was sewing this tapestry, which in no time at all, it seemed, would cover every square inch of the examination room.

Placing a gentle hand on the back of the chair, Kathryn stopped its movement. A head sat atop the torso. The hands continued their rapid work, but the head lifted slightly at Kathryn's touch. As it turned to face her, Kathryn saw that the oval area where she had expected to see some semblance of eyes, nose, and mouth was a void of blackness.

As she tried to take this in, a gruff voice spoke from the void.

"You can help me, or you can help them," it said. "You can't do both."

"What are they trying to do?" Kathryn asked.

"Solve the problem," the faceless face replied.

"But I don't see the problem," Kathryn said, her frustration mounting.

"Then you had best stay out of our way," the sewer replied, returning its attention to its work and resuming its rocking.

One of the planets came zooming toward her. Kathryn

caught it instinctively, as if it were a perfectly aimed hover-ball. The moment she touched it, an unexpected sense of power flowed through her. Suddenly, all of the equations on the padd were part of the fabric of her mind. She could see them in their infinite possibility and realized at once that this planet was not a planet at all.

This planet was her mind's representation of the entire universe, in dozens of different dimensions. She suddenly remembered Seven of Nine, standing before her in her ready room, exactly when she could not recall, describing a computer that could hold every quantifiable fact of all living and nonliving things in the galaxy. It had sounded like an impossibility at the time, but in this moment, her mind contained the processing power of that computer.

This universe was hers . . . to do with as she would.

She could not deny that she was tempted to play. The rest of the cadets seemed to be enjoying their work, and given the vast possibilities at her fingertips, she could hardly blame them. What would this universe look like if one removed all but ten dimensions? The fact that she could conceive of ten dimensions was dizzying, but as she thought it, she watched the planet begin to erupt violently, losing its spherical form in favor of an irregularly shaped mess.

"Stop that!" the gruff and ageless voice from the chair commanded. "You don't know what you're doing. None of them do."

"But . . ." Kathryn started to protest.

"Give it to me!"

And with that, the misshapen planet flew from Kathryn's hands, and with it went her ability to understand not only what she had been doing but why she had cared to do it at all. She watched, fascinated as the planet flew into the hands of the creature in the chair and evaporated into countless threads, which were busily woven into the ever-expanding tapestry.

Kathryn thought back.

The beginning.

The strings.

And now . . . the fabric of the universe.

She studied the tapestry more closely and realized that the edges crawling toward her were starting to fray. No matter how fast the creature in the chair sewed, it seemed some inevitable chaotic force was determined to unravel its work.

The imbalance.

"PHOEBE!" Kathryn shouted at the top of her lungs.

Phoebe rose from her position at one of the hundreds of workstations. Taking the steps that separated them two at a time, Kathryn rushed to her side.

"Are these your people?" the captain demanded.

"Yes," Phoebe nodded.

"And that thing in the chair?"

"It is also of us."

"What I did . . . with the planet . . . or what I thought I could do . . ." she stammered, struggling to find the right words.

"Is all within our grasp," Phoebe finished for her.

Kathryn didn't know which was worse, the ignorance or the arrogance she saw before her.

"And you are the Nacene?" Janeway asked.

"Before we opened the gateway, we did not understand that there were others. We did not call ourselves anything as there was no need to differentiate ourselves from any other sentient life-form. Only those who remain in your space-time construct understand that term as you do."

"This power you wield . . . you enjoy it?" Kathryn demanded.

"It is of us. It is what we do," Phoebe replied.

"But it is dangerous," Kathryn said slowly as if she were trying to explain quantum mechanics to a very small, very stupid child.

"To you, certainly," Phoebe said. "But we can undo what has been done."

Janeway remembered the Caretaker, the first Nacene she encountered. She remembered how he had dismissed her as a "minor bipedal species." Given what she now knew . . . what it was to be Nacene, she could hardly blame him. But she had never imagined hundreds or thousands like him, randomly experimenting with the fabric of space and time, matter and antimatter, life and death, *simply because they could.*

"Who is the Nacene in the chair?" Kathryn asked.

"They are the Others . . . the ones who locked themselves inside our former home when the gateway was closed."

"The gateway . . . ?" Janeway said, and as she did so, realized that Phoebe could be referring to only one thing . . . the entire artificially constructed Monorhan system.

Phoebe smiled, pleased at her pupil's progress.

"The gateway is no longer stable, is it?" Janeway thought aloud. "When we collapsed that star and the singularity was formed . . . the singularity that is growing larger by the microsecond . . . we broke something we didn't even know was there, didn't we?"

"You couldn't have known," Phoebe said. "What you experience as 'Monorhan space' is unstable in ways you do not fully comprehend. Its instability is now unacceptable. The initial imbalance was temporarily corrected by closing the gateway, but I, and many others, believed that the patch would not hold. Those, like me, who remained in your construct did so in an honest effort to solve this problem, and now we require your help."

Kathryn hated to rush to judgment, but based on what she had already seen, she had a hard time imagining herself helping Phoebe or her people do anything. The only being she had ever encountered with anything approaching their destructive capability was Q. But for all of his irritating arrogance, he had never done anything to her knowledge as massively careless as the Nacene.

Finally she asked, "Why must I help you?"

"Because you are the only one who can."

Chapter 13

Chakotay hadn't spent much time alone in the captain's ready room. Apart from her quarters, Kathryn had only this modest space off the bridge to call her own. Though most Starfleet captains serving aboard smaller Federation vessels made do with similar accomodations, *Voyager* had been designed with other amenities for the captain's exclusive use, including a private dining room, which had been sacrificed to the necessity of *Voyager*'s circumstances and become Neelix's kitchen. The uneasy first officer paced the area between the entrance and the windows, awaiting B'Elanna's arrival, and did his best to avoid even looking at the empty chair behind Kathryn's desk. She had disappeared over ten hours earlier, and though he was a long way from losing hope, every moment that passed without finding her, or even a solid lead as to where she might have gone, added to the weary burden he bore.

He respected Kathryn. She was a force of nature who had entered his heart four years earlier and taken up permanent residence. Her absolute certainty that *Voyager* and her crew would overcome all of the odds stacked against them and return to the Alpha Quadrant someday reinforced his faith and transformed his doubts to hope.

Without her . . .

He would do what he could and what he must. He would not dishonor her by failing to live up to her fierce and lofty expectations. But her loss would break his spirit in a way he would never be able to express . . . *to anyone but her.* He was not willing to even consider that possibility at the moment. Duty demanded that he push it from his mind until every alternative had been exhausted. The tightrope they had walked daily together since their journey home had begun was suspended above a pit of uncertainty, and Chakotay had always secretly suspected that the rope would snap without their unflinching mutual resolve.

His gaze strayed again to her empty desk. Despite the room's illumination, the faint blue light of the docking bay pouring through the room's observation windows cast a pulsating glow across its lonely surface that beat in rhythm with his heart. Each beat marked the distance between them, and with their inexorable passing pushed him closer to accepting the unacceptable.

A chiming at the door pulled him from these thoughts and he called, "Come in."

To his surprise, Neelix entered, asking, "Am I disturbing you, Commander?"

"Of course not," he replied. "Report."

"I have finished my study of the Monorhan documents we recovered, and there are a few things I felt I should bring to your attention."

"Certainly," Chakotay nodded. He remained standing, shifting his weight slightly from side to side.

Neelix could sense his discomfort, and, keeping his eyes fixed on Chakotay's face so as not to even suggest the loss that hung heavy between them by acknowledging the emptiness of the rest of the room, began to speak.

"I believe that the entity we came to know as 'Phoebe' may very well be related to the entity the Monorhans call their Blessed All-Knowing Light. At the very least, she . . . or they . . . will most likely be fighting on the same side of the battle that is to come."

"What battle?" Chakotay asked.

"Are you familiar with the Heresy of Gremadia, Commander?" Neelix asked.

"Of course," he replied. "That was the belief in the promised city called Gremadia . . . the belief that caused division between the Fourteenth Tribe and the other tribes of Monorha."

"That's almost right," Neelix said. "Had that belief been the only difference between the Fourteenth Tribe and the others, I don't believe the Fourteenth Tribe would have been so difficult for the rest of Monorha to accept."

"Explain," Chakotay said.

"The real problem with the heresy is not its assumption of the promised city. The problem is the suggestion that the Blessed All-Knowing Light, the one god worshipped by all Monorhans, would have had to build the city in the first place in order to do battle with other entities, or gods. You see, for most of Monorha, monotheism is an essential tenant of their faith."

"I see," Chakotay said.

"Dagan said that the All-Knowing Light would restore the 'harmony that was broken.' But that harmony could only be overcome at the end of a battle between the All-Knowing Light, and his followers, against some he called the Others."

"Are you suggesting that we have found ourselves in the middle of some kind of civil war?" Chakotay asked.

Neelix nodded. "I am, Commander. Naomi's description of Phoebe in her true form and the effect on the Caretaker's remains mean that Phoebe was probably Nacene. Just as the Caretaker unintentionally destroyed Ocampa and devoted the rest of his existence to compensating for that *broken harmony*, I believe the Nacene were also instrumental in damaging Monorhan space. There are too many properties to this system that do not obey natural laws. Ensign Kim was kind enough to explain in some detail the few that I could understand. But with the Caretaker and Suspiria, there was disagreement between them as to how to proceed once the harmony had been broken. The Caretaker remained aboard the array so that he could tend to the Ocampa. Suspiria took some of the Ocampa with her. Phoebe and the Blessed All-Knowing Light must have found themselves in a similar disagreement with these Others."

"But we don't know why Suspiria took . . ." Chakotay interrupted.

"Kes did," Neelix added.

This was news to Chakotay.

"Kes and I talked many times about her experiences while in contact with Suspiria. Though Suspiria was able to exponentially heighten the natural abilities that Kes and all of the Ocampa share, and that was alluring to her, Kes always believed that ultimately Suspiria's intentions toward her people were malevolent. Suspiria didn't care for her people, the way her mate did. She took them so that she could continue experimenting with them. Kes sensed a need for power and control in Suspiria that went far beyond the more nurturing, if misguided, efforts of the Caretaker."

"If what you're saying is correct," Chakotay said, "then one Nacene, or group of Nacene, may be functioning like the Caretaker, stabilizing Monorhan space, while the other, Phoebe and/or this All-Knowing Light, are working to undermine their efforts for their own ends."

"Which is where the Key comes in," Neelix added.

"How so?"

"The Key opens the conduit of light," Neelix continued.

"Assylia told me that her people believed that was merely a metaphor for the truth the Key revealed," Chakotay said.

"I think they might have been wrong about that," Neelix said. "Dagan does describe the mechanism where the Key fits and I have found something very similar to what he described aboard the array."

"Where?"

Neelix handed Chakotay a padd that showed a diagram of the mechanism's location. It took Chakotay only a moment to realize that the mechanism was centered at the base of the spore sack he had discovered aboard the array.

Neelix continued as Chakotay tried to work this piece into the puzzle. "According to Dagan, the 'owner' of the Key is the only one who can use it to unlock the conduit of light. This will destroy the boundary that separates the All-Knowing Light and his followers from the Others."

"So if the captain were to place the Key in this mechanism . . ." Chakotay began.

"And if the boundary that separates them is Monorhan space . . ." Neelix added.

"Then Phoebe and the Nacene who are with her will be forced to fight the battle with the Others who are trying to maintain this space," Chakotay finished.

"That's why she took the captain," Neelix said. "She has to keep the captain away from the Key and the lock."

"Why didn't she just kill her?" Chakotay wondered.

Neelix hesitated before he said, "If Seven was right about Dagan's death causing the changes in the Blue Eye, then it is possible that the captain's death might destabilize the system in a similar way. Perhaps Phoebe was trying to prevent that from happening. At any rate, we don't know the limits of the Nacene's abilities, but if this array is any indication, they go far beyond what we know of the Caretaker or Suspiria. Bottom line, Commander, if the captain is still alive, I doubt very much that Phoebe will ever return her to us."

Chakotay swallowed hard. Much as he hated to admit it, Neelix was probably right.

But even as the fragile shards of hope that he was clinging to began to slip from his grasp, Chakotay realized that he still had at least one final card to play in this game.

"What would happen if someone other than the captain placed the Key in its lock?" he asked.

Neelix paused to consider.

"I honestly don't know. Probably nothing," he replied.

"Or Phoebe might come back to stop us. If the captain is dead then the next person to touch it should be the new owner."

"I don't know, Commander . . ." Neelix said warily.

But Chakotay felt his spirits reviving as he continued. "If the captain is the only one that can use the Key, and we place it in the lock . . . it won't work. And we'll know she's still alive. If it works . . ."

"But won't that be worse . . . for all of us?" Neelix asked.

"I doubt very much that Phoebe will let us get that far," Chakotay said.

The door chimed again. Chakotay called, "Enter," and B'Elanna strode quickly into the room, Tom and Harry at her heels.

"Chakotay," she began without waiting for permission to speak, "you have to see this."

"What is it?" he asked, somewhat unwilling to be derailed from his present line of thinking.

"Tom and Harry . . ." she said before obviously realizing that in her enthusiasm she was stealing their thunder. She nodded to Tom, who was beaming from ear to ear.

"Lieutenant?" Chakotay directed at Tom.

"We've discovered how the tetryon transport system works," he said.

"Can we use it to leave the array safely?" Chakotay asked.

Things might be falling into place after all. If we can force Phoebe to return the captain, and we can use the array's transporters to leave . . .

Chakotay's mind was racing with new possibilities.

"No," Harry jumped in.

Chakotay looked between the three of them, crestfallen and curious as to why, based on this statement, they were all still smiling.

"Then what . . . ?" he said, at a loss.

"We can use it to get a lot farther than that," Harry said.

Tom stepped slightly forward. His bright blue eyes blazing, Tom finally made their enthusiasm clear for Chakotay.

"We can use it to get home, Commander."

Vorik felt better. As he rested on one of sickbay's empty biobeds, the crushing weight that had descended so suddenly upon his mind had begun to lift, thanks in large part to the neural inhibitor that the Doctor had placed on his forehead. The Doctor stood beside him, running a medical tricorder around his head and neck and clucking softly at the readings he was seeing.

Taking several slow, measured breaths, Vorik tried to remember exactly what he had been doing before the painful interruption . . . something about the singularity's event horizon . . .

Vorik.

The voice was in his mind. The shooting pain that had so recently brought him to his knees threatened to cripple him again as the Doctor stopped in midscan to ask, "What just happened, Ensign?"

"I don't know . . ." he managed through gritted teeth, clutching his head in both of his hands to keep it stabilized atop his neck.

"I'm detecting a drop in neuropeptide production in your limbic system," the Doctor said, attempting to hide his alarm.

The Doctor quickly coded a hypospray, and with a soft hiss the medication flowed from Vorik's neck directly into his bloodstream.

A few breaths later, Vorik again seemed calmer.

"Can you tell me when . . ." the Doctor began.

But Vorik couldn't hear him. This time, what entered his mind was a fragment of a memory. He was seated across from Tuvok in the mess hall, long after his duty shift had ended. They were playing *kal-toh*, a Vulcan strategy game where several small pieces were arranged to form a semblance of a sphere, but only the proper alignment of each piece in relation to the others would result in perfection. Tuvok was a master of the game. This particular match had taken place over several days and, if this moment was any indication, would take as many more as Vorik's dense brain would require. It wasn't that Tuvok was letting him win, though Vorik knew full well that had Tuvok so desired, their game would have ended within hours of its inception. This was meant to be instructional for the young Vulcan, an exercise in disciplined strategic thinking more than a test of the players' respective skills.

What differentiated this moment from his actual recollection of the game was that as he sat staring at the configuration of metal pieces, he could actually see the solutions.

All of them.

The complexity of the game lay partially in the fact that hundreds of different combinations could result in a victory. A skilled player could see several dozen steps ahead of any given move. Tuvok could probably see twice that many.

But when Vorik played, he was, invariably, making a best guess with each move.

Until now.

Somehow the precise order of nineteen moves that would lead to the quickest victory, no matter how Tuvok chose to counter, was as clear to him as any text on a padd. Fifty variations that would draw the game out longer but lead to the same conclusion were also vividly playing out in his mind.

What was overwhelming about this experience was the absolute peace that accompanied the certainty which consumed him. It was unlike anything he had ever known before.

Vorik.

The voice again.

This time Vorik knew it was Tuvok's voice.

Turning his head slightly to the right, he saw Tuvok lying behind the forcefield, a mass of pulsing tentacles obscuring most of his body. But Tuvok . . . whole and separate from the entity that was joining with him . . . was still an individual apart from that creature.

And Tuvok needed him.

Over the Doctor's strenuous objections, Vorik sat abruptly up and crossed to the forcefield.

"You must allow me to pass," he said with a soft urgency.

"I'm afraid that's impossible, Ensign," the Doctor replied. "Now kindly return to your biobed. You may be in serious danger . . ."

With uncharacteristic rage, Vorik slapped his hand against the forcefield. Willing himself to endure the pain as his fingers began to fry, he stared hard at the Doctor, who called within seconds, "Computer, lower the forcefield around station one."

Without another glance, Vorik moved to the head of the bed and gingerly placed his hands on what little flesh of Tuvok's face remained visible.

"Ensign, what are you . . . ?" the Doctor stammered, fully aware that he was not in control of this moment but somehow flabbergasted just the same at how quickly the worm had turned.

"My mind to your mind," Vorik said softly, initiating the mind-meld that he somehow knew would be Tuvok's last link to the living world. "My thoughts to your . . ."

But before he could complete the last word . . . *thoughts* . . . the meld took him and he returned to the state of peace and harmony that he had never before known.

The Doctor stood by, virtually helpless. True, he could have overpowered Vorik had he chosen and forced him to comply with his wishes. He was not a huge fan of mind-melds in theory or practice, though he had to acknowledge that this skill had come in handy on a few occasions in his practice aboard *Voyager*.

But the simple fact of the matter was that he had run

out of options for treating Tuvok. The creature would be fully formed in a few hours, perhaps less. Tuvok was about to die, and there was nothing . . . absolutely nothing . . . that he could do about it unless Tuvok stopped resisting his only treatment option. He allowed himself to nurture a silent hope that whatever Vorik was doing might somehow bring Tuvok to his senses. After his last disastrous attempt to separate Tuvok from the creature, he had been forced to conclude that the cause of his failure had been Tuvok himself. He did not want to be cured. He had indicated in every way imaginable from the moment he had been brought back on board that he wanted this transformation to happen. At the very least, should Vorik succeed, he might gain some insight into Tuvok's thoughts. The Doctor had faced failure of this magnitude on precious few occasions and didn't like to admit to himself that he hesitated to stop Vorik because the attempt was the lesser of all evils he was currently facing.

Vorik stood perfectly still, his eyes closed, his head lifted slightly. The Doctor thought he saw the faintest hint of a smile playing across the ensign's face, but that seemed unlikely. Vorik reminded him of nothing so much as himself, when he stood alone in his sickbay on a quiet morning listening to Mozart or Puccini.

Moments later, Vorik nodded his head, still entranced. He did not open his eyes until he had removed his hands from Tuvok's face, but when he did, they burned with a fire he had seen only once before in the ensign, a tempestuous passion that could have been mistaken by a less experienced hologram for the onset of the *Pon farr*.

"I have been asked to relay two messages, Doctor," Vorik said evenly, his calm, cold voice bringing the more typical mask of Vulcan restraint over the rest of his face.

"By all means," the Doctor replied, not bothering to hide his annoyance.

"Tuvok intends to complete this transformation. He does not wish you to take any further steps to prevent it."

"*That's* the message?" the Doctor said pointedly. "Was there anything else? Perhaps something I hadn't already intuited from Tuvok's behavior over the past ten hours?"

"You will not understand," Vorik replied, crossing to the Doctor and gazing at him with something that resembled pity.

"Try me, Ensign."

"Are you familiar with the Vulcan principle of the *Kol-ut-shan*?" he asked.

"It means infinite diversity in infinite combinations," the Doctor answered matter-of-factly. "For most Vulcans it is a philosophical concept or a focus for meditation. However, I believe that there are certain Vulcan . . . what would be the word. . . . *mystics*. . . . who have gone so far as to suggest that it is also a state of being which a Vulcan may aspire to. Of course this experiential *Kol-ut-shan* is practically impossible to achieve, not unlike a human mystic achieving Nirvana, or the Questran notion of *Slou-mantica*."

Vorik's next words were difficult for the Doctor to accept, despite the uncharacteristic passion that burned behind the young Vulcan's eyes as he said them. "Once the transformation is complete, Tuvok will live as one with the new life-form that is gestating within him. In this state he will achieve *Kol-ut-shan*. What is happening to Tuvok is a gift. It is not something any Vulcan would willingly refuse."

"Does he also understand that his body will die? What use is it to experience infinite diversity in infinite combinations if one won't be around long enough to enjoy it?"

"But he will," Vorik replied, the light flaming again in his eyes. "The man we have known as Tuvok will die, but his *katra,* his essence, all that makes him truly what he is, will survive. We will suffer, but he will never again know the torment of life . . . only its possibilities."

The Doctor frowned.

Vorik's words painted a pretty picture. What he described was something akin to the fulfillment of his most secret desire to actually become human. But he could not believe such a thing was really possible.

"That is comforting to know, Ensign," he finally replied. "Especially since there is precious little I can to do prevent it." Tossing his tricorder on the workstation, he was about to raise the forcefield again when it occurred to him to ask, "What was the second message?"

"Before his body dies, Tuvok wishes to speak to someone called Assylia."

Janeway stood on a gently sloping rise above a dimly lit plain. The field below was awash with chaotic activity. It was a battle. That was easy enough to see. The two opposing sides appeared to be equally matched. The dying lay strewn about like discarded playthings.

She turned to see Phoebe standing beside her.

There were a thousand questions she wanted to ask.

What was this place?

How did this moment fit into the picture that was coming dimly into focus, the image of the Nacene, fighting among themselves to find the solution to the problem posed by the strings?

She wondered whether or not this struggle was still ongoing, until a deeper fear struck her.

Perhaps this was a vision not of the past, but of the future . . . a future in which she now had a hand to play.

A flutter of motion caught Janeway's eye. Turning to look over her shoulder, she saw a vast army arrayed behind Phoebe, standing on the rise, watching the battle below, just as she was. She recognized some of them . . . which was to say, she recognized their species. Among the throng were Hirogen, Borg, Ocampa, Illiderians . . . almost every race she had encountered in her voyage through the Delta Quadrant, and countless others she could not name.

One of them who vaguely resembled a Monorhan male pushed his way through the throng, and called to those assembled in a commanding voice, "Where will you stand?"

The assembly stared blankly at him. It was as if they were all certain that to enter the fray unleashed on the field was certain death, and though they clearly had a stake in the outcome, they were unwilling to sacrifice themselves to assure their victory.

"We are one!" the Monorhan cried again. "We have experienced life beyond time and know now that our infinite existence was still too small. The Others will force you to choose between slavery and exile. I would make another choice, here and now. I would choose victory!"

Janeway felt her heart rise to the call of this stranger's words. Though she had no obvious personal stake in the outcome of this battle, the force of his passions called out to her to stand with him and face death rather than shrink from this fight.

But the faces of the listeners did not flame with the same passion Janeway felt surging within her. It was difficult to place a single name on so many disparate and alien expressions, but the best description that came to Janeway's mind was *pity*.

Turning his back to the others in defiance, the valiant and doomed speaker ran to the edge of the cliff and leaped.

Though from this height Janeway could only assume that he had already met a violent death when he fell to the ground below, moments later she saw him clearly join the battle.

Finally it dawned on her that, like Phoebe, these must all be Nacene who had taken other forms. In their more "natural" state, they appeared as flowing masses of translucent energy like the thousands who were engaging one another on the field below.

In a flash of light, something shot upward from amid the Nacene assembled behind Janeway, and took flight into the sky. It was a strange sight, a star rising with the same speed it might have fallen from the heavens. Moments later, other members of the crowd began to follow. For a dazzling minute, the sky was filled with their beautiful exodus. Many of those on the battlefield turned to witness the spectacle. Once the last had fled, the battle was resumed, though it seemed to Janeway that this desertion had given one side energy and enthusiasm to pursue their ends that had been absent in the more evenly matched battle that had been waged moments before.

Janeway and Phoebe were alone upon the rise.

"Why didn't they follow him into battle?" Janeway demanded.

"We were afraid," Phoebe replied simply. "We wanted to live. . . . to explore . . . it is our nature. We did not understand that this was our moment. In Exosia, time does not force us to make such choices."

Exosia?

Janeway had heard that word before.

"Exosia is your realm?" she asked.

"It is our home."

"Wait a minute," Janeway interjected hastily. "When we encountered the Caretaker's mate, Suspiria, we were told that Exosia was her realm. It was the place she went to when she wasn't present with the Ocampa she had taken to her array."

"Who told you that?" Phoebe asked with barely concealed contempt.

"The Ocampa who led us to her . . . his name was . . . Tanis, I believe," Janeway replied, annoyed.

"Then he was misinformed," Phoebe said flatly.

"I beg your pardon?"

"The Nacene you knew as Suspiria was a liar," Phoebe said. "I am certain she was attempting to reenter Exosia . . . she was probably using the life force and abilities of the . . . what did you call them . . . ?"

"Ocampa . . ."

"Yes, the Ocampa, to create some crude key of her own. But she has been barred from Exosia along with the rest of us for tens of thousands of your years. Whatever the Ocampa who followed her were told . . . whatever they believed . . . neither she nor any of them would ever have been capable of entering Exosia without us and the Key."

Janeway considered this and spared a moment of regret for those Suspiria had misled before another question rose to the surface of her mind.

"Did you say Suspiria *was* a liar. . . . as in, she is no longer . . ." Janeway let the thought trail off.

"I can no longer sense her among us."

"Then she's dead?" Janeway asked, as the faint hope of ever encountering her again and perhaps helping her to see reason and return *Voyager* to the Alpha Quadrant started to fade.

"Not as you understand it. But I am confident that if Exosia was her goal, the Others have found a way to put a stop to her efforts that would be more permanent than death."

Janeway paused and looked again at the tumultuous field. "Is this a vision of Exosia?" Janeway asked, taking in every detail of the field and the outcropping of rock on which she stood.

Phoebe smiled.

"Of course not. You could not survive there in your present form. Our existence there is beyond you. This is the place between . . . the place where the last battle was fought and lost."

Janeway struggled to piece together the fragments of information she had gleaned through her journeys with Phoebe.

"Let me see if I have this right," she said. "You and the Others were once in Exosia, where you discovered the strings. You learned to interact with them and somehow that knowledge allowed you to leave Exosia and enter our dimension?"

"We played with them, as you played with your toys when you were a child. But as you saw, to touch one, was to disrupt them all."

"So the strings which somehow form the fabric of all space-time were disrupted by your . . . *play*?" Janeway asked, incredulous.

"We meant no harm," Phoebe replied.

Neither would a five-year-old who picked up a phaser, Janeway thought. But that wouldn't change the outcome at all.

"Be that as it may, you created the imbalance and your choice to remain in our dimension so that you could continue *playing* forced the Others to close the gateway between Exosia and our dimension to prevent the imbalance from getting any worse?"

"Yes," Phoebe replied.

"What is the nature of the imbalance?" Janeway asked.

"You have seen part of it for yourself," Phoebe answered.

Janeway thought back. She had forced the children out of her mother's home, just as some of the strings must have been forced from Exosia when the opening between Exosia and what Janeway considered normal space-time was created.

The light.

Suddenly she remembered vividly the strange glowing balls that had approached the house once the children were gone, and the icy inexplicable terror their presence created in her.

"It has to do with photonic energy, doesn't it?" Janeway theorized.

"It does," Phoebe replied. "There can be no photonic energy within Exosia. It is disruptive to our natural state. Before the gateway was closed, it began to bleed into our existence in a way that was . . . dangerous."

Turning again to the battlefield, Janeway realized that the struggle had ended. A host of Nacene—*the victors,* she did not doubt—were rising into the sky, much like those who had abandoned the fierce and valiant warrior who had tried to lead them. As they did so, the landscape began to take on a form that was somehow familiar. What had been an anonymous rock face and a barren field took on a more specific quality. The colors . . . the textures . . . she could not put her finger on this place, but she knew beyond a doubt that the familiarity was real.

A lone figure rose from among the dead. It was the vaguely Monorhan warrior. He cried out in a voice that echoed throughout this new creation. In any language, the sound would have communicated clearly his utter despair.

As his cry died out, two stars rose above the horizon. Janeway had spent several days analyzing them and knew them at once. They were the two suns of the Monorhan system, Protin and the Blue Eye. But even with her naked eyes, Janeway could see that the Blue Eye at its birth in no way resembled the warped, collapsed star they had discovered only a few days earlier.

"Monorhan space was the place ... *in between*," Janeway said in recognition. "It was the first place in our space-time that was damaged by your play, wasn't it?" she asked.

"It was. Those of us who remained behind chose exile rather than return. This reality was created after the Others had retreated to Exosia. Life was not meant to exist here. The Others had forbidden it."

"But why?" Janeway asked. "Why not return to Exosia with the Others?"

"And spend eternity tending to the strings?" Phoebe asked.

Janeway remembered the strange figure seated in the chair and its constant fruitless sewing. Compared to Phoebe and her fellow Nacene, those who were actively engaged in constructing and deconstructing an entire universe, she could easily understand Phoebe's choice, however irresponsible it might have been.

Another thought struck her.

"You said life was not meant to exist here. But Monorha is filled with life. How did that happen?" she asked.

"Our life gave life to this place. It is of us, though the creatures that arose once we had left are not," Phoebe replied.

"Is that why the Monorhans, and the ships that they built using their natural resources cannot leave this system?" Janeway asked.

"They are anomalous, just as you consider this region

of space to be anomalous," Phoebe answered. "They should not exist here. The one that gave our potential for life to them did not foresee that the very life he gave them would bind them to this place for all eternity. Though that which is impossible exists here through his will, that will did not stretch beyond the gateway and could not sustain them beyond its borders."

"Who is the one that you are speaking of?" Janeway asked.

"Look . . ."

Janeway turned again to the field. The single Monorhan-looking Nacene was moving among the dead. As he did, he collected them, gathering up their remains and forming them into an object he held firmly with both hands.

"The Key," Janeway said in utter disbelief.

"Yes," Phoebe answered.

"And what does the Key do?" Janeway asked.

"It was created so that when we learned from this existence how to solve the problem, how to balance the strings without destroying this dimension or countless others, we could return home and share our knowledge with the Others. Without it, those who remained behind and undertook this great cause will be trapped here forever. The Key opens the conduit, and is the only safe way for us to return home."

Janeway didn't want to sympathize with Phoebe. The reckless abandon with which her entire species had wreaked havoc on their own dimension and now hers, was unpardonable. But the simple truth of Phoebe's words resonated in a way she could not help but relate to.

Home.

Every moment of whatever life Janeway had left would be selflessly devoted to the same quest. Here, at least, she finally met Phoebe on a small shard of common ground.

"If the Key was made by your kind and left here to be used when you had collected the knowledge you seek, why am I important?" she asked.

"It was unforeseen," Phoebe replied. "The Key lives still . . . in its way . . . and has the right to choose its owner."

"How is that possible?" Janeway asked. "The first Nacene we encountered, the entity known as the Caretaker, told us he was dying. The form that he reverted to at the end . . . that was death, wasn't it?"

"In this dimension, yes," Phoebe replied. "We are eternal, but the longer we stay here, the more energy is required to sustain our existence. The entity you encountered waited too long. Had he returned to Gremadia, he would have found the energy he required to continue his existence in his chosen form. But he has never known death as you understand it."

Suddenly another truth was clear to Janeway. "That's why you built the array, isn't it?" Janeway posited.

"Gremadia is a place where all the exiles must return from time to time in order to replenish themselves if they wish to continue their explorations."

"And those who do not . . ."

"Some have chosen to cease the struggle. They wait at Gremadia for our number to be complete again and for the conduit to be opened when the Time of Knowing is upon us." Phoebe answered. "Those who fell on the field of battle were forced to remain behind. They lacked sufficient energy to rediscover their true form. The formation of the Key was a gift given to them by the one I have spoken of; the one we call the Light."

"The one who tried to lead you?"

Phoebe nodded.

"Kind of ironic name, isn't it?" Janeway mused.

Ignoring her, Phoebe went on, "The form he gave them is a vague reflection of the oneness they knew in Exosia. And only in that form can they continue to exert any kind of will. Through that power, they choose their owner. They first chose a Monorhan called Dagan. They did not understand that their choice would kill him. The Monorhans feared the Key, and locked it away. By refusing to touch it, they also denied the Key the right to choose its next owner."

"Why is it necessary for the Key to have an owner?"

"So that there will always be one with the power to open the conduit. Without that, there is no hope for any of us."

"What happened to the Light?" Janeway asked.

"I do not know," Phoebe said almost sadly. "He has been lost to us for longer than I can remember. Some believe he died. Some believe now that he never really existed, that this memory of us is some kind of hopeful illusion. All I know for certain is that I cannot sense him or his power among those of us who are left."

Phoebe paused to let this sink in, then pleaded, "Do what I ask, willingly, and I promise no further harm will come to any other life-form that inhabits this space and time. Help me open the conduit."

Janeway was about to agree. But one final disturbing question remained.

"Are you ready to return home?" she asked. "Have you solved the problem?"

As she waited, breathless for Phoebe to respond, she thought of the array, the technological miracle that she knew the Nacene who had remained behind could only be responsible for. She thought of the power structure, the adaptive life-support system, and the computer core capable of holding every fragment of data about the entire universe in one place and hoped silently that Phoebe would say yes.

But as she watched this face, a face whose subtlest thought had been plainly read by her since the day her sister had been born, she knew that she wasn't going to get the answer she was hoping for.

"We have not," she replied. "But it no longer matters. Your actions here brought me to the gateway. I have called the exiles and we must use the Key now. If we do not, the Others will return."

"How do you know that?" Janeway demanded.

"When you destabilized the gateway, they were drawn here as we were. I told them I would destroy the Key. They gave me three days to do so. In less than twenty-seven hours they will be back to make sure I have upheld my side of our agreement. If we do not use the Key and return to Exosia before that time, we will not even be allowed to choose to remain exiled in this dimension. The Others will destroy us, Kathryn, and all that you and I both hold dear, just as they did once before."

"But you said the gateway was closed. How can the Others come back, if you cannot pass through it without the Key?" Janeway asked.

"The will of the Others in Exosia keeps the gateway closed. They are the only beings who can enter or leave as they please, though to my knowledge they have never chosen to do so until now."

Janeway looked again at the field. She shuddered at its barrenness. Even the masses of "dead" had been somehow more comforting than the wasteland that stretched as far as she could see. There were ancient lessons of war which were still taught at Starfleet Academy. The one that came to Janeway's mind now was first taught by one of the earliest races of humans in recorded history to successfully civilize their small corner of the planet Earth.

"They made a desert and called it peace," Janeway said softly.

"And will do so again," Phoebe added. "Even we, sometimes, fail to learn."

Janeway sighed deeply, raised her eyes to meet Phoebe's and said, "Take me back to my ship."

After the third successive probe test had been completed to Chakotay's satisfaction, he was almost as excited about the prospect of the tetryon transporters as Tom, Harry, and B'Elanna were.

Harry had been right. The tetryon field emitted by the system actually bent space and as long as the appropriate coordinates were transferred to the system, they seemed able to set a specific end point that extended far beyond the realm of any transporter he had ever seen . . . theoretically . . . all the way to the Alpha Quadrant.

Tom had also been right. The system was designed to accept telepathic commands for coordinates, and even in species, like humans, who were generally not telepathic, their thoughts took them to any destination they desired. Chakotay's biggest concern had been trusting any human mind with such a huge variable. On his best days, when he felt most calm and serene, he had rarely been able to experience only one thought at a time. With so much riding on the outcome, he would never have agreed to the test had not B'Elanna solved the final problem to his satisfaction.

Voyager stored dozens of organic containers that were used in transport tests when an operator was uncertain whether or not a life-form could safely transport to a specified area owing to interference or distance. Harry had been the first to come up with the idea of using the organic matter inside the probes to take the place of a human and add the "thought" variable to the equation, but B'Elanna had been the first to successfully code the organic material to emit a specific frequency of "thought" that the tetryon transporter could read. By piggybacking *Voyager's* long-range sensors to the array's much more powerful sensor grid via the data-interface cable still tethered to *Voyager,* they had successfully detected three successive probes containing the coded organic matter at their appropriate coordinates. The third, their most ambitious test, had been transported a distance of almost twenty thousand light-years. It wasn't the Alpha Quadrant, but it was twenty years closer to home. Chakotay would have been thrilled with one-quarter of that distance.

The final test would be a shuttle test. Since Tom and Harry had volunteered to pilot the shuttle, all had agreed that this manned flight should be set just beyond the borders of Monorhan space, the closest destination possible that was outside the system, but within twenty hours of the array at impulse speeds. In order to avoid any potential pitfalls of using human thoughts to control the test—no one could say for certain with two men aboard whose thoughts would take precedence, should one's concentration fail—the shuttle's navigational array and been routed through one of the coded organic canisters, exactly as had been the case with the probes.

"See you in a few hours," Tom said jauntily as he stepped inside the shuttle. If all went as planned Tom and Harry would immediately reenter Monorhan space once the shuttle had arrived at the coordinates and return to the array at full impulse.

Chakotay planned to use that time to force Phoebe's hand by taking the Key back to the array and placing it in the "lock." Assuming the captain did not return of her own accord, he was still unwilling to accept the idea that *Voyager* would leave the array without her . . . especially when their next stop might be home.

Chakotay gave Tom a nod of good luck, then left the shuttlebay to monitor the test with B'Elanna in astrometrics. Neelix, who had been as thrilled as the others at Tom's potential discovery, had also asked to attend the test and was pacing nervously about the staging area before the main viewscreen when Chakotay arrived.

"Shuttle *Homeward Bound,* you have clearance to transport," B'Elanna said over the comm as Chakotay joined her at the sensor control console.

"*Homeward Bound?*" Chakotay asked.

"Tom renamed the shuttle while we were reconfiguring the navigational array. Somehow *Monticello* just didn't have the ring he was going for," B'Elanna replied with a smirk.

Chakotay nodded with approval and took a deep breath. In seconds, at least one of their problems might very well be solved.

"*Activating enhanced navigational array,*" Harry announced.

"*Coordinates locked in,*" Tom replied.

This was it.

"*Activating tetryon transport system on my mark . . . three . . . two . . . one . . . mark.*"

The shuttle lifted from the bay deck and inched toward the invisible plane created between the two transport alcoves, now separated a wide enough distance to accommodate the shuttle's width. In a flash of brilliant white light, *Homeward Bound* disappeared from the shuttlebay.

A pregnant pause . . .

. . . long enough for B'Elanna to confirm the shuttle's arrival . . .

. . . silence . . .

Chakotay's jaw tensed.

"Where are they, Lieutenant?" he asked.

B'Elanna's fingers were flying across the sensor controls. Grid after grid was being searched, each replacing the last on the viewscreen as the computer confirmed quicker than the eye that the shuttle was nowhere to be found.

"I can't . . ." B'Elanna stammered, then slammed her fists onto the panel in frustration.

"I have no idea," she finally said.

"Does that mean they didn't reach the edge of the system . . . or . . . ?" Neelix asked, hurrying to join them.

He was interrupted by a call from Ensign Brooks over the comm. *"Shuttlebay one to Lieutenant Torres."*

"What is it, Brooks?" B'Elanna snapped.

"The tetryon transporter has been . . . well . . ." He paused, as if searching for the right word.

"Has been what?" Chakotay demanded.

"It melted, sir," Brooks replied. *"There was no explosion. I can't imagine where the heat necessary to generate something like this . . . both of the alcoves from the array were completely destroyed, and they took two meters of conduit and panels in every direction with them."*

"Begin an immediate analysis of the debris. I'll expect a full report within the hour. Chakotay out." Turning to B'Elanna he said expectantly, "Well?"

"They didn't arrive at the set coordinates," B'Elanna said stoically, "and they're not within a hundred light-years in any direction of the coded end point of the transport."

Before any of them could give in to an inkling of despair, Chakotay raised his shoulders and snapped, "Find them, Lieutenant."

B'Elanna's eyes were brimming with tears. Refusing to allow them to fall, she managed a firm "Aye, sir," and turned back to the console to begin her search.

In the last few months B'Elanna had lost too much. The first news she had received from the Alpha Quadrant while she had been building a new life for herself aboard *Voyager* had been about the massacre of the Maquis she had served with. The Maquis had taken something with them when they died, something she had never forced herself to clearly name. It was her passion, and her hope . . . the fire in her belly that had seen her through every impossible situation she had encountered as *Voyager*'s chief engineer. For months she had suffered this loss in silence, unsure how or where to even begin to make peace with it.

She would be damned before she would also lose one of her best friends, and the man she loved.

Not today, anyway.

Chapter 14

Seven of Nine intercepted Neelix en route to join Commander Chakotay in transporter room three.

"Oh, hello, Seven," Neelix said somberly as she fell into step beside him.

"Are you unwell, Neelix?" she asked, more out of curiosity than concern.

"Oh . . . I'm fine." He shrugged unconvincingly.

"You disapprove of the commander's plan?" she asked. She had seen thousands being led into assimilation chambers. Neelix resembled those who already knew what they were facing.

"Well, let's see," Neelix said, "in the last ten hours we've managed to lose the captain, Lieutenant Paris, and Ensign Kim, and we're about to intentionally antagonize at least one, possibly many of the Nacene while risking another encounter with the creatures who led Tuvok here and infected him with the parasite that is about to kill him. I don't know if 'disapprove' is the right word," he finished, shifting his modified phaser rifle from his right to his left shoulder. "I suppose if it were up to me, I might seriously consider just calling this the disaster that it's been and getting out of here as soon as possible."

The ocular implant seated at Seven's brow rose quizzically. She had rarely known the Talaxian to be so vehement or pessimistic.

"The commander is attempting to see that the captain is returned to us," Seven observed. "You do not believe the potential for success outweighs the risks inherent in the mission?"

Neelix sighed.

"Part of me does. But the rest of me keeps thinking about Naomi. There's only so much I am willing to sacrifice, Seven," Neelix said defensively.

"I understand," Seven replied.

"You do?"

"The officers and crew aboard this vessel volunteered for the services they are performing. Naomi Wildman did not have the opportunity to make such a choice," she stated with typical detachment. "It is . . . unfair," she finished.

"I am certain of only one thing," Neelix said after a thoughtful pause. "There are forces at work here that are more powerful than we are. And I don't believe those forces have any of our interests at heart. The longer we stay, and the more we do to irritate them, the worse this is going to get. I don't take our losses lightly. But we should accept them and move on, before there is no one left to grieve for those who are gone."

Seven's placid gaze remained fixed on Neelix.

"You are proposing an efficient method of resolving this crisis," she said.

"Well, thank you," he replied, not sure if she was actually complimenting him.

"Unfortunately, in my experience, *Voyager*'s collective is rarely concerned with efficiency," she added as the doors to the transporter room slid open before them.

Chakotay had already returned the Key to its ceremonial box and placed it on the transporter pad. He was configuring his tricorder when they entered.

"I've analyzed the schematics of the array and found a way to take a little time off of our journey," Chakotay said as they joined him.

"The pattern enhancers Seven and B'Elanna set up on the *Betasis* are still functioning. Once we're there, we'll travel a few hundred meters on foot to the nearest tetryon transporter."

"You're not actually suggesting we use them again?" Neelix said in disbelief, before adding a somewhat respectful "Commander? I mean, after what happened to Tom and Harry?"

"There is no other way to get from the first to the second ring where the lock for the Key is located. We've used them before and I'm reasonably certain that as long as we use them as they were designed, we should be safe."

Neelix didn't appear to be convinced, but hesitated to voice another round of doubts.

"From there, we should be able to transport to the series of transport alcoves nearest the room where the lock is located," he indicated, pointing to the schematic. "Thanks to Tom's experiments with their transport system, we have figured out how to manually enter our destination into their system and bypass the telepathic controls, as long as we are moving from one transport hub to another within the array. Otherwise, we're talking about a journey through the array on foot of almost two kilometers. I don't want to risk exposure to the creatures that infected Tuvok for that long, but if either of you disagree, now's the time to say something."

"I have been tracking the multiphasic life-forms for the past several hours," Seven noted. "Most of them are

currently located in what we believe to be the array's engineering center, located on the first ring. By following the
course you have set, we run very little risk of confronting
them," she said, adding, "Assuming our presence does not
disrupt them in any way."

"Neelix?" Chakotay asked.

"The quickest route sounds best to me," he said as enthusiastically as possible.

"Very well," Chakotay replied, taking his place on the
transporter pad. "B'Elanna and I reconfigured the modified phaser rifles you are carrying to stun the multiphasic
life-forms. My rifle is equipped with the neural agent that
is toxic to the Nacene. If we should encounter Phoebe, or
any other Nacene, mine is the only weapon that will harm
them."

Seven and Neelix nodded their understanding as they
joined him on the pad.

When they were set, Chakotay ordered the transporter
officer to energize.

Once aboard the array and then on to the second ring,
the away team made its way through a few short winding
corridors, some lined with the strange pattern-shifting
portals Chakotay had discovered, until they reached the
hallway that ended with the large metal doors that led to
the chamber they were seeking.

Seven had kept her eyes glued to her tricorder as they
walked, continuing to track the movements of the multiphasic life-forms. Neelix, whose thoughts were clearly
elsewhere, managed to run straight into Chakotay at the
turn to the final corridor.

"I'm sorry, Commander," he began to apologize, but
Chakotay cut him off with a quick "Shhh!"

Neelix stepped aside and followed Chakotay's fixed
stare.

"Commander?" he asked, the remnants of his undigested ration pack making its uncomfortable presence in his stomach known to all three.

The end of the corridor was shrouded in darkness, but Chakotay had come to an abrupt halt at a faint flicker of movement in the shadows.

"Seven?" Chakotay asked, ignoring Neelix for the moment.

"One of the multiphasic creatures has just appeared at the entrance to the chamber," Seven said evenly, stowing her tricorder and raising her rifle to its ready position.

Neelix immediately did likewise, and they allowed Chakotay to move into position behind them before they continued cautiously down the corridor.

Chakotay knew what to expect. The first creature had been terrifying to encounter, but he was confident that the shrieking approach he knew had to be imminent would not be sufficient to unnerve Seven, and for all his bluster, Neelix was both tougher and shrewder than he usually let on.

Placing his faith in both of them, he tread softly behind their formation, willing his nerves to silence their call for him to order all three to turn around and run for their lives.

The creature passed out of the shadows. Seven and Neelix got their first glimpse of the life-form they had seen up to this point on sensors only.

Chakotay's expectations, though well founded, were nonetheless disappointed.

To Janeway's surprise, she and Phoebe rematerialized inside engineering, a few meters from the diagnostic station where she and B'Elanna had been studying the Key shortly before *Voyager* had boarded the array. Janeway's breath caught when she remembered that the Key had gone missing just before she had confronted Phoebe in her quarters, but Phoebe calmed her with a reassuring hand.

"I had to hide the Key in order to protect it," she said, crossing to the station and rerouting transporter controls to remove the Key from the warp core.

As Janeway moved to join her she heard Ensign Glenn tap her combadge and call, "Glenn to Lieutenant Torres."

"Torres here," B'Elanna replied.

"Lieutenant, the captain has returned. She and her sister are in engineering."

Moments later, B'Elanna entered engineering and crossed briskly to confront them.

"Captain," she said as she approached, her eyes alight.

But Janeway silenced her, raising her right hand and saying, "A moment, Lieutenant."

"The Key is gone," Phoebe informed Janeway.

"You didn't think we'd leave it in the warp core, did you?" B'Elanna snapped.

Both women turned on B'Elanna at these words, but only Phoebe's face contained suspicion.

"Where is it now, Lieutenant?" Janeway asked calmly.

"Captain," B'Elanna began, somewhat unsure of her footing, "permission to speak freely?"

"Of course," Janeway replied.

B'Elanna's eyes darted to Phoebe, and Janeway added, "Phoebe and I have come to an understanding, B'Elanna. You may say whatever you like in front of her."

"She's Nacene," B'Elanna said, as if unsure whether or not Janeway had forgotten, or was merely overlooking this fact for the moment.

"And I have agreed to help her," Janeway answered her unspoken question.

B'Elanna's next thought was easy enough to read on her face, though Janeway appreciated the fact that she refrained from voicing it.

I just hope you know what you're doing.

"When you disappeared, we did all we could to discover the purpose of the Key," B'Elanna said.

Janeway nodded. She would not have expected less.

"It's our understanding that it opens a conduit of some kind between our space and . . ." B'Elanna faltered. "To be honest, Captain, we don't know exactly where it leads."

"Exosia," Janeway replied. "Phoebe and her people intend to use the Key to return home."

"Commander Chakotay wanted to use the Key to find you. He's taken it to the array to place it in the mechanism designed to open the conduit."

Janeway threw a questioning glance at Phoebe, who was obviously perturbed at this development.

"He will not be allowed to do so," Phoebe said. "Only your captain can use the Key to open the conduit."

Janeway tapped her combadge and called, "Janeway to Chakotay."

There was no answer.

After another unsuccessful attempt, B'Elanna said, "I'm sorry, Captain. Our communications have been spotty at best aboard the array."

"I will find him," Phoebe offered. "I know where he has gone."

"Return him to the ship immediately," Janeway ordered. "Bring the Key with you. And make sure the rest of your people know we have only a few hours to open the conduit."

Phoebe vanished, and B'Elanna finally found voice to ask accusatorially, "Captain, why are you trusting her? You know what she did to all of us."

"There is more at stake here than our personal regard for her or her tactics," Janeway replied. "I agree she's a threat, but she's by no means the most significant one we are facing at present."

"I hope you're right," B'Elanna replied.

"What's the ship's status?" Janeway asked.

B'Elanna took a moment to gather her thoughts.

"All systems are operating at maximum capacity, Captain. Repairs from our entry to the array have been completed. Our interface with the array's control systems is stable and assuming we can navigate the singularity's event horizon, we should be able to leave on your order."

"I'm sure Lieutenant Paris is up to the task," Janeway said, intending her words to be comforting.

With self-restraint that was palpably painful, B'Elanna informed the captain of their attempt to harness the tetryon transporters and the subsequent loss of Tom and Harry without coming completely unglued.

"As soon as this is done, we'll find them, B'Elanna," Janeway said once B'Elanna had finished. "You have my word on that."

"Yes, Captain," B'Elanna replied.

Janeway's reassurances, even in a situation as dire as this, obviously did a little to lift her withering spirits.

"What's Lieutenant Tuvok's condition?" Janeway asked next.

"I honestly don't know," B'Elanna answered. "With everything else going on . . ."

"Is he still in sickbay?" Janeway asked.

"I believe so, Captain."

"I'm going there now to check on him. Ask the commander and Phoebe to meet me there when they return," Janeway ordered.

B'Elanna acknowledged this with a nod and as Janeway turned to go said, "Captain?"

Janeway halted her steps.

"It's good to have you back."

Janeway offered her a tight smile.

"It's good to be back."

She had almost made it to the door when the Doctor called over the comm system, *"Sickbay to Lieutenant Torres."*

Janeway stopped again to hear his transmission.

"Go ahead, Doctor," B'Elanna replied.

"Can you tell me who Assylia is?"

"She was the commander of the Monorhan ship we discovered, Doctor."

"Then perhaps you can also tell me why Lieutenant Tuvok is asking to speak with her?"

Janeway's eyes widened as B'Elanna hurried to join her at the door. "I'm on my way, Doctor. Torres out."

"What is he talking about?" Janeway asked.

"I'll explain on the way," B'Elanna said.

In the short distance that separated engineering from sickbay, B'Elanna gave the captain a complete report on their discovery of Assylia's consciousness and the means they had devised to trap it in a holomatrix. She was also able to give Janeway a rough summary of all that Assylia had discussed with Chakotay, including the fact that she had been responsible for *Voyager*'s near destruction when they boarded the array. Chakotay had left a standing order before he left the ship that under no circumstances was Assylia's program to be brought back online.

The Doctor appeared pleasantly surprised to see Janeway enter sickbay along with Lieutenant Torres. But his obvious relief at this development was short-lived.

"Doctor, report," Janeway requested, taken aback at the sight of Tuvok's body covered by the pulsating mass of translucent energy.

"As you can see, Captain, the transformation begun when Tuvok was infected by one of the parasites is almost complete. A short time ago, Tuvok called to Ensign Vorik telepathically. Vorik initiated a successful mind-meld with him. He was able to communicate Tuvok's wishes to me, including his request to speak with Assylia. As there is no record of her in the ship's manifest, I have been at a loss as to how best to fulfill this request."

Janeway turned to face Vorik, who was still standing beside Tuvok's biobed.

"Why does Tuvok wish to speak with Assylia?" she demanded.

"I do not know, Captain," Vorik replied. "He has a message for her, but that is all I was able to learn before he terminated our meld."

"Captain," B'Elanna interjected, "Tuvok has been unconscious in sickbay since he was brought back on board."

"That's not entirely true, Lieutenant," the Doctor said. "He did regain consciousness long enough to disable my program, and even unconscious has successfully fought off each attempt I have made to separate him from the parasite."

"My point, Doctor," B'Elanna said with barely concealed irritation, "is that there is no way Tuvok could have known that Assylia is on board."

Janeway didn't know what to make of this, but for the moment, she had a more pressing concern.

"Doctor, you said Tuvok has resisted your attempts to separate him from the parasite. Does that mean . . . ?"

"According to Ensign Vorik, Tuvok is well aware that his body will die when the transformation is complete. He is willing to sacrifice his life in favor of a new state of being which Tuvok believes is somehow superior to life as you know it."

Janeway's mind reeled. She had last left sickbay completely confident that the Doctor would be able to save Tuvok's life. Nothing could have prepared her to accept the idea that Tuvok would willingly commit suicide.

"I'm sorry, Captain, but there isn't much time left," the Doctor said. "If it is possible for Tuvok to speak with Assylia, he should do so right away."

Janeway nodded.

"Transfer Assylia's holomatrix to sickbay, B'Elanna," she said.

A few moments of tense silence later, Assylia appeared before them.

"Where am I?" she asked. "Where is Commander Chakotay?"

Janeway addressed her. "I am Kathryn Janeway. I am the captain of this vessel. We have transferred your program to our sickbay."

"I was told you had departed," Assylia said flatly.

"And as you can see, I have returned," Janeway replied. "One of my crewmen has been infected by a parasite . . . a creature like that we believe was responsible for the death of your people."

"Chakotay spoke to me of this," Assylia replied. "I am sorry for your loss."

Janeway winced at her premature condolences.

"My crewman, Lieutenant Tuvok, wishes to speak with you. Are you willing to do this?"

Assylia seemed disconcerted by the request, but replied, "Of course," adding, "On one condition."

"I beg your pardon?" Janeway said.

"I requested your Commander Chakotay's aid when

last we spoke. Have you discussed my request with him?" she asked.

"To what request are you referring?"

"I offered to help your ship escape the array in return for your help in destroying it. Are you willing to assist me?"

Janeway was dumbstruck. Only a few moments in Assylia's presence had answered any question she had as to why Chakotay had terminated her program and ordered it to stay offline. She was demonstrating an appalling lack of sensitivity to their situation. She tried to allow for the horrible fate this woman had suffered, but even so, could not see herself acting the same had their situations been reversed.

"We will be leaving the array shortly," Janeway said. "If you wish for us to transfer you back to your ship before we do so, I will be happy to comply. But this array is not yours or mine to destroy. I have been in contact with the beings who created it, and I have no doubt they would respond with deadly force should either of us attempt such a thing."

Assylia accepted this all too willingly for Janeway's liking.

"I understand, Captain," she replied evenly. "Where is your Lieutenant Tuvok?" she asked.

Janeway gestured toward the biobed where Tuvok lay motionless.

"How am I to speak with him?" she asked.

Vorik stepped forward to offer, "I will initiate another meld. You may communicate through me."

"That will not be necessary," Tuvok said.

Everyone in the room turned in disbelief at the sound of Tuvok's voice.

With slow, deliberate movements, Tuvok rose unassisted from the biobed and stood to address them. The creature that engulfed him did not hinder his movement, or the clarity with which he spoke. Indeed, it seemed that it had intentionally wound its way over his body in order to facilitate such movement, disengaging itself from Tuvok's head and neck. Tuvok stood before them now, wearing a vibrant suit of pulsating light.

"You are Assylia," he began.

"I am," she replied.

"I have a message for you . . . from your people."

"My people died fifty years ago, just as you are about to die," she said in a cold, measured voice.

"No," Tuvok contradicted her. "They did not. Your entire crew . . . *all of them* . . . are still alive and well within Gremadia."

The creature that glided delicately toward the awestruck Chakotay, Neelix, and Seven was in every way the polar opposite of the first multiphasic life-form that Chakotay had encountered aboard the array.

Its face was familiar. But only now could Chakotay see that the soft rounded eyes set above the extended jaw were definitely Monorhan. From the uppermost section of the torso, several pairs of delicate wings guided its serene movement. Only one set of arms was visible, extending from the lower portion of the creature's body, and folded with the palms of the hands together, reminiscent of meditation or prayer.

It made no sudden movements, halting its progress when it had come within a few meters of Chakotay and his team.

"Commander," Neelix asked nervously.

"Hold your fire," Chakotay said softly. His thoughts and feelings flew in the face of all logic, but nonetheless, he could not sense a shred of hostility emanating from the creature.

With one hand, Seven of Nine pulled out her tricorder and scanned the area.

"Commander," she said, "I am detecting thousands of multiphasic life-forms approaching our area."

Chakotay had a theory. The creature's face and demeanor had locked into place a piece of the vast puzzle he had been trying to solve, and all he needed now was a way to test it.

Stepping in front of Seven and Neelix, Chakotay walked a few paces closer to the creature. It betrayed no sense of alarm at his approach.

"We mean you no harm," he said. "But we must enter this chamber."

He could have sworn that joy, mixed with unutterable longing, radiated from the creature's eyes.

"Will you allow us to pass unharmed?" he asked.

In response, the creature retreated, leaving an unobstructed path between the away team and the door of the chamber, which still hung slightly ajar after his last forced exit.

"Thank you," Chakotay said, and gestured for Seven and Neelix to follow, adding, "Lower your weapons."

"But Commander," the terrified Neelix persisted.

"That's an order, Neelix."

With Chakotay in the lead, all three passed unhindered by the creature and crossed the threshold of the vast chamber where the tattered sphere hung suspended in midair. They stopped almost as soon as they entered and their eyes confirmed the tricorder readings Seven had detected moments before. The entire chamber was filled with the creatures. The fragile light that emanated from their bodies bathed the vast chamber in an eerie silver glow. Through its dimness they could make out that a clear path to the base of the sphere lay open before them, but Chakotay hesitated for a moment to continue.

"Commander, I don't understand," Neelix said under his breath.

"B'Elanna was right," he replied. "The parasites that infected the Monorhans did not kill them. They were transformed, just as Tuvok is being transformed. They mean us no harm. The Doctor said that Tuvok should not have survived his injuries. They might have infected him to save his life. We've been here long enough that had they wished to do the same to us, they could easily have found a way."

"But you said the creature you and Tom saw . . ." Neelix began.

"These creatures retain physical aspects of the host bodies that were infected by the parasites," Chakotay answered. "The first one we encountered was different. It displayed none of the serenity or self-control we are seeing here."

"Maybe they're just waiting for us to get a little closer," Neelix suggested.

"I do not believe that is so," Seven said. "The Doctor described the transformative process in Tuvok as a merging. The original parasite must merge with the consciousness of the host. The more horrifying creature you saw could have been created if a parasite infected a body that was devoid of such consciousness."

"Assylia," Chakotay nodded.

"Quite possibly," Seven replied.

There was a flutter of motion near the base of the sphere. Though the creatures kept their distance from the away team, their anxiousness was palpable.

"Let's go," Chakotay said, starting toward the sphere.

They were within a few paces of it when the creatures closest to the base retreated from their position in a flurry of motion.

As they cleared an opening, Phoebe appeared amid the rapidly retreating throng and placed herself between Chakotay and the lock.

"You have taken something that belongs to me," she said solemnly. "Your captain and I have reached and understanding. You will return with me to your ship and bring the Key with you."

Chakotay hesitated to respond, but the creatures did not. They closed the space around the away team and Phoebe, cutting off all access to the chamber's exits.

"I'm not sure we're going to be allowed to do that," Chakotay finally replied.

A faint smile lit Phoebe's face . . . a smile that did not touch her eyes.

"Is the captain alive?" Chakotay demanded.

"She is awaiting our return to *Voyager* as we speak," Phoebe replied.

Chakotay tapped his combadge.

"Chakotay to Janeway."

The only response was a sharp burst of static.

Phoebe took a step toward him and said, "Take my hand, Chakotay. It is necessary for me to return you to your ship. Your captain is waiting."

The agitation of the creatures was palpable. They closed the circle, floating within a meter of the away team and the Nacene. The only path open to Chakotay led past Phoebe, directly to the lock.

"Do not be afraid of these abominations," Phoebe said. "I will not allow them to harm you. They are of no consequence. Only the spores that live within them matter."

As if to prove her point, a razor-sharp tentacle flew

from Phoebe's side, encircling the torso of the first creature it encountered and forcing it to the floor of the chamber. For a few tortured seconds it writhed in obvious
agony, until it ceased to struggle. Once it was dead, a small
translucent worm emerged from its belly and crawled toward Phoebe's feet.

Phoebe bent and collected the small wriggling spore.

"Do we understand each other, Chakotay?" she asked.

Chakotay didn't honestly know whether the captain
was alive or dead. But he was certain that if she was, whatever "deal" she had struck with Phoebe did not include the
arbitrary sacrifice of innocent lives.

"Do we understand each other?" Phoebe asked again.

"Perfectly," he replied.

Lowering his phaser rifle, he aimed it directly at
Phoebe and fired.

Chapter 15

"You lie!" Assylia shouted, closing the small distance between herself and Tuvok.

B'Elanna and the captain instinctively reached for their phasers, sensing the hostility buried for so many years within Assylia and now given leash. But Janeway also immediately realized that their phasers would have no effect on the hologram. Janeway's eyes locked with B'Elanna's and a subtle nod communicated her wishes. B'Elanna moved silently to the holomatrix control station located near the entrance to sickbay and waited for the situation to develop. With the flick of a finger, she could deactivate Assylia's matrix from here and eliminate any threat she might pose.

"No, I do not," Tuvok replied.

"I watched them die, hundreds at a time. Our surgeons confirmed their deaths, and my helplessness," Assylia choked.

"What you witnessed was the first stage of their transformation. During that time, their bodies died. But their consciousnesses, all that they are apart from their bodies, were merged with the beings that had entered them. I have heard their thoughts and their memories. In our new existence, there are no barriers between us. Once the completeness of their new existence was clear to them, they . . . like me . . . welcomed this process.

"We enter the final stage of transformation in complete willingness. It cannot be achieved otherwise. Your people exist now as pure consciousness in a form which allows them to experience the universe in ways you cannot imagine. Once they have returned home, they will never again know or fear death.

"They share only two regrets. The first is that you have suffered needlessly these fifty years. Had you not separated your mind from your body just before your body was found by the spore, you would be one with them now. They would have you know that they can feel your concern, but it, like your pain on their behalf, is unnecessary."

Assylia listened, apparently unmoved. It was as if she could not . . . or *would not* . . . accept his words. "You contradict all I have been taught of life, death, and the will of the Blessed All-Knowing Light. If what you say is true, then the faith which has sustained my people for thousands of years is false," she said haughtily.

"Your faith was imprecise. It was based on an understanding of space and time which your people have now transcended. Their belief in your Blessed All-Knowing Light has never wavered. They understand now, as I do, that his existence is as real as theirs. He is not, as you could not help but believe, a god. He is merely a more evolved state of consciousness and energy with whom they will now be able to enter into dialogue. They await his return to this city he created, and desire nothing more than to follow him home when the Time of Knowing is complete."

Janeway followed Tuvok's words with a mixed sense of regret and relief. She understood now that the god of the Monorhans, their Blessed All-Knowing Light, was in fact the Nacene who had tried to lead his people against the Others, and that he had been trapped in this dimension against his will, the same entity Phoebe had referred to more simply as the Light. Despite the slight panic rising within her, she also began to understand the allure of the transformation that Tuvok had described. She had often wondered at the life he and all Vulcans were resigned to live. She understood the delicate line they were forced to walk. Their experience of emotions was an overwhelming and all-consuming one. They had been able to evolve into the rich and advanced society they were only by imposing total control on those emotions. Their cult of logic had undoubtedly served them well. And she knew that despite their inability to express themselves as emotional beings, they did possess feelings, and that when they permitted themselves to feel them under strict controls, it was a satisfying experience.

But if she was hearing Tuvok correctly, the existence he was about to accept would be far superior to the constant battleground that had been, up to this point, every moment of his life. Pure logic was a state every Vulcan would aspire to but understood was impossible to attain in any practical form. Tuvok's new existence would be, by definition, an experience of this purity, and much as she hated to admit it, she could not deny that to hold him back from this opportunity would be both selfish and cruel.

Assylia paused, then spoke again, saying, "How is it possible that you could have sensed my people and their need while I, who was bound to every single one of them from the moment I became their *rih-hara-tan,* have known nothing of this?"

Tuvok cocked his head to one side, his gaze curious.

"You have heard them, just as I did. But your pain and anger blinded you to their truth. You were incapable of understanding."

"I heard nothing," she said flatly. "I sensed . . . from time to time . . ."

"Your connection to your people was broken in the transformation. But nonetheless you were aware of their presence . . . and of their need."

Though Janeway did not truly understand the finer points of the argument that was happening in front of her, she could sense Assylia's inability to deny Tuvok's words try as she might, as well as her unwillingness to accept the entirety of what he was saying.

"What need?" Janeway interjected.

"Their existence within this dimension is . . . incomplete. They are meant to pass beyond this place, through the conduit of light described by Dagan. They *need* to go home."

Janeway's mind spun at the thought. This was something Phoebe had obviously failed to mention on their little educational sabbatical. Clearly the spores that infected the Monorhans were meant for the Nacene. Now that the two species had unintentionally joined, the transformed Monorhans also believed that Exosia was their true home. The question was, if the Nacene needed the spores in order to undergo a similar transformation before they could traverse the conduit, were there enough left on the array to facilitate this for Phoebe and the others who had been exiled?

Throughout this entire exchange, a small corner of Janeway's thoughts had been fretting over the fact that Phoebe had not yet returned with Chakotay. That worry began to blossom into fear.

Tuvok continued to address Assylia, unperturbed. "I, too, misunderstood at first. Our fragile minds cannot hold but a fragment of their truth. Nonetheless, I felt their need and answered it. They honored this by saving my life and offering me a place among them."

Finally Assylia said, "I require proof. What you are asking me to believe is impossible."

"What proof could I offer you?" Tuvok asked.

"The beings that I have sensed are capable of exerting their will upon the controls of this station. I have a request to make of my *shi-harat.*"

"What is it that you wish Naviim to do?" Tuvok asked, noting that Assylia was shocked that he would know her servant's name.

"There is a dataport on the *Betasis* which has been compromised by the creatures you speak of. It tethers my ship to this station. Have them remove it so that I may send the *Betasis* back to Monorha. Those we left behind have a right to know of our fate."

Tuvok closed his eyes, and for a silent moment, all stood by, breathless, awaiting his response.

Finally he opened them and said, "It is done, my *rih.*"

Horror cascaded across Assylia's stern face.

"Naviim," she whispered.

"Be at peace," Tuvok said, then clicked his tongue in a manner Janeway recognized was meant to communicate a deeper, more personal thought meant for Assylia alone.

For Assylia, this moment was a living nightmare. She had never forgotten Naviim's face as he stood beside her, willing to face death to protect her rather than seek out the safety of one of the preservation pods. As her final words to Naviim before the transfer that had trapped her within her ship were echoed back to her through this alien's lips, she saw, sensed, and knew that in this moment, she was speaking to her beloved *shi-harat*.

"Naviim . . ." Assylia said again, and for the first time it was clear to Janeway that Assylia had seen the truth in Tuvok's words.

"NOOOOOO!" A frantic wail erupted from Assylia's throat, and she fell to her knees, clutching her face in her hands.

Janeway moved immediately to Assylia's side, unsure how best to console her, or why this moment was so devastating to her.

"Assylia . . ." she said softly.

"*Rollins to Torres,*" a sharp voice interrupted over the comm.

"What is it?" B'Elanna asked.

"*We're reading a massive energy buildup within the docking bay where the Monorhan ship is berthed. It looks as if an autodestruct system of some kind has been activated.*"

Janeway knelt beside Assylia and grasped her by her forearms, forcing her to look directly into her eyes.

"What have you done?" she demanded firmly.

"I didn't know," Assylia stammered through her sobs, "I didn't . . . what he said isn't possible."

"Why are your ship's systems suddenly overloading?" Janeway pushed.

"The dataport connecting my ship to the array regulated the flow of information between the two systems," she began.

"We are maintaining a similar connection now, Captain," B'Elanna offered.

Shuddering, Assylia continued, "Thanks to that connection I have been able to monitor the array's systems and interact with them from time to time."

For example, when you disabled the array's guidance system and almost destroyed my ship, Janeway thought, but thought best to keep to herself. Nodding sternly, she willed Assylia to continue.

"My ship and I were one. It knew my thoughts and wishes. The only thing which kept it from acting on those wishes all this time was the cable that connected us to the array. The dataport regulates all commands between the *Betasis* and the array and will automatically override commands that could damage its systems. It would never allow my ship to execute my final order."

Janeway didn't have to ask what that order had been.

B'Elanna had moved to another computer interface and re-rerouted the sensor data.

"Captain, Rollins is right. The *Betasis* is going to explode."

"How much time do we have?"

"Ten minutes, no more," B'Elanna replied.

Janeway wanted to shake Assylia but forced herself to remain calm.

"Can you stop it?" she asked. "Is there an emergency override?"

Assylia shook her head weakly. "It was my last wish . . . to die here . . . as they did."

"But they're not dead," Janeway said, then turning to B'Elanna asked, "Will the explosion be contained within the docking bay?"

"No, Captain," B'Elanna replied. "It will destabilize the ring's structural integrity. Once the explosion hits the singularity's event horizon it will set off a chain reaction. . . ."

"Can we return Assylia's consciousness to her ship? Could she counteract the command from within the system?"

"The bioneural systems of the *Betasis* were infected with Borg nanoprobes. It was the only way we could force her consciousness into the holobuffer. I don't think she could survive within . . ."

Janeway raised her hand. She didn't need to hear any more. She had less than ten minutes to get *Voyager* a safe distance from the array.

Seven watched in alarm as Chakotay fired on the entity known as "Phoebe." Had she been in command of this mission, it would certainly not have been her first choice. Though she would not have hesitated to defend herself, or the team, she sensed vulnerabilities in Phoebe that Chakotay seemed oblivious of. Why had she not simply killed them and taken the Key if that was her goal? To Seven it seemed obvious that the captain was, most likely, just as Phoebe had said, alive, and that up until the moment Chakotay fired, might still have the upper hand in her dealings with the Nacene.

Nonetheless, Chakotay's aim was true. The blast from his phaser rifle stuck Phoebe's chest, and she was thrown to the deck, where she remained motionless for a full five seconds.

"Good shot, Commander," Neelix offered too soon.

The Monorhans were agitated, fluttering about the room but keeping a safe distance from Phoebe's inert body and Chakotay's team.

"Commander?" Seven said.

"Take Neelix and get back to *Voyager*," he ordered, kneeling to remove the Key from his pack.

"You may yet require our assistance," Seven replied.

"That's an order, Seven," he snapped.

But even as she turned to comply, courses of bright blue energy began to stream visibly through Phoebe's body. At first it appeared as if she was undergoing some sort of primitive electroshock treatment. But when her eyes opened and she started to sit up, Seven's curious fascination was instantly replaced by a solid and sharp sense of self-preservation. The problem now was that Chakotay held the only weapon that had any chance of damaging Phoebe at all.

As Chakotay moved to fire again, a burst of invisible energy shot from Phoebe's hand and impacted his chest, sucking the wind from his lungs and knocking him several feet from his prior location.

Seven tried to aim her weapon at Phoebe, who was rising from the floor, but the Monorhans, attempting to aid the away team, were rushing to surround Phoebe and denying Seven a clear shot. Seven did not truly believe her weapon would damage the Nacene, but she was certain it would kill the Monorhans and hesitated to injure or anger her only allies.

She glanced aside to see Neelix searching the room for cover, a safer place from which to attack Phoebe or repel her next onslaught. Spotting a long, low bank of computer stations along the room's edge, he rushed to Chakotay's side and began to pull him to safety.

Seven saw his actions and intuited his destination. Keeping her aim fixed on the last spot where she'd had an unobstructed view of Phoebe, she moved to cover Neelix as he pulled Chakotay to the relative concealment of the station panel.

Dozens of the Monorhan creatures where thrown from Phoebe's immediate vicinity. Poking her head above the computer station, Seven watched as Phoebe's head and torso, still arcing with flashes of brilliant blue light, began to destabilize. Her face appeared first to flatten, then elongate. Her arms extended, losing their hands and fingers in favor of several longer cilia-like appendages. Several similar tentacles emerged from her chest until all that had been vaguely humanoid in Phoebe's appearance dissolved in favor of the nightmarish creature Naomi had described to the captain when she awoke from her surgery. The Doctor had dutifully recorded Naomi's description in his logs, and Seven had committed them to memory in preparation for this away mission.

The toxin still flowed through Phoebe. The translucent tentacles now pulsed with an inky black sludge, and the flashes of light gradually intensified from a cool blue to an angry red hue.

Phoebe, in her true Nacene form, was capable of inflicting substantially more damage upon her attackers. Monorhans were grasped by her powerful tentacles, and one after another, the life was drained from them. In each case, the small wormlike spores emerged in the final throes of death and began to collect in the center of the floor beneath Phoebe.

At this point, the only advantage the away team had was numbers. But given the rate at which the Monorhans were succumbing, Seven could not predict how long that advantage would hold.

Chakotay was stirring. Seven helped him to kneel, saying, "We are pinned down. The Monorhans are keeping Phoebe busy for the moment, but are taking heavy losses."

"We have to get the Key and get out of here," he said firmly.

"An interesting tactical choice, when you had that option only moments ago," Seven replied.

"Don't tell me you trust her?" Chakotay asked.

"I do not," Seven said simply. "I was merely pointing out to you . . ."

"Later," Chakotay cut her off. "I'm going back for the Key."

"I will make the attempt," Seven replied.

Chakotay next thought process was clear enough to read on his face. He was considering the fact that this had been his foolhardy idea, as well as Seven's relative value to the crew and *Voyager*'s mission, and was obviously sorely tempted to contradict her.

"You are barely able to sit up, Chakotay," Seven chided him.

"Go ahead," he nodded. "But try and stay down." Raising his rifle to his shoulder, he moved to Neelix's side to cover Seven as she moved quietly away.

The scene playing out before Chakotay's eyes was chaos. One after another, the Monorhans made suicidal runs toward Phoebe, and each time she managed to capture and subdue most that crossed within reach of her tentacles. The collection of . . . what had Phoebe called them? . . . spores beneath her was growing. Between Phoebe's words and Assylia's, it seemed safe to assume now that the Nacene's spores and the Monorhans' parasites were one and the same. Assuming Chakotay and his team managed to somehow return to *Voyager*, if Phoebe's intent was to allow the spores to attack their crew as the Monorhans had been attacked, Chakotay didn't like the odds of their survival.

"I guess it could be worse," Neelix muttered.

Suddenly there was a low cracking noise from behind them both. Once, years ago, Chakotay had agreed to go ice skating on a holographic lake with a fellow Academy cadet he'd found charming. Apart from confirming his bitter distaste for cold-weather activities, Chakotay had received a near-hypothermia-inducing lesson in the sound thin ice made when it was about to give way. The sound that was now meeting his ears from more than one location behind him indicated in no uncertain terms that something solid was slowly weakening and about to rupture.

He didn't have to turn his head to understand what was happening. He clearly remembered the stasis chambers that lined the room and the hundreds, probably thousands of beings which were held in those chambers.

"It's worse," Chakotay replied.

The creatures continued their attacks on Phoebe. Chakotay could barely make out Seven's lithe form, staying as low to the floor as she could, but failing to find a clear path through the throng. Dozens of Monorhans had surrounded Chakotay's rucksack and seemed intent on thwarting anyone who might approach.

"We have to get away from these walls," Chakotay shouted to Neelix.

"Why?" Neelix asked.

The answer came in the form of a deafening crunch as a casing gave way. It had housed a creature more than three meters high with four appendages attached to its exoskeleton, each terminating in sharp pincers. Disoriented, the creature stumbled from its stasis chamber, barely missing Neelix's head as it fell.

More loud crunches followed, as Chakotay pushed Neelix toward Seven, into the melee.

"Don't look!" he ordered. "Just run!"

Janeway's first response was to order B'Elanna to the bridge.

"Bring the impulse engines online and release the docking clamps. Force your way free if you have to. Take shields and structural integrity to maximum, and wait for my order. If you don't hear from me in eight minutes, get *Voyager* to safety."

"But . . ." B'Elanna started to argue.

"There's no time for explanations, B'Elanna. I have to get to the Key. If Phoebe was serious about bringing it to me, she'd already be here. If I'm not back with Chakotay's team by then, we're not coming back."

B'Elanna forced a stoic nod and an "Aye, Captain" before calling for Vorik to join her and hurrying from the room.

Assylia was still crouched on the floor, sobbing. The Doctor had moved to her side and was attempting to murmur some words of comfort, which were obviously having no effect whatsoever on the broken woman.

Tuvok stood immobile, watching Assylia with the same curious eyes that had been fixed upon her since her strange request of someone called Naviim.

Moving directly into his line of sight, Janeway said, "Tuvok?"

His eyes blinked rapidly and then took on a more familiar expression.

"Captain," he replied.

Physical displays of affection had never been part of the unspoken vocabulary of their long relationship, but the bittersweet pain of this moment overwhelmed her and she placed a delicate hand on the area of the glowing creature that rested above his heart as her eyes brimmed with tears.

"You said that you would enter the final stage of transformation willingly," she said.

"That is correct," he replied.

"Then it isn't too late?"

"Too late for what?" he asked.

"The Doctor might still be able to save you," she said urgently, "If you will allow him to."

Tuvok met Janeway's fervent gaze. His eyes, usually filled with cold and dark resolve, were lit with an emotion Janeway was certain she had never seen there. It was a mixture of kindness and regret.

"I would not choose another course, Captain, nor would I have one chosen for me," he said.

"But, Tuvok . . ." Janeway implored, the breadth and depth of the loss she was faced with tensing between them.

Doubt and confusion played across Janeway's face as she tried to push her own heart out of the way and consider this choice only from Tuvok's point of view.

Finally she offered a weak, semi-serious "I could make it an order."

"You could," he replied.

"But though that might change your course of action, it would not change your choice, would it?" she asked.

"It would not," he replied.

Removing her hand, she looked directly into his eyes and said, "I will miss you. But I would not deny you this. Goodbye . . . my friend."

"Goodbye . . . Kathryn," he replied. "Live long and prosper."

Without another word, she turned and rushed from sickbay.

Ensign Clayton was halfway through her third straight duty shift in transporter room three when Janeway entered, slinging a modified phaser rifle over her shoulder. Clayton had followed the away team's progress from the

Betasis into the first ring. But once they had used the alien transporters to move to the second ring, she had lost a stable lock.

She had noted with surprise and relief when Chakotay's team had activated a set of pattern enhancers within the second ring. She watched, bleary-eyed, for the first moment she might detect their signals within the range of the enhancers, certain that their arrival there might indicate a need for a rapid evacuation, and she had no intention of disappointing them.

Clayton was the first in her family to enter the Academy. The second daughter, one of three children, she had been taken to Bajor by her parents when she and her siblings were just toddlers. Because her parents were Federation citizens not affiliated with Starfleet, the Cardassian authorities had granted them permission to work as teachers within the occupied territories. This was one of many positive faces they tried to put on the Occupation for many years. But Clayton knew intimately the true methods and means of the Cardassians, and their unspoken determination to crush Bajor's people and civilization. Her sister and brother had died fighting for the resistance not long after their parents had been stripped of their status as "neutral advisors" and thrown into a labor camp. Clayton had been smuggled off on a cargo vessel and, once returned to the safety of the home of her father's sister on Earth, had immediately transmitted her application to Starfleet Academy. The years on Bajor had left an indelible mark upon her spirit. Human by birth, a Starfleet officer by choice, in her heart she was, and always would be, Bajoran.

Voyager had been her first assignment, and Clayton had done her best by Captain Janeway. She had served for four years in relative obscurity as a nameless, faceless, but nonetheless integral part of *Voyager*'s survival up to this point.

"Ensign," Janeway barked as she entered, "do you currently have a lock on Commander Chakotay's position?"

"No, ma'am," she replied. "His last known location was section fifty-seven epsilon of the second ring, where he activated a set of pattern enhancers, but I haven't had a clear signal for the past eleven minutes."

"Show me that section of the array," Janeway requested, stepping shoulder-to-shoulder with Clayton to examine the display. As she pondered the schematic, Janeway said softly, "Where was he headed?"

"There is a large storage bay only a few hundred meters from the pattern enhancers, Captain," Clayton offered. "I believe that was his intended destination."

"What's in that storage bay?" Janeway asked.

Overlaying a sensor display on the schematic, Clayton answered, "There are muted biosignatures and . . . *oh, my* . . ."

"What is it?"

"The multiphasic activity in that room is off the charts."

"What does that mean, Ensign?"

"We've been tracking the life-forms Commander Chakotay discovered, and from the looks of it, almost all of them are now located in the storage bay where the away team was headed."

"Can you transport me directly there?" Janeway asked.

"Maybe."

Janeway raised an eyebrow. Clayton knew full well that when the captain posed a question she was accustomed to receiving either a definitive answer or a lot more information.

"Explain."

"The mineral compound that blocks our transporters has an unusual crystalline formation. It refracts the beam, thereby destabilizing it. But there are sections of the array that do not contain the compound, less than ten percent. If we use the pattern enhancers the away team set up and direct the beam from there through the unaffected sections, I think I can get you in the room."

"You think?"

"I've run a few simulations . . . in the event the away team couldn't make it back to the enhancers. I'd just have to reverse the settings," Clayton replied. "Of course you might want Lieutenant Torres to check my calculations."

"There isn't time," Janeway said, stepping up to the transporter pad. "Do it."

Clayton took a deep breath and reset the transport parameters. When it was done she said, "Ready, Captain?"

"Energize, Ensign . . . Clayton, isn't it?" Janeway asked.

"Yes, Captain," she replied. "Ensign Grace Clayton."

"Good work, Grace," Janeway replied with a tight smile. "Now energize."

Chapter 16

In Janeway's abrupt exit she had missed the wave of emotions that washed over Tuvok's face following her departure. Tuvok's gaze had shifted to Assylia, still wailing and rocking back and forth inconsolably.

Her pain was a magnet, tearing at the powerful and new emotions that he had discovered in his communion with the transformed Monorhans. His thoughts turned back to the fire . . . the certainty and peace that now lay within his grasp. Their cool firm simplicity bathed him in peace, bringing him one step closer to the acceptance that would mean his death and release.

But something else, equally powerful, stayed him. He had intentionally severed his link with the Monorhans, those who were waiting so anxiously for him to join their vast and brilliant harmony. He had opened himself to them only once in the last several hours, at Assylia's request. And though he had sensed Naviim's presence, and allowed Naviim to move through him for a moment to address his *rih*, Tuvok was now alone, standing on the precipice of complete abandon and wondering why, now that he had come so far, he was hesitating.

Other than to deactivate the holomatrix, the Doctor

was helpless to ease Assylia's suffering. She was beyond his ministration, or any that could be offered by anyone else.

Except for Tuvok.

He had never before *felt* compassion.

He understood it. He had seen it in action many times, particularly in his interactions with Janeway and her crew. He knew its value and the absurd lengths to which it often led humans.

But he was completely unprepared for the selflessness of the emotion.

His first contact with the transformed Monorhans had been a tangle of confusion. But once his mind had been opened to them . . . or by them . . . he had allowed the struggle to cease and given way to the torrential rain of emotion that had always been buried within him.

This was part of the allure of the new life that was being offered to him. Pure logic was only part of the experience. Logic balanced with emotion . . . the end of the struggle . . . was the elusive prize he so desperately sought.

But now that he was no longer able to submerge his feelings beneath a solid layer of logic, he found, much to his surprise, that the choice that lay before him was not as simple as he had believed up to this point.

He could accept that his friends and family . . . those who *loved* him . . . would feel pain when his body died. It was a testament to their devotion to him that they would willingly suffer this pain so that he might take the final step in this journey he had chosen. And it was appropriate that they honor his choice.

But Assylia's suffering moved him in a way he had never experienced. Even with all of the promise that lay before him, he was not certain he would be able to find complete peace in it, if it meant he had failed to relieve the

pain of another whose tortured existence demanded that
any being who was sentient of it respond with *compassion*.

The realization hit him.

He would always regret this choice.

But not as much as the alternative.

His arms were bound to his side, constricted by the
presence of the life-form awaiting the final transfer of his
consciousness. He gently requested release, and the creature rearranged itself so that he could place his hands on
Assylia's face.

Kneeling before her, he said quietly, "My mind to your
mind . . ."

The meld was initiated. He was all too aware that the
enhanced mental abilities he was currently enjoying, the
same abilities that had allowed him to call to Vorik and
find the strength to deliver the Monorhans' message to
Assylia, would be lost to him forever if what he was about
to attempt succeeded. But the part of him that knew compassion did not care.

Once his mind was firmly linked to the consciousness
that was embedded within Assylia's holomatrix, he
opened the door that linked him to the minds of Assylia's
people. For a moment, both were bathed in a sea of conflict and terror.

Something was wrong.

Protect them.

The Key has been recovered.

Danger.

It is the Time of Knowing.

It must be stopped.

Blessed be the All-Knowing Light.

Resist.

Surging through the sea of these vast conflicting fragments of thought, Tuvok saw the chamber where the

Nacene known as "Phoebe" was slaughtering the Monorhans.

His despair was overwhelming. But from Assylia he received an infusion of righteous rage.

She knew what he knew.

These were her people, and they were once again under attack. But this time, there was something she could do to help them.

Tuvok?

He heard her words clearly in his mind.

The choice is yours, he answered her.

This responsibility is mine. I must help them, she replied.

Then do so.

Tuvok was again seated in front of the fire, grasping the hand of his mirror image. Assylia sat beside him, and as he made his wishes clear to the creature that had shared every aspect of his being since the transformation had begun, the image of the face across the fire began to shimmer.

For a brief moment, Tuvok knew sadness. The features of the face distorted and were replaced by a mirror image of Assylia. Though Tuvok did not remember releasing the hand of his counterpart, he saw now that the entity firmly grasped the hand of Assylia.

Then, the fire was gone. He was alone again in the darkness of his mind. But the anticipated and familiar loneliness did not ache within him as it had so recently. An icy wave washed it away as the pain, regret, and compassion buried themselves deep in the recesses of his mind where they belonged.

The Doctor watched in amazement as the glowing creature that had engulfed Tuvok began to writhe and wriggle, moving down Tuvok's arms and beginning to envelop the holographic body of Assylia.

She did not seem to resist the transfer. In the space of a few short moments, the creature completely disentangled itself from Tuvok and covered every visible portion of Assylia.

Force of habit called the Doctor to scan both of them with his tricorder, but it wasn't necessary to understand what was happening. Tuvok had said that the final choice to accept the creature was his and his alone. Clearly he had made the choice to allow the creature, now fully formed, to merge with Assylia's consciousness rather than his own.

The transfer was complete.

Tuvok fell unconscious to the deck as the creature formed itself into a tight cocoon around Assylia. A few moments later, the Doctor watched in awe as an organism of unspeakable beauty burst forth from the cocoon, unfolding its massive wings and beginning to beat the air with them to hold a stationary position above Tuvok's supine form.

Two delicate arms emerged from the creature's torso. Long tapered fingers reached for Tuvok's face and gently caressed him. Then, in a brilliant flash of blinding white light, the creature was gone.

The Doctor knelt over Tuvok and activated his tricorder. The readings were impossible, but confirmed when Tuvok opened his eyes and started to sit up.

"Gently, Lieutenant," the Doctor said in his most soothing voice. "It appears you are going to be fine."

The first thing Janeway was conscious of as she materialized in the center of the chamber where Chakotay, Seven, Neelix, and the Monorhans were battling for their lives was a complete inability to breathe. There was simply no space around her which was not occupied by billowing rapidly beating wings. After a few seconds of tumbling through this disoriented jumble, she threw herself face-down on the floor of the chamber.

Through the confusion she heard the unmistakable hiss of weapons fire.

That would be the away team, she thought, and the fact that at least one of them was still alive and wielding a weapon steeled her resolve. With one arm raised above her head to shield it from the relentless onslaught of frenetic activity, she started to crawl toward the only opening she could make out within the swirling mass. Within a few meters, her hand struck something solid. Raising her eyes, she saw a standard-issue rucksack, and within it the rough edges of the ceremonial box in which the Key to Gremadia had been presented to her.

Frantically, she opened the pack and pulled the box free. With a loud click and hiss, she released the ceremonial lock and cracked the box open.

Blinding rays of pink light—accompanied, perhaps only in Janeway's imagination, by a screeching wail—poured from the box.

I guess they're glad I'm back, Janeway thought, relatively undisturbed by the fact that she was now accustomed to thinking of the Key as many living things.

The frenetic efforts of the creatures that surrounded her increased exponentially when the Key was revealed. The box was pulled from her fingertips and lifted from the ground, then abruptly clattered back to the floor as the creature who had grasped it was pulled from the melee by an unseen force.

This time, Janeway managed to rise almost to her hands and knees, and in one quick motion threw her body over the box, clutching it to her chest and folding herself around it in a fetal position.

The creatures ceased trying to grab the box and instead

turned their efforts on her. Sharp fingers plucked at her from all sides as she struggled by feel to pull the box open and release the Key.

Finally, her palm found its smooth warm surface and she was able to shift herself into a position to pull it free.

The moment her entire hand was positioned securely on it, she had the strange sensation that it was stuck there. She wouldn't have risked testing the theory by letting go, but she definitely didn't like the feeling.

Like a piece of metal drawn to a powerful magnet, Janeway's other hand was pulled without aid of her will to the sphere. Squinting her eyes automatically to shield them from the powerful light emanating from the Key, she rose, or was pulled by its force, to a standing position. She folded her arms over the Key in a protective gesture, pulling it into her abdomen, and for the first time since her arrival was able to take a full breath, and then see exactly what kind of disaster she had transported into.

The first thing to strike her was the sudden comparative stillness and silence of the moment. She now had a clear vision of the creatures who had been buffeting her about the floor as they cleared a space around her, revealing the rest of the room to her sight and further illuminating it by the glow of their bodies, which seemed to pulse with light.

She knew instantly that these were the Monorhans. The structure and translucent glow of their bodies were similar to that of the creature that had been joined with Tuvok. But the faces that now turned to her with expressions of mingled awe and reverence were unmistakable both in their physical character and in the spirits that spoke to her through their large haunting eyes.

On either side of her, down the sides of the room as far as she could see, hundreds of aliens were wrestling with the creatures. She recognized some of them. There were many she could not place. But the memory of the field of battle Phoebe had shown her and the mass of Nacene who had assumed other forms in order to facilitate their explorations was still vivid in her mind.

The exiles have returned, she thought, but almost as quickly corrected herself when she saw the stasis chambers lining the walls and dozens of alien life-forms forcing their way through the barriers that separated them from the battle.

Or these are the ones who gave up the struggle, she realized.

Neither thought was particularly comforting.

But even as she realized this, she saw at the same time that, like the Monorhans, they had ceased to engage with one another and were turning their attention to her instead.

From the far end of the chamber a familiar voice called, "Captain!"

"Chakotay," she replied, searching the scene for him and smiling with relief when she saw him pull himself free from the clutches of what looked like a large green spider. When the alien's eye stalks were directed toward her, it seemed to lose all will to engage Chakotay and stood quite still as her first officer hurried across the room toward her.

From the opposite flank, Seven and Neelix came into view and likewise began to run in her direction.

No one, neither the Nacene nor the Monorhans, seemed inclined to stop them. The all stood still, many openmouthed, staring at Janeway.

At first this was difficult to understand. Then the intensifying heat of the Key clutched firmly in her hands reminded her that, at least for the moment, she was holding the only ace in the room and nothing seemed as important to either side in this conflict as how she was going to play it.

"You're all right," Chakotay said on ragged shallow breaths as he reached her.

Janeway nodded, managing a weak smile.

There was still one all important factor in the equation that was missing, and Janeway was impatient for her to show herself.

A large wriggling pile pulled her attention to her left. *The spores,* she knew in an instant. Lifting her eyes above the wormlike organisms, she saw Phoebe, a mass of writhing black tentacles floating above the spores. Her first reaction to Janeway's presence was to release several Monorhans who were held in her grasp. Once they were free she gently glided to the floor and slowly lurched toward Janeway and her officers.

"Kathryn," her voice boomed, echoing throughout the chamber.

At least Phoebe no longer looked or sounded like her sister. In some ways this made what must come next much easier for Janeway.

"You didn't return to *Voyager,*" Janeway began, then quipped, "I was starting to worry."

"Captain, the life-forms we detected . . ." Chakotay began.

"Don't worry, Commander," Janeway halted him. "I think I know everything about this situation I need to for the time being."

"You will return the Key to its box, Kathryn," Phoebe said in a tone more commanding than supplicating. "We will not allow it to be used until the rest of the exiles have returned."

"That was our understanding," Janeway replied, nodding slightly, but making no move to release the Key, still clutched to her stomach.

"Then why do you hesitate now?" Phoebe demanded.

"It appears this situation is a little more complicated than you described to me," Janeway replied.

"You refer to the abominations," Phoebe said.

"And the fact that this array is about to be destroyed," Janeway added.

The filaments of red light that had been coursing through Phoebe's undulating form were transmuted to a vivid shade of violet. Something in this change gave Janeway the distinct sensation that Phoebe was attempting to verify what Janeway had said.

A moment later, her suspicion was confirmed. "It cannot be stopped," Phoebe said with resignation.

"I didn't think it could," Janeway replied. "You will allow Commander Chakotay and his team to return unharmed to *Voyager,*" she said in a tone which clearly indicated that this was a demand, not a request.

There was a pregnant pause as Phoebe appeared to consider her options.

"Of course," Phoebe finally replied.

Chakotay opened his mouth to protest but didn't have a chance before Janeway said, "Thank you," adding, "Commander, if I'm not back on board in five minutes, I'm not coming back. Your orders are to get the ship as far away from the array as possible and resume a course for the Alpha Quadrant."

Chakotay's head was pounding. The sudden relief he'd felt when Janeway appeared in the chamber, heightened when she addressed Phoebe in the calm commanding voice that had seen them through situations worse than this, evaporated in a flood of conflicted pressing needs.

She had a plan. That much was obvious. But if she was honestly willing to give her life in the execution of it, the biggest part of his heart felt it was his duty to stand by her side while she did it.

"Send Seven and Neelix," he said quickly. "But let me stay," he said.

"This isn't up for discussion, Commander," Janeway replied. "Assylia activated her ship's self-destruct mechanism. This entire place will be destroyed in the next six minutes. Tuvok is dead. Tom and Harry are missing. *Voyager* needs you more than I do right now."

She was right and he knew it.

But he couldn't force himself to accept it.

"*Now,* Chakotay," Janeway commanded.

There wasn't time to think of all the things he wanted to say to her. The truth was he had never allowed himself to imagine saying goodbye to her. With an emptiness in his heart that threatened to suffocate him, Chakotay turned to Seven and Neelix and nodded for them to join him in moving quickly toward the exit. The creatures cleared a path, and within seconds the chamber was behind them as they ran as quickly as they could toward the waiting pattern enhancers.

Phoebe moved closer to Janeway, saying, "I have done as you wished. Now put the Key away."

"Tell me one thing first," Janeway demanded.

"What is it?"

"Why didn't you tell me about the Monorhans?"

There was another pause as Phoebe considered the best way to answer this question. There wasn't a truthful answer that was going to get her anywhere, but as she tentatively pushed herself into Janeway's mind, searching for an alternative, she saw all too plainly that there was also no point in lying. The exiled Nacene who were not already here were still en route to the array. By the time they arrived the array would be destroyed, but neither Phoebe nor those already present would use the conduit until their number was complete. That left precious few options but one.

Janeway would have to die aboard the array.

Her death would further destabilize the gateway, but the Key would remain intact to be used in another time and place.

Phoebe was spared the need to explain this to Kathryn as a high-pitched screech filled the chamber. Every head in the room snapped toward the far entrance where the soulless creature, *the unknowing one,* floated forward, propelled by its ragged, misshapen wings, heading straight for Janeway.

Chakotay's team had no difficulty reaching the pattern enhancers they had set up near the chamber. Clayton transported them from the array directly onto *Voyager*'s bridge. Rising from the captain's chair, B'Elanna rushed forward.

"Chakotay, what happened?" she demanded. "Where's the captain?"

There was, unfortunately, no time to answer her question.

"Chakotay to transporter room three," he barked.

"Go ahead Commander," Clayton replied over the comm.

"Do you have a lock on the captain?"

"Yes, sir," she replied.

Finally, some good news.

He debated calling for an emergency transport right that second. But Kathryn had asked for five minutes. If they were his to give, he would.

"Computer," he called, checking the time on his armrest console. "Begin a four-minute countdown with audible confirmation every sixty seconds, starting now."

"Countdown enabled," the computer replied.

Turning to B'Elanna he asked, "What's our status?"

"All systems are standing by, Commander," she replied. "Impulse engines are online, shields and inertial dampers at maximum. Our interface with the array's docking controls is stable. We've plotted a course that skirts the edge of the singularity's event horizon and we're ready to depart."

"Excellent," Chakotay replied. "Seven, you're on tactical. B'Elanna, take the helm."

"Aye, sir," they replied in unison, taking their stations. Chakotay took half a second to appreciate that it was the first truly harmonious moment they'd shared since their mini-collective state had ended.

"Commander," Neelix said.

"Get down to sickbay, Neelix," Chakotay ordered. "Tell the Doctor to prepare for casualties. Boarding this godforsaken place was almost a disaster. I don't expect we'll have an easy time on the way out either."

"Yes, sir," Neelix snapped, heading immediately for the turbolift.

Taking his seat next to the captain's chair, he opened a comm channel to the entire ship.

"Three minutes remaining," the computer said.

"This is Commander Chakotay to all hands. We are ready to depart the array. Red alert."

As the bridge was bathed in the pulsing red glow of the emergency lights, B'Elanna said, "Commander, the tractor net controls that run along the outer edge of the docking bay are still active. We haven't tried to disable them yet, but I believe we should do so before we attempt to leave."

"Why would we do that?" Chakotay asked.

"Once we initiate our separation from the docking bay, our link with the array's systems will disconnect. If the tractor controls should be activated automatically or *by anyone else* before we clear the bay, we won't be able to pull free and maintain our exit vector, and once our link is terminated we won't have any control over the tractor system."

Chakotay weighed the pros and cons. Since the entire array was going to be dust in a matter of moments, he didn't think it mattered one way or the other.

"Can we target them from here?" he asked.

"Yes, sir," Seven replied. "Their coordinates are locked in and phasers are ready."

Chakotay was about to order Seven to fire when the most unexpected of voices cut softly through the tension enveloping the bridge.

"That would be most unwise, Commander," Tuvok said, emerging from the turbolift.

Chakotay's head snapped toward him, along with the head of every other bridge crewman present.

"Tuvok," he whispered, then spoke up, saying, "the captain said you were dead."

"She had good reason to believe I would be the last time we spoke," the Vulcan replied with characteristic restraint. "But as you can see, she was mistaken."

"Are you fit to return to duty?" Chakotay asked.

"I would not be here were I otherwise," Tuvok replied.

Chakotay shook his head, a faint smile crossing his lips. He and Tuvok had never been the best of friends, but at this moment he was struck by how much he'd missed him over the past few days.

"Take your station," Chakotay said. "Seven, replace Collins at ops."

"Two minutes remaining," the computer reported.

Seven complied as Chakotay continued, "So why shouldn't we destroy the tractor net controls now?"

"Because if we do so, we will not be able to safely leave the array," Tuvok replied. "The tractor net functions as a guidance system, shepherding vessels along the singularity's event horizon. Our navigational systems are not sophisticated enough to calculate the required course adjustments, nor could the most skilled pilot successfully plot the appropriate course. It is one of many safety features created for this array and will activate automatically when we cross the docking bay's threshold."

Chakotay thought back to his conversation with Assylia and her conviction that the creatures had brought *Voyager* safely on board.

"How do you know that?" Chakotay asked.

"It is one of many things I learned from the life-forms who first brought me to the array," Tuvok replied without a hint of remorse.

"Did they tell you that they were responsible for our safe arrival?" Chakotay asked.

"Yes, Commander," Tuvok replied. "Assylia briefly disrupted the automated system when *Voyager* approached the array. They were able to counter her efforts only moments before the ship's imminent destruction."

"I hope you thanked them for us, Tuvok," Chakotay replied, resuming his seat.

"I did, Commander," Tuvok replied.

"Transporter room to the bridge," Clayton's voice announced.

"Go ahead, Ensign," Chakotay replied.

"Commander, there is a highly localized subspace dissonance field forming in section fifty-seven epsilon of the array's second ring," she informed him.

Kathryn, Chakotay thought silently.

"Does it pose any danger to the captain?" Chakotay asked.

"I don't know, sir," Clayton replied. *"But it is effectively jamming the captain's signal. I can't keep a stable lock."*

Chakotay considered his few options.

Much as every cell in his body demanded that he find a way to return to the array, he knew that Kathryn would never forgive him if he did so.

"One minute remaining," came the computer's maddeningly calm voice.

Closing his eyes, Chakotay forced himself to take a deep, measured breath. Kathryn's face and last words rose unbidden to his mind.

Voyager needs you more than I do right now.

He knew what he had to do.

Acceptance and peace with this choice would have to come later.

"Lieutenant Torres," he said softly, "release the docking clamps and go to stationkeeping."

"Aye, sir," B'Elanna replied.

A heavy metallic clank assured him that they were one step closer to putting this debacle behind them.

But at what cost?

"We are clear of the docking clamps and have terminated our interface with the array's systems," B'Elanna announced. "The bay forcefield is down and we are ready to depart on your order, sir."

The ship rattled, and bucked. At first Chakotay assumed that they were having difficulty maintaining their position within the bay.

That changed when the bridge was plunged into sudden darkness.

~

What the . . . ? Janeway thought as the horrific creature unfurled its arms and shot toward her.

She sensed the confused flutter of activity among the others, but none came immediately to her aid.

This isn't good.

Phoebe spent an entire half-second debating within herself as to whether or not she should intercept the creature and temporarily save Janeway's life. Phoebe knew that the presence of the Monorhans had irreparably damaged the fragile peace she had made with the captain. Janeway hadn't come to the array with the intention of honoring her agreement with Phoebe.

No. The captain had made her choice.

It was so predictable as to be nauseating.

She was going to try and help the abominations. She either did not know or did not care that that course would certainly lead to her own death when she became the conduit. Nor did she weigh this more heavily than the reaction of the Others in Exosia, who would only be able to see Janeway's actions as a declaration of war.

Which meant that Phoebe also had a choice to make. The unknowing one was acting on instinct. It sensed the unclean blood of the lesser being in its path and yearned to purify it with the gift of the newly generated spore resting in its belly. It was acting on a primal Nacene drive which tied it more closely to the Others than to Phoebe or the exiles, an ignorance rooted in their unwillingness to interact with the life-forms beyond Exosia. Had its transformed body been tempered by a consciousness, it would have understood, as the rest of the transformed Monorhans did, that the spore wriggling within it and yearning for release was not meant for a lesser being. It would have sensed the Key and the promise it held as it poured its light into the chamber, waiting for Janeway to press it into its lock. But the unknowing one could act only on its most basic drives. It would infect the captain and she would begin the transformation. Within hours, if such time existed, another abomination would be born.

But once the spore was implanted in the captain's body, the Key would sense her oneness, her newly born Nacene-ness, and would disconnect itself from her will.

No Nacene could actually "own" the Key, because no Nacene could become the conduit and use the conduit at the same time. The fatal flaw in the Light's grand plan had been to tie the Key's activation to a *lesser being,* a flaw Phoebe and the other exiles had attempted to compensate for by gently suggesting a mythological origin to the ancient Monorhans which included godlike beings that had created and cared for them. It was not exactly a lie. And as the Monorhan belief system had evolved to include a rudimentary understanding of the Key and Gremadia, Phoebe had rested content in the certainty that whenever she and the exiles chose to use the Key, any number of Monorhans would willing have sacrificed themselves to make this happen. After all, it would have been the will of their Blessed All-Knowing Light.

The course that lay before Janeway and Phoebe now, as the unknowing one surged forward, deviated somewhat from the master plan, but was, Phoebe had to acknowledge, a better means to the same end. Janeway would not die, at least not right away, but she would no longer be the Key's owner. This would briefly forestall the further destabilization of the gateway Phoebe had worked so hard to avoid if Janeway died without opening the conduit. This would also buy Phoebe the time she needed to gather at least a few of those who had been waiting at Gremadia to take them to join the exiles in preparation for the battle that was surely to come.

In the meantime, the abominations would die, with all the others Kathryn held dear when the array was destroyed.

All in all, an acceptable compromise.

Too late Janeway realized that though her phaser rifle was still slung over her shoulder, she could not use it and hold on to the Key at the same time. She made the attempt anyway, but found that her hands were firmly glued in place around the Key. Casting a quick glance behind her, she saw the massive tattered sphere floating there. She took an instinctive step back, but almost tripped when her heel met the solid base that circled the floor beneath the sphere.

She didn't know what the creature was, or why, unlike the others, it seemed to show no deference to her position as they Key's owner. Its rage and hostility were palpable, and it took only a few brief seconds for her to resign herself to the inevitable.

Twenty meters.

Ten.

Oh, hell.

A brisk blast of noxious air assaulted her nostrils, but at the last possible moment, the creature was pulled from its intercept course.

Janeway lifted her eyes in awe as one of the Monorhans, one with a curiously familiar face, grasped the unknowing one it its arms and carried it safely away from the captain.

Assylia, she realized, her heart catching in her throat.

Then what became of Tuvok?

Janeway watched as dozens of others, seemingly on Assylia's command, joined the fight, tearing at the creature's wings and literally ripping it apart in a frenzied dance of survival. She was reminded of a holovid she'd once seen which showed in graphic detail the fury with which a pack of hyenas would descend upon a wounded lion.

Within moments, the horrific spectacle ended as the creature emitted a final weakened shriek and fell lifeless to the chamber's floor.

It landed mangled, facedown. One of the small worm-like spores that Janeway had seen piled below Phoebe emerged from its remains and in a flash joined its companions.

Throughout this the Nacene who had emerged from their stasis chambers had begun to assemble themselves in a large group surrounding the pile. The Monorhans collected themselves in their own formation along the other side of the chamber.

Janeway repositioned herself beneath the sphere. In the apparatus at its base she could clearly see a half-circle indentation. She did not know exactly how she knew, but nonetheless she was absolutely certain that this had to be the lock that the Key was meant for, and that once the Key was placed there by her, the conduit would open.

"Kathryn," Phoebe called.

"These life-forms," Janeway asked, referring to the Monorhans, "how were they created?"

The death of the unknowing one had frustrated Phoebe's plan yet again. She was forced again to face the lesser of the evils before her.

Just keep her talking until the array explodes. As long as it takes so that she doesn't use the Key and open the conduit. . . .

~

"The Monorhans who discovered the station were taken by the spores intended for my people," Phoebe said.

"Taken?"

"We can only enter Exosia in a purified state," Phoebe said. "To do otherwise would further unbalance our two realities. The spores were created to facilitate our final transformation. But as the Monorhans were created through us, the spores mistook them for us. They are not sentient. They were drawn to the Monorhans instinctively."

"Another unforeseen effect?" Janeway asked.

"They are of no consequence," Phoebe thundered.

"How can you say that?" Janeway replied in disbelief. "Just because they weren't a part of your highly flawed plan, that doesn't change the fact that they exist in their present form because of choices you and your people made. Like it or not, they are now *of you*, and they belong in Exosia. Not to mention the fact that unlike you, they are clearly mortal and will be destroyed when the array explodes. Any that might escape would at best be damned to eternal purgatory within this system, wouldn't they?" she demanded.

"Each of them has the power to generate another spore," Phoebe replied. "That which lives within them is necessary for us to reenter Exosia. I will lead them from this place and harvest the spores they possess."

"Will they survive that process, and will you allow them to follow you into Exosia when you do return?" Janeway asked.

"Of course," Phoebe said.

Janeway wasn't fooled. She studied the chamber. Its floor was littered with dead Monorhans, and she didn't imagine for one moment that the pile of spores wriggling at the feet of the Nacene had materialized out of thin air.

"I'm sorry, Phoebe," she said finally. "I wanted to help you. I truly did. But you and I both know that in order for you to get what you need, one way or another these beings will die."

"Why do you care?" Phoebe demanded.

"Because I'm not in the habit of placing my own needs above those of innocent life-forms. I would think you'd know that by now. Their rights are no less important to me than yours. And I share a sympathy with them that I cannot find for you or your people. They are not responsible for what has happened here, and they do not deserve to die now because of your ignorance or arrogance. I'm sorry, Phoebe," she said again. "Our reality is bound by time, and yours has now run out."

Raising her voice to address the Nacene assembled behind her, Janeway called out, "Those of you who wish to return home should make use of the spores that remain. Those who do not will have to find another way."

"Kathryn . . . you can't . . ." Phoebe said.

"Oh, but I can," Janeway replied.

Janeway fell to her knees at the base of the sphere and moved to put the Key in its place.

But Phoebe had one final card left to play. "You will not survive this," she warned. *The conduit can only be opened by its owner because the life force of the owner is required to sustain it."

Janeway paused for a fraction of a second.

She'd known this too. Not the mechanism of her death, but the probability of it. Her gut impulse to make sure Chakotay and the others were returned safely to *Voyager* had risen from the belief that whatever course she chose, she was probably not going to leave this chamber alive.

She thought of the Caretaker.

He'd had another choice. He could have left the Ocampa to the Kazon and saved himself by returning to Gremadia. But his sense of duty and responsibility, values that he could have learned only from his interaction with the *lesser beings* of this dimension, values that Janeway was certain Phoebe had failed to truly absorb despite the depth and breadth of her experiences, had led him to sacrifice himself to ensure the survival of those whose planet he had all but destroyed.

"We are more alike than you think, Phoebe," Janeway replied. "I have seen the compassion other Nacene have been capable of. I suggest, when this is done, you look harder at yourself and the options before you. Find a way to solve the problem that does not include the wanton destruction of those you think of as *lesser beings*. We may not be immortal, but there's a lesson in our mortality that you still need to learn."

"What is that, Kathryn?" Phoebe asked.

"There are some things worth dying for."

Phoebe was, as Janeway had said, *out of time*. But in the split second it took her to martial her energy to stop Janeway's heart in her chest and prevent her from this final fatal step, every single Monorhan still alive came together and formed a protective barrier between Phoebe and the captain.

Janeway sensed their motion and intent, took what she believed would be her final breath, and placed the Key into the lock.

Chapter 17

There was a faint click as the Key snapped into its place. The moment it did, the pink light was transmuted to orange, then yellow, finally resolving into blinding whiteness.

Janeway's hands fell to her sides. The first thing she felt was an inexplicable sense of relief. It was as if the weight of a thousand worlds had been lifted from her shoulders.

She thought for a brief moment of Tuvok, and the peace and clarity of his final moments. She could not feel anything so absolute, but in the few seconds that were still hers and hers alone, she did feel something similar as a kind and loving face filled her mind's eye. It was not the face of her former fiancé, Mark, or her father, who had died so many years ago and whom she'd missed terribly since. It was not the face of her sister, stolen by the Nacene she could only think of as "Phoebe," or the face of her beloved mother, Gretchen.

For reasons only the deepest recesses of her heart knew, the face that rose to her consciousness as she released herself to whatever must come of this choice was the face of her first officer, Chakotay. Perhaps this was her mind's way of assuring her that she had left her crew in the best possible hands. Or perhaps he was the last person she thought of because his was the heart and spirit that had become the most important if unacknowledged part of her own in the joys and sorrows of the past four years.

And now he will never know, she realized with an overwhelming sense of regret.

But as the light emanating from the Key enveloped her, all thoughts of herself were wiped from her mind. She was lifted from the floor where she had knelt, her arms stretching out at her sides as her legs unfolded. The whiteness surged around her. She felt certain that it was pulling her apart. The tattered remains of the fragile spherical casing that had housed the spores disintegrated around her in a cascade of fiery sparks as she was drawn to the center of the ring and held aloft by the force of the Key.

And then, *they* were moving through her. One after another, the transformed Monorhans forced themselves into the center of her body. They sought out the impossibly small space between the subatomic particles of her being and passed through like tiny threads through the eye of a needle.

She did not know what awaited them on the other side. But in their passage she knew utter and complete joy. Somehow, they understood the sacrifice that she was making on their behalf, and in the fraction of a second that the essence of each was mingled with her own, she felt their gratitude.

It entered her mind and soul as the most beautiful of songs. Surging to a perfectly resolved crescendo within her, the fragmented and dissonant music that had first called to Tuvok now took its rightful place among the larger symphonic tapestry of the ever-resonating universe.

~

Phoebe watched this spectacle with rage. Janeway had betrayed her, just as she had attempted to betray the Others. The few spores that remained were drawn in their present form not to the Nacene who stood by, helplessly witnessing the end of their hopes, but to the conduit. Given the choice between the dimension where they had been trapped and that to which their true nature belonged, they sought Exosia, burrowing through Janeway's chest, unaware that when they arrived, they would immediately meet their destruction.

The exiles who had been left behind were crowding around one another, a mass of confusion. They had chosen to return to the array and enter stasis because they had grown weary of their struggle. None of them would dared have disrupted the spores, but were content to wait patiently for the number to be complete before they attempted to reenter Exosia. Though they were, for the moment, trapped in whatever alien form they had last embodied before entering stasis, Phoebe sensed that they could nonetheless share in her rage, and suffer some in the knowledge that the existence now granted to the Monorhans was probably lost to them now for all eternity.

There were too many to contain, but Phoebe gathered those she still had strength to sustain within her, granting them a small fraction of her power and will, and left the array in search of a place to safely collect her thoughts and plan for the coming eventuality.

She could not know for certain exactly what the Others would make of this intrusion into Exosia. She was absolutely certain, however, that this would speed Vivia's return and that the next time they met there would be no hiding the truth from her. The Others would have their revenge, and Phoebe knew beyond a shadow of a doubt that it would be both swift and final.

The only comfort she found as she traversed the frigid barrenness of space-time was in the thought that whatever she and her people were about to suffer, it would be nothing compared to the fate that would certainly befall those that Kathryn cared for.

The passage of the Monorhans through the conduit seemed to stretch itself over countless lifetimes. In reality, it took less than two minutes.

The last creature to move through her made more than her gratitude known to Janeway in the fraction of a second that they shared as one. Fully aware of the lengths to which Janeway and her people had gone on behalf of not only the Fourteenth Tribe but all Monorhans, the *rih-hara-tan* Assylia paused for an infinitesimal moment within Janeway's expanded consciousness to give the only gift she could. It was less than Janeway deserved, but all that Assylia had left to offer.

Certain that her children were finally safe, having tasted all too briefly the song of her people as they found the home they had longed for, Assylia transferred the entire life force within her to the failing systems of Janeway's body, which had been completely drained, as Phoebe had rightly predicted, in the process of becoming the conduit for the Monorhans.

For a brief moment, Assylia stood on the precipice of eternity and glimpsed the bright and peaceful fulfillment of her people. Then, with a prayer of gratitude to the Blessed All-Knowing Light, she asked that if her life could be taken that Janeway might survive, He, in his infinite wisdom, let it be so.

Assylia never entered Exosia.

Much to the amazement of the Nacene who were too weak to follow Phoebe, when the conduit was closed and Janeway's body fell in a heap upon the floor of the chamber now filled with an inky blackness, the captain was still breathing.

The few seconds it took for the ship's emergency lighting system to compensate for the shipwide blackout were interminable to Chakotay. When the bridge was once again awash in the rhythmic pulse of red light he called, "Report!"

"Commander," Seven's measured voice called from ops, "the *Betasis* is reaching critical mass. It will explode, setting off a chain reaction which will destabilize the array in less than one minute."

"What happened to the lights? Are we losing power?" he asked.

"No, sir. The subspace dissonance field coming from the array expanded to a large enough area to disrupt *Voyager*'s power grid, but it has now collapsed and I have rerouted nonessential systems to compensate for the temporary drain."

"Chakotay to transporter room three, have you recovered the captain's signal?"

"Aye, sir," Clayton replied.

"Thirty seconds remaining," the computer reported.

"Chakotay to Janeway," he called over the comm.

A sharp burst of static was the unwelcome but nonetheless fully anticipated response.

Forgive me, Chakotay thought, unsure whether he was addressing the spirits who watched over his people, or Kathryn.

"Tuvok, drop our shields . . . Clayton, initiate transport!"

Five quick heartbeats later Clayton called, *"I have her, Commander."*

"Raise shields. B'Elanna, get us out of here."

Under B'Elanna's calm hands, *Voyager* glided steadily forward, passing through the docking bay's entrance, headed straight for the swirling destructive mass of the singularity. Just as the aft section was clearing the bay, the familiar deep green tractor net flickered to life and surrounded the ship in its stabilizing energy web.

At the same time, the central core of the *Betasis* reached critical mass, and the finest technological achievement of Monorha's Fourteenth Tribe exploded, taking with it the docking bay where it had rested for fifty years, and vaporizing the upper ring's stabilization field controls.

Voyager careened to starboard.

"Can we go to impulse?" Chakotay barked.

"Not yet, sir," B'Elanna replied. "We haven't cleared the . . ."

But the end of her statement was lost as the ship jutted abruptly to port, and the tractor net blinked out of existence.

Suddenly, the intertial dampers were pushed to the brink of their capacity as the ship skidded along the edge of the event horizon. The ops and engineering consoles erupted in a shower of sparks, and those who were able to keep their seats or their footing did so only by holding on for dear life to whatever was nearest.

"Shields at sixty percent," Tuvok called from tactical.

The chain reaction that Seven had predicted was swift. Like falling dominoes, each bay to the right and left of that which had housed the *Betasis* crumpled in upon itself.

Huge shards of metal were pulled free and plunged into the inexorable gravity of the singularity. Within seconds, the lower ring was also affected. The perfect circles were ripped from their orbit as the first sections to collapse were pulled first toward the center, then caught in the singularity's gravity and plucked like petals from a flower and sucked into oblivion.

Massive pieces of shrapnel flew before the main viewscreen as B'Elanna nudged the impulse engines from one-quarter to one-half, silently becoming one with the ship as she gently did her best to find the ever-narrowing course to safety.

She managed to avoid the event horizon by less than a hundred kilometers and for a heart-stopping second dropped the nose forty-five degrees, heading straight toward one of the only sections of the array that was still relatively intact.

"Shields at forty percent," Tuvok said.

Chakotay saw it rushing toward them and silently cursed himself for waiting too long. Their rapidly disintegrating shields would never protect them from head-on impact.

"B'Elanna?" he called shrilly.

"Don't worry," B'Elanna said softly. At the same time she had been entering one slight course correction after another, the rest of her brain had been calculating trajectories for the array's debris. Though she couldn't have given Chakotay the odds to the decimal point, as Seven of Nine would no doubt have done in her place, she was fairly certain that in six out of ten possible permutations, the mass of metal they were soaring toward, which began spitting plasma as they approached, would not be in the same position in less than two seconds.

"Come on," she hissed under her breath.

One of the struts that had extended from the array shot past them like a spear.

One second.

B'Elanna closed her eyes . . . and thought of Tom.

They had spent four years as chief engineer and conn officer debating and testing the limits of *Voyager*'s flying capabilities. She wondered for a fraction of a second if he would have chosen the same course.

It doesn't matter now.

As *Voyager* reached the last obstacle separating them from relatively open space, the cumulative gravitational pull of the singularity upon the remaining solid fragment of the array forced the section out of their path and B'Elanna punched the engines to full impulse.

The main viewscreen was filled with calm star-filled space.

As the ship hurled itself toward safety, bucking under the protests of the singularity's residual gravitational field, Tuvok called up optical controls at his station and the entire bridge crew watched in awe as the swirling mass of particles that had been the stable sight of the singularity was lit by the final death throes of the exploding array. For a few seconds, it erupted into a vortex of orange and green fire.

A final shock wave shot out, nudging the ship forward in its wake, but compared to the last few minutes, the impact was relatively mild.

Chakotay found voice to say, "Good work, B'Elanna."

"Thank you, sir," she replied.

"Set a course for . . ." He paused as if honestly unsure where they were supposed to go next. "Set a course for the nearest border of the Monorhan system. We'll stop there for repairs and begin a thorough search for the *Homeward Bound*," he finally said.

"Aye, sir," B'Elanna replied, her heart sinking.

They were headed for the exact coordinates where Tom and Harry should have reentered Monorhan space. B'Elanna didn't know what they would find there. But she was certain it wouldn't be the lost shuttle. There was only so much she was willing or able to confront right now. As much as she knew they needed to complete the search, some small part of her knew it was going to be fruitless.

And once that happened . . .

For the moment, she allowed herself to disconnect from these painful and unspeakable thoughts and with lead-tipped fingers entered the course as ordered.

Captain Janeway had materialized on the transporter pad lying unconscious on her side. As protocol demanded, Clayton had immediately initiated an emergency site-to-site transport to get the captain to sickbay without wasting a second. Of course, in the brief moments between her successful retrieval of the captain and her input to activate the site-to-site transport, the entire transporter system had automatically locked down to prevent catastrophic cascade failure as emergency systems were rerouted to accommodate for the requirements of the primary shield, structural integrity, and inertial dampening systems.

Clayton hadn't wasted a moment in rushing to the captain's side to check her for injuries that would make moving her unwise, and when she found no obvious cause for concern, she lifted the captain unceremoniously over her shoulder and carried her to sickbay.

In the chaotic minutes that ensued, Clayton had struggled to keep her balance, moving as quickly as possible through the dimly lit corridors that separated the transporter room from the medical bay. By the time she reached the doors, her uniform was sticky with sweat and the muscles of her neck and right shoulder were screaming in protest, but she entered sickbay both proud and relieved that she had accomplished her task.

"Computer," she called, gently lowering the captain on the nearest biobed, "activate Emergency Medical Hologram."

At the same time, Crewman Dalby entered, supporting Ensign Davidson, who was holding his right arm, streaked with a nasty-looking plasma burn.

"Unable to comply," the computer informed them.

"Where's the Doctor?" Dalby asked.

"I don't know," Clayton replied, hurrying to the holographic control panel and taking note of the Doctor's mobile emitter sitting in its case on his desk.

"Computer, was the Doctor's program damaged?" she asked.

"Negative," the computer replied.

Clayton wasn't the holographic wizard that Lieutenant Torres was, but her first casual glance at the Doctor's initiation file shed at least a little light on the computer's cryptic response to her inquiry.

"What is it, Grace?" Dalby asked, crossing to join her.

"The Doctor's program . . ." she stammered in disbelief. "It's gone."

Acting Captain's log
Stardate 52019.1.

> *It's been twelve hours since we left the array. We've set a course for the border of Monorhan space where we will begin our search for Ensign Kim and Lieutenant Paris and are en route at full impulse. Repairs are already under way. Primary systems are functioning at eighty percent and shields have been fully restored.*

*The subspace dissonance wave that impacted the ship
just before we escaped the array caused a catastrophic failure
in the ship's holoemitters. All holographic programs running at the time, including the Doctor's, were damaged.
I've ordered Lieutenant Torres to reconstruct what she can
of the Doctor's program. Apparently even the backup modules we created were lost, and she believes it will be several
days before we are able to initialize a replacement program
. . . if ever.*

*Captain Janeway was recovered from the array, but for
the time being is . . .*

Chakotay paused. He couldn't even bring himself to
say it. He was relieved when a chiming at the door of the
captain's ready room made continuing his log unnecessary
for the moment.

"Come in," he called.

B'Elanna entered, pausing at attention before the
captain's desk. He rose to greet her, moving from the chair
he could not yet find any comfortable position in and saying, "Report." He crossed to the rail that separated the
main area of the room from the low benches that lined
one wall and ran his hand along its cool surface.

"I think I know at least part of what happened to the
Doctor," she said.

His head snapped up. She didn't sound pleased by
whatever she had discovered.

"Just before we left the array, there was a shipwide
blackout," she began.

"I remember," he said.

"For reasons that aren't entirely clear to me, when the
dissonance field hit the ship, all photonic energy in its path
was pulled into the field. I assumed we simply suffered a

brief power drain, but the only systems affected were those that utilize photonic energy."

"Which explains the loss of the lighting systems and the holographic emitters," Chakotay said.

"Right," she nodded. "But in the case of the Doctor, the field's impact was unique. All of the other holographic systems simply went offline. But the Doctor's program was extracted. There isn't a single subroutine remaining . . . and given the nature of the event, that shouldn't have happened. None of the other holograms were deleted. I've never seen anything like it."

"What do our most recent scans show about the singularity that Gremadia was orbiting?" Chakotay asked. "Is there anything that suggests . . ."

But B'Elanna cut him off, saying simply, "It's gone."

"What?" Chakotay asked in disbelief.

"I can't explain it. Within minutes of the array's destruction, the singularity disappeared."

"That shouldn't have happened, should it?"

"I stopped asking that question soon after we entered this system," B'Elanna replied wearily. "Of course it shouldn't have happened. All I know is that it did. And now there's nothing to scan in order to help me confirm my hypothesis about the Doctor's disappearance."

Chakotay took this in, gazing out at the starfield that rested in an illusionary static position beyond the window.

"Neelix," he muttered.

"I beg your pardon?" B'Elanna asked.

"Neelix said something a few days ago . . . he mentioned in passing . . . one of those sort of impossible suggestions you just tend to write off because it's Neelix."

B'Elanna smiled faintly. Obviously she too had been guilty of this on more than one occasion.

"Naomi did a drawing of the Monorhan stars, and gave it to the captain," he continued, crossing to the credenza. He found the drawing resting in a cleared space and made a mental note to replicate a frame for it. "Then she did another, for her mother, and Neelix got a little concerned because the drawings were different. She was using a view from the mess hall for her model, and at the time the area of space where we collapsed the Blue Eye was still visible. Neelix thought some of the stars were missing."

B'Elanna considered this.

"What are you suggesting, Commander?" she asked.

"I'm not really sure," he replied. "There's so much about this system that we don't understand. We've theorized and hypothesized and all but decided that there is something artificial about Monorhan space, that it was probably constructed by the Nacene, and that somehow it is a boundary between what we consider 'normal' space and Exosia. I'm beginning to think that we need to know more about the exact nature of this artificial system. The microsingularity created when we destroyed the Blue Eye might be evidence of some kind of serious destabilization of the boundary."

"Because in normal space the Blue Eye would have simply collapsed," B'Elanna interjected.

"And not only did a singularity form instead, but we know it's getting bigger," Chakotay continued. "If Neelix was right, and for some reason photonic energy is being sucked through the instability in the boundary at the microsingularity . . ."

"And if the captain did succeed in opening some kind of direct conduit between our space and Exosia . . ." B'Elanna picked up.

"A similar effect was observed. For a brief moment all

photonic energy present in the vicinity of the conduit might also have been pulled into Exosia," he concluded.

"I'll do an astrometric scan," B'Elanna said. "If the microsingularity is producing the same effect as the dissonance wave . . . it might . . . I don't know . . ." She trailed off.

"Give us a place to begin to get a better understanding of this system," Chakotay suggested. "If the Doctor's program was taken intact into Exosia, we might still be able to find him and get him back."

B'Elanna paused before asking, "Should we alter course and just begin our examination of the microsingularity now?"

It was a painfully difficult choice. The captain had been unconscious since her return from the array. She was still in sickbay, where Seven of Nine was doing all she could to stabilize the captain's condition, but every moment that went by without the Doctor was one more moment lost in the battle to save her. On the other hand, *Voyager* was also missing her best pilot and senior ops officer. No one—least of all B'Elanna, Chakotay realized—was anxious to see that priority dropped down a peg either.

"Maintain course for now," he replied. "But let me know what the sensors show. If there's reason to alter course then, I'll consider it."

"Aye, sir."

"Have the sensors picked up any evidence of further Nacene activity?" he asked.

"No." She shook her head.

"Well, that's good news, isn't it?" he offered.

He looked back at the computer station on the desk. He needed to finish that log, but for the moment simply couldn't face it.

"If you need me, I'll be in sickbay," he said.

B'Elanna nodded mutely as he left.

When he arrived, he was somewhat surprised to see Tuvok standing beside the captain's motionless form. Seven of Nine stood opposite him, indicating a reading on the neural monitor that suggested minimal brain activity.

"Commander," Seven greeted him, "there has been no change in the captain's condition since my last report."

"Thank you, Seven," he said, joining them. "I know you're doing all you can."

"She is stable, for the moment. But she has suffered severe neurological damage. I have thoroughly studied the ship's medical database and do not believe it will be possible to reverse her injuries. We can continue to artificially support her body's systems indefinitely, but she is, to all intents and purposes, brain-dead."

Chakotay nodded, his jaw clenching involuntarily as his stomach churned.

"Do you have anything to add, Tuvok?" he asked.

"Only that while I did not wish to see the captain come to harm, I am certain that her sacrifice was not in vain."

Chakotay locked eyes with Tuvok. At some point, many, many years from now, he might find this thought comforting. But for the moment, he was struck with an intense irrational desire to wring the Vulcan's neck.

Tuvok did not miss the hostility flaring in Chakotay's eyes, but was, of course, unaffected by it.

"If the captain was successful in opening the conduit between our space and Exosia, the Monorhans who had been transformed aboard the array were able to pass through into the existence for which they were meant. They are now at peace."

"And how do you suppose the Nacene feel about that?" Chakotay demanded harshly.

"I cannot speculate," Tuvok replied. "They are a complex species, and I do not believe our limited understanding of their actions or their nature suggests any conclusive answers to that question at this time."

"Of course, we don't know if the captain succeeded," Chakotay said bitterly. "We may never know."

"That is not entirely true, Commander," Tuvok contradicted him.

"What do you mean?"

"The Monorhans were not bound by the physical constraints of the array. They remained there by choice. Though most of them would surely have died in the destruction of the array, had even one of them survived, I believe I would still sense their presence."

"And I take it you don't?" Chakotay asked.

"No, Commander. I do not."

The tension flaring between them was dispersed when the doors slid open and Neelix entered, leading Naomi Wildman by the hand.

"Commander," Neelix said, "Naomi was wondering if she could speak to the captain?"

Chakotay's brow furrowed. He worried that this would be a traumatizing experience for a child.

"She understands that the captain is *resting*," Neelix added quickly, "but I didn't think it would do any harm."

Chakotay shifted his gaze to the young girl's solemn little face, then saw that she was holding a sheet of drawing paper in her free hand.

"I've drawn a picture of one of my favorite stories for her," Naomi said seriously. "Even if she can't see it yet, I thought I could tell her about it, the way Neelix tells me every night when I fall asleep."

"That's very kind of you, Naomi," Chakotay replied.

Forcing the hot rush of despair rising within his chest

to a standstill, Chakotay watched silently as Seven set up a stool on level with the captain's bed where Naomi could sit and describe her drawing to the captain. Seven then retreated to the Doctor's office while Neelix moved to Naomi's side and Tuvok remained standing his serene vigil opposite them as Naomi began her story.

"This is the Great Forest," Naomi said softly, holding the picture between them so that had Janeway been capable of opening her eyes Naomi's drawing would have been the first thing she would have seen.

"And in the middle of the forest is the Great Tree. The sun is always shining there . . . see . . . that's the sun. And it's always warm, but not too hot. When you get to the Great Tree you will always know because everyone you love will be there waiting for you. This is me, and my mother, and that's Neelix . . ."

Chakotay saw Neelix raise his hand to brush a tear from his eyes.

Turning away, Chakotay allowed those forming in his eyes to fall freely.

He didn't know if it would ever be possible for Kathryn to return to those who loved and needed her.

All he could do was ask the spirits that lived between the unnamed stars of the Delta Quadrant to guide her on the dim and rocky path that separated life from death.

That . . . and wait.

Please Kathryn, he silently prayed, *find your way back to us.*

Epilogue

The last thing the Doctor remembered was standing over the translucent remnants of the creature that had gestated within Tuvok and been transferred to Assylia. He had begun pondering the safest means of disposing of them only after he had released Tuvok from sickbay and added a brief subroutine to remind himself to consult with Tuvok once this latest crisis was past. He did not believe the ship's disposal systems would be capable of recycling them. For all he knew, B'Elanna and Seven would want to study them. But for him they were simply in the way.

That wasn't exactly true.

Yes, the remains were in the way.

But the last thing he remembered . . . *was impossible.*

He had explored as many aspects of humanity as his program allowed, interacting with the crew, creating a holographic family, engaging in physical intimacy with Danara Pel, fantasizing about physical intimacy with . . .

Had this been a fantasy?

Or, perhaps . . . a vision?

Impossible. Holograms didn't have visions.

Nonetheless, the last thing the Doctor clearly remembered was the sight of Captain Janeway, suspended in midair and surrounded by a blinding white light.

One minute he had been in sickbay, and the next before the captain.

No.

Drawn toward the captain.

Which meant . . . now . . . he was . . .

Where?

Suspended in the absence of light, he could find no immediate answer.

Tom's eyes fluttered open. He was disoriented by the sensations that floated into his groggy consciousness.

His head rested on a pillow, soft, but . . . stale. It reeked of something . . . a foul smell he found hard to place.

Is that cigar smoke?

Tom was, of course, not a smoker. But from time to time his holodeck programs included characters who smoked cigars, cigarettes, or pipes. Only when the holodeck safeties were off had he ever smelled the sickening fumes, and had never understood the attraction or felt the slightest inclination to try them himself.

Bright multicolored lights flashed in rhythmic patterns on the ceiling. Rising, he found the source of the illumination. A large window on the room's far side exposed a dark sky filled with signs resting atop dozens of large, ornate buildings. The signs flashed and burned in vivid hues, many of which included the words "Casino" and "All You Can Eat Buffet."

The only furnishings in the dingy room were two beds, the one where he had been and a second, where Harry lay snoring softly. They were separated by a small wooden table, atop which sat a truly ugly lamp in the shape of a smiling circus clown riding a bucking elephant.

A low dresser sat opposite the beds with a strange box adorned with push buttons and a crude handset.

Is that a telephone? he wondered in dismay. It was an ancient communications device, one which had long ago gone the way of the combustion engine and fossil fuels.

Where are we?

The last thing he remembered was the shuttle. He and Harry, doing the first test flight of the tetryon transporter.

Whatever this place was, it had to be a simulation of some kind. It looked and felt like a motel room, one he might have found appealing in his younger, wilder days. But where was the shuttle? And how could Harry sleep at a time like this?

"Harry," he called, crossing to the ensign and shaking him roughly. "Wake up."

"Huh . . . what?" Harry jumped, startled.

"We have a problem," Tom said.

Shaking the sleep from his eyes, Harry sat up and glanced curiously around the room.

"Where are we?" he asked.

"That's the problem," Tom replied.

There was a loud knocking at the door.

Both of them jumped, but were reluctant to answer immediately.

The knock was repeated . . . louder.

Nodding to Harry, Tom crossed to the door and as casually as he could asked, "Who is it?"

"Room service," a male voice replied, with the oddest combination of condescension and glee it was possible to project in two words and three syllables.

Tom couldn't place the voice immediately, but casting a questioning glance at Harry, could see in his alarmed eyes that Harry recognized it.

"Oh, no," Harry said.

"What?" Tom asked.

"Don't open it," Harry replied.

CONTINUED IN
STRING THEORY, BOOK 3:
EVOLUTION

GLOSSARY OF MONORHAN TERMS

ati-harat: artisan in service to the *rih-hara-tan*

hara: group or pack

harat: male leader of a *hara*

haras: female leader of a *hara*

haran: male or female member of a *hara*

kuntafed: wild Monorhan animal

linuh-harat: seer/prophet, advisor to the *rih-hara-tan*

Protin: Monorha's primary star

rih-hara-tan: leader of an entire Monorhan tribe who can establish the same psionic link with all tribe members that a *harat* or *haras* can with his/her *hara*

shalla: head of a secular committee of Monorhans, established by the Interim Emergency Council

Shi-harat: personal bodyguard to the *rih-hara-tan*

The Blue Eye: Monorha's second star

wantain: snow

ACKNOWLEDGMENTS

Who's to blame?

Well, it's usually safe to start with the parents. Mine were horribly supportive and encouraging of everything I wanted to do, particularly my artistic endeavors, so I'm sure a lot of this is their fault. My father, Fred, was the first to consciously and thoughtfully critique my work, which always made me feel like he took it seriously. Since his death, everything I've done, including retaining his name for professional purposes, is a tribute to his love and fierce spirit. My mother, Patricia, has always been my biggest fan and assures me to this day she's not the least bit biased.

My older brother introduced me to *Star Trek,* so he had a hand in it. Since TOS was the only show we could agree on to watch on a regular basis, those nights in front of the TV gave me my earliest appreciation of story-telling on an epic scale. Thanks, Matt.

My younger brother, Paul, teaches me more than I can say about dedication and discipline. Our father lives on in him, which is a daily inspiration.

I then had the misfortune to marry into a family of intelligent, generous, and insanely supportive people.

Special thanks to Vivian, my blessed other mother; Donna, for the grammar and content notes and constantly making me feel like not just an in-law but a true sister; Chris and Derek, for not complaining while we spent those hours on the phone; Debra, Bill, Michael, and Justin, for being genuinely thrilled when I told them about this project; and Ollie Jane, for giving me back what I'd lost eleven years ago, a living grandmother.

Then there's the extended family and friends who might not know how much a comment here or a suggestion there, or just a willingness to share the ups and downs of this life, has meant to me: Beth, Candy, Allan, Christiana, Carolina Joy, Sean, Katey, Maggie, Jack, Fred, Marianne, Freddie, Erin, Greg, Ralph, David, Katie, Tony, John Mitchell, Adrian, Julie, and most recently, Katherine. A special heapin' helping of blame goes to Sam, who knows I wouldn't be alive without her love of so many years.

Of course I can't leave out Maura, who has never failed to take me seriously and in whose debt I plan to be for as many years as she'll have me as a client.

And Jessica, who first invited me to turn my pitches into prose.

Oh, and let's not forget Jeri Taylor, who actually poured copious amount of fuel on a small fire when she invited me to Paramount to pitch for her when *Voyager* was still in production; her cohort in crime, Bryan Fuller, who kept asking me to come back with more stories; and, finally, Mike Taylor. Sometimes negative feedback is more empowering than positive feedback.

learned that lesson at his hands, and what had been one of dozens of stories I'd created for *Voyager* over the years became a mission, then a teleplay, and finally the core story of this book.

Jeff was way too accommodating to a first-time writer to go without mention. Now I just have to wonder, why was he listening to me? He gets the shame of changing what he had done so I wouldn't have to. Does he now begin to see how wicked I truly am?

Heather bears the lion's share of responsibility. She answered an email and I found a soul sister I'd never imagined could exist in this world. She knows what she's done and that I couldn't have written a word of this without her constant love, support, comments, suggestions, and belief. I honestly don't know sometimes how I got through a day before we were writing partners. An extra-special heart-stopping thanks for the moment she said, "I'm thinking we could incorporate *Siren Song* into this project. What do you think?" Somewhere inside, she knew better than I did how much I wanted this story in the world.

I notice Marco there, trying to fade into the woodwork as if all he did was his job, but oh, no . . . he's not getting off that easy. He had no good reason to believe in me or hand me such a glorious project my first time at bat. I'm going to spend the rest of my life trying to figure out how to repay that faith and to live up to his high regard. It means the world to me.

But always, at the end, it's the husband's fault, isn't it? Deciding who to dedicate my first book to wasn't hard.

He's listened to every word I've ever written. But more than that, he's walked this road with me, constantly by my side, and his love has given me strength and courage I didn't know existed. There are no words for my gratitude to him or the daily wonder that is our life together.

So, if you enjoy any of what you are about to read or have just read, you know whom to call.

ABOUT THE AUTHOR

Here's what happened.

Kirsten never wanted to be a writer. Nothing against writers, you understand. She's a voracious reader, as the many groaning bookcases in her house will attest, along with the nice folks at Brentano's, Barnes & Noble, Waldenbooks, and Amazon.com.

But writing is hard.

The problem was she loved to tell stories. She'd been doing it as long as she could remember, and by the time she was in her teens she had figured out that telling stories onstage was her favorite thing in the world to do. So she pursued her dreams of acting all the way to Los Angeles and was having a marvelous and reasonably successful time.

Then, one night, she was bored. Her husband had the audacity to get cast in a play while she was between productions, and this left her in an unusual spot: home . . . alone . . . for hours and hours . . . with nothing to do.

Roughly the same time this realization hit, *Star Trek Voyager* premiered on UPN. After a couple of episodes she found herself imagining story ideas. So she completed a story in her head and one day over lunch told her husband about it. His response . . .

"Sounds great, but what are you going to do . . . write it?"

Umm.

Yeah.

Ten years and lots of writing later, she has teleplays, screenplays (currently not produced but stay tuned), the beginnings of two original novels, and, finally, her professional science fiction debut: *Fusion* and a contribution to the upcoming *Voyager* anthology *Distant Shores*.

A word to the wise: Don't ever tell a storyteller what they can or can't do.

STAR TREK®
STRANGE NEW WORLDS

08

EDITED BY
DEAN WESLEY SMITH
WITH ELISA J. KASSIN
AND PAULA M. BLOCK

All-new *Star Trek* adventures—by fans,

for fans!

Enter the *Strange New Worlds*
short-story contest!
No Purchase Necessary.

Strange New Worlds 9 entries accepted
between June 1, 2005 and
October 1, 2005.

To see the Contest Rules please visit
www.simonsays.com/st

SNW8.01